The Isa Project

A novel

Gina R. Briggs

Copyright © 2022 Gina R. Briggs
All rights reserved

The characters and events portrayed in this book are fictitious. Any similarity to real persons, living or dead, is coincidental and not intended by the author.

No part of this book may be reproduced, or stored in a retrieval system, or transmitted in any form or by any means, electronic, mechanical, photocopying, recording, or otherwise, without express written permission of the publisher.

ISBN-13: 9798849980140

Song lyrics by: Gina R. Briggs
Music by: Matthew Briggs
Photography by: Gerry D'Arco

Printed in the United States of America

A Note to My Readers

This is my first attempt at fiction-writing. I have zero formal training in this art form, which is perhaps why I gravitated toward it. I understand that this story will not be everyone's cup of tea. For that, I won't apologize. Instead, I hope that the next novel you pick up suits you better, and I humbly thank you for giving mine a chance. This work is a labor of love; I began in the aftermath of losing my first child and finished while I waited on my second. Art is therapy. For those of you that are lost, broken, and grieving, my advice is to write it out, act it out, play it out, paint it out…Just create. It gets better.

With gratitude,

Gina

Content Warning
Please be advised that this book contains references to alcohol consumption, sexual situations, addiction, assault, and mental health topics that may not be suitable for all readers.

For Poppy, Baby Briggs, and Matthew.

My wish, my hope, and my realized dream.

When falsehood can look so like the truth, who can assure themselves
of certain happiness?
—Mary Shelley
Frankenstein; or, The Modern Prometheus

***

I shut my eyes and all the world drops dead;
I lift my lids and all is born again.
(I think I made you up inside my head.)

—Sylvia Plath
"Mad Girl's Love Song"

Prologue

"**Are you ready to fly?**" I nodded and the stagehand whispered into his headset, "She's ready."

Barefoot, my toes gripped the cold backstage floor. It was a ritual—I'd scrunch up my toes as tight as I could and then ever so slowly release the tension just as I was hoisted up and up and up… Until I was hovering ten feet above the X of neon glow tape, my launching pad.

"…I saw the loveliest small white bird. Come quick! It's flying this way," Angela Brandon, the actress playing Nibs exclaimed.

"What kind of a bird is it that could be so lovely?" Tootles, AKA Glenn Roscoe, squeaked.

"I don't know, but as it flies it chirps, 'Poor Wendy,'" Nibs replied, my cue to cut over the false trees, dip daringly towards the lip on the proscenium, and soar across the third row of spellbound audience members.

Isa's luminescent white-blonde plait shone like the north star in the back row of the orchestra. I'd notice her anywhere—that amused smirk transformed by wonder and awe. She was always an untamable beauty, but in the darkness, she appeared almost sane again…or as sane as she ever was. The glance that locked our eyes but for a mere instant was an entire friendship replayed, turned upside down, and suspended in time. There she was, ironically, dazzled by *me*. And I, whipping through the air with my pearly white nightgown fluttering behind me, was still fixated on *her* and immune to the onstage cacophony. Isa was the one-woman show, forever and always drawing my attention elsewhere. Stealing my thunder even when *I* was the one flying.

"Go on! Shoot it! Bows and arrows!"

"Out of my way, Tinkerbell! I'll shoot!"

I wanted to wrap my arms around her and carry her away; I'd unbuckle the harness—I didn't need the rigging system—and fly us straight out of the playhouse. Was I rescuing her or trying to lose her? I didn't know. I will never know.

"I have shot the Wendy bird! Peter will be pleased with us Lost Boys!"

My final glimpse was over. I was pulled back towards the stage, still so high above the set that I could make out Steve leaning against the dressing room door. His lecherous smile as my stage mom giggled at one of his jokes turned my stomach. I had to put Steve out of my mind. I had to put Isa out of my mind. I was landing now. It was my turn. It was finally my turn. I loved her. No, I hated her. No, I… It didn't matter. For once, this was not about Isa. For the next page and a half of dialogue, I would shut my eyes, listen for my cue, and drown out the mess that Isa dragged in with her when she decided to reappear.

"This is no bird. It's a lady."

"Wendy has an arrow right through her heart! Poor Wendy is dead!"

"I thought it was only the daisies and wee flowers that die…"

I fluttered my eyelids closed in Wendy's overdramatized, childlike fashion. Equally compelled to smile and cry, I saw daisies dancing against the black. Daisies in her white-blonde hair.

Isa.

Even while in character…no matter who I was pretending to be…

Isa haunted my dreams.

1.

Reunion

"K? Hey! K!"

Tucking my Vitamin Water under my chin, I grabbed the Kind Bar from the register. I slowly spun in the direction of the voice to avoid textbooks flying out of the unzipped backpack that was precariously hanging from my shoulder. My eyes locked with his. Like a fish out of water. The signature goofy grin like a buoy in the dead sea of weary college kids cramming for finals week.

"Miss? You forgot this!" the cashier called after me.

I mumbled an apology as I attempted to grab my dining card but, disoriented as I was, managed to drop my Vitamin Water, lose my lit and crit textbook, and fling the card six feet across the floor instead. I knelt down to collect my things, but he got to the card first. Curiously surveying the name and face on the plastic, his already out-of-place grin broadened with confirmation.

"It *is* you. K Statham in the flesh. I've been here all semester and I was wondering when I was going to run into you."

Lincoln. Lincoln DeLuca. Standing right next to the bruin statue.

"Lincoln."

"Yes, K, that's still my name," he beamed.

He laughed. *That grin.* It was akin to the warmth of a chai tea latte on an overcast autumn morning. My stomach did an unprecedented somersault. Lincoln DeLuca after three years.

"Is it okay if I...I don't know...hug you?"

He handed me my dining card back, zipped my backpack for me, and spread his arms with eager anticipation.

"Um, yeah. Sorry."

Why was I blushing? Beet red, I leaned in for a hug—Vitamin Water and makeshift cram session dinner occupying both hands. He smelled...grown up. A warm, cleanness radiated from his flannel. Or maybe it was an aftershave? Cologne? Did college guys wear that stuff? His face was the same, but the stubble was new. The round framed glasses made him look slightly older too; he was a sandy haired Harry Potter (from at least movie #5, to be exact). All that was new hinted at the amount of time that had passed, so why was I still—

"You look exactly the same! I mean, I didn't expect...I don't know. It hasn't been that long, but still. You...you look great, K."

I was the same, at least by outward appearance. He was right about that much. Same unruly curls twisted into a long braid. Still sporting my vintage thrift store standbys; still convinced that ankle-length, high-waisted skirts and Peter Pan collars gave off an aloof enough presence to avoid being hit on when I went out or accosted by sales reps who wanted to give me samples at the mall. I had learned years ago that I was hopeless at convincing people I was *cool*, so I settled for convincing them that I was *smart* by dressing like a librarian from another era.

"It's so good to see you," Lincoln continued as I racked my brain for what to say next. "I would've reached out...I mean, I *did* but... Did you change your number? Sorry."

He was rambling. Clearly, he was as nervous as I was. Okay, this was the Lincoln I remember.

"Yeah, sorry. I did. Change my number. But yeah...Lincoln...what are you doing here?"

"I transferred! Do you want to sit down? Get dinner or… It'd be great to catch u—"

"I've really got to—" I indicated the backpack stuffed to the brim.

"Study. Yeah. I should do that too. 'Tis the season," he laughed. "For studying. Cause, finals."

More nervous chuckles. Where was this going? I wasn't prepared for this reunion, but there we were—in the middle of the Caf, fumbling over our words and probably looking like idiots. Grief certainly changes a person, but I suppose we were already socially awkward to begin with.

"You know what? Sure. I have to eat anyway."

As if I just told him that he'd been given a free pass to skip finals altogether, that all-too revealing grin resurfaced.

"Oh, okay! Yeah, yeah me too," he said, beaming. "But can we go somewhere other than the Caf? I mean, I've been playing out this moment in my mind since I got here, and I didn't imagine this all going down *here*."

"You always were a romantic. What's more idealistic than being engulfed in bruin pride?" I asked, perfectly timed if I may add—a gaggle of cheerleaders dressed to the nines in blue, crimson, and gold brushed past him.

"Ah, and you still love to tease."

God, that smile.

"What about Casa Grande?" he asked. "As a romantic, I insist on treating you with *my* dining dollars...at a restaurant that is at least somewhat off campus. We can just pretend that it's not across the street."

I guess you never can tell when the tide will turn—when the course of your life will take on a new direction. It was no secret that I had done my best to block out every reminder of her that remained, but I always knew in the corner of my mind that I would find myself facing what was lurking. I suppose you can only hide for so long. So yes, I didn't know this was coming. I didn't think I'd be caught off guard by

Isa's brother in the cafeteria of a university that I didn't even know he attended on a Thursday night when I had planned to study for my Islamic Luxury Arts final. But at the same time, my entire body from the split ends of my curls to the chipped nail polish on my toes knew. I knew this was coming and it was time to face it.

"Okay, Lincoln. Let's do this."

Lincoln put his palms together and tilted his head down, performing an awkward gratitude bow of sorts.

"Great. Just gotta grab my backpack."

He hoisted his backpack off the table he occupied before I unknowingly changed his plans. When he smiled, I felt the corners of my mouth twitch into what could vaguely be identified as something similar. Weaving through the sea of crammers, we left the gaudy bruin statue and the blue, crimson, and gold pull of academia behind.

"I feel bad for these waiters. You gotta know that half their business is probably college kids that plow down free chips and salsa, order water, and leave without a tip."

I raised my eyebrows in agreement as I submerged my own chip into the could-be-spicier-but-this-would-do salsa that Lincoln and I shared. Our hands did an awkward dance as he maneuvered his chip around mine and haphazardly lost it in the small pool of cilantro, onion, and tomato. He drooped his head and sighed.

"Don't you hate it when that happens?" he groaned.

In his classic good-natured Lincoln way, he dug out a "rescue chip" from our basket and proceeded to scoop out the castaway. In this ordinary exchange it dawned on me how odd it was to share something so intimate as a bowl of chips and salsa—to perform the awkward and potentially messy act of consuming food—across from a person that I had avoided the mere memory of for years. I'd punish myself for allowing my thoughts to wander down the rabbit hole of, "I wonder what Lincoln is up to?" just a month ago and now here I was—passing him the Cholula so he could douse his chicken quesadilla. Simultaneously, it was absolutely normal and utterly foreign. Wasn't it yesterday that I sat on the barstool in Lincoln's kitchen, laughing at him for microwaving his Wendy's hamburger—aluminum foil and all? In the span of 30 seconds, my mind cycled through the events of that exact day.

It was the summer before sophomore year and one of those torturously hot days where even your bare skin felt like an unnecessary layer obstructing you from cool air. Isa stood indignantly in front of the fridge after we recovered from our laughing fit and declared that we needed better entertainment than Lincoln's half-assed attempt at blowing up the house. In my mind's eye, I could see every detail of the sombrero that Lincoln revived from a box in the basement and his goofy grin when he suggested we host a "fiesta." I remember the startling shade of lime green Kool-Aid that Isa mixed with tequila, preparing makeshift margaritas. And I felt a melancholic pull at my heart when the scene of us falling asleep on the couch resurfaced. The glow of the DeLuca's basement tv in the background and the coffee table consumed by remnants of chips, queso, "margaritas," a lone child-size maraca, and the Sombrero of Truth. I filed that one in the "Good and Safe" memory drawer then found myself literally shaking my head to release the sweetness of the memory from my mind—to loosen its grasp on my heart before it became hard to breathe.

"Are you cold?" Lincoln asked.

"Just a chill."

"Hey. Remember the Sombrero of Truth?"

Get out of my mind.

"No…not really." I laughed nervously and took a sip of water.

Maybe he'll move on to something else. Please God, let him move on to something else.

"Oh, come on! Sombrero of Truth! Whoever wears the sombrero has to tell an embarrassing secret. And wasn't it a drinking game somehow?"

"Everything was turned into a drinking game back then."

He laughed knowingly, "Yeah, you're right. Good thing we've grown up since then. Look at us—sensible semi-adults about to embark on the trials and tribulations of the real world."

"Pretty much."

I didn't know what else to say. Where do you start when you haven't seen someone in three years and there is so much space and time to fill, yet only one real question between us? Or rather, only one name—an entire life unlived nestling between us as casually as the salsa bowl.

"Do you graduate in May?" he asked.

"That's the plan," I said.

"Are you still studying theater?"

Bringing another chip to his mouth, I thought of the sombrero resting ridiculously atop his shaggy high school head of hair.

"No, no, no. I don't act anymore. I changed my major. Art history. I like it. It's…calming." I shrugged. "Way less stress. History's comforting, you know?"

"The dates never change," he offered.

And less pressure when it came to choosing an identity, but I didn't tell him that part.

"Exactly. The great works stay the same. The names, the dates, the time periods. And preserving that is…important. I think. Remembering the artist and the life behind the work. Someone needs to remember their stories, so why not me? It's much safer than creating art of my own. Or, you know, being scrutinized by casting directors."

I half-heartedly chuckled but the seriousness in his eyes told me that my attempt at self-deprecating humor did not land.

"K, I…well, you know I've always thought you were a great actress. And I never thought there were limitations to the roles you could play."

His sincerity was almost oppressive. Why did I have to get weird and word vomit my elevator speech? I should have known that I couldn't pull the wool over Lincoln's eyes. He wasn't like the people I'd befriended in the last few years and kept at a convenient distance. I knew what it meant to accept this dinner invitation; I couldn't hide behind sarcasm because, with Lincoln, my scars were on display.

"Tell that to the old white guys that run the theater department…and the world," I laughed.

He gave me a knowing, slightly sad smirk.

"But besides, it's just not for me anymore. I had a…bad…episode. After. Well, after everything happened," I admitted, more to my refried beans than to him.

He nodded soberly and I knew he could read between the lines.

"Well, art history sounds really nerdy. Which you are. So, I'm sure it's a good fit."

His smile confirmed that the crack in my armor was okay.

"What are you gonna do after graduation?" he asked casually.

The dreaded question. If I were able to answer with any semblance of certainty, maybe I'd finally be able to wean off my antidepressants. But alas—today was another day of averting my gaze from the terrifying abyss of post-graduation life; today was another day popping 150 milligrams. Although who am I kidding? The expected and completely ordinary fear of the unknown after college life was not the reason I had to visit Dr. McPherson once a month. I groaned.

"I know, I know. We all hate that question. I'm sorry," he repented.

"No, it's okay," I said, feigning cheeriness. "I'm just hoping Lenny will let me stay on until I get my life together."

"*Lenny*?" Lincoln nearly did a spit take. "You're working at Chubbie's?"

"Yup." I shrugged. "Since sophomore year. It's something to keep me busy. It's, you know, just a block away from campus. And money's a thing we all need, I guess."

I didn't feel it necessary to provide the detail that this part-time barista job wasn't just a resource for "fun money," but a lifeline…especially on the days when getting out of bed seemed like a ridiculously tall order.

"Man, I haven't been to Chubbie's since…I don't know when."

His eyes lingered on mine for a bit. Swiftly, I diverted my gaze to my plate.

"Let me guess," he said, jovially. Switching gears, he put his elbows on the table and leaned in. "That loot you're making goes straight to thrift stores and books."

I laughed, grateful that we were moving onto lighter subjects.

Dipping a chip in the guacamole, I continued, "Honestly, though, I'll probably apply for grad programs. When in doubt, do more school, right? The loans and real stuff can wait."

The "real stuff" most definitely could not wait as worries about money, survival, and purpose played out on a continual loop in my mind at all hours of the day and night. But he didn't need to know.

"Amen to that," he cheered, tipping his water glass towards mine.

I picked up my glass and together we created a satisfying clink that instantly brought me back to old times. How many obscure things did we cheers to back in high school? I'm sure an actual list would make us laugh—and cringe—now.

"What about you? The bright and promising Lincoln DeLuca. Where has he been? What has he been up to? Inquiring minds want to know."

I held my knife out in front of him, a la microphone. I didn't know why, but it was natural to be playful even if the atmosphere had been heavy moments before.

"Well, ma'am, if you must know," he began, "I spent an entire semester at Columbia barricading in my dorm with adult beverages that I was too young to legally purchase. I more or less trashed my GPA then got back on track at TCC. Which, by the way, is the most depressing place on the planet. I think they purposefully paint the walls pukey, beigey yellow to inspire you to get your grades up and get the hell out of there. Anyway, after TCC I transferred here. Playwriting. I took a butt-ton of summer courses so now I should be able to graduate in May."

Playwriting? I wasn't surprised. Out of all of us, he was the most unafraid. His sketches in high school were at least something new. Lincoln's voice as a playwright was like a drop of honey sweetening up the stale white bread of our high school theater department, which exclusively performed Golden Age musicals. Of course, he had stuck with it. But an alcoholic downward spiral? That would definitely have stumped me four years ago. I could never have envisioned the contagiously optimistic Lincoln DeLuca falling into a pit of despair, but then again, I could have never imagined the event that put him there. Knowing what I know now, I didn't flinch.

"Next..." He let out a sigh as he continued, "I might try out another city? Freelance and find a survival job? It was easier to stay put for a while, but I really want to—"

"Escape your hometown," I finished.

"Yeah. That. But this time I'll be in a better place before I do it," he said. "I was a wreck in New York. I could blame it on Isa but, if I'm being honest, I probably wasn't ready to go that far. There was a lot of...unresolved stuff."

I knew exactly what he meant and, from my own experience, knew that he probably didn't want this moment to linger for fear of giving in to the impulse to unpack that dark thing in the corner of his mind. Besides, I didn't want to open the door to what I knew was unresolved. There were things he didn't know and perhaps I would leave them that way no matter how much time had passed.

"So," I teasingly broke the silence. "Should I expect a character with my name up on a Broadway stage anytime soon?"

Only it wasn't exactly a joke. When Lincoln said he would do something, he did it. People like Lincoln demanded others to believe in them and if you got caught up in that optimism long enough, you sometimes found that you believed in yourself with that same ferocity.

"Oh, come on, K. You've got to know that you inspire all of my stories," he said a little too earnestly.

I ignored what could very well have been some sort of confession by busying myself with shredding the wrapper of my straw. We all have things we wish we could get off our chests, but I wasn't quite there yet; I was just warming up to the idea that Lincoln DeLuca was at my school, sitting across from me at Casa Grande, and handing the waiter his dining card to pay for my meal. I knew that we'd get there eventually—it was inevitable, right? —but now I just wanted to enjoy the simplicity of occupying the same space.

After dinner, we meandered down the street toward my apartment—another technically on-campus oasis that was just far enough from the chaos to comfortably let loose.

"Well, this is me," I said, gesturing to the second story apartment behind us.

"Fancy," Lincoln observed.

"Ha. Not really."

My apartment was nothing remarkable, but it wasn't my parents' house and that in itself was an improvement.

"Could be worse. I share a place with two blokes that leave their pizza rolls out on the kitchen counter for weeks. You got roommates?" he asked.

"Just me. And F. Scott," I said.

He raised an eyebrow.

I found the mangy orange tabby loitering outside my apartment the winter of sophomore year. He didn't put pressure on his front right paw, and he had a collar with a tag that read, "Scottie." I fed him and gave him water, but after three days of routine visits, I began to wonder if Scottie was *supposed* to be outside… He started sleeping on my fire escape and every time I opened the door, he tried to sneak between my legs and hobble inside. I'd never owned a pet, but Scottie seemed in need of an owner. He had a mouth on him like no cat I'd ever known—meowing like he was holding a debate with a courtroom of unmovable jurors.

"Scottie, where's your house?" I'd say.

"Meoooooow." Was his reply.

"Who's your owner? Don't you need to go back home?"

"Meoooooow."

Finally, I called the number listed on Scottie's tag. The voice that picked up the phone told me that the cat belonged to his grandma who had died over a week ago. And no, he did not want him back. He had let Scottie out when he boxed up his grandma's apartment. He was allergic and apparently too inconvenienced to take the poor thing to the humane society.

That was how I came to have a roommate. After spending most of my savings on the cutest ever cat-sized cast to repair his broken leg, I renamed him F. Scott Fitzgerald. His judgmental eyes and quick tongue made me think he was criticizing the debauchery of the jazz age and humanity at large. We were both shipwrecked by loss, which gave us a natural understanding for one another. We've been inseparable ever since.

"My cat," I explained. "And he's a neat freak, so we get along."

As we said goodbye, we exchanged those generic promises to stay in touch and "grab coffee soon," but I knew that he would actually follow through with the sentiment. ("Hey! Now *you* can make me a caramel macchiato!" he had joked. But I totally could. I made a mean caramel macchiato.) We hugged again and this time my complexion didn't betray my emotional turmoil—it's funny how you can develop a deeper level of comfortability in a matter of a few hours with some people. Time, distance, and even trauma are barriers that can either be indestructible or, in an instant, melt away depending on the person.

I had dinner with Lincoln DeLuca and my world hadn't collapsed. I was still about to walk into my apartment, say hello to F. Scott, study for my final, and this little world I built for myself was still intact. On a whim I thought that maybe I could have both—I could reinvent myself and hold on to some semblance of who I used to be. Even though I knew Lincoln to be the kind of person to throw pebbles at a window and send letters by carrier pigeon, if need be (what a freak), I wanted to *make sure* that a coffee date actually happened.

"Wait!" I said just as he turned to walk back to campus. "You don't have my new number."

The smile he gave must have made his jaw ache. We traded phones and I typed in my new number. I knew this meant that I might see the name "DeLuca" pop up on my screen again and that might, at first, make my heart sink. I knew this meant that, probably, eventually, we'd get around to talking about the reason why we hadn't seen each other in three years. I knew these things, but because the weather was in the pleasant mid-50s, the sky was turning my favorite shade of orangey-pink, and Lincoln's eyes were so full of hope and eagerness, I decided it was okay to feel a little bit of hope too.

"So, this means that you're officially not lost forever? Because if you disappear again after tonight then I insist that we ditch our finals and do something more epic than destroy two and a half baskets of tortilla chips," he joked.

"And what would constitute 'more epic'? If we *were* the kind of people to blow off finals, what would we do instead?" I urged.

Why not? I didn't quite feel like climbing the stairs to my front door just yet.

He seemed slightly taken aback but decided to play along.

"Okay," he mused. "I would say, let's go to Jeni's—"

"All the best reckless ideas begin with ice cream," I inserted.

"Yes, obviously," he agreed. "Although the *best* begin specifically with butter pecan."

My faux vomit reaction was instinctual.

"Gross. No. Mint chocolate chip. You know this," I said.

He sighed. "You can get whatever toothpaste favored weirdness you want," he continued. "After that, we'd go to the walking bridge. You gotta admit that the view of the river…the lights of the cityscape…pretty epic."

"Go on."

"Then we'd end the night at the Parthenon," he said.

"The *Parthenon*? Can we even get in there now?"

"Get *in*? What? No. Did you think I wanted to tour the museum? No! We'd sit out on the grass and watch the stars. Climb a tree. That place is so much better at night. No elementary school field trips or tourists," he said.

"You mean, sneak in? Isn't it gated?" I asked. "And what are we…17?"

"Well yeah, it's gated…but it's not a particularly *tall* fence. Even you can manage it." He winked.

It was a reflex—I punched him in the arm, and we *were* 17 again. Only this time I felt something different. That tiny flip in my stomach from earlier in the evening was back.

I will not be caught off guard, I told the unfamiliar sensation inside myself. "Well," I said, attempting to take back the reins, "too bad we aren't the kind of people to blow off finals."

The sky had morphed into a subtle lavender streaked with deep violet. The books in my backpack were heavier than before and the ache in my back reminded me that I still needed to study, or I'd surely regret it at 8:45 tomorrow morning. Now it was actually time to say goodbye.

When we parted, I climbed the stairs, unlocked my door, and was greeted by F. Scott rubbing up against my legs—no doubt inquiring for food. The unglamorous efficiency was just as I left it at 8:00 am, but I surveyed the space with a different perspective. The curtains, tapestries, books piled to the ceiling—all of it felt claustrophobic. I had an intense desire to open the windows. I had been holding my breath for three years, but now I was ready to inhale possibility.

Later that night, I woke up with a start—laying on my futon next to the open window with my Islamic Luxury Arts notes scattered on the floor. I was cold, as always. I shut the window and sat back down with my notes. Without the noise of the street and my tv on mute, I took in the sudden, uncomfortable silence and the sensation of being utterly alone. I remembered F. Scott purring on the windowsill before I dozed off, but now he was somewhere else. Probably under the bed. The chill wouldn't go away. But the spare blanket was on top of the stack of freshly folded laundry, wedged in the corner between my nightstand and the closet.

Isa wasn't there. Isa had never been there. She wasn't lingering in that far left unlit corner. She wasn't beyond that gaping black hole of the closet door frame. The wisps of silky white-blonde hair visible out of the corner of my eye were figments of my imagination. "The brain's way of making sense of an inexplicable situation," as Dr. McPherson would say. Still. It was unnecessary to look in that direction. The mere thought of a sideways glance caused my skin to prickle and arm hairs to stand wildly at attention. The only solution was to reach for the remote, unmute the tv, drown out the disconcerting voices, and concede to inevitable shivers.

"Did you take iron pills?" Isa would have asked if she was here. But she wasn't.
Isa isn't here.
My phone buzzed until it tumbled off the ledge of the tv stand.

Lincoln DeLuca [12:56am]: Maybe we aren't the kind of people to blow off finals, but...

Three dots popped up. He was composing another message.

Lincoln DeLuca [12:57am]: what kind of person can say no to ice cream?

A tap on my window announced Lincoln's arrival and prompted F. Scott to dart from under the bed. He stood on the fire escape with a pint of Ben and Jerry's in each hand—one butter pecan and one mint chocolate chip. The sight of the streetlights illuminating his grin may have appeared stalkerish if I didn't know him so well. Showing up on my doorstep unexpectedly with ice cream didn't used to be an out of the ordinary occurrence but more of an unspoken expectation.

"It's one in the morning. What are you doing?"

"Why are you whispering? I don't think we have to worry about parents grounding us. Unless…do you share this place with Tim and Azrah?" he joked. "And I know you must have missed our Walmart runs. Especially since I always paid for the ice cream."

"Not true. I paid. Once."

"Yeah, and that time you showed up with Great Value brand. I got the good stuff."

"Okay, but how did you know I was awake?"

"That," he said, gesturing to the glow of the tv. "And I just hoped."

"Lucky you," I said. I pulled a hoodie over my head, grabbed a beanie, and met him at the front door. "Um…let's sit out here," I suggested, "my place is a mess." A lie: I never left my space in any state of disarray, but I didn't want that intrusion just yet. "Now, show me the loot."

"Cute pom-pom." Lincoln flicked the knit poof ball on the top of my hat. It was an oversized knit beanie from the 80's that I recently found at a garage sale. Lincoln had always loved poking fun at my fashion choices.

"Hey, quit." I swatted his hand away. I couldn't decide if the overpowering wave of déjà vu was welcoming, creepy, or just plain bittersweet.

We sat on the fire escape, popped open our Ben and Jerry's, and lamented about the last several hours spent studying. The gripe session turned into general observations about our school, the student population, and the professors that we each admired or hoped to never see again after May. We discussed the books we'd been reading and the shows we'd been watching. We speculated about where our high school classmates were now and reported any recent sightings or gossip. Discovering that we were both dead to the social media world, we admitted that this decision made stalking old acquaintances an actively embarrassing task rather than something we could write off as information acquired by route of passive scrolling.

We were stumbling through the motions of getting to know each other for the first time after a long time, while finding small pockets of familiarity to park in briefly along the way. Somehow, we got on the topic of the new hobbies we'd taken on or longed to when time would finally permit.

"What do you paint?" he asked.

"Oh, I don't know. Just abstract stuff. I'm not really *good*. I'm, you know, an admirer. Not an artist."

"You are an artist. That doesn't just go away. It doesn't matter how you choose to express it. But whatever—I won't ask to see your portfolio if you want to be secretive about it," he said.

I laughed. In simple terms, painting made me feel good. It made me feel free to explore and not "get it right." It was different than theater because I didn't need to follow someone else's script.

"What about you? Italian?" I asked. "How'd you get into that?"

"Whitney got me started with lessons a while back. An effort to coax me out of my 'slump' as she called it." He laughed halfheartedly. "She's always a little pushy about offering help, but this actually stuck."

"Whitney? Your dad's girlfriend? They're still together? I didn't think that would last," I mused.

A picture of the last time I saw Whitney bubbled to the surface from somewhere in the depths of those untouched memories. Her manicured nails, black shift dress, and polite, practiced smile. Her airy voice reciting overused scripture and insisting that while "we may never know this side of heaven" the explanation for tragedy, "peace can still be ours." She was so easy to dismiss, but still, her presence—maybe more accurately, those empty words—enraged me on a cellular level that I couldn't understand.

"Stepmom now," he corrected.

"*Really?*"

"Yup... She's still, well, you know—the way she is," Lincoln said. "But she's actually been good for Dad. I mean, *I* don't get her, but...she's calm. And consistent. That's what he needs."

I nodded. How could I argue with the appeal of consistency after so many years of chaos?

"What about you?" he asked.

"What do you mean— 'what about you'?"

"Are you...seeing anyone?"

All I could do was laugh. *Seeing* anyone? I had never properly seen *anyone*. Why now, of all times, would I choose the aftermath of...everything...to give that a whirl?

"Nope," I said, simply. "And you? Are still with...Sarah? Sidney? Shit. Sorry..."

"Samantha. But close enough." He laughed. "No, we broke up years ago."

I got the feeling that he would rather not discuss the details of the breakup, and I didn't particularly want to know.

"Why Italian?" I said, changing the subject.

"Switzerland," he said to the now empty pint of butter pecan.

There was a weighty silence in which we watched two cars pass. Switzerland was a much more loaded topic than Samantha, and yet I had unknowingly opened that door wide open.

"I'm still going to go..." he continued. "Don't know when, but soon. I think it's time."

It wasn't that I had forgotten about Switzerland, it was more like the entire idea was kept in a protective folder in that special filing cabinet in my mind. If I was obligated to go about my real life and perform the expected tasks of going to class, conversing with others like a normal human being, and even executing the simple chore of brushing my teeth, I had to abide by the unspoken agreement with my mind that I would pretend this folder didn't exist; this particular folder was in the back of a drawer that I didn't feel safe opening.

"You'll have to send me a postcard. And some chocolate," I contributed rather lamely.

"Or you could come with...like you said you would…" His tone took on a seriousness that I knew was coming but had managed to avoid all evening.

I stood up and leaned against the railing of the fire escape, looking out to the street and the lights of campus.

"I guess I thought you would've already done something…with...it…"

"No. I was… Well, I already said: I was pretty messed up for a while. It's not that I'm *okay* now but—"

"But it's bearable," I offered.

The sky was getting lighter as I blinked away the sudden tears that started to form in the corner of my eyes. I wasn't surprised by their unwelcome arrival. In the last three years, I learned that I had little to no control over when I might start crying. I also learned the answer to the question that my four-year-old self asked when we moved out of our Chicago townhouse: "Do you ever run out of tears?" No. No, you don't.

"Yeah. It's bearable," he agreed. "I guess because it has to be. And anyway, I know that eventually I need to do it."

Lincoln rose and stood next to me, crossing his arms on the railing in the same fashion.

After a minute or so of each of us roaming through our own private, but likely similar memories, he spoke up, "Whoa. What time is it? Did we really talk that long?"

"No idea," I said to the sky. "It's pretty though."

The predawn glow blanketed us like a secret. The streetlights were fading, and the gentle sounds of waking started to replace the silence of those mysterious early morning hours. I was wide awake and the necessity of a restful night's sleep before this upcoming final was not just fading, but altogether lost. The rich hues above us and the brisk December chill made the encounter feel purposeful. I didn't want the warmth of my comforter or to be dragged into consciousness by my alarm. I wanted to be on this fire escape…escaping.

I glanced up at him. His eyes were transfixed on the sunrise that was more prominent between the law school and nursing department. I felt sad, but calm. Studying his face in the early morning sun while restraining my desire to reach out and what? —I didn't know—but I knew that squashing the desire was agonizing. He was Lincoln—my best friend's brother. But more than that—he was my *other* best friend, even if we unfairly treated him like an annoyingly tag-a-long.

I never noticed just how much he resembled Isa. The shape of the eyebrows. The hazel eyes with the ring of gold around the pupil. I stared at him, and I wanted to surrender—to let the tears flow freely. I had a strange thought: *He is beautiful.* Like she was beautiful, but also in a different way that I hadn't realized when we were younger. Maybe it was because he had that early twenties lived-in look going for him with the facial hair and "I've been through some shit" weariness behind the eyes. Maybe it was as simple as the fact that I missed her. But I had missed *him* too. How could I not? Lincoln—with the daisy that matched mine. I missed him before he ever left.

Sensing my eyes on him, he broke the silence, "But K, what about you? What happened to you? After Isa died."

2.

The Sparkler

"Are you awake?"

    I had my back turned from the rest of the group. The tent in Blair's backyard was suffocating. I couldn't sleep; I still couldn't shake the brutal humiliation of only hours before.

    "One school play and she's already preparing for Broadway!" Savannah had laughed, holding up my spiral Spanish 1 notebook for the rest of the girls to gawk at.

    The evidence was clear as day—my amateur first-attempt at an autograph decorated page after page in childish, unpolished cursive. "K Statham" a hundred times over, like entries from a serial killer's diary.

    "But she's marked up this entire page with 'Sister Sarah Brown!'" Deanna exclaimed, grabbing the notebook from Savannah, and pointing at the page where I, to my present horror and their delight, had practiced the autograph of my on-stage persona. I cursed my past self who daydreamed of appeasing a line of eager audience members when I should have been taking Spanish notes.

    "You know it's just a play, right? I mean, I know it's confusing, K. Jason Calbots basically *is* as much of a playboy as Sky Masterson, but sweetie, he's not about to waste his time with a freshman in real life. You know?" Blair chimed in, eliciting explosive laughter.

"Yeah, like that's such a loss. I'm sure K has zero interest in jocks that had to retake standard level English twice. He can barely remember his lines, let alone write an essay on Moby Dick," Isa jumped in. She was the only one not laughing.

"Calm down, Isa," Savannah interrupted. "We know our precious wittle K wouldn't stand for Jason's advances. She'd slap him just like Sarah."

"Oh my god. K," Blair asked, feigning interest. "Have you ever even been kissed? Or will the play be your first time?"

I wanted to die. My nightgown with the tiny cherry buttons seemed vintage in a trendy way ten minutes ago. Now it felt babyish, more Shirley Temple than Ann-Margret. My naivety was on full display. Why did I come to this sleepover with these girls that I barely knew anyway? Why did my mom have to sign me up for this dumb play? Why did I have to be cast as the lead? And *why* did I ever think, "Hey, maybe this will be fun. Maybe I'll make some friends. Maybe I am actually talented." I could have—I *should* have—dropped out. It would have been so easy to use the "I'm new and I just want to adjust to my workload" excuse. New girls shouldn't draw attention to themselves. What false confidence made me think it'd be okay to deviate from that social norm?

To be fair, I didn't ask for this. My mom had the audition flier sitting on the kitchen counter when I got home from school one day and proudly declared that she had already emailed the drama teacher about how I could "get involved."

"There was a stack of these in the front office. I grabbed one when I dropped off your lunch. The gal at the front desk—Mrs. Ford—said her daughter has been doing the plays for years. Her name's Blair. She *loves* it," my mom explained. "And by the way, honey, we've got to remember to give you some cash so you can buy your lunch in the cafeteria if you forget your lunch again."

I had only been half listening, but when she reported that she'd taken it upon herself to promise Ms. Morris, the drama teacher, that I'd be at auditions Friday afternoon, I spoke up to protest.

"Honey, this will be good for you!" Mom assured me two months ago. "All those years of dragging me and Daddy to those crazy musicals. Now is the time, honey! Remember we said that this move was an opportunity for a fresh start? And Blair's mom told me this school has a *fantastic* drama department. Best high school theater in the district, apparently. And wouldn't you know that Lanette Ford is also the vice president of our HOA? They live on Hammersmith Court. Maybe we can both make a new friend, huh?"

New friend alright. I didn't foresee Blair and I exchanging friendship brackets in the near future. I lunged for the notebook that was still in Deanna's hands and fumbled with the zipper of my backpack before shoving it back in.

"It's a good thing you don't need to draw on too much imagination to play the role, K," Blair said. "Most freshmen are already in love with Jason, but not all of them are as prudish as Sarah."

And you're perfectly typecast as Adelaide because you're the dumbest slut of the sophomore class.

At that, the girls started to complain about how Ms. Morris was incompetent at her job and "didn't get it" because she wouldn't allow the Hot Box Girls to wear actual lingerie-esque showgirl costumes. That was the whole point of this get together. We weren't gathered at Blair's to sing kumbaya and braid each other's hair; we were attempting to add a bit of modern flair to the tired old costumes Ms. Morris had left over from that last time the school performed *Guys and Dolls*…in the 80's. Not that it mattered to me. Sarah's conversative frocks suited me just fine and I had no desire to turn her Save-a-Soul band uniform into a crop top set. Instead, with the focus now directed back onto the costume dilemma, I seized the opportunity to retreat to the house for the bathroom. I just wanted a moment to sit in my embarrassment without onlookers pointing and staring. Surely, they would think tears were a sign of weakness—possibly pointing out that I wasn't a good fit for Sarah after all. Anyone that had ever seen *Guys and Dolls* knew that Sarah was supremely poised and controlled.

When I opened the bathroom door, Isa was standing right outside.

"Sorry. It's all yours," I mumbled and tried to brush past her.

"Hey," Isa said, placing her hand on my shoulder to stop me in my tracks. "If I said, 'Don't listen to them.' would that sound too cliché?"

"I… um…"

"I know. It would. But don't listen to them. I would hate to see them recruit a perfectly capable person into their squad of insecure followers. Look, I don't know you, obviously. But I'm assuming you have better things to do than vie for their approval."

"I mean… It's not a big deal. It was stupid anyway. The…um…autographs or whatever."

She stared at me for a moment like she was trying to use her eyes as a lie detector test. Apparently, I didn't pass.

"Can I be candid?" Isa asked, as if she hadn't been already.

I nodded, dumbly. I had maybe spoken two sentences to this girl before tonight. Something unmemorable along the lines of, "Do you know what time rehearsal is?"

"They're jealous that a freshman got Sarah. I mean, look at Deanna. This is her senior year and she's been in chorus every. Single. Year. And Blair—this is the first time she's ever had someone rival her position on the throne. Everyone thought Savannah would get Sarah and we all know Blair totally dominates her so that wouldn't have ruffled any feathers. But *you*. You intimidate them. You're good. They know it. And they hate it."

"Thanks?" I didn't know what else to say.

"And look," Isa nodded towards a framed photo of a chubby toddler in the bathroom. "Blair's always been kind of a porker. She's probably jealous that you're way skinnier than her too. Just saying."

I couldn't help but laugh. My change in demeanor seemed to satisfy Isa because she started to laugh with me. The noise that erupted from her was melodic and unexpected. Husky yet bright, it was unlike anything else I'd ever heard. When my eyes met hers, I saw a kind of assurance that was hard to pin down. Sure, I had noticed her before. She was a Hot Box Girl, and I knew she was older than me—a sophomore. Her brother (Lincoln? I wasn't sure at the time.) was a freshman like me and the assistant stage manager. She wore a lot of tie-dyes, carried her books in a large canvas satchel, and she had long, loose white-blonde waves that were sometimes adorned with daisies from the Freshman/Sophomore courtyard. Her arms were usually covered with noisy bracelets, seemingly handmade.

At a distance, she seemed the carefree, free-spirited type. But up close, there was something more. This girl knew herself. This girl was grounded. She was more than confident; she was wise. We got a hold of ourselves and the smirk that replaced her giggle fit encompassed the perfect juxtaposition of sarcasm and knowing severity. Whatever was in her that made her shine like that—I wanted it too.

"Are you awake?" Isa whispered now. Her voice, a crystal clear and daring whisper, pierced through the nighttime sounds of crickets and soft snoring.

For a split second I thought about ignoring her, shutting my eyes, and pretending to be asleep like the rest. Maybe I'd be telling a much different story if I did. But I didn't. I rolled over to face her.

"Yeah, I guess."

"Have you ever gone streaking?" she asked.

"Um…what? No. You mean like—"

"Come on," Isa hissed.

Without any idea about what I was getting myself into, I unzipped my sleeping bag and followed Isa as she crawled silently out of the tent. We dodged the limbs of the sleeping girls sprawled around us and slowly zipped the tent shut before letting out even the shallowest of exhales. Void of explanation, she darted to a nearby oak and motioned for me to follow.

Crouched down in the grass, Isa whispered, "Let's leave our clothes here. Better than out in the open."

"Are you serious? What if we get caught?"

"Who's going to catch us?"

I hesitated. "I don't know? The police? *Blair's mom?*"

It was obvious to everyone that knew her that Lanette Ford was a stage mom to the extreme and, as a consequence, overwrought by even the most minor of calamities. I pictured her calling our moms immediately and sounding an Amber alert within five minutes of discovering us missing.

Isa snorted. "Seriously? Lanette sleeps like a rock. And she probably has her overnight anti-age creamer on. God forbid she risk the neighbors seeing her in that state."

"How do you kn—"

"Come onnnnn."

"But what if one of them wakes up and sees that we're not here?" I asked, throwing my arms towards the tent. And then a horrifying thought dawned on me. "What if they find our pajamas and *take* them?"

The possibilities for further humiliation seemed endless. Not to mention, the biggest question was: "Why are we even doing this?"

"K, live a little, will you?" Isa urged.

She started to pull her *Bye, Bye Birdie* cast tee over her head and somehow it felt wrong to stand there and watch her disrobe without making an attempt to join in the harebrained scheme. I suppose I could have refused altogether and crawled back into the tent, but I knew that if I did, I'd wind up laying on the ground wide awake and wondering what life would be like if I was as adventurous as Isa. And so, I started to strip. Isa tossed her pjs in a sloppy pile, but I attempted to fold mine, as if tidiness would somehow save me if I was caught and forced to deliver an excuse for myself.

It was the most alien feeling—to become bare under the moonlight, completely outdoors and in front of a near-stranger no less. I had always been a modest person. I had no siblings—no sisters whom I was used to undressing in front of. I don't even think my own mother has seen me naked since I was maybe eight years old. But there I was—bare straggly legs (Of course, I had forgotten to shave. A mistake that only furthered my vulnerability.), exposed chest, and tummy out on display. Slouching and crossing my arms over my chest, I felt every bit of the awkward fourteen-year-old that I was compared to Isa's perfectly relaxed and upright form. I assumed that she wasn't the kind of girl to stand in front of the mirror pinching the baby fat on her stomach or wondering if her current cup size was really *all* she was ever going to get. But before I could properly tumble down a rabbit hole of body shaming, Isa strode in the direction of the road, and I had to catch up.

The mild October air enveloped my skin. The pleasantness of the sensation overshadowed the fact that keeping up with Isa's pace necessitated that I allow my arms to hang loose instead of functioning as a shield. I was thankful that the neighborhood streets were dim except for the soft amber glow of a streetlamp in front of every third house. It had to be close to 3:00 am at this point and every house appeared to be in a deep slumber. The entire neighborhood was our ghostlike playground. Isa started to run.

"K! Keep up!"

Even if I lived just two blocks away, Isa clearly had a better sense of direction. The quintessential suburban Colonials were more like a fading dream than a reality with the absence of broad daylight. If I happened to remember the route my mom took to drop me off at Blair's several hours earlier, there was no chance of me recollecting it now in this darkness, at this pace, and amidst this pulsating adrenaline. If I stopped, I wouldn't be able to find my way back; I had to stick to my erratic companion or face the horror of wandering the McMansion maze alone. Though, to be perfectly frank, it wasn't that logic that magnetized me to her. My feet pounded against the pavement, I leapt over flowerbeds, and I delighted in the feeling of the forbidden night wind flapping against my ponytail.

Isa was a Fourth of July sparkler darting ahead of me with her wild blonde waves illuminated by the streetlights. She was soaring too high to scrutinize or judge me and I was too hyped myself to think twice about how vulnerably exposed we were anymore. A deviation from her chaotic dashing, Isa took a sudden turn to the right and weaved between the gap in the fences of two houses. We were at the top of a small hill and before us was a large expanse of meticulously landscaped property. The question of *"Where are we going?"* was on my lips, but I decided that it wasn't worth letting the thought escape. Isa had a mission, and I was just along for the ride.

As we continued to sprint further down the hill, I began to make out the soft outline of the neighborhood's clubhouse. There was a pool on the other side of the clubhouse in the direction that we were approaching.

I could sense Isa's intention even before she paused to say, "Since you've never been streaking, I can assume you've also never been skinny dipping."

Any other time, I'd have a million objections— "We can't break in." "What if there are alarms?" "It'll be way too cold." Tonight, however, I just burst out laughing. Of course, I had never been skinny dipping. Did she know who she was talking to? I never stayed up past 10:00 pm if my parents told me "Lights out." She laughed her husky laugh but simultaneously silenced me by placing a hand over my mouth. In the playfulness of the moment, I sobered abruptly and listened for instructions.

"Okay, this is what we're going to do," she explained, just inches away from my face. "I used to hang in this neighborhood all the time and I know that the gate is literally always unlocked. There're motion sensors right above the windows, so if we just stick to the far right and swim on the deep end, we'll be fine."

We stealthily approached the gate that surrounded the pool area. Just as she said, the gate was unlocked, and she easily pushed it forward. She tip-topped along the gate until she reached the far-right side of the pool, and I imitated her every move. My heart raced as we crept towards the edge of the deep end. She was the first to dip her toes in. I didn't immediately follow suit because it all at once struck me that we were now committing another level of deviance. If an alarm sounded or an insomniac neighbor happened to see us, trespassing was far worse than gallivanting naked through deserted streets. But then again—I had come this far. I was already inside the gates and, if caught, couldn't argue my way out of being her accomplice. I watched Isa lower her body over the edge and into the turquoise abyss. She let out a comical silent scream.

"Cold?" I asked.

"No. It's great."

She splashed me. It was definitely cold.

"Come onnnnn," Isa whined. That seemed to be her chase phrase of the evening. "You'll get used to it." She submerged her entire body underneath and then popped back up with force. "Ahhh. Refreshing!"

I scooted towards the lip of the pool and draped my legs over. Icy pangs shot through my entire body. "Oh my god. No way. How are you doing this?"

"Like this," Isa said.

Before I had time to retreat, Isa grabbed both my hands and pulled me in. Luckily, I had the presence of mind to hold my breath before going under. Completely engulfed by chlorine, I squinted my eyes open. Isa's eyes were fully alert. The pool lights gave her an ethereal presence. She was something out of a fairytale or a dream. Despite the bitter shock to my system, I was calm. In unison, we resurfaced.

"Isn't this amazing?" Isa asked. I had to admit that it was. "K, we're so *alive* right now." And we were. Her laughter confirmed that we were indeed very much alive.

"Where did you move from?" she asked as if we were having a conventional get-to-know you conversation over coffee.

I had waded off to the other side of the deep end. My mind was far from the world I had left behind just a few months ago.

"Oregon. A little town outside of Portland. But before that—Philadelphia. And before that—a suburb of Chicago. This is supposed to be the last move though."

"Ugh. Lucky. I'd give anything to get out of the south."

"I just want to…stay put I guess," I admitted. "And Tennessee's not so bad."

"Yeah, maybe. If you didn't grow up here."

I didn't know how to argue that. It was such a common theme with everyone I had met—they were all envious of my having moved across the country and I was envious that they knew the same people since pre-k.

"At least you have good weather here. No way we would be doing this in Oregon. By this time, it's snowmageddon back ho—I mean, back there." It felt dishonest to call St. Helens home.

"Do you have a lot of friends there?" Isa asked.

She was listening, but also appeared to be performing some sort of improvised synchronized swimming routine with her eyes closed.

"No," I answered honestly before I could stop myself. "No really *close* friends, anyway."

"It's hard to find your people. Most people are dreadfully ordinary if you know what I mean."

I think I did. But I also feared that I too belonged in the "dreadfully ordinary" category.

"Lincoln is my best friend," she continued.

"Lincoln. He's your—"

"Baby bro," she finished. "I mean, yeah, you could say I have 'friends.' But Lincoln is the only one who's really awake. I just don't want to waste the energy. That stuff is precious. You have to be careful who you give it to."

I wasn't entirely sure what she meant, but I murmured a semi-confident, "Yeah. Yeah, definitely."

"You have any brothers? Sisters?"

"Um...no it's—"

"Just you," Isa completed. She liked to finish thoughts. "That's fine. I mean, you create your own legacy. Poor Lincoln is forced to walk in my shadow. It's hard to live up to infamy."

I laughed. Was this girl extremely self-aware, brutally honest, or existing with a dominant screw loose? Maybe it was all of the above. I couldn't tell. She closed her eyes and spun, her wet locks creating ripples all around her.

"Shoulda been a ballerina. Don't you think?" She laughed that characteristic laugh again. "I know, I know. My boobs are way too big for a leotard."

That made us both laugh. Whatever the underlying cause of her freedom, I liked it. She was so blunt. So free. I don't know why I was normally ashamed by the mention of "female" topics, but in Isa's presence, I was laughing along with her.

"Probably for the best," I said. "My mom once told me that ballerinas are crackheads who live on coffee and cigarettes. Actors can actually eat."

"Actors?" Isa asked, looking me dead in the eye. "Oh K, I don't want to *be an actor*. I just do the plays for something to do. Lincoln's the real theater freak."

"What do you want to do?"

At that moment, I decided that there was nothing more important than learning as much as I could about her.

"Oh, so many things," she said, floating on her back now and staring up at the moon. "I want to live in Switzerland and play acoustic guitar. I want to read tarot for strangers. But I guess if I had to have a *real* job, I'd be a traveling yoga instructor and Reiki healer. No, maybe a ski instructor or a tour guide. But I've also always had a thing for stargazing and being one of those live statues—you know, the ones that are totally painted? Or even a nude figure model...that's probably pretty lucrative.

"I don't know. There's plenty of time to see what the universe will throw at me. But I'll start in Switzerland. I'll just be some rich widower's au pair, make him fall in love with me, and then he'll fund my next expedition. Either way, I want at least three dogs and two cats. Maybe an alpaca. What about you?"

How was I to compete with that? I knew it was senseless to try.

"I have always…loved art. All kinds," I managed.

"You're an artist," she stated, like it was as plain a fact as the deep hickory brown of my hair.

"I…I guess? I was in the children's choir when my parents were going through their Catholic phase. And then, in second grade, our school took a field trip to see *Charlotte's Web* at the Arden. I became obsessed after that. I always wanted to see shows, but I was…I don't know. I never thought I could *be in them*. This is my first play, actually, but…I think I really love it. I've always been sort of…shy? So, I didn't think—"

"So do it! K, 'shy' is a label somebody gave you at some point in your life, probably. I see you at rehearsals and you are *in it.* Maybe you just haven't had the right people to listen to you and that's why you've felt 'shy' or whatever. But let me tell you—when you're making art up there, people are listening."

Who was this girl that apparently knew more about me than I knew of myself?

"I'm a little bit psychic," she said in response to my thoughts. "Trust me. Don't stop creating."

"I'll remember that," I promised.

My sometimes-contrarian teenage disposition softened as I privately vowed to thank my mom for signing me up to audition in the first place.

"Let's get out of here," she said suddenly. "I'm starving."

Running back to the tent dried us off so our pjs—which, thankfully, remained untouched—weren't sopping wet when we at last pulled them back on.

"My car's here," Isa said. "Let's get some Taco Bell. They won't miss us."

At this point, my muscles were aching, and my eyes were drooping. Sleep beckoned me, even if it was only to sleep in a cramped tent on the cold, hard ground. But her eyes bore into mine and that somehow energized me. That same depth of intensity from our moment outside the bathroom was there. But there was something else too. A longing? A loneliness? In some incommunicable sense, I felt needed and for that, I wasn't about to refuse her. We climbed in her forest green Subaru.

"Tamara's old car," she declared. "I'm pretty sure her work boyfriend got her the new one."

"Tamara?"

"My mom. At least, that's who she claims to be," Isa clarified.

"Your parents are divorced?" I asked.

"Nah. Well, not yet."

"I'm…sorry."

"K, how can you be a downer right now? We're about to get crunch wrap supremes!" she said as she scrolled furiously through her iPod for the right ambiance. "I don't care what anyone says, *The Bends* is Radiohead's best album."

She put the car in reverse, and we were free once again, venturing out into that special time of late-night-early-morning that feels somewhat sacred because you know you're not supposed to be awake.

"Don't leave me high…Don't leave me dryyyyy…" Isa rolled down the window and bellowed the lyrics into the crisp early morning air.

The speed limit in the neighborhood couldn't have been more than 25, but her dash read 50mph. I'll never forget learning the words to "High and Dry," sticking my hands out of her open sunroof and the thought that ran through my mind: *This could be my person.*

3.

To See Without Looking

Finally, I had made it to the last question of my never-ending final:

> *Describe the symbolism behind the Arabesque inlays on the photo below.*

My Chubbie's double shot espresso had fought admirably to hold my eyes open for the last two hours, but I sensed the defenses crumbling. I powered through another short paragraph—chicken scratch at this point—and succumbed to an intense yawn. My professor raised her eyebrows in my direction.

"All done, K?"

"Yes, thank you," I said as I handed her my exam.

"Get some sleep these next few weeks, yes? Be kind to yourself."

"I'll try."

Dr. Mirza was one of the good ones and had been with me since I changed majors freshman year. Not only was she the art history chair, but I was lucky enough to have her as my academic advisor.

***

"Why art history?" she asked.

I took a deep breath and tried to recall the answer I had prepped for the occasion. I wanted the college of art to take me seriously. I wanted them to see me as a fully-functioning, albeit fledgling, adult that was dependable and certainly not "overwhelmed by my circumstances" (as the head of the theater department had said).

No—come January I would walk onto campus a new person. A capable person. Not someone marked by grief. No one in the art department knew me and so no one would have reason to avoid my gaze or, worse, shower me with looks of pity.

"I have always…I have always…"

"You're an artist," I heard her whisper.

No. No. No. Hot tears were forming. Damnit. I had prepared for this. Art history. Come on, come on. *Why* art history? Because I want something safe. I want to explore art from a safe distance. No. I knew I couldn't say that...

I'm interested in the cultures of ancient civilizations, I remembered.

Right, that was it. And I had a good bit about how I believed studying an individual's art can reveal so much about…about what? I swallowed hard. Was she to accompany me everywhere I go now? No. That was crazy. Surely, that had to be crazy.

"…loved art..." was all I could stammer.

Dr. Mirza tilted her head and gave a faint smile. This woman was stunning and, in my opinion, very easily could have been a model if she hadn't become a professor. In fact, she almost looked like my mother but maybe ten years older. This observation was mildly off-putting and comforting at the same time. Her skin was the color of caramel, her round dark brown eyes were kind and soft, and her thick black eyebrows were flawlessly arched. One fundamental difference—two, actually—was that Dr. Mirza wore a hijab. And a small gold hoop pierced her right nostril.

"Not to worry, Ms. Statham. Or should I call you… K?" She glanced down on my transcripts that were sprawled on her desk. "It's K, is it? Do you prefer—"

"Yes. Yes. Sorry, yeah. It's…I just go by K."

"Got it, thank you," she continued. "I don't want you to feel as though this is a scary job interview. We are happy to have you in the art history department and nothing you say to me today would persuade me to recommend otherwise. We're meeting today so we can make sense out of your spring semester schedule, yes? You were accepted ages ago, so the hard part is behind you!"

She was waiting for a response before continuing her spiel, but my thoughts were centered on that final bit— "the hard part is behind you." I knew she was referring to the whole three ringed circus of admissions essays, the ACT, and scholarship applications, but that wasn't what came to mind. "The hard part is behind you." Was it, really? My incessant 3:00 am thoughts told me that the hard part had only just begun. I wouldn't classify perfecting an intro paragraph for a personal statement as "hard" anymore, not after enduring the last month and a half.

"You have the first semester under your belt, and we've had many students come to us much later in the game, I'm afraid," she comforted. "Quite a mess to untangle without having to add on a summer semester or two. But you—you are just in time."

A rogue tear trickled down my cheek. I wiped it away with the edge of my cardigan sleeve almost as quickly as it had sprung loose, but not without Dr. Mirza's notice. I could sense that she was about to speak—maybe offer me one of the tissues on her desk or ask me what was the matter. Instinctively, I found something in the room to comment on and divert the attention off my obvious inability to cope in perfectly normal social situations.

"That looks just like one of the Thorne rooms," I noted, pointing at the miniature display of an art studio sitting on the bookcase behind Dr. Mirza.

Like an intricate dollhouse for a child that appreciated fine detail, this model included tiny easels with half-finished paintings and a teacher's desk littered with miniscule art supplies and papers to be graded.

"Oh this?" Dr. Mirza spun in her chair to face the teensy work of beauty. "Yes, the Thorne miniatures. Exactly! I am quite an admirer. This was made for me by my friend and colleague, Dr. Pacala. She teaches most of the sculpting and 3D visual arts courses. She knows how I love Thorne's work. She did a good job, yes? You see," she pointed at the delicately hung whiteboard at the rear of the tiny room, "my name is right there."

Indeed, "Dr. Mirza" was written in what resembled a dry-erase marker scroll; a charming personal nod that was barely perceptible from my seat on the other side of her desk.

"That's incredible," I said.

"She's somewhat of a genius. I always tell her. She's too bashful to admit it, I'm afraid. Where have you seen Thorne's rooms?"

"The Art Institute of Chicago," I explained. "My cousins, aunt, and uncle came to visit us when I was four or five. My cousins are both around my age and they were not having it; the museum is a lot for little kids, I guess. But I loved it. Especially the Thorne miniatures in the basement. It was like a hidden playhouse. My cousins just thought the rooms looked like 'boring Barbie houses,' but I don't know…I just kept imagining the lives that would live in those rooms and the stories the little walls would tell.

"It's hard to explain, but it was personal for some reason. Like I was peeping into someone's private life. Kind of melancholy in a way because where did the people in the rooms go? I'm an only child and…well, my parents work a lot so…I guess I've also spent a lot of time in empty rooms… Anyway, it's always been my favorite exhibit."

Dr. Mirza had leaned back in her chair as I lost myself in recalling one of my fondest memories. She was now nodding her head and thoughtfully fixating on the ceiling. I wasn't sure what to say next; I started to pick at my cuticles, waiting to take her cue. When the silence that filled the room began to linger longer than was natural, I wondered if my babbling had made me appear childish. I wanted to kick myself for that brief admission of childhood loneliness. Sure, my emotions had been unpredictable lately—almost as if the ice palace that I spent nineteen years building around my heart had thawed under the pressure of everything that I was forced to process.

I was raw, exposed. In the first few months after it happened, my every thought and feeling was balancing dangerously on limp, open palms. Anyone could take what they wanted; I was only a vessel to this grief that simply couldn't be contained. But that was no excuse. Dr. Mirza was not just a stranger, she was a stranger that needed to think of me as capable so that I could move forward. I *had* to move forward. Taking a semester off was not an option, lest I allow this blackness to swallow me whole.

Please. I need to go forward, I pleaded silently, picking away at my cuticles.

"You see, K," Dr. Mirza said, interrupting my anxious descent. "That is the job of an art historian—to see beyond looking. Some merely look at what's in front of them, while others strive to see what's inside. Others ask questions. My favorite poet, Henry David Thoreau said, 'It's not what you look at that matters, it's what you see.' You understand? I think you are in the right place. And pardon me for suggesting, but this could be the right time, yes? There is so much to see that is outside of ourselves. And often one finds it useful to get outside of themselves."

I was almost positive that this woman knew nothing of my "current circumstance," but I welcomed her discernment. I wanted to be anyone other than myself. I *needed* to see outside of myself. For a moment, I gave myself the permission to imagine that I could very well be in an entirely different state of mind by the end of the spring semester. Perhaps it wasn't just the wild delusion of a desperately depressed person that I may be able to reinvent myself—maybe I actually could. Maybe if I focused less on what was inside and devoted myself to studying what was around me—what was beautiful and *only* that—I could let go of this grotesque secret. Maybe it would all simply fade away.

***

It was that vignette of meeting Dr. Mirza that played in my mind as I lazily weaved through my peers en route to my apartment. I still had to pack before I drove back home. I also needed to return all the books I checked out from the library for finals, stop by Chubbie's to pick up my schedule (Lenny didn't like to schedule me much over break; he wanted me to "enjoy the holidays" even though I always objected), spend probably twenty minutes coaxing F. Scott into his cat carrier…maybe I'll have time for a nap too. Hopefully. I was tired and fading fast. So tired, in fact, that I was barely aware of where I was going.

"Oh! Oh sorry. I wasn't paying atten—"

"K?"

Lincoln turned around after my face collided with his back. He was waiting at the crosswalk I needed to take to get to my apartment, a few textbooks under one arm and a guitar case slung over his other shoulder. I noticed that he was still wearing the same blue, gray, and juniper green flannel from the night before. He had a gray beanie over his sandy blonde hair, probably to mask the fact that it was unlikely he had time to shower between our marathon catch-up session and his first final of the day.

"K!" he said again. "I guess I'm going to run into you every day now. Or *you* run into *me*."

"Sorry. I was somewhere else. I'm pretty tired."

"Hey, I'm not complaining. I just don't want to get my hopes up with all these chance encounters." He grinned and I wondered how he could possibly look so chipper on approximately zero hours of sleep.

"How was your exam?"

"It went shockingly well, actually. But I'm crashing. What about you? And what's this?" I said, referencing the guitar. "You play now?"

"Could hardly call myself a liberal arts student on this campus without toting an instrument around, right? It's just a prop so I fit in."

He wasn't wrong. Moody artist-types strumming their hearts out on the quad only until they secured a record deal and dropped out was the dream turned cliché for many of the students at this school.

"Kidding," he continued. "It *is* a prop though. I can't play this thing. Devised Theater final. Long story."

I had an intense urge to listen to Lincoln tell me this long story. For some reason, the thought of his voice giving me a play by play of his creative mind sounded like the perfect white noise to lull me to sleep. But that was just an idiotic thought. I hadn't pulled an all-nighter in a while and my brain was foggy and betraying me with sentimentality.

Go home, pack your bags, then go to sleep before you embarrass yourself.

"What are you doing for break?" he asked.

"Probably just…"

Probably just taking 2-4 baths a day, rereading the Ariel poems, ignoring grad school deadlines, and thinking up excuses to avoid social interaction with family members.

"…just catch up on some reading. I have some family stuff. And a department party," I managed.

"Well, we should hang out? …If you want. If you're not, uh, too tied down with family stuff," Lincoln offered. "We're having the Christmas party again. You could stop by? Or just…we could watch a movie? Whatever you wa—"

"The Christmas party?" I asked. "I didn't know your dad still did that."

The last DeLuca Christmas party took place junior year of high school. Bookended by two notorious Tamara DeLuca meltdowns, I'm pretty sure the memory of that holly jolly occasion will be ingrained in the minds of all who attended, resurfacing every holiday season.

"Oh yeah," Lincoln rubbed the back of his neck, apparently uncomfortable. "It's…yeah…it's not like it used to be. Whitney's all into decorating. Looks like the seasonal aisle of Hobby Lobby just barfed all over the place." He laughed nervously. "But anyway, it's really chill. There's going to be a lot of food. Her whole women's group or whatever brings over a ton of pies and casseroles and junk."

"Well, who am I to refuse a Baptist woman's chicken and rice casserole?" I joked.

Lincoln laughed sincerely this time. Whatever social hurtle he had to jump through to extend the invitation was behind him now and his body visibly relaxed. It was adorable, in a sense. Just knowing that he was going out on a limb to spend time with me. And it was equally so odd how time and emotional distance can, without our consent, build invisible walls of awkwardness between us and what would have been a totally normal occurrence just a few years ago. In high school I had a standing invitation to the DeLuca residence. Nobody asked me to come over; I just showed up.

"So, you'll be there?" he ventured, readjusting the guitar case on his shoulder. Those familiar hazel eyes bore right into mine. Who was I to refuse them?

4.

Act Too

Strands of sweaty curls clung to my forehead as I tried to squeeze past my hormonal peers. When it came to flirting, my locker neighbors had no self-awareness; they chose directly in front of my locker and in the dead center of the hallway as the ideal spot to tickle and taunt each other.

"Oh my goddddd, Todd. Ewwww! Your locker smells like an armpit," Cassandra, the owner of the locker to my right declared.

"Yeah, it's my practice uniform. Coach is running us real hard to get ready for the game on Friday," Todd said as he slammed his locker shut and, inconveniently for me, leaned against it. "You're gonna be there, right?"

"But like, do you even take your filth home and wash it? That shit reeks," Megan—bottom locker—asserted.

Mrs. Santiago had held us past the bell talking about the grave impact tomorrow's Spanish 1 exam would have on our overall GPA (why was it that every teacher thought their class was the most critical?). If it weren't for that, I would have been able to race to my locker, grab my stuff, and bolt to the south wing of campus before my moronic locker neighbors sauntered out of their respective classrooms. This was a tactic I tried to utilize as often as possible because I'd found that even minor social interaction and the act of physically plowing my way past them when they never heard/ignored my requests to get by would inevitably make me late for rehearsal. Ms. Morris liked to start at 2:50 pm on the dot.

"Sounds like Meggy Meg needs to take her potty mouth home and wash it," Enrique taunted.

Enrique's locker was below Todd's, and he took every opportunity possible to offend Megan or poke her ribs. This sickening display of attraction was sometimes welcomed with playful snickers and faux attempts to fight back, but today Megan rolled her eyes to the popcorn ceiling.

"Excuse me..." I tried.

It was useless. Enrique poked Megan and she proceeded to swat him with a textbook. In the blink of an eye, a tickle war had ensued between the two of them and my voice was lost among the shrieks, squeals, and general hubbub of hallway traffic. I hated my own kind. After only a year and a half of teenagerhood, I was already looking forward to my twenties and beyond.

Come on. MOVE.

Then, I found my escape route. In the raucous, Todd's football helmet toppled out of the locker and skid across the floor. As both Todd and Cassandra lunged forward to grab his precious crown, I was able to dart past.

"Looks good on me, doesn't it?" I heard Cassandra coo behind me as I sped away. I guess she beat him to it.

They irritated the hell out of me, especially when their mindless banter made me late to rehearsal. But if I was being completely honest, what bothered me most was feeling invisible. My locker was at the focal point of the madness, but I may as well have been a ghost. What would it have been like to be a Cassandra or a Megan? What would it have been like to have guys notice me, flirt with me, try to get my attention? Nobody asked me if I was going to the football games.

Not that I wanted to go, but still—maybe it would feel good to be asked. These were the complicated thoughts of my 14-year-old brain as I shifted into full suburban mom speed walking mode. It was 2:52 pm.

Ms. Morris greeted latecomers by pausing mid-sentence, clearing her throat, and declaring with every ounce of grandeur her body could muster, "Nice of you to grace us with your presence." After just one high school theater rehearsal, I already knew half of the Actor's Equity rules and guidelines thanks to Ms. Morris's insistence that we all hold ourselves up to a professional standard. She never actually enforced these rules. That is, she didn't *actually* expect us to give her five dollars for showing up late or dropping a line, but she always made sure to remind us: "In the real world, you'd be fined for that. That's the business, folks!"

I wasn't looking to draw even more attention to myself from tardiness. But, as luck (a thing that I usually had in short supply) would have it, I wasn't the only drama kid who was standing outside the auditorium when vocal warmups were supposed to be taking place. Several of my castmates huddled around the closed auditorium doors and some were even leaving the building.

"What's going on?" I asked no one in particular as I approached the group. A tall kid with shaggy blonde hair was blocking my view of the door. I didn't realize until he turned around that it was Isa's brother, our assistant stage manager.

"Hey!" he said, then cleared his throat theatrically. "I mean, Sargent Sarah." Bringing his hand to his forehead, he gave me a salute. "A little late? I'd normally have to charge five dollars for that, ma'am, but I'll let it go just this once."

He was joking; the enormous, toothy grin gave him away instantly. Before I could respond, Isa emerged from the crowd. When we locked eyes, I blushed. I hadn't seen her since the sleepover Friday night or, technically, Saturday morning.

Did she tell anyone we went streaking? I thought before my brain could process what the next socially acceptable response might be. How does one interact normally after such an abnormal experience? But awkwardness—which had to have been radiating from my pores—

didn't faze Isa. She flashed me a smile then turned to whack Lincoln on the back of the head.

"Give it a rest, Lincoln. K, rehearsal's been canceled. See?" Isa nodded at the now-visible notice on the auditorium door.

THESPIANS, I REGRET THAT REHEARSAL MUST BE CANCELED. MY ELDEST NEEDS EMERGENCY TREATMENT. WE WILL RESUME TOMORROW. LEARN YOUR LINES!!!
CHEERS!
MS. M

"Is her kid sick?" I asked.

"Well, if you're the kind of person that considers felines 'kids,'" Lincoln snorted. "Ms. M has, like, seven of them. You gotta admit—she's the type."

He swirled his finger in the air and tilted his head from side to side—a gesture to indicate that Ms. Morris was a total wacko…which she was. Everybody knew that and it was one of the reasons she was so good at her job.

"She has *three*," Isa corrected. "Just because she's a woman of a certain age and single, doesn't mean she's a cat lady."

"How many cats does it take to be a 'cat lady'? I thought just more than one would get you in the club," Lincoln responded.

Isa rolled her eyes and I laughed.

"Ms. M is an eccentric who prefers the long-term company of soulful creatures. You've seen her—she's a total babe for a woman in her fifties. She probably still has an exhilarating sex life," Isa justified.

Lincoln shuddered and retorted, "No one was thinking about her sex life, Isa."

"Insinuating that she's a cat lady also implies that she's a recluse who doesn't get any and I'm simply defending her lifestyle by saying that she's still a woman of the world, even if she has a few cats. That's all. Anyway, Cleo is sick. We should be helping, not gossiping."

"What are we gonna do? Bring her cat some chicken noodle soup?"

Unlike the morons I had for locker neighbors, I found Lincoln and Isa's banter amusing. But their brother-sister comedy routine went unnoticed by everyone but me. Drama kids were loudly talking on their cell phones, making alternative plans, and trying to catch rides all around us. Blair, Savannah, and Deanna were sitting on a bench a few feet away, all glued to their phones.

"Yeah, mom, just pick us up now… Ugh, yes, it is a big deal. We've really got to run 'Bushel and a Peck,'" Blair whined into her phone. "I wish Ms. Morris took this seriously. There could be agents in the audience, and I told you I want to start doing commercial work so I can build a film reel."

Savannah and Deanna looked up sympathetically right as Blair snapped her phone shut.

"She'll be here in ten. And we're going to Starbucks," Blair told the others.

"Blair, 'Bushel' is in good shape. Stop freaking," Savannah said.

"Yeah, well, it would be in *better* shape if all the Hot Box Girls knew the choreo," Blair scowled, glaring at Deanna.

"Is the PSL out yet?" Deanna asked, oblivious.

"Uh *yeah*, Dee. It's been out since *September*. You got one last Friday, remember?" Blair responded.

For some of us, the play was an escape. Saying someone else's words and stepping into a different world was what we daydreamed about as we dragged our feet from one class to the next. A select few—but mostly just Blair Ford—lived in the delusion that the next logical step from Middle Tennessee high school theater was Broadway. For others still, drama club was an excuse to add an easy extracurricular onto their college applications or a chance to goof off with friends. Jason and his buddies were the latter. When I saw him clapping his friend—one of the gangsters in the ensemble—on the back and whooping loudly about how he's free to go, I wasn't surprised.

Trying to maintain focus when Jason and I were in a scene together was arguably the most challenging part of the whole experience. I'd rather monologue until I was blue in the face. Everything was a joke to that kid. And yet, part of me still wanted to impress him. I wanted him to think I was "cool" or…whatever. I didn't want to let on how much this play meant to me. If you cared—really, *really* cared—you were a Blair-style primadonna. So rather than roll my eyes when he'd make farting sounds as his buddies came on stage, I patiently smiled and waited for him to stop laughing so we could move on with our dialogue.

Jason caught me staring at him and walked over to me. I swallowed hard. There was no mistake that he was definitely looking directly at me, but what did he want? I'd never actually held a conversation with him that wasn't scripted.

"Hey," he said.

"Hi. Jason. Did you, um, see that rehearsal is canceled?" I stammered like an idiot.

"Yeah. Sad. But hey, maybe we could run lines or something?" Jason asked, revealing a side smile that dripped with enough charm to warrant Ms. Morris putting up with his shenanigans.

Put that smile and muscular physique on a stage and bam! You sell tickets. He was a pain in the ass, but he had mastered that particular cocky swagger and sense of owning the room that is only attainable by straight white males that know they're in their prime. And smart girls like me weren't supposed to fall for that kind of crap…but my social anxiety bested me yet again.

"Oh um, well, I'll have to call my mom. Where…um…where did you want to run lines? Here? Or…"

"Hell no." Jason playfully pushed my shoulder. "Let's get out of here," he replied, leaning in a little closer than necessary.

My face was scorching. Isa and Lincoln were watching the whole awkward scene unfold. I met Isa's gaze, then my eyes darted to my Keds as I laughed nervously and tucked a stray curl behind my ear. Why was it so impossible for me to talk to people like a normal, functional human being?

"Hey, you know what? I just realized…" Jason paused to chuckle and slap his palm to his forehead. "My place is *literally* just up the street. My parents aren't going to be back for another couple of hours. Let's do it there."

"Ha. Ha. Good one, Jason," Isa interjected as she looped her arm through mine. "K is actually coming with us."

"Whoa, my bad. I guess I didn't know you were her *mom*?" Jason rebuffed.

A couple of his friends snickered, and I noticed that Blair and her friends were looking over at us now too.

"K, let's go. Jason, find someone else to prey on, okay? Toodaloo!" Isa waved at him, bearing a sarcastic smile that gave her the appearance of a deeply cynical beauty pageant contestant and pulled me toward the door.

She laughed in her uniquely bright and husky fashion, but now there was a hint of devilish delight. I had to admit, leaving Jason with his mouth hanging open, struggling to find a comeback was pretty satisfying even if I had been caught like a fly in his web only moments before.

Busting through the double doors, Isa exclaimed, "The world is our oyster. What do you say…Chubbie's? K, have you been?"

Her arm was still linked with mine as she led the way to her car.

"Yes!" Lincoln shouted to the sky as though he'd been waiting all his life for someone to make that suggestion. "They have the fall flavors now. Caramel apple macchiato, oh how I missed you!"

"Sorry, I should probably actually call my mom and get a ride," I began as we approached the same forest green getaway car that delivered us to Taco Bell at three in the morning just a few days ago. "She doesn't know that rehearsal is canceled and tomorrow I've got this Spanish exa—"

"Okay, so call your mom," Isa said, matter-of-factly. "Tell her you're studying with us at Chubbie's. I'll drive you home later."

She opened the driver's door and threw her satchel in the backseat. Lincoln started to open the passenger door, but she stopped him.

"Dude. Be a gentleman. K gets shotgun."

"Oh, excuse me. Your chariot, milady…" Lincoln said, holding the door for me like a stuffy British chauffeur.

"You dork. You're gonna scare her off," Isa laughed.

"Um…are you sure you don't mind driving me home?" I asked.

"K, come on! Trust me, you're going to freaking LOVE Chubbie's," Isa urged.

Once again, I did what Isa said. I was being invited somewhere. Comforted by the fact that, in broad daylight, wherever we were heading most likely wouldn't involve full frontal nudity this time, I got in the passenger seat…and promptly forgot to call my mom.

"Do you know what he meant by *run lines*?" Isa said, scrolling through her iPod with one eye on the road. "No doubt he just wants to do the nightclub scene."

The scene she was referring to was right before the act one finale. It was a pivotal moment in the plot where Sky convinces Sarah to go on a date with him in exchange for "one dozen genuine sinners." Sarah, desperate to keep the Save-A-Soul Mission that she works for afloat, accepts the bargain only to be made a complete fool. She winds up getting accidentally drunk, kissing Sky, and belting "If I Were a Bell" before confessing her love and discovering that Sky's friend was hosting a party with a bunch of shady gamblers at her mission while they were out. In typical Golden Age musical fashion, it all works out in the end, but the notable part of this scene—especially for someone like me who had never been kissed—was, The Kiss. We hadn't yet rehearsed it.

"Guys like Jason are tools," Isa continued. "They might be nice to look at, but there's not much going on upstairs. And once they've had their fun, they'll throw you out like trash. I know that sounds brutal, but you're too nice to see it. You always have to show them who's in control. Anyway, that's why you've got us to protect you."

I felt my face flame up again. I didn't particularly appreciate speculation of Jason trying to get in my pants with Isa's brother listening.

"Yeah, remember what he did to Megan Sanders?" Lincoln chimed in.

I turned to face him in the backseat.

"Megan Sanders?" I asked.

"You know her?"

"No, she's just… Her locker is below mine."

"You're stuck with the S's. That's unfortunate. Let me guess: Todd Sutten, Cassandra Shubbler…"

"Enrique Santana," I finished.

"Idiots. Every one of them," he declared.

"Oh my god. Right?" I laughed. Hard.

"Stick with the theater freaks," Lincoln said. "Popularity kills brain cells."

It sounded like a practiced mantra. One that perhaps he'd used to soothe himself in the past. He shot me his toothy grin and I pulled a long strand of hair in front of my face, playing with it to hide my sudden nerves. There was something about that smile... I decided at that moment that I liked him. Sharing a mutual disdain for your peers can bond you to a person. In a way that only teenagers understand, that sort of connection makes you feel like you're not alone. Someone else knew what it was like to feel ignored and perhaps hurt by the people that we tried to dismiss.

As much as I was beginning to admire Isa, deep in the core of me I knew that she didn't experience the same push-pull effect of wanting to fit in while, at the same time, resenting the desire to fit in. Her waist-length white-blonde waves with flowers tangled throughout soared in the breeze as we sped through green lights. She wore a baggy t-shirt with a colorful graphic of Frieda Kahlo, and I noticed that her jeans were ripped in places—which was technically on trend—but unusual were the pen marks up and down the legs. It looked like she had doodled on herself while bored in class—a daisy here, a rainbow there. And there were quotes too. I recognized Emily Dickenson at once because I did a project on her in 8th grade English. "Hope is a thing with feathers" was etched right above her left knee. By appearance alone, you could tell this girl didn't care what people thought of her.

"Megan Sanders sent Jason a nude over the summer," Isa recited as though it were a news report. "Then he sent it around to the whole football team."

"Dude, it was on Myspace too. Jason's a dick," Lincoln concluded.

"Correct. So, you'll stick with us, and we can let the Blairs of this world flock to him," Isa said, again, like it was an indisputable fact.

"Do you really think Blair's into him?" I asked, dumbfounded. I assumed Blair was too self-absorbed to have a crush.

"Drawn to him like a moth to a flame. Has been for years," Isa said.

I thought I saw the hint of a cruel smile trace her lips, but just as quickly, it vanished.

It turned out that the acclaimed Chubbie's was more or less a hole in the wall—an old Victorian house that would make a perfect candidate for one of those HGTV renovation shows. Isa must have seen the question in my eyes when we parked.

"Shabby chic," she said.

A large white Persian cat sat doorstop-style on the wraparound porch directly in front of the entrance.

"Here, Chubbie Chubbie…" Lincoln coaxed the cat.

"Ahh," I said, understanding, "Chubbie's a cat."

"The most famous fluffball in the city. And she brews the best $1.50 cup of coffee." Isa winked.

The wooden sign above the front door said, "Chubbie's Coffeeshop" and featured a caricature of Chubbie herself wearing a black beret. Chubbie stared blankly at Lincoln with her huge, round blue eyes then stood and stretched luxuriously as if she had been asleep for centuries. Afterward, she proceeded to plop down on the porch and expose her rotund belly for Lincoln to stroke.

"She's purring," Lincoln whispered to us, as though he was afraid to disrupt the preciousness of the moment.

"Who's the cat lady now?" Isa said snuggly as she held the door open for me. "Come on, K. Let's give them a moment."

Whoever decorated the interior of Chubbie's couldn't decide between a grandma's house or an eclectic hippie aesthetic. The massive bay windows had lacey curtains tied off with bows and the window seats were adorned with frilly mismatched pillows. In contrast, the artwork on the walls consisted of psychedelic blobs confined in assorted frames and Bonnaroo posters from years past. The air was thick with the smell of warm spiced apple muffins, but there was a subtle trace of patchouli incense underneath. It was about as far from Starbucks as a coffee drinker could possibly get, but I felt slightly cooler and more alternative just by standing inside those worn-down walls. It was a place threaded with history and, I noticed when I surveyed the colorful chalkboard, boasted a menu as diverse as the decor.

Witch's Brew Pumpkin Spice, Crazed Caramel Apple Macchiato, and Bone-Chilling Cold Brew, to name a few. Isa directed me to a table by the front stained-glass window and slung her satchel over one of the rickety wooden chairs. None of the painted wooden chairs matched and every table was collaged with different magazine clippings. Our table had an array of tropical birds, ordinary sparrows, graceful swans, and peaceful doves all harmoniously intertwined in an impossible ecosystem.

"The bird table is our favorite," Isa said proudly. "And there's never anyone here from school since it's in college town. It's a hidden gem. Come on, I'll introduce you to Lenny."

"Why Miss Isa! What can I do for you today?" an elderly black man with a gray goatee and an ironic French beret asked from behind the counter.

"Happy spooky season, Lenny," Isa chimed as she leaned herself onto the counter.

"Finally, October! Best time of year!" Lenny laughed and the crow's feet around his eyes deepened.

"This is K. We're in the play together," Isa said and pushed me forward. "She's the *star*."

Predictably, my face turned crimson.

"Hi," I said sheepishly.

"No kidding?! Well then, this one's on the house. For bringin' a celebrity to my shop. I always say you DeLucas are my best customers."

Lincoln walked in, dropped his backpack on the bird table, and joined us at the counter.

"Lenny!" He greeted him with that same toothy grin.

Did he really look at everyone that way? As if he were genuinely delighted to be in their presence? It was unabashedly sincere.

"My man!" Lenny exclaimed. "Crazed Caramel?"

"You know it."

Lenny started whipping up Lincoln's drink and Isa and I scoured the menu.

"I get something different every time," Isa explained. "The chai's amazing. Cold brew too. Anything, really. Even just straight up black. Just a regular old cup of black coffee is only $1.50."

"Same price since we opened in 1989," Lenny declared above the crackling espresso machine.

I wondered how Lenny was able to make a profit with prices that low, but that thought didn't linger for long — the place was full to the brim with artsy looking college students reading thick books and older adults on their laptops. Eventually, I settled on a chai tea latte and Isa asked for a concoction of espresso, almond milk, mocha, and cayenne pepper. Lenny brought our steaming mugs to the bird table. Mine had a print of Starry Night, Isa sipped from a Victorian teacup with delicate roses, and Lincoln's was a fat bowl of a mug that read "Save the Animals. Eat a Republican."

"Don't you love it here?" Isa asked me after taking a long sip of her latte.

I nodded enthusiastically. I had just been introduced to the best chai I had ever tasted—complete with the design of a sleeping cat embedded into the foam.

"This is… magic," I said.

"They opened the year I was born. Chubbie and I are both Leos. But 16 is basically 70 in cat years. I think the universe put Chubbie's here just for me. She knew I would need it someday. The universe, that is. I don't think Chubbie herself is all that interested in the coffee business," Isa said.

"Wait. 1989? Shouldn't you—" I began.

"I'm supposed to be a junior, yeah," Isa stated, finishing my thought.

"Oh, sorry. That was rude…" I stared down at the birds who now seemed to be judging me with their beady little bird eyes.

"I don't care," Isa said. "I was held back in Kindergarten."

"It's great because she's like the only sophomore that already has her license," Lincoln pointed out. "No more bus rides."

"I didn't even think about that, but I guess you wouldn't be allowed to drive with only a permit," I said.

"Oh, I drove plenty of times before I got my license," she said, waving the confession away like everyone casually broke the law from time to time. "But yeah, I turned 16 July 23rd. My Kindergarten teacher held me back because I played with my crayons like they were Barbies. You know, I'd create voices for them and stuff. Well, apparently that's not 'normal' behavior for a five-year-old. They were all, 'She has ADHD. She's mentally delayed.' The typical load of BS they tell parents anytime a kid isn't a cookie cutter model of perfection. I was *bored* for crying out loud. Who wants to sit there and listen to monotonous gibberish about the alphabet and days of the week all day long? That's not how I learn."

"But you'd be surprised how many kids that were held back in Kindergarten go on to discover planets and win Pulitzers and junk," Lincoln added.

He then took a sip of his coffee and apparently burnt his tongue. I couldn't help but giggle when he squirmed uncomfortably in his seat, held out his tongue, and started fanning it.

"Duh, you dork. I'm smart as hell. Anyway, I'm grateful for it. I can alphabetize anything without singing the song in my head like the rest of those bozos that just did one round of kindergarten."

Before I could embarrass myself with an inappropriate follow-up question, Lincoln suddenly dug into his backpack and pulled out a small, black leather notebook.

"Ooo!" was all he said as he frantically jotted something down.

"He does that sometimes. His 'Idea Book.' Every writer has one," Isa leaned over to me and explained.

Lincoln was absolutely transfixed with whatever idea was spilling from his brain onto the paper. To be so absorbed in the act of creation to just do it anytime, anyplace without fear of who was watching gave me pause. Meanwhile, I had a hard time admitting that I wanted something even to myself. I guess on a subconscious level I knew that once you said you liked a thing, a place, a person…it had more potential to be ripped away. I liked the boy that I saw at Friday prayers, but then we stopped going to mosque. I liked our townhouse in Chicago and then we moved. I liked the Children's Choir in Philly but there wasn't a program like that in our little town in Oregon.

"Hey, check this out," Isa interrupted my private self-analysis.

She got up and motioned for me to follow her to the alcove on the other side of the dining room. The built-in bookcase filled with tattered board games held much more potential for entertainment than my Spanish 1 flashcards.

"Wanna play Chinese checkers?" she asked.

Two rounds of checkers later, the sun was starting to descend.

Isa had taken to reading a copy of *The Bell Jar* that she found in the Little Free Library box on the front porch (she exchanged it with her Geometry textbook) and I, at long last, pulled out my flashcards.

"I'm starving," Lincoln said, standing from the table and stretching. "You ready to go, Isa?"

"Umm hmm," she muttered vaguely without looking up.

"Oh, I almost forgot!" Lincoln said, rummaging through the mishmash of notebooks, stray assignments, and textbooks in his backpack again. "The show poster!"

He pulled out an advertisement for our production of *Guys and Dolls*. My stomach flipped at the reminder that actual real, live people from the community might be coming to this thing in a little under two months.

"Lenny, do you mind if I put this up?" Lincoln asked Lenny, who was bussing tables nearby.

"Go right on ahead, young man. You know I am an avid supporter of the arts," Lenny replied.

I started to pack up my backpack, put on my coat, and gather my trash when Lincoln exclaimed, "Hey! Isa! What day is it?"

"October 15th. Why?" she replied without looking up from her book, evidently engrossed.

"The *Rent* tour opened tonight," Lincoln said, pointing to another show poster. This bit of information seemed to be the only thing capable of pulling her from the intricacies of Esther Greenwood's quarter life crisis.

She gasped and shutting her book, said, "If we leave now, we can—"

"But can we go through a drive-thru on the way? I'm seriously starv—" Lincoln moaned.

"Lincoln. No time. You know they have the opening night apps after the show. Last time they had crab and all that fancy shit. Get your stuff. Let's go!" Isa insisted as if she couldn't leave fast enough.

"Oh yeeeeah. Those crab cakes," Lincoln mused aloud and performed a chef's kiss into the air.

I, of course, had no idea what was going on. Obviously, I knew what *Rent* was—an edgy 90's rock musical about the AIDS crisis. Not that the topic had any relevance to my lived experiences and an overly sheltered 14-year-old, but I was entirely obsessed. I listened to the soundtrack every day; I'd shove my earbuds in and forge my way through the maze of students en route to my next period while jamming out to "La Vie Bohme." I insisted that my parents accompany me to loads of musicals over the years, but I knew without a doubt that I'd never be able to convince them to take me to a show like *Rent*. The topics were too "adult" and "vulgar," my mother would say. And that train of thought should have reminded me to call my mom. After all, she would be driving to the school soon to pick me up from the rehearsal that I never told her was canceled, but the allure of seeing one of my favorite musicals of all time was too great.

"How do we get tickets?" I asked, trailing behind as they practically sprinted to Isa's car.

"We don't," Isa said, hopping in the driver's seat. "We 'Act Too' it."

"What?"

"We call it 'Act Tooing,'" Lincoln clarified while Isa pulled out of the parking spot. "As in 't-o-o.' We see the second act of a musical—they don't check tickets when you come back from intermission—so *we* get to see it *too*. For free. I came up with the name."

"*Working title*," Isa teased.

"Hey, you didn't have any ide—" Lincoln started to protest.

"Wait. *What*? How many times have you done this?" I asked, incredulous.

"Loads of times," Isa said with a smile.

"We've seen *Into the Woods, Cabaret*..." Lincoln continued.

"*Little Shop of Horrors*. But that was horrible."

"Okay, Isa and I can never agree on this. *Little Shop* was hysterical. She was just overly critical because it was understudy night."

"And you've never gotten caught?" I prodded.

"Never," they answer in unison.

"It's the easiest thing in the world," Isa explained. "You just waltz right in the front door. If anyone in the lobby questions you, you just say, 'I had to run out to the car' and, like Lincoln said, the ushers don't scan tickets for act two. You can just pop into any entrance—but really, most of the empty seats are in the upper balcony or the front two rows of the orchestra, that's your best bet—and watch the second half for free.

"Sometimes it's confusing as hell because you've missed the first part of the show, but most of the time we've already listened to the soundtrack anyway, so we have some idea what's going on. And you know what—I don't know what I don't know. I'm comfortable living in ignorant bliss…for free."

I was too impressed to be concerned about breaking the rules. The second act still had "Take Me or Leave Me" and "Seasons of Love." Not to mention, this was a national tour. That meant real professional actors. It was the closest you could get to seeing a Broadway show without going to New York. I wasn't going to pass that up.

"So, you game?" Isa asked, taking her eyes off the road briefly to look at me.

"Let's do it." I said.

I smiled wide and my stomach fluttered. I was going to see *Rent*. Or at least, part of it. These were the most thrilling, interesting, and possibly, in Isa's case, insane people I'd ever met, and they wanted to hang out with *me*. They were into the same nerdy Broadway stuff that I was into. Seeing both of them—especially Isa, who I was convinced at this point was definitely Cool with a capital "C"—excited about something that I only privately poured into on lonely walks through the hallways and alone in my bedroom, planted a seed.

It is acceptable to like things, to have interests, to have a passion. I was going to make this mine. After years of just watching, I was *doing*. I was the lead in a musical and there I was, spontaneously checking off a show from my bucket list. But what's more, when they both started cheering at my acceptance of their plan, I felt like I was flying.

I think I have friends now, I thought and preemptively turned off my cell phone—we were going into a theater after all.

I didn't know how much time had passed—an hour, maybe? — all three of us were too transfixed by Johnathan Larson's masterpiece to give the time a second thought. We emerged into the performing art center's lobby with tears streaking our cheeks and snot coming out of our noses. One day, as a jaded theater major, I would look back at this time in my life and sigh at how I fangirled over the most overdone shows. But for now, I liked what I liked. In as much as a 60-minute live performance can change a person, I was transformed.

"Are those tears I see? Everyone, gather round! A rare display of emotion from the Ice Queen herself!" Lincoln teased Isa as she hurriedly wiped her cheeks.

"Feelings are for freaks," she said and punched him in the arm.

"That was—I don't even know. Incredible seems too bland," I said, still reeling as we surveyed the cacophony of the lobby which now included buffet tables and cater waiters walking around with champagne flukes.

Isa grabbed a glass from a distracted waiter before anyone could stop her.

"Out. Of. This. World," Lincoln contributed. "Hey! I see crab cakes!"

He charged across the room, standing out like a sore thumb among the well-dressed and considerably older theater patrons.

And then it hit me. My mom. Oh my god. Oh *shit*. What time was it? I never called my mom.

"You okay?" Isa eyed me digging frantically through my backpack and turning on my cell.

"My mom. I forgot to call my mom. My parents are probably having heart attacks," I practically panted as I waited for the screen to light up. Sure enough—a gazillion missed calls and five voicemails. Isa peered over my shoulder.

"Oh damn…that doesn't look good," she said, then downed the rest of her champagne.

I mustered the bravery to hit play on the most recent voicemail from my mom and brought it to my ear.

"Now I am beyond worried—I am *furious*. I called Mrs. Ford and she said that she picked up Blair and the girls *hours* ago. Rehearsal was *canceled*? Call me back immediately. Daddy and I are going to call the police if we don't hear from you soon."

My mother's voice was stern but wavering on the verge of a waterworks explosion. I couldn't remember the last time I'd made her that angry, if I ever did. I was not the kind of kid to forget to call, show up late, or do anything unexpected at all, really. I only just got my cell phone a few months prior when I started my freshman year, and my parents made it unmistakably clear that it was for emergency use only. I didn't even have the capability to send more than 50 texts a month, so its sole purpose was to let them know when things like this—canceled rehearsals—came up and I needed a ride.

"Isa, can you take me home, like, *right now*? My mom is totally freaking out. I think she showed up at the school looking for me," I said.

"Where do you live?" Isa asked.

"The Crockett Springs neighborhood. Same as Blair—"

"Easy. That's the neighborhood across from ours. I can get you there in 20. Yo! Lincoln! The ball's over; K's going to turn into a pumpkin if we don't get her home!" Isa called across the lobby.

Lincoln, who had just stuffed his face with crab cakes, grabbed one more for the road then jogged over to us.

"I'm sorry to rush you guys. It's just that my mom is really strict sometimes and it was stupid of me to forget to call her," I explained as we hustled out the doors and across the street to Isa's car.

This was my first time downtown and if it weren't for the fact that I was in a blind panic, I would have wanted to gawk at the bright lights of the honky-tonks and the hilarity of the cowboy hat-clad tourists.

"Don't sweat it. Did you get one of these?" Lincoln handed me a crab cake as we buckled our seatbelts and set out for suburbia.

I waved it away. I couldn't eat when I knew I was facing the lecture of a lifetime in 20 minutes. Instead, I sent my parents a quick text:

Me [9:20pm]: Sorry. Was with friends. On my way.

No way was that halfhearted excuse going to get me out of the hole I dug for myself, but I at least had to let them know I was alive.

"Are your parents going to kill you?" Lincoln asked.

"Don't worry—I'm great with parents. I can talk to them," Isa offered.

"My mom grew up in a super traditional Pakistani household, so yeah… Sometimes she's real laid back. She wants to prove she's the opposite of my grandparents, I guess. But other times, she's really high strung. I mean, she probably thinks I'm pregnant or dead right now. And my dad is probably freaking out because she's freaking out. He's a lot more chill. But he'll still be pissed…mostly because I'm sure he's spent the last few hours talking my mom off the ledge. God, I'm such an idiot," I said.

I wasn't typically one to pour out the details of my nuclear family dynamics, but here I was—blabbering away.

"Your mom's from Pakistan?" Isa asked, interested.

"She immigrated with her parents when she was three, so she basically grew up as an American," I explained.

"Dope," Lincoln approved and took another bite of crab cake.

"So, you're half…" Isa tried.

"Half Pakistani. Half white. My dad's family jumped right off the Mayflower."

"I knew there was something exotic about you," Isa said.

"Uh, Isa, hello? That's racist," Lincoln said, sending a bit of crab cake flying from his full mouth.

"It's oka—" I began.

"What? I didn't mean it in a bad way. It's a very good thing. You're... 'ethnically ambiguous.' You could be Greek, Hispanic, mixed race... Your opportunities for casting are limitless. And there's an edge of mystery. Like, 'Where is this girl from? Wouldn't *you* like to know?'" Isa elaborated. "I totally thought you were white. But now that you say that, I can see it. I can definitely see it. Eyebrows that luscious can't be drawn with pencil."

"Isa! What the hell? You're being a legit racist right now," Lincoln said. "K, I apologize on behalf of this insensitive woman. I claim no blood relation."

"What?" Isa exclaimed, "My eyebrows are basically invisible. It's a *compliment.*"

"No, it's okay," I said. And it was...kind of. "I'm used to it. I'm white passing. I don't really identify with being Pakistani, anyway. We haven't spoken to my mom's side of the family in years. It's not a big deal, though. I never really knew them."

That part was true. I hadn't seen or heard from my maternal cousins, aunts, uncles, or grandparents since before we left Chicago ten years ago. But the other part—the white passing and identify part—that I hadn't quite figured out how I felt about just yet. That's a big puzzle for a 14-year-old...for an any-age-year-old.

"But what about your parents?" I said, diverting the attention from myself. "Aren't your parents going to freak out too?"

Isa snorted and Lincoln was silent. Did I say something wrong?

"Dad's on a business trip," Lincoln said after a beat.

"And Tamara—" Isa began.

"Mom..." Lincoln said under his breath.

"*Tamara* won't be home."

"She's a lawyer. She likes to hang out with her work friends at her practice sometimes and she gets home late," Lincoln clarified.

"Sure. Work *friends,*" Isa said, flashing her turn signal and staring daggers into the road in front of her.

The car was silent for the remainder of the drive and, with the tension in the air, I almost forgot to fear for my life until we pulled into my neighborhood.

"It's the house with the blue shutters," I said, "on the left."

"Okay," Isa said, breaking her silence, "let's all get out of the car and apologize profusely. We stole K from the school parking lot, dragged her to Chubbie's, and when we got there, she dropped her phone in a puddle. It was busted, but we put it in some rice and then it came back to life. We're so very sorry."

"But why didn't she just borrow one of our phones or ask Lenny—"

"Because, Lincoln, we were so busy studying for this damned Spanish 1 exam! You better not screw this up with your 'honest Abe' routine. We'll say we're all so overwhelmed with our schoolwork. It's hard being a teen these days. These teachers put too much pressure on us!" Isa lamented.

Her eyes were glassy, and I thought for a second that she was going to cry. Then she turned to me and winked. I swallowed. We pulled into my driveway. All the lights were on in the house and my parents immediately ran out of the front door.

"K! Oh my god! Are you…? Oh my god!"

My mother ran to me and pulled me into a teary embrace before I could say anything.

"Where have you been? Your mother and I have been worried sick. What happened to your phone?" my dad, the more composed of the two, asked.

He looked from me, to Isa, to Lincoln, then back at me.

"I was…um… This is Isa and Lincoln and they—we—went to a coffee—" I pulled away from my mom's suffocating embrace and began to stutter.

"Mrs. Statham. Mr. Statham. I'm Isabel DeLuca. This is my brother, Lincoln. We're in the play with K," Isa stepped forward and began her performance.

"Hi," Lincoln said, extending a hand to my dad, "Nice to meet you."

"Tim Statham." My dad shook Lincoln's hand. But when Lincoln turned to my mom, her hands remained tightly secured on my shoulders. "This is my wife, Azrah," my dad said on my mother's behalf.

"We're SO sorry about this," Isa continued. "I take full responsibility. K told us she needed to call you, but I was rushing for us to get to this coffee shop—it's a great place to study—and when we got there, well, K's phone broke."

"It broke? But you sent us a text?" my mom exclaimed.

"It's…it's fine now. But I dropped it—"

"In a puddle," Isa finished. "But luckily, we were able to save it with the rice trick! It's really a lovely coffee shop. If you haven't been to college town, I highly recommend it. Loads of artsy boutiques and cafés. I know you're new in town. You should definitely check it out. Anyway, the owner helped us. He gave us a bag of rice and now it's good as new."

"Uh huh…" My mom nodded and I wasn't sure if she was buying the story or not.

Still with a smile plastered on her face, Isa looked at me. I knew it was my turn to jump in. My palms were sweating, and I was glad that I wasn't face to face with my mom or I wouldn't have been able to say what I said next.

"I just completely forgot about calling after that. I was upset about my phone. I know it was expensive. And then—the Spanish test. It's going to be insane. Mrs. Santiago is the hardest teacher I have, and this test is basically going to make or break my overall GPA. I'm sorry, I was just so focused on the test. We studied for hours," I lied.

That was the first real lie I had ever told my parents. As an only child with limited playmates, the opportunities to lie, get in trouble, and be naughty in general were few and far between. I was always a goody-two-shoes and too painfully shy to cause any kind of disturbance. So, why was it so easy to just take Isa's lead and…tell a story?

"Once your GPA goes off the rails—good luck getting it back on track, am I right?" Isa said.

My mom was still frozen, but my dad seemed completely satisfied. Bored, almost.

"That's what I always tell K," he agreed. "You have to watch that GPA like a hawk right from the start."

We all nodded a little too agreeably, but he didn't seem to mind the brown-nosing.

"Alright now, Isabel, Lincoln, I'm sure your parents are waiting on you. We won't keep you. Thank you for bringing K home."

My dad patted Lincoln on the shoulder, nodded at Isa, and made eyes at my mom to follow him into the house.

"Thank you for understanding, Mr. Statham. And again, we are SO sorry for the inconvenience this has caused. You too, Mrs. Statham," Isa said emphatically as my dad started up the driveway.

"Please, call me Tim!" my dad called back. "Glad K's got herself some study partners. And, uh, play acting friends too. How about that?" He chuckled.

My dad had a habit of referring to my chosen extracurricular as "play acting" even though I told him on multiple occasions that the descriptor "play" was unnecessary.

"Thank you," was all my mom said and she steered me up the driveway. I could tell the conversation was far from over.

"Bye. And thanks," I managed to say before dragging my feet to face my sentence.

Isa winked and mouthed, "You're welcome."

"See you at school," Lincoln said and waved.

As I closed the front door, I heard Radiohead blaring from Isa's car speakers.

"K," Mom began, "before you spend any more time with that girl, I want to meet her mother. I don't like the idea of you driving around in a stranger's car."

"You let me spend the night at Blair's house and Isa's actually *nice*. Blair's kind of a—"

"That's an entirely different situation and you know it. I've spoken to Lanette on several occasions at HOA brunches and every time I drop something off for you at school, she's in the office. A few times Blair's been with her. She's a lovely girl."

"Well, of course she's nice to *you*. But she's kind of a brat at rehearsal. She's just…mean."

"What are you talking about? Has Blair done something to you?"

I was stuck. I was too embarrassed to tell her about the sleepover incident and without that as evidence, I didn't have much to stand on. So, I shrugged.

"I don't know, I just…I just prefer hanging out with Isa."

"Well, I don't have a good feeling about that girl. Something seems off. I want to meet her mom. Until then—cell phone." She held out her hand, expectantly. "You're smarter than this, K. Why didn't you borrow one of your friend's phones?"

"I—"

"She was cramming for her test, Azrah," Dad called from the living room sofa. "Give the kid a break."

"Just go to your room," Mom said, ignoring him. "And…you're…*grounded.* Okay?" She said the word like she was trying it out for the first time, which she was.

There was a silence between us. We were both uncomfortable, stunned. She sighed and straightened up. My mom and I were both 5'1" but at that moment, her presence completely dominated mine.

"Yes," she continued, more confident now. "you're grounded."

"What?"

"You heard me."

"Azrah, she was studying," my dad campaigned on my behalf during the commercial break. "Our girl's gonna get an A on that test. Right, honey? *Grounded.* Bologna. Let's just take a break from hanging out with friends for a while. Alright, K?"

And at that, he switched his attention back to the evening news.

"That's what being grounded *is*, Tim," Mom said, annoyed.

Only I didn't make an A on that Spanish test. Because I didn't actually study like I said I did. I nearly passed with a C-. But I never forgot that second act of *Rent*.

5.

Swings and Streetlamps

Being that neither of my parents had practiced organized religion since I was in elementary school, I was always spared the rigmarole of holiday services. In recent years, my winter break consisted of six to seven hours a day spent alone in my room with only an occasional shift at Chubbie's to break up the monotony. I'd sleep, read endlessly, sleep, do a bit of painting if I was feeling frisky…and sleep. Most days, I didn't feel like creating anything at all. Rather, I'd spend the majority of the day in bed beating myself up for not taking advantage of my limitless time to create, all while being physically, emotionally, and mentally incapable of manifesting a single creative thought.

    This inability to *do* anything but *think about doing* then feeling *guilt about not doing* was a pattern Dr. McPherson had been trying to break for three years now. What I didn't tell him was that the Zoloft he prescribed made me feel as though I woke up already at 50%. I didn't want him to know, of course, because I was scared of going off the Zoloft. And even if things appeared to be getting more "bearable," I still wasn't keen on feeling at full capacity.

    "It seems that you thrive best with structure. Most of us do, in fact. It's nothing to be ashamed of. Routines are very healthy for us. That's why pediatricians recommend parents set routines for their children right away. It's also why recent retirees suddenly experience signs of depression. Straying from the routine can make some of us feel unbalanced," Dr. McPherson had said at one of our appointments the summer before my sophomore year.

"I thought I'd be happier without homework," I told him then. "Art history is a lot of reading. So many term papers and all the research… I thought I needed a break."

"It can be disorienting to come home from college and realize that you aren't necessarily the same person you were when you left, or that those around you—your environment even—have changed," he offered.

"But I didn't really leave. My college is 40 minutes from my parents' house."

"And does it feel the same?" he pried.

"…No. It feels…I don't know."

Sitting in Dr. McPherson's office, I thought of the summers of years past. Images came tumbling out of the filing cabinet in my mind before I had a chance to stop them—lazy days spent binging black and white movies, listening to Isa play her guitar while sunbathing on the roof, dreamily browsing the clothing racks of our favorite vintage thrift store until close… The summer when Isa had to get her wisdom teeth pulled out popped into my head. Lincoln and I were her personal chauffeur, chef, and nurse for two weeks. She made us sign a document saying that we would not, under any circumstances, film, photograph, or record in any way the embarrassing things she might say or do post-surgery. To our disappointment, she was ever the unfazed, self-possessed flower child as she always was—just a bit loopier.

I could still see her slouched low in the backseat of the car as Lincoln drove us home from the dentist. She seemed to have dozed off, but after several minutes, she shot up and pointed urgently at the sky ahead of us. She was trying to form words, but her speech was slurred beyond comprehension. "It…pretty…sk... See it? K? Abe? Look!"

"You feeling good, Isa?" Lincoln laughed.

But I knew exactly what she was trying to say. I had been on too many car rides with Isa not to recognize the "Look at the sky!"

gesture—always spastic, always dire. It was as if she needed whoever she was with to experience that divine moment in time as desperately as if her very life depended on it. "Nature's showing off," she used to say. "Look at our girl go!" Because nature, the universe, God—in Isa's mind—was undoubtedly made of feminine energy.

Back then, I didn't have a routine. I didn't need one. And although I liked Dr. McPherson and found most of his advice to be reasonable, I severely doubted that something as tedious as scheduled activities would make the fog, I had been wading through for six months magically disappear. What I *needed* right then and there was something to do with my hands. I started picking at my cuticles—a habit that Dr. McPherson told me was activated by social anxiety.

"How about theater? Is there a summer production you could get involved in? The dinner theater perhaps? You worked there once before, not long ago."

"I can't act anymore," I said, avoiding his eyes and digging into the puffy reddened skin below my right thumb.

He knew this already. Why would he even suggest that?

"K, would you be open to something more tactile? Painting? Or drawing? Maybe knitting?" he asked. When I met him with a blank stare, he continued, "It could prove useful for you to explore a creative outlet that is separate from what you've done in the past. In other words, let's keep theater on the backburner for now—until you're ready to touch it again—"

If I'll ever be ready to touch it again, I thought hotly.

"And let's explore something new," he finished, eyeing one of my now bleeding hangnails. "I also want us to work together to establish a routine for your breaks from school."

And that was how I got into painting—a positive consequence of Dr. McPherson's homework assignment. But that was also how Family Dinners came about. In addition to scheduled "outdoor time," a reading list, and required journaling, Dr. McPherson told my parents that it would be helpful for me to more or less be forced to engage by having family meals when I stayed with them. The nature walks and journaling I neglected within a matter of weeks, but painting and, to my irritation, Family Dinners stuck.

In the past, my parents and I ate together, but it was mostly around the television, and we hadn't even done that since I started theater freshman year of high school. For four years straight, it was typical for me to stand over the kitchen counter, plow through leftovers and multitask with a homework assignment all while barely saying no more than three brief sentences to my parents. The three of us were always preoccupied. There was never much "intentionality"—as Dr. McPherson said—in our household, even when I was a kid. I was a textbook hermit before I had a reason to be and would hunker down in my room or watch hours of cartoons. (This was before parents thought to enforce screen time limitations. Or maybe my parents were just too busy to care…) Mom spent a lot of time on the phone yapping to clients or gossiping with friends. And Dad, a senior-level corporate economist, worked pretty much constantly—both at the office and at home.

So that was why, even after roughly three years of this practice, the Family Dinners still felt a bit strained. My dad would say, "Doctor's orders," anytime I attempted to feign a migraine or claim I wasn't hungry enough for dinner. Although I knew full well that the definition of insanity was to repeat the same actions and expect different results, I tried to get out of the whole charade at least a few times each and every time I came home for school breaks.

"Dinner's ready!" Mom called up the stairs.

I had been in the bath but instead of getting out and drying off, I sat in the tub hugging my knees to my chest as I watched the water drain.

"Honey! Did you hear your mother? Dinner!" my dad shouted after a few silent moments.

The bath water was almost entirely gone. The first day of break was always the worst. They would be putting on their most overt "We're Super Involved and Interested Parents" performance and I found that tired song and dance exhausting. I didn't know how I was going to handle it today of all days. Despite a two-hour nap, I was still paying for that all-nighter with Lincoln. I didn't trust myself not to snap at my parents when they inevitably got under my skin.

"I'll eat later! I'm not hungry!" I called back and held my breath, praying for a favorable response.

"Let's go, K! Doctor's orders!" Dad replied, predictably.

I took a deep breath, counted ten of the tiles on the bathroom floor, then finally stood and toweled off. I threw on a pair of pajama pants and my dad's old University of Chicago hoodie—the same one I had been wearing since Lincoln showed up with the ice cream. Twisting my wet curls up into a messy bun, I longingly stared at F. Scott who was curled on my pillow and fast asleep. How I envied what little expectations society placed on cats. Finally, I trudged down the stairs, as ready as I would ever be for what I had coined the "First Day Back Third Degree."

"Sweetie," Mom said as I sat down at the table, "did you try on the new clothes I got you?"

Ever since we moved to Tennessee, my mother had been on a "Southern Belle" kick to blend in with all the other neighborhood moms. She always looked primed and ready for Steeplechase or a spontaneous chicken and waffles brunch and operated under the delusion that I was also inclined toward this aesthetic. It annoyed me how much of a chameleon she was—perhaps because, despite her blood running through my veins, I could never achieve her level of social prowess. And even now, I couldn't stand her wearing those obnoxious shirts with phrases like, "Raised on Sweet Tea and Sunshine!" when I was privy to the knowledge that she grew up in Chicago…where the tea was served hot, and the sun was mostly in hiding.

"I will. Later," I said, referring to the small pile of in-your-face magenta that was folded on my bed when I got home.

I had no intention of wearing either of those dresses. Or trying them on. We both knew this, but pretending had become our truth. She just smiled patiently and started spooning linguine onto her plate.

"Oh, and, honey," she piped up after a brief uncomfortable silence where my dad passed me a serving platter of baked chicken breast, "did you read the email I sent you?"

She was forever sending me emails, most of which included articles related to grief and mindfulness. This was another habit of hers that I didn't appreciate but tolerated.

"No, actually," I said, now drowning my plate in alfredo sauce. "I've been really busy with finals."

"Study, study, study!" Dad chimed in before bringing a heaping forkful to his mouth.

"I think I may send it over to Lanette," Mom continued and took a casual sip of chardonnay.

I was about to take a bite of chicken, then paused. "Why?" I asked, the fork suspended in front of my mouth.

"I think it's very applicable. It talks about processing grief through the lens of those that have departed. There's a link to a guided meditation where you visualize peacefully entering the afterlife," she explained, but the more she talked, the more I could sense my appetite fading. I put the chicken back on my plate and started mindlessly twirling my noodles. "It's healthier if those of us that are left behind actually come to terms—"

Please stop talking.

She was obsessed with using terms like "the departed," "pass away," and "no longer with us." It was as if she thought my fragile state of being couldn't fathom the brutality of calling a spade a spade. "No longer with us" implies that the dead have briefly left the room, but they'll be right back. "She's no longer with us—she just ran out to get a carton of milk at Kroger. But she'll be right back." "Dead," to me, was more palatable. "Gone," even. At least that was honest.

"I don't think Mrs. Ford wants to hear that…" The comment was under my breath, but the damage was done.

My mom stopped mid-sentence. "What did you say?"

"I just don't think Mrs. Ford needs some bullshit article to tell her how to grieve."

My dad, a skilled pro in this department after twenty-three years of marriage, jumped in the moment he sensed my mother's nostrils flaring with tension. "Hey, K, you got any appointments with Dr. McPherson on the books? How's therapy going anyhow?"

"Just dandy, Dad," I said, holding my mom's gaze. She sighed, relenting, and then took another sip of her wine. "I see him again after New Year's."

"Good. Good." He nodded approvingly. "I'm—*we're*—proud of you, honey. For keeping up with that."

I never knew what to say in moments like these, so I brought my water glass to my mouth and took a huge gulp, so I wasn't expected to reply.

"You know what I was thinking," Dad continued. "Why don't we go to the historic district and do the Dickens of a Christmas thing this year? We can pick out a tree and everything. It'd be nice to have a real tree this year, don't you think?"

He glanced at my mom who looked horrified. I knew what she was thinking—our cleaning lady, Mitsey, didn't come frequently enough to keep up with all the pine needles that would end up covering mom's pristine white living room carpet.

"But I thought you hated Dickens," I said, slightly amused.

"Oh, you know me. I'm just a Scrooge about the traffic. And nobody knows how to drive through that damn roundabout." My dad chuckled.

"Well, Tiffany *does* always comment on our fake tree every time she's here…" my mom thought aloud, swirling her wine.

My aunt Tiffany was my dad's older sister, and my mother's not-so-secret rival. Every other year aunt Tiffany came to visit us for Christmas with my uncle Mark and my cousins, Paisley, and Kinsley. And every time, my mother would jump through hoops to make the house look like the cover of *Home and Garden*. Tiffany's family was a picture-perfect and predictable upper middle-class example of the all-American life. Tiffany was a stay-at-home mom, Mark ran a store that sold golfing equipment, and Paisley and Kinsley, who were my age and three years older, respectively, were both high school cheerleaders turned dental hygienists. I was pretty sure they were both engaged to business majors before their junior years of college. Apparently the "ring by spring" and "M-R-S degree" fad extended beyond the south because their family lived in Michigan.

    I had absolutely nothing in common with any of them, especially Paisley who used to write love letters to the vocalists of *NSYNC when we were little and now, dreamt of quitting her day job to become an Instagram influencer. Kinsley had a better head on her shoulders. She at least read—or listened to audiobooks, rather—during her morning runs. But we rarely had anything to recommend each other as she was solely focused on Nicholas Sparks…and I could say with confidence that if I never read *The Notebook*, I wouldn't die in regret.

    "I just thought it'd be something for us to do," my dad said. "We need some together time while you're here, K. Some Christmas spirit with just the three of us before Tiff and the family get here."

    "Dickens of a Christmas" was a festival that the historic part of town put on every December. Thespians from the local high schools adorned 1800s garb and roamed the streets singing carols. There were hot chocolate vendors and carriage rides, a lot that sold real pine trees, and a guy dressed as Santa for the kids. The highlight of the event was the candle lighting ceremony for the enormous Christmas tree in the center of the town square's roundabout. It was charming if you were into that sort of thing.

    No doubt the whole festival would be more enjoyable as an anonymous participant rather than as a high schooler sweating in a stuffy costume and being mocked by other kids from school. Isa, Lincoln, and I had been roped into it once by Ms. Morris. Breaking character, even if one of our idiot peers tried to mess with us, was strictly forbidden. I remembered, then, how Isa had hidden a flask in her petticoat so we wouldn't have to endure the experience sober. Lincoln and I were juniors, Isa was a senior, and that was right before everything fell apart…how had I forgotten?

"I don't know…" I said, making a mental note to store Dickens of a Christmas in the "Do Not Open" folder of my filing cabinet. "Maybe we could just go to the movies or something."

"Whatever sounds good to you, honey," my dad smiled and started to clear the table.

That was the difference in my parents—one wanted me to grieve perfectly while the other seemed to want to help me through my grief at my own pace, on my own terms. I had to give my dad some credit. Since Isa died, he had "stepped up" I guess you could say. It was as if the very reality of a young person—a young person that was only two years older than his only child—dying shook him out of his passive parenting style. Death is such a permanent thing. One day you're here and the next…well, do any of us know where we go next?

"Are you finished, K?" Mom asked, rising from her chair, and pointing at my mostly untouched chicken alfredo. I nodded. She took my plate and brought it over to the sink saying, "You and I still have to go shopping for Daddy. We can go this weekend and do lunch."

"Yeah, maybe," I said, waiting for a lull in the conversation that would serve as an appropriate time to go back upstairs.

"I need to get my nails filled," my mom observed as she put on her dish gloves. "Come here, K. Dry for me." Begrudgingly, I walked over to the sink. When I grabbed the dish towel, she noticed my raw hangnails and chipped polish. "K, when was the last time we got your nails done?" Without waiting for me to reply, she continued, "Let's do our nails this weekend too. We can make it a girl's day. Oh, and I'm hosting the HOA's Christmas party next week. I figured I could also combine it with a little Mary Kay. Last minute gifting! It's going to be ugly Christmas sweater themed," she said the last bit in a sing-song voice.

"Ugh, Mom. Really?"

"Oh, honey, I'm sorry. It was a last-minute switch. Lanette just wasn't feeling up to it again this year. But while you're home, you might as well help me play hostess?" She looked over at me expectantly and I grabbed a soapy wet plate from her gloved hands.

My mom had always sold something—Pampered Chef, Mary Kay, Avon, etc. Name a multilevel marketing company and she has bought into it with the fiery passion of a thousand suns. When I was younger, she used me for unpaid grassroots marketing—insisting that I bring her business cards to school and hand them out to my friends and teachers.

Azrah Statham
Helping *You* Become a Happy Homemaker

Unlike most of the airheads that sold this crap, my mom was actually somewhat of an evil genius. Putting her social butterfly persona into overdrive, she was always the top salesperson in her district and constantly hosting events. The problem, though, was that when she hosted these buying parties at our house, she always expected me to help her in some way. Bring in the appetizers at the appropriate moment, refill glasses of chardonnay, or worse—act as a living dummy when she demoed beauty products. "This is fun, right? It's like acting. This is what it must feel like to be on the stage!" she'd say before every party. But my parents' living room crammed with tipsy, gossipy housewives was not my idea of a stage.

"I'm going to take a bath," was all I could say in reply. I placed the dish towel back on the counter and headed for the stairs.

"Didn't you already take one today?" she called after me.

"Hey, K!" my dad said, pivoting to face the stairs from his seat on the sofa. The evening news was blasting as was his usual post-dinner routine. "Whenever you're ready, I can look at those grad school applications with you. Deadlines have to be coming up soon!"

"Yeah, okay. Thanks," I said and shut my bedroom door before the conversation could go any further.

I plopped down on my bed next to F. Scott. He startled, then proceeded to knead the comforter and settle back down into an impossibly twisted knot that would only be comfortable for a cat. Staring up at the ceiling, I absorbed the quiet. I could almost convince myself that I was normal…and then I came home. There was no escaping the past when my parents still treated me like a mental patient.

"Are you awake?"

My entire body shuddered, and my eyes snapped open.

Isa?

My heart raced and beads of sweat populated my forehead. I sat up, but a little too quickly and instantly my vision blurred. The steam from my scalding bath water was overpowering, but I was determined not to pass out. Did I take my iron pills today? Cursing my anemia, the last hour or so started to come back to me as I gripped the edges of the tub. I had fallen asleep in the bath. My tattered copy of *Ariel* laid on the mat and the eucalyptus candle I lit was still flickering. The last thing I remembered was reading "Lady Lazarus" and thinking, bitterly, that Ted Hughes must have been such a dick to Sylvia.

> "Out of the ash
> I rise with my red hair
> And I eat men like air."

And then, I closed my eyes. I must have been dreaming, of course. Isa wasn't here. Isa was gone. I knew this.

Initiating slow, steady breaths, I reached for my cell and began to scroll through the notifications that I had missed. A couple of texts from my friend, Julia, an art history/German double major.

Julia Visser [9:15pm]: Do you know if we have to bring something to Dr. Mirza's party?

Julia Visser [9:20pm]: Would it be lame if I just picked up something from Kroger?

There was also an email from Tufts University's Department of Art History and Architecture with the subject line: RE: Your request for more information. I knew opening that email would cost me energy that I didn't have at the moment, so I left it unread. Then, a push notification from Hulu: "Don't miss The Bachelor Season 17!" I cleared it. Paisley had obviously been using my account again and tainting my recommendations. Irritated, I felt an urge to turn off my phone. Instead, I found myself composing a message on autopilot.

Me [9:46pm]: Hey. What are you up to?

Within the space of a breath, I saw three dots.

Lincoln DeLuca [9:46pm]: Watching National Lampoon's with Dad and Whit

Lincoln DeLuca [9:46pm]: you bored already?

Me [9:48pm]: I was just thinking about the bachelorettes

Me [9:48pm]: and the time you were kidnapped

Lincoln DeLuca [9:50pm]: OMFG the pedal tavern! Highlight of my young life

Me [9:50pm]: LOL

Surprising myself, I audibly laughed at the memory of 16-year-old Lincoln getting bamboozled by a flock of drunken bachelorettes. The three of us had been downtown that night watching the New Year's fireworks by the river. Lincoln, chatty Cathy that he was, struck up a conversation with the group of scantily clad twenty-somethings.

"I'm just curious. Why is this a sought-after destination for bachelorette parties?" Lincoln had inquired.

The funny thing about it was that he wasn't some pervy teenager trying to hit on older women, but a writer conducting research. At the time, he was working on a skit that parodied the tourists in our city for our drama club's version of Saturday Night Live. We called it "Comedy O'clock" and sold tickets for a night of sketches, monologues, and music acts to benefit the department. Most of the money went towards future sets and costumes, although one year we all agreed that the proceeds go directly to Ms. Morris so she could pay for one of her cat's expensive UTI procedures.

The bachelorettes were obsessed with Lincoln. "Isn't he adorable?" they squealed. One girl, who must have been freezing in her mini skirt and "Bridesmaid Babe" tank top, snatched the soon-to-be bride's sparkly pink tiara and placed it atop Lincoln's shaggy blonde head.

"You should totally come with us! Tracey's fiancé would be soooo jealous ohmigod!" the bachelorette exclaimed as two others grabbed his arms and pulled him onto a pedal tavern.

I looked at Isa cautiously, but she just shrugged.

"Let him have his fun," was all she said.

We found him 45 minutes later on the corner of Broadway and Jefferson, hopping off the pedal tavern with a look of crazed distress. His cheeks were covered in lipstick prints and his phone's photo album now contained 50 or more selfies and group shots with the unnamed party girls.

"Happy 2008!" a bridesmaid babe screamed from the moving tavern.

"WE LOVE YOU, LINCOLN!" shouted the bride herself.

"*Never. Again.* Are you two allowed to let bachelorettes kidnap me," he said to us, his face stone-cold.

As he tossed the pink plastic penis lei from his neck into a nearby trash can, Isa and I laughed so hard that I think she may have peed herself.

Lincoln DeLuca [9:51pm]: You up for a moonlit stroll? I have to walk Ella after this. Come with?

I hesitated before typing my reply. What excuse did I have to say no? And anyway, something compelled me to reach out to him in the first place. It was as if the last three years of silence didn't matter anymore. The time I spent avoiding him and allowing our friendship to fizzle out suddenly felt stupid if all along it had been this easy to just…jump back into our old rhythms.

Me [9:53pm]: meet you at the swings

When we were teenagers, the elementary school playground located between our neighborhoods was where Isa, Lincoln, and I would meet up…usually in the middle of the night, and usually for some purpose that involved alcohol smuggled from our parents' liquor cabinets, pranking our classmates, and the like. It was a two-minute drive and about ten minutes by foot. On more tame occasions, we simply met at the playground then walked through the neighborhoods or sat on the swings, talking for hours about matters of grave importance or absolutely nothing at all. One night, in the spring of sophomore year, my mom caught me sneaking back into our house from one of our rendezvous.

She had asked, "Why don't you just call each other if you want to talk? I don't get it. Why do you have to sneak out and risk getting picked up by the police?"

I didn't say anything to her at the time, but I knew exactly what Isa would've said— "Because we can."

I hadn't been back to the swings since the night of her funeral. I tried to push that detail from my mind as I made my way down my darkened street, cutting through the elementary school's soccer field and, finally, to the deserted playground. Isa and Lincoln had gone to that elementary school. More often than not, they would exchange memories of their time there when we were messing around on the swings or the monkey bars. I was jealous during those times. Isa and Lincoln wouldn't have said that their upbringing was better in any shape or form because they had always lived in one place but, from my perspective, that worldview gave them a groundedness that I longed for. Where I was expected to continuously adapt, my heart straddled between one home and the next, they knew this city like the back of their hands. Maybe I mistook that for knowing themselves… As it turned out, none of us knew anything about who we were or where we were going…

"You came!" Lincoln smiled broadly and I saw his breath float into the pitch black. "It's a little colder than last night."

Definitely an understatement.

"What do you mean? Of course, I came," I said, approaching him.

Even with a beanie, mittens, and a chunky scarf, I hugged myself around the middle.

"I just have to get used to you being…around. Again. It feels good," he said rather sheepishly.

He let out an awkward laugh and a cloud of frozen breath billowed from his mouth. We locked eyes.

I started to respond—to say what, I didn't know—but I was interrupted by Ella's nose bumping into my calves, sniffing incessantly. The DeLuca family dog, Ella, was a white and auburn Cavalier King Charles Spaniel and the friendliest dog you'd ever meet. I fell in love with her when I first came to their house. She had jumped on my lap to cover me in slobbery kisses without so much as a "hello." Ella's pleading chestnut eyes and gentle nature would turn even the most uptight of people into a puddle of mush. Especially now, after three years, I felt my heart melt as she wagged her tail and let out a few gleeful barks.

"Ella! I missed you!"

I bent down to give her some love and her tail swished back and forth so fast, it looked like it was going to pop loose. She jumped up, placed both paws on my peacoat, and licked my face furiously.

"She remembers you," Lincoln said.

"Of course, she does. She's my girl! Who's a good girl? Yes, *you* are. *You* are." I snuggled my face into her fluffy coat. "You want to go for a walk, Ella? Come on! Let's go for a walk!"

Ella jumped and ran in a circle. Lincoln and I stood there laughing. He was right—this *did* feel good. Normal. I could almost convince myself that there was nothing to be afraid of.

"Only Ella can bring out the dimple smile," Lincoln observed.

"Hey, if you're going to get sappy on me then I'm goi—" I protested in mock annoyance.

"Okay, okay…jeesh!" He held up his hands in surrender. "It's nice to see you smile, K. That's *all*."

I shoved him. Mostly because those reflexes of us taunting each other like old friends had kicked back in. But also, because my stomach was performing an unwelcome gymnastics routine and I didn't want to analyze what it meant. And more…I couldn't remember the last time I felt like smiling the "dimple smile."

"Shall we promenade?" Lincoln extended his arm to me and though I rolled my eyes, I took it.

"Why, Mr. Darcy, how bold of you to call on me so late at night. What will my father think?" I said in a British accent as we began to venture into the neighborhood.

"No, I want to be Willoughby. That's the hot one, right?"

"Different book, but yes. And also, the *douchebag*. You're more of a Mr. Knightley from *Emma*, actually, now that I think about it."

"Who's he?"

"Ugh. Never mind. Read your Austen."

"Fine," he said, pausing at someone's mailbox for Ella to sniff. "Give me a reading list and I'll consider it."

"Maybe I will."

We continued walking through the streets, casually commenting on the variety of Christmas decorations ranging from tasteful twinkling white lights to gaudy blow-up santas. I wondered if Mrs. Ford and the HOA approved of holiday spirit in the form of gigantic inflatable packages but realized that Mrs. Ford probably couldn't care less now.

"Hey, how's…um…your mom?" I asked.

I knew it was a touchy subject—Lincoln never purposefully started a conversation about his mother—but I also knew that if we were properly going to do the "let's move on and be friends again" thing, then we needed to start piecing together what had happened in the last three years of each other's lives. Lincoln was always emotionally braver than I was, so I figured he wouldn't mind if I volunteered him to go first.

"Well, for starters, she's back now." When he saw my furrowed brows he continued, "Oh yeah…I guess you didn't know that she left in the first place. So, Mom kinda dropped off the face of the earth after the funeral. Turns out that she went on a trip. I don't really know where, but she was gone for, man…six months or so?"

"Whoa, what? And you don't know where she went? Like, at all? She didn't call or anything?" I asked, not knowing if I should have been as shocked as I was; Tamara had always been prone to impulsive behavior.

"She called," Lincoln said, "once. About a month later. Told me she was in the Caribbean, and she had finally met the man of her dreams." Lincoln paused to chuckle sarcastically then bent down to clean up Ella's mess with a doggie bag. "She went on for an hour or so about how she wanted so badly for me to meet the guy and be in their wedding—oh yeah, she was also supposedly engaged—and I just let her talk. I—and I know this sounds stupid because after all she's done to us and… Anyway, I just let her talk because I guess I missed her voice. She's still my mom…"

"I don't think that's stupid."

"Well anyway," he rubbed the back of his neck and his gaze diverted up to the stars.

I sensed that what he was about to say next was going to be difficult for him.

"Anyway, then she started talking about Isa. 'I got your sister this shell bracelet!' she told me. And 'You and Isa have to meet us here. Isa would love the water.' It was like…like she didn't know Isa was dead. She must have been drunk or something."

I had no idea what to say, so I just stared at our shoes and kept in time with his pace for a few breaths.

"So, after that," he began again, "I didn't hear from her until she got back. She didn't have a husband. She wasn't engaged. I still have no idea who that guy was that she told me about. She moved back into her condo. I think she's working again? I don't know. She'll invite me over sometimes for dinner. Sometimes, when she's manic I guess, she's super 'oh Lincoln, my baby, I miss you!' and other times she'll just text me this really toxic shit when she's in one of her moods."

"Like what?" I asked but knowing all too well that Tamara's moods could get dark.

"Last month she sent me this message out of the blue: 'You know Isa was my favorite, don't you? Every mother has a favorite and she was mine.' I didn't respond. She hasn't said anything since. But I guarantee she'll reach out again soon like nothing ever happened. Probably begging me to come over and meet some deadbeat guy that's living with her."

There were no words. We had stopped walking and were both fixated on Ella, who was now sniffing profusely at a particular spot in someone's flower bed. She started digging and Lincoln jerked her leash.

"Hey, Ella! Quit." We continued to walk, circling back to the playground. "It's okay, K," he said, evidently sensing that I didn't know how to proceed. "Thanks for listening. I guess that's been the hard part, you know? Not having someone around to listen. Someone that knows what Mom is like. And…someone that knew Isa."

"Well, you shouldn't have to deal with that. Your mom being…the way she is," I said.

"It's okay. You don't get to choose your family. But at least I still have this good girl!" Lincoln said, ruffling Ella's floppy ears. He pulled a small dog treat from his jacket pocket. "Sit, Ella, sit…" Lincoln held out his hand and Ella placed her paw eagerly against it. "Good girl!" he cooed and gave her the treat.

Always the optimist, Lincoln never harped on the negative for too long.

We climbed up the grassy hill that led back to the playground and the image of him carrying that guitar case randomly popped into my head.

"So, what was that guitar all about? From this morning? Are you writing something, or…"?

"Oh yeah! I wanted to tell you about that." His face brightened.

"Get Lincoln talking about writing and he'll never shut up," Isa used to say.

"I'm working on a devised piece," he continued. "It started out as an assignment for class, but now I think I'm going to expand it and make it my senior capstone. I want to get real people in the community involved. Not people from the department or anything like that. It has to be honest and the performance majors here are just—well, I guess you know, right? You were a major. They're just—"

"Kind of phony?" I ventured.

Though my first semester was mostly a blur, I'll never forget the feeling of having been thrown in a boxing ring every time I walked into an acting class. Every minute of the school day was one long, drawn out audition where everyone was fighting for the same role. I found it mind-boggling that Lincoln could put up with it, but then again, maybe the playwriting majors were less competitive than the performance majors. In either case, Lincoln wasn't the kind to claw his way to the top, knocking others down along the way.

"Yeah, exactly," he agreed. "And they just want big credits on their resumes to show off to casting agencies and whatnot. Most of them probably wouldn't even be interested in an original piece, especially along the lines of what I'm thinking."

"So," I said, sitting down on a swing now that we were back at the playground, "tell me about it."

It had been years since I'd had a conversation with someone about theater. I had my friends in the art history department and we would nerd out over our favorite Surrealists and Van Gogh's Blue Period, but none of them had any interest in going to the theater, let alone discussing it. And I found that refreshing. By the time I switched majors, I was burnt out on all things performing arts related. I didn't want to act in plays, read plays, or watch them. I truly wanted nothing more than to leave that part of my life in the past. Maybe, I figured, I'd be a season ticket holder at a regional playhouse later in life—when I was well off enough to afford that sort of thing, in my mid-forties or something, more self-assured and able to love art for art's sake without any residual personal trauma looming over me. But for the time being, I wanted to avoid it.

Although now…swinging gently in quiet darkness with just Christmas lights from the neighborhood below casting red, green, and blue hues on our faces, I had forgotten about how cold it was and wanted nothing more than to hear about Lincoln's play. To "talk shop," as they say.

"Well, it's an examination of loss, really," he started as he tied Ella's leash around the jungle gym. Tuckered out from her walk, she happily laid down on the playground's synthetic turf.

"Okay…I'm intrigued. I think…" I laughed nervously.

He jumped onto the swing next to me, began to twist around in circles, and continued, "The idea is that I get members from the community to write their own—cause, it's a devised piece and all that—reflections on loss. They'd basically write their own monologues, stories—whatever they feel comfortable calling it—and perform them for an audience. With some **improvised** scenes too, maybe. Sort of an intimate storytelling scenario where we're all processing and working through our losses, but it also extends the invitation for the audience to reflect too…if that makes sense?

"It'll be interactive somehow. And I want to include multimedia elements. So, I'm talking projections, sound design, installations… The cast would work together to come up with this stuff. Like, maybe we have a sculpture that's made of old clothes from someone's grandpa that died, or…something like that. And the guitar, well, it represents my loss."

"Isa's guitar?"

"Yeah." He finally took a breath. "It is. Was. I want to incorporate it into the show somehow. Still working on that bit, but it'll all be informed by the cast. Once I get my cast together, we'll go from there and it'll take shape."

He stopped spinning and I watched the chains of his swing unravel counterclockwise before speaking.

"Lincoln, I think that's brilliant." It was practically a whisper, but I knew he heard me because that goofy grin was all too visible, even in the dim, festive ambiance.

"My hope is that it provides some sort of…I don't know, exactly. Healing? Release? Or at least just *acknowledgement* around loss. That it's universal. And most of us are living with it," he said, and I saw that telltale glimmer in his eyes—the one that manifested when he was talking about something he was truly, deeply passionate about.

Then, something else. A mischievous smile and the whites of his eyes widened. I knew this look too. An idea was about to explode.

"Wait a minute. Wait a minute. Wait a—" He stood abruptly. "K! What if—I mean—YES. Why didn't I think of this as soon as I saw you in the Caf? K! You have to be—I mean—" He now knelt in front of me and clutched the chains of my swing. "K, would you be in my play?"

His arms framing my waist, his warm breath hitting my face…that jubilantly hopeful look he was giving me. As if things were finally clicking into place for him. Suddenly, I wanted to backpedal.

"What is this, a proposal?" I joked to mask my discomfort. "Where's the ring?"

"K, I'm *serious*," he said. "You're technically a 'member of the community;' you're not a theater major anymore. And I *know* you'd help me make this what I really want it to be. Think of everything you could bring to the rehearsal room!"

The last time he asked me to be in one of his plays, I failed him. I realized then as our eyes locked, that I never apologized. That was junior year of *high school* and after all this time…a semester away from graduating *college*, and I never apologized to my best friend for breaking my promise. He stood now and began to pace. Sensing his energy, Ella jumped to her feet and wagged her tail.

"We could use your nerdy art history stuff somehow…blend that in there." He stood still and turned to me. "Painting! We'll do some cool shit with paint and—and—"

"Lincoln," I tried. But he was lost in thought, pacing again, and getting Ella stirred up in the process. Once the wheels started turning, it was hard to pump the breaks on Lincoln's creative engine. "Lincoln!"

"Yeah?" he said, the trance broken.

"I don't know if I can. I haven't been on stage since the first semester of freshman year."

"That wasn't *that* long ago. Are you telling me you're nervous?" he asked, now climbing to sit on top of the monkey bars.

I sighed and kicked the AstroTurf. Buying my time before I had to come clean, I leaned backwards in the swing, letting my unruly curls touch the ground. The sky was so clear. Every star was on display. I watched my exhale evaporate into oblivion, then sat back up to face him.

"*Hamlet* was my last play," I began slowly. "I was the Ophelia understudy."

"I remember." He nodded.

I didn't remember telling him about *Hamlet*. I don't know when I would have, given that we weren't speaking all that much back then.

But maybe I did? Maybe at the funeral? I lost a lot in the fog, so it was hard to say.

"Well, I didn't finish the run. I dropped out."

"Okay…"

"It was…a couple of days after the funeral. It was an understudy performance. The, um, second Tuesday of the run."

I was stalling, but the last time I had spoken about that night was in Dr. McPherson's office years ago. In the frigid air, my palms started to sweat, and I fought the urge to rip off my mittens and devour my cuticles.

"I was…very…um…*distraught.* You know. I mean, everything had just happened."

"Right," he encouraged.

"And well, I wasn't in a good head space to go out there. On stage, I mean. I had some vodka before. But I wasn't dru—"

"K, I'm not judging yo—"

"No, no, I know. But I wasn't. I wouldn't do that before a show. I just needed a bit to get out of bed and, I don't know, trick myself into going to the theater. Does that make—"

"No, yeah. I get it. I do."

I took a deep breath, but still couldn't quite relax. There was no way out but through. I was in this memory now. I had opened the filing cabinet and gone straight to the folder labeled "Things I Used to Love."

"Well, I did most of the show and it was fine. I put everything out of my mind, somehow. But then. Act four, scene five. Ophelia's final scene."

Lincoln nodded. We studied *Hamlet* and *MacBeth* in Honors English junior year. We were both Shakespeare obsessives. He knew exactly which moment I was referring to.

"And then," I said, uneasily testing the waters, "when I sang her little song…

'He is dead and gone, lady,
He is dead and gone;

At his head a grass-green turf,
At his heels a sto—'"

I choked back a sob. Tears stung behind my eyes. I saw the stage lights blinding me once again. The sympathetic faces of the actors playing Gertrude and Claudius…the fear in their eyes when they realized that maybe, just maybe, I was no longer acting. I saw the wilted flowers in my shaking hands.

"There's rosemary, that's for remembrance," I was supposed to say. "And there is pansies, that's for thoughts"—on that line I was supposed to hand Gertrude a limp pansy. I saw the whole scene in my mind. Just as vivid as the day it all imploded, live and in full view of a 300-seat audience. Lincoln sprang from his seat atop the monkey bars and sat on the swing next to me.

"And—and—" I stuttered.

The tears barreled down my cheeks. I tasted snot, salt, the very bitterness of the cold air itself. The Christmas lights had muddled together hideously. Red. Green. Blue. White. Pounded into my head. I shut my eyes. Lincoln took my mittened hand in his.

"And" I finally managed, "I got to the line, 'There's a da—there's a dais—'"

"There's a daisy," Lincoln finished, gently.

"And, I completely lost it," I said, wiping my face. "I had a panic attack on the stage. I didn't finish the last line. I just…I just wailed. Like a wounded animal. It was…so…it was mortifying. And the…um…actor playing Laertes carried me offstage."

I let out a long, heavy exhale. Both of us staring at the ground, we were silent. Lincoln squeezed my hand.

"K," he whispered.

I couldn't meet his eyes.

"K, hey. Look at me."

He knelt in front of me again and took both hands in his. Relenting, I unwillingly met his gaze. His glasses were foggy and there were tear tracks running down his cheeks. I could see them shining against the night.

"You have nothing to be ashamed of. I promise you. I *wouldn't lie to you.*"

There was more to the story, of course. But I couldn't tell him that yet. So, to fill the silence, I just said what I should have said junior year of high school.

"Lincoln, I'm sorry I broke my promise. When I…quit your play."

He smiled a small, melancholy smile.

"You know what? I haven't thought about that for years. Ancient history," he said.

"I don't want to disappoint you again. If I…if I were to help you with this play."

"You won't," he said seriously. And then, his smile expanded. Whatever joke that was on his lips was already betraying his faux severity. "You think I'd let you bail on me again, do you? I don't want you thinking that every five years you can screw me over. This tomfoolery mustn't become a *thing*, you know."

I started to laugh, and he knew he had reeled me out of my dark place.

"What is it that they say these days?" His British accent was far less convincing than mine, I have to admit. "Ah yes, fool me once and shame on you, but fool me twice…and you'll remain a spinster, Elizabeth Bennett. No more gentleman callers for you."

I plunged into his chest and hugged his neck. Tight. Like you're supposed to hug someone you care about, not the haphazard way that I had hugged him the day before in the Caf.

"Elizabeth Bennett is an independent woman, you moron. Didn't you at least watch the movie?" I laughed into his shoulder, leaving wet blobs of tear stains. "Your threats are useless."

We broke our embrace and stood—the physical release of tension, sorrow, nervous energy, memory, and all that was in between.

"Nay, woman. Your tricks will not get the better of me!" he exclaimed into the night as he went to untie Ella's leash.

Ella sprang into action, happily trotting beside Lincoln as we made our way down to the street. He needed to go left, and I needed to go right, but we lingered underneath a streetlight both unwilling to be the first to say goodbye. The purging of emotion that I had held secret for so long made me feel tired but weirdly... Was "free" the right word? I couldn't understand how the retelling of a painful memory had actually drawn me closer to him. Wasn't unpleasantness to be avoided? Didn't you get closer to a person by sharing secrets, inside jokes, and ice cream? Singing along to Les Mis in the car, rolling the neighbors' houses, and binge watching dumb tv shows until dawn. Those were the kinds of things that made a friendship.

I didn't want to relive that night as Ophelia even alone in the cobwebbed corners of my own mind, and only yesterday I was skirting around the truth. I was a road-raging manic navigating my way through that conversation at Casa Grande; taking unprecedented sharp turns and segueing past troubling subjects before he had a chance to infer too much. I had endured last night's conversations with the same disciplined emotional distance I used on everyone else. And that's when it hit me. Endure. That's the only word that I could use to describe what I had done for the last three years. I had *endured*. But I hadn't really lived. I hadn't really felt.

I learned from the hours spent in Dr. McPherson's office that there was something necessary about having others bear witness to your grief. But Dr. McPherson didn't reciprocate the pain that I would pour out (or dribble one drop at a time, never *entirely* comfortable with sharing) during our sessions. He couldn't—I'm pretty sure that would be crossing a line professionally. You'd go mad if you were a therapist that wept with each and every client as they gushed about their issues.

But it was different with Lincoln. What I shared with him on those swings, that cost something for me—privacy or pride, I guess? — but it cost something for him too, to see me suffering. To see me grieving, that must have stirred up unresolved grief for him. How could it not? We grieved for the same person. And yet, he did it anyway. He stayed. He listened. He didn't just bear witness, which would have been enough, but he *felt* also.

In the way that profound revelations sometimes do, all of this seeped over me like a warm bath. I now understood why it felt good and right and normal to be in Lincoln's company again. The missing piece in my journey to moving forward was to experience this grief with someone else—someone that knew exactly what it was (and who it was) that I missed. Maybe I had my reasons for shutting him out before, but now I couldn't argue against letting him in. It all boiled down to one word…

"Thanks," I said.

"For what?"

"You know."

I stuffed my hands in my coat. He was doing the same. Slightly rocking from the balls of his feet to his heels, he looked shyly at an icy patch on the road between us. I stepped just a hair closer to him.

"For forgiving me."

"We were kids. It's okay."

"What are we now—*actual* grownups?" I teased.

"God, I hope not," he replied, his toothy grin busting at the seams.

We both laughed and then fell silent. His nose was pink from the cold, but that was probably nothing compared to my cheeks, which I assumed were scarlet. My insides were boiling, and my stomach felt like it had dropped to my butt, but I took his gloved hand anyway. It just felt like the next right thing to do.

"*Also*…thanks for forgiving me for disappearing. I won't do it again."

"I'm glad you're back, K," he said softly and then ever so subtly glanced down at my lips.

At the same time, I sensed a teeny sensation of wetness on my bottom lip.

"Is it snowing?" he asked, breaking whatever momentary spell that was between us.

And it was—snow was on my lips and in my eyelashes, in my hair. I glanced up at the streetlamp and saw tiny snowflakes dancing in the light. There was no way it was going to stick. We were never so lucky to get real white Christmases here—just ice. But it was pretty.

"Look at nature showing off," I said to the sky.

I felt the warmth of Lincoln's eyes on me as I closed mine. I tilted my head skyward and stuck out my tongue, tasting the fresh snow as it melted. I figured Lincoln must have been doing the same because I heard him chuckling. How can you not laugh when you're catching snowflakes? Then I heard a distinct tinkling sound.

"Ella!" Lincoln exclaimed.

Ella had squatted in front of the streetlamp to mark the spot as her own.

"Nothing like a spontaneous pee to kill a mood," Lincoln laughed.

I smiled. The "dimple smile." My cheeks were aching since I was out of practice. And we left all that was unsaid between us, unsaid.

"Night," I said, turning to go.

"Slept tight," Lincoln waved, "Don't let the bedbugs bite."

Several feet ahead now, I turned around one last time to say goodbye to Ella.

"See you later, Ella!" I called.

Hearing her name, Ella looked back at me. With her mouth partly open, she had the appearance of a smile. And I allowed my mind to wander…

✳✳✳

It was the morning after Jason's party. I was sore and exhausted, but mostly angry. I didn't want to speak to her, to even look at her. But I followed Isa out the front door, nonetheless. Ella had been whining to go out. It was already 11:00 am and, hung over, we were still in our pajamas and shading our eyes from the sun. Ella must have seen a squirrel and she bolted—the leash shot from Isa's hand before either of us could register what was happening.

"Ella!" we yelled.

We ran after her in our bare feet. Quickly, the chase developed a chaotic, exhilarating energy—akin to the night we went streaking at Blair's, years ago at that point. We were calling after Ella, but she was blissfully ignoring us and sprinting down the sidewalk at record speeds with her leash trailing behind. Isa started laughing. I started laughing. Dads mowing their lawns and moms driving by in their family vans stared at us as we ran like feral children. We could have been six or seven years old. We were rowdy and euphoric. Isa jumped over garden gnomes, and I ran headfirst through a sprinkler, drenching myself.

Finally, Ella slowed to a steady trot, and we caught up with her in a neighbor's front lawn, ten houses or so from Isa's. We collapsed into the grass, Isa grabbed Ella, and we laid there panting and laughing until tears were springing from the corners of our eyes. I forgot I was angry at Isa—so angry that I wondered if I hated her. But in the grass, there was nothing complicated between us. There was no distrust. We were two friends sharing a laugh in a moment in time that we would never again recreate.

"Ella, you naughty girl!" Isa said.

She snorted and that made us cackle all the more.

"Excuse me! What's going on out here?"

The woman whose lawn we had collapsed in was standing at her front window, eyeing us suspiciously.

"I'm sorry, ma'am. We jus—We just saw a squirrel and decided to take care of it for you," I called to her.

The look she gave us only made the laughter cascade in faster and faster waves. We were roaring as we stumbled to our feet, grass in our hair…leaving what was lost behind.

***

I let the scene play out in my mind as I watched Lincoln and Ella walk away. If I could bottle uncomplicated, unadulterated joy, I would have that memory—the one of me and Isa rolling around in the grass, laughing like banshees—in a vial around my neck. And now, I'd include me and Lincoln under the streetlamp in that vile too.

6.

Opening Night

"**Five minutes until places!**" Ms. Morris bellowed into the green room.

"Thank you, five!" the cast replied in unison.

Opening night of *Guys and Dolls* finally arrived on December 10th. The cast gathered in the makeshift green room, which, by day, served as the high school's band room. The space was congested with nervous energy; some of us were doing lip thrills, some of us were singing our solos to the walls, and others were still applying pounds of stage makeup.

"Time calls are technically *my* job…" Lincoln said as he approached us.

Isa and I were reviewing the script. Or, rather, Isa, who was alternating through yoga poses with the script in one hand, was on book for me as I frantically spat my lines at her. I feared that if I didn't study this script in earnest until the very last second before curtain, I would forget it entirely. I couldn't risk humiliation and I had to prove myself. Blair might have been the instigator, but she, Savannah, and Deanna weren't the only ones whispering about the audacity of a freshmen as the leading lady.

"Well look at you—Mr. Bigshot with your headset," Isa said, transitioning into a downward dog.

As the assistant stage manager, Lincoln was dressed in all black and wearing a headset to communicate with members of the stage crew from the light and sound booth over the auditorium. When he found out that he'd have the privilege of wearing one of the department's three headsets, it was all he had talked about for a week.

"Don't you need to be in the booth?" I asked.

"They'll survive without me for two more minutes," Lincoln said nonchalantly.

"But. The sound—" I started.

Not exactly knowing what tasks to delegate to an assistant stage manager (she'd never had one before), Ms. Morris put Lincoln on the sound board. He was responsible for running the music tracks. If he wasn't there to press play, I could be onstage about to open my mouth and be forced to sing acapella.

"K, come on." Lincoln raised his eyebrows then put a reassuring hand on my shoulder. "This isn't my first rodeo; I told you, I've been doing plays since 6th grade."

"A seasoned professional, you might say," Isa asserted from child's pose.

"Exactly," Lincoln continued, "and I will personally see to it that your solos go off without a hitch. But if Jason's tracks don't start on time… Hey, it's live theater…what can be done?"

Isa's husky laugh bounced off the walls, but I stared at him wide-eyed. My panic was mounting. If Jason screwed up in one of our duets, that would also make me look bad. Surely Lincoln wouldn't jeopardize the show just to prank Jason. Over the last several weeks, Jason and the male ensemble had been, in Isa's words, "total dickwads" about the Havana nightclub/kissing scene and I knew that angered Isa and Lincoln just as much as it mortified me. But to intentionally miss a sound cue…

"Kidding. Only kidding," Lincoln chuckled. "He doesn't need my help to look like an ass."

And that was true. To any sane and well-adjusted person, Jason *was* an ass. As immature as they come. But to many of the girls in our cast—and the guys for that matter—he was a hero and comedic mastermind. He would wink at me from across the room while his friends made kissy faces behind him. The ridiculing began when he pulled away from me the first time, we ran the kiss and shouted, "Whoa! Whoa! Ms. Morris, tell her we can't do tongue! Children will be in the audience!"

For the record—I did no such thing. In fact, being that it was my first kiss, I barely made contact with his lips at all. Hence, shoving my tongue down his throat was the furthest thing from my mind. But Jason couldn't resist a laugh. I privately decided that a stage kiss didn't count as a real first kiss and that was the only way I could stop myself from spiraling into a pit of disappointment.

I knew Jason didn't like me and I told myself that I wouldn't have given him a second look if we hadn't been playing romantic opposites, but still—I thought the *first* time would hold a little more magic. At least a tiny tinge of a spark? But it was brief, bland, barely there and, frankly, didn't get much better as rehearsals continued. ("An indication of what he's like in bed, I'm sure," Isa joked at lunch once.) And from that moment forward, Ms. Morris had to add fielding inappropriate comments to her list of duties as director. The number of times in a rehearsal when she had to pause to say, "Children, please! We came here to tell a story! That is our *job* as thespians," was innumerable.

Ms. Morris was never, however, privy to Blair's snide remarks. It wasn't Blair's style to get the entire cast rolling around on the floor, clutching their sides because that took up valuable rehearsal time. Blair, the consummate "professional," preferred to make quick jabs that went straight for the gut at inopportune moments.

The week before opening and conveniently right before we went onstage to sing "Marry the Man Today," she leaned in close and whispered, "I know Ms. Morris doesn't want to crush your spirit, but I'll be straight with you—you were pretty pitchy last time we ran this.

Just don't think about Jason watching you from the wings and you'll relax."

"She's just trying to psych you out," Isa had said to me when I told her. "Don't let her have that satisfaction. Ms. M would tell you if she had notes for you."

While I knew this was more than likely an accurate assessment, I found it difficult to dig up the seeds of doubt that Blair planted before they took root. If I liked acting any less, I would have been tempted to quit altogether.

"Irish wristwatch! Irish wristwatch! Whether the weather be cold…or whether the weather be hot…" Blair's vocal warm-ups pierced my eardrums as she pranced by us in her flouncy blonde Adelaide wig.

"Okay enough of this stress-talk," Isa said after releasing her tree pose. "K, we need to get you pumped the hell up. You only get one first opening night."

Standing close enough to me that our noses nearly touched, she stared me dead in the eyes, grabbed my sweaty hands, and started shaking my arms like they were made of Jell-O.

"Come on, jump with me!" She began to bounce. "Jump, Abe!"

Lincoln put one hand on Isa's shoulder and the other on mine and started to bounce. Hesitantly, I began to bend my knees ever so slightly.

"I'm going to puke," I said.

"Nope. No, you are not," Isa closed her eyes and said serenely. "You are not gonna puke. You're gonna kill it. You are going to make them laugh, cry, and beg for more."

Lincoln let out a few supportive whoos and they both continued to bounce with me lamely half-squatting along.

"Now stop," Isa said, abruptly. We all stood completely still. "Squeeze my hands as hard as you can."

I squeezed.

"Harder," she demanded.

I squeezed again.

"Harder!"

I squeezed even harder.

"Whoo! You got this, K!" Lincoln rallied.

"Now, close your eyes. Breathe in," Isa instructed. I did as she said. "Hold your breath at the top of the inhale…now release and let it all out."

Like thawing ice, my firm grasp on Isa's hands dissolved and I intuitively let out a long, satisfying exhale. When I opened my eyes, I saw that she was fixating on me with intensity. It was as though she was trying to give me a bit of her own inner strength.

"You're going to be okay," she said. Her soft half-smile carried the weight of the world.

And maybe it was the adrenaline. Maybe it was the breathing exercise. Or maybe Isa and I were connected in some inexplicable spiritual sense. But I felt ready. I knew I could do this, and I wasn't even a little bit afraid. Since my mother still hadn't met Isa's mom—Isa had a million and one excuses for why her mom was unavailable or just incapable of calling my mom back—I only spent time with Isa at school and rehearsals. But between lunches together every day, passing notes in the hallway, and being attached at the hip during rehearsals, our friendship gained momentum at lightning speed. If she said I was going to be okay, then dammit—I was going to be okay.

"Lincoln! Where are you?" Ms. Morris' voice in Lincoln's headset was so loud that it almost startled the Zen right out of me.

"Hey, I gotta go," he said. "Let's do the thing."

"Wha—" I began to ask.

"We have a tradition," Isa explained. "Before every show, we say this chant. We've been doing it since middle school. Ready?"

Lincoln and Isa grabbed hands and reached for mine.

"Oh, and there's a handshake thing that goes with it," she continued. "It goes…"

They both began to chant, "Break a leg…"

They swung their arms (and mine) forwards and backwards.

"…don't make me beg…"

They put their hands together in a pleading position.

"...drop a line..."

They drew an invisible line across their necks, indicating cutting their own throats.

"...and they'll whine..."

Balled into fists on either side of their eyes, they made a crying baby gesture.

"...so, raise your cup..."

Hands were raised into the air holding an imaginary glass.

"...and don't screw up!!" they shouted and pumped their fists into the air. Isa surprised Lincoln with a swift spank and then wacked me as well.

"Break a leg, K! Isa don't screw up," Lincoln said and made his exit for the booth.

"Places!" Ms. Morris' voice, like an unseen and omniscient god, echoed from the intercom system over our heads.

"You're going to be great," I told Isa.

"Not as great as you."

I took one last glance at myself in the mirror. With my normally frizzy hair smoothed into sleek depression-era curls and my lips painted with "Scarlet Stiletto" red (a color my mom was overjoyed to let me borrow...on the condition that I tell my castmates she sold Mary Kay), I didn't recognize the gangly, insecure teenager I was underneath my character. I decided then and there that "Shy, Lonely New Girl" was a role that I had outgrown.

"A star is born!" my mom squealed as soon as she and my dad spotted me. Pumps click-clacking against the cement, she rushed over to me with her arms already extended for an embrace.

The cast had lined up outside the auditorium after bows for the "petting zoo," as Isa called it. Apparently, it was a routine event after every show; an opportunity for the audience to greet the cast— "Every now and then, we *must* indulge them" Ms. Morris had said, referring to our "fans." But more accurately, the petting zoo was a photo opp for the parents. My dad was carrying what looked like a large stuffed animal and my mom was wearing her million-dollar smile. Our dimpled smiles were essentially the only thing we had in common. Mine only surfaced sporadically, but mom used hers to secure sales with clients.

"Honey! Oh, I'm so proud of you!" she said, squeezing me. "I can't believe it was *you* up there! In front of all those *people*! Who kidnapped my child?" She laughed at her own joke and gave me a pretend pinch. "Is that really *my* daughter in there?"

Luckily, my dad interrupted by stepping forward to kiss me on the forehead.

"My girl!"

He beamed and presented me with a very large and very silly looking teddy bear. With the words "Break a Leg!" embroidered on the bear's tummy and a small cast wrapped around its leg, it looked like something you could win by playing Skee-Ball at a carnival.

"I told Daddy that women prefer flowers, but he said they'll just die anyway," my mom explained. "Men. They never listen!"

It was gaudy and certainly dorky but imagining my dad selecting this teddy bear himself and sitting it on his lap throughout the performance made me feel like I might start blubbering. My parents had busy lives and I so rarely did anything to elicit attention. It was a significant moment for me to bask in their praise, although I would have preferred to redo the whole scene without onlookers.

"How did you memorize all those lines? And the singing. Sweetie, I didn't know you could do that. Where did you learn how to sing?" my dad gushed.

"It was because I signed her up for children's choir all those years ago," my mom said, loving the opportunity to take credit in any situation.

"She's a natural," Isa piped up.

She had been standing beside me, but my parents hadn't even noticed.

"Isa, it's good to see you again," my dad said. "And congrats! What a terrific show."

"So glad you could come, Mr. Statham."

"We wouldn't have missed it for the world. This is K's first play, you know."

He put his arm around my shoulders and pulled me close.

"You did a lovely job, Isa," my mom said, albeit stiffly. "Are we still on for dinner tonight? Where are your parents?"

"Oh, my dad's here somewhere," she said, standing on her tiptoes now to survey the crowd. "But my mom's probably going to meet us at the restaurant."

She was smiling, but I knew now that it was the kind of look she put on for authority figures—polite and practiced. There was something distressing her underneath the calm exterior, and though I didn't know for certain, I guessed it had something to do with her mom. It was like pulling teeth to finally arrange this dinner. Isa's mom had either been out of town, sick, or Isa had "forgotten" to talk to her about it. But every time I begged my mom to let Isa drive me home from rehearsal *just for today* or *just once* let me go with them to study at Chubbie's for *only an hour*, the answer was always the same— "Not until I meet her mother."

"You freaking DID IT!"

Before I knew what was happening, my feet were off the pavement. Lincoln had run up behind us, grabbed me around the waist, and hoisted me into the air.

"Whoa! Put me down!" I protested through laughter.

"Oh, sorry, hi, Mr…um…K's dad," Lincoln said, sobering after he placed me back on my feet and saw that my parents were right in front of us.

"*Statham,* you idiot," Isa whispered, elbowing him in the stomach.

My dad smiled warm-heartedly and extended his hand to greet Lincoln as a man carrying a bouquet of daisies walked up. Though it was dark, and I was nearly blinded by the swarm of parents using flash photography, I knew this man had to be Mr. DeLuca. This man *was* Lincoln in twenty-five years; he was just as tall, just as lanky. The only difference was that he was wearing a blazer and smart, black-rimmed glasses.

"Dad!" Isa smiled and nearly bounced into her father's arms. "Are these for me?"

"Who else?" Mr. DeLuca said, handing Isa the daisies.

She brought them to her nose and executed a dainty twirl.

"My favorite!"

Radiating youth and joy, I hadn't seen her so childlike.

"Good job, Lincs," Mr. DeLuca said, bringing in his son for a hug. "Another great show."

"Oh, Mr. and Mrs. Statham," Isa yipped excitedly, completely out of character, "this is our dad."

"Tony," Mr. DeLuca said, "Pleasure to meet you both."

Mr. DeLuca shook hands with my parents. It was finally happening. The parents were meeting and now my mom could relax.

"And you must be K." Mr. DeLuca turned to me. "You're quite the actress. The kids were right."

"Um…thank you, sir," I stammered.

"K, come on. Let's get changed so we can get out of here," Isa said, grabbing my hand and pulling me towards the backstage door.

"I'm *starving*! Where are we going again?" Lincoln asked, trailing behind us.

Dodging the entanglement of our castmates taking photos and talking eagerly with their friends and family, we almost made it to the double doors before Ms. Morris stopped me in my tracks.

"K," she began, "I wanted to say, 'Brava!' Exceptional. Truly exceptional, my dear."

Ms. Morris patted my cheek in a grandmotherly fashion then waltzed back into the post-show cacophony before I could reply. Blair stood feet away, and I assumed by the look on her face, overheard my private moment with Ms. Morris. Her face was the very picture of defeat; and given that she was balancing three massive bouquets in her arms and was still wearing Adelaide's outrageous wedding dress from the act two finale, I couldn't help but find her pout rather comical. Festering in a world of her own, she didn't notice when someone's grandma bumped into her, sending one bundle of roses flying just as Jason glided between us to catch up with his buddies.

"Oh, Jason," Blair said, eyes fixed on me, "could you carry these for me?"

"Yeah. Sure." Jason knelt to grab the roses before anyone could trample them.

Blair gave me a decisively wicked grin before turning to walk off with Jason. But I could care less. Let her have Jason. I didn't want him. I was on cloud nine and nothing—not even a snot like Blair—could bring me down to earth.

"I thought the entire production was wonderful. From start to finish!" my mom exclaimed, picking up a breadstick.

Thirty minutes after being seated at Michelangelo's Pizzeria, we were still waiting for Mrs. DeLuca.

"Looks like my wife is held up at the office," Mr. DeLuca said as we took our seats. "Sometimes she has to put in overtime. The college interns don't do their jobs." He had laughed effortlessly, but there was something suspiciously unconvincing about it.

"The set was remarkable, too," my dad chimed in. "Lincoln, did you help out with that?"

"Yup," Lincoln said, nodding his head and swirling his breadstick in olive oil, "Ms. M had me doing basically everything backstage-related. I'm sort of the drama club underling."

The olive oil that dribbled down his chin and onto his cast t-shirt only added to the self-deprecation.

"You're proving your worth. Ms. Morris will have you assistant directing and then taking on your own shows in no time," Mr. DeLuca said. "Could you pass the water, Tim?"

"Sure, sure," my dad said, handing Mr. DeLuca the pitcher. "That's what I tell K—you have to make yourself indispensable. Learn as much as you can while you still can."

My dad winked at Lincoln. Just as my mom loved to claim credit, my dad loved to dispense advice... And he loved to remind everyone of said advice, especially when you realized later that you should have listened to him all along.

Absorbent as a sponge, Lincoln reached behind him to fish his writer's notebook from his backpack and started to jot something down. I noticed that tiny ripples were forming in my water cup and glanced at Isa, who sat next to me. She was gripping the sides of her chair and jiggling her leg so wildly that the table was shaking. I followed her gaze to the entrance, and that was when I first laid eyes on Tamara DeLuca.

A platinum blonde woman pushed open the door carrying a large leather handbag in one hand and clutching a cellphone to her ear with the other. Her smoky charcoal eyeliner created a winged cat-eye appearance and layers of magenta blush accented her high cheekbones. She looked like Barbie when Barbie decided that her profession of the day would be corporate law. It wasn't that she was fake in a Botox and spray tan kind of way, but there was something...off.

Like she was playing dress up, but underneath the power suit was a frightened little girl trying to impress everyone. Her spastic eyes darting across the restaurant in search of us made her at once commanding and terrifying. I could easily see her leading a board meeting or sobbing hysterically in the bathroom, clumpy mascara tracking down her cheeks—either version would have been believable.

"Muah!" Tamara bent down to give Isa a kiss on the cheek. "Darling, how was the show? Oh, Linky Loo! How's my future Woody Allen?"

She collapsed into the empty chair between Lincoln and Mr. DeLuca, dropped her cellphone in her bag, and ruffled Lincoln's shaggy head. Embarrassed, he raised a hesitant hand to smooth out the disturbed hairs.

"Oh my god. Where are my manners! I'm Tamara!" She stood up again and extended a hand, crowded with imposing jeweled rings, to my parents from across the table.

In this exchange, she pushed over the saltshaker, which Lincoln righted. My dad was natural, but my mom was visibly skeptical as she shook Tamara's hand, eyeing the small pile of salty mess on the tablecloth that Tamara had created.

"Tim Statham," my dad said.

"Azrah," my mom greeted, "I'm so glad we could finally connect."

"*Ara*. What a beautiful name!" Tamara cried as she focused on flipping through the menu.

"It's actually Az-rah," my mom corrected, but Tamara didn't take her eyes off the menu.

I glanced at Isa. She hadn't said a word and had barely moved an inch aside from her right leg, which was still jiggling with nervous vigor.

"Tammy, we were just discussing the sho—" Mr. DeLuca began.

"Double martini. Dry," Tamara said to the nearby waitress, who was not the woman assigned to our table. "Have we ordered yet? I think I'll get the Bolognese." A parlous chiming sound exploded from Tamara's purse. "Ugh, so sorry dears, it's work again. I'll dash off to the ladies. Be right back." She stood, slung her purse over her shoulder, pushed her chair in, then said by way of parting, "Tony, please make sure they don't use Gordon's, okay? If it's Gordon's, send it back."

Two large pepperoni pizzas later (and an untouched plate of Bolognese for Tamara), the meeting of the parents hadn't exactly made an upswing. At least my dad and Mr. DeLuca hit it off—both were avid Chicago Bulls fans, and they were businessmen through and through.

Mr. DeLuca was a financial advisor and my dad, the economist, could talk about money and the fluctuating stock market all evening if it were up to them. Isa, Lincoln, and I remained mostly silent.

I was busy studying Tamara DeLuca—watching her clumsily stagger her way through conversation while repeatedly checking her cellphone and downing martinis was not too different from witnessing a car crash.

"It was unfortunate about that poor boy playing…what was that character's name? Nathan…?" my mom tried.

"Nathan Detroit," I finished.

"Yes, yes. That poor boy must have forgotten his lines in that one scene close to the end. You could see it all over his face," my mom said, taking a sympathetic sip of wine.

I noticed that she avoided looking Mrs. DeLuca in the eyes as she talked, preferring to focus on everyone else at the table.

"That's Jon Seong. We've been friends since 5th grade," Lincoln said, wiping pizza grease from his mouth. "He was super nervous."

"He did look like he was trembling a bit at times," Mom observed.

"Probably because Blair threatened his life if he jumped her lines," I whispered to Isa, but she didn't seem to hear me.

Her eyes were glued to her mom who was now reapplying her lipstick using a compact mirror. With a shaking hand, Tamara smudged a bit of deep pink beyond the barriers of her lip line but didn't appear to care as she closed her compact and picked up her martini once again.

"Jon's a good guy," Lincoln went on. "He's not the best actor, but at least he's trying. Great musician though. And he's not all cocky about getting a big role like Jason."

"Jason. Was that the one you were supposed to be in love with, honey?" my dad asked.

I nodded and looked down at the checkered tablecloth.

Why wasn't Isa talking?

"Well, I thought that kid was a hoot!" Dad added.

"And Blair was just really *something* in that role, wasn't she?" my mom asked the group.

"Oh *Blaiiiir*! Blair Ford? Now I *really* wish I could have seen—uh—this little *show*," Tamara slurred. "Isabel, when was the last time you had *Blair* over? You should have Blair come by sometime. Oh, I miss you girls. You pretty little girls."

Isa was blank-faced, and the rest of the party fidgeted uncomfortably in their seats at the sight of Tamara's now watery eyes. That ear-piercing chiming sound started up again. This time, Tamara upturned Lincoln's Pepsi as she retrieved her phone from her bag.

"Jesus Christ," Isa muttered under her breath.

"Tammy, what are you—" Mr. DeLuca started.

"Whoopsies!" Tamara giggled. "I've got to take this one and then I *promise*, I'll be back and ready for dessert, or do you kids want to go to go Chuck, um, what is his name again? The mouse with the games and all that?" She hiccupped. "That's right! Chuck E. Cheese. I think you *deserve it*. You've worked *so hard*."

"We're not ten," Isa spat into her lap.

"Be right back." She almost tripped over my mom's chair as she made her way to the women's restroom. "So sorry, Az-er-ia."

"Tammy!" Visibly anxious, Mr. DeLuca stood, but then sat back down when Tamara waved him off.

Watching Tamara stumble her way to the restroom, it didn't seem—to me anyway—that she was on a work call. Who guffaws like that on a work call? Maybe she was just really personable with her colleagues? Or maybe it was the gin. Either way, I decided it wasn't my place to point it out to Isa.

The dads fought over who would pay the bill, but Mr. DeLuca won in the end—probably because he didn't want to burden my dad with his wife's bar tab. We exchanged farewells and parted ways to our respective vehicles. I tried not to think too much about how Mrs. DeLuca was getting home. That wasn't my business. My mom, on the other hand…

"That woman is a drunk if I've ever seen one," she said as soon as she shut the passenger's side door.

"We don't know her well enough to make a statement like that," my dad reasoned. "Who knows what kind of pressure she deals with at her job. Lawyers are always go-go-go."

"Did you see her lipstick? Smudged clear across her face!" Mom snorted, then turned to face me in the backseat. "K, I don't know if I want you around those people. Mrs. DeLuca is clearly unstable."

"Mom! What doe—" I began.

"Now, Azrah, really." Stopped at a red light, my dad jumped in to diffuse the situation. "We shouldn't make such harsh judgments from one meeting. Tony's alright, wasn't he? *I* liked him. And the kids—your friends, honey—both respectful. Good heads on their shoulders."

"I don't know." My mom was clearly frazzled. "I don't want that girl putting bad ideas in your head. K, you need good influences. The apple doesn't fall far from the tree."

"What's wrong with Isa?" I argued. "Just because her mom's a little bizarre doesn't make her a bad person. You said we couldn't hang out until you met her parents and now you have. I mean, what if people didn't want *their* kid to hang out with me because of *you*? Wouldn't that be totally unfair?"

"What would make you say that, K?" my mom asked. She was stern but as she continued, I could detect just the faintest quiver in her throat. "What is so *different* about me that would make someone judge me? I'm an American, just lik—"

"Mom! God! I didn't mean—"

"That's enough!" Dad interjected. He rarely raised his voice, so when he did, we listened. "Azrah, K needs to socialize." He placed his right hand gently on my mom's leg while the left remained on the steering wheel. "Isa and Lincoln are good kids. Now K, apologize to your mother."

"But I didn't—"

"K, I mean it. Disrespect your mother and you won't be spending time with any friends. I don't care who their parents are," my dad said.

"I'm sorry," I muttered and slouched down in my seat.

I stared out the window, silent, for the rest of the ride home. I tried to relive the memories of just hours before—onstage, taking my bow during curtain call.

"No day but today!" my phone sang.

A persistent buzzing and the lyrics from *Rent* stirred me out of a light slumber later that night. I pushed back the comforter, grabbed my cell phone, and silenced it before my ringtone could echo through the sleeping house again.

Missed Call [2:12am] — Isa DeLuca
Missed Call [2:14am] — Isa DeLuca
Missed Call [2:15am] — Isa DeLuca

Racking my mind as to why Isa was calling me in the middle of the night, I was distracted by a small "*plunk*!" at my window. Seconds later, I saw a pebble hit the glass. My phone started to buzz again. This time, I answered immediately.

"Isa?"

"We're outside! Open up!" Isa whispered into the phone and promptly disconnected the call.

I opened my window and found Isa and Lincoln standing below me, bundled up against the December cold. Isa carried a large, lumpy pillowcase. Lincoln steadied a bike with one hand and had a fist-full of the tiny pebbles my parents used to decorate their backyard flower beds in the other. With his signature goofy grin, Lincoln smiled up at me.

"Come down!" Isa whisper-yelled.

"What are you guys doing?" I called back then my eyes instinctively shot to my bedroom door. Any minute disturbance might prompt my parents to come in and check on me.

"We're roll—" Lincoln started, but Isa put a hand over his mouth to silence him.

"We'll tell you when you come out!" Isa said.

"But my parents have an alarm system."

"Can't you turn it off?" she asked.

"Not without waking them up."

She thought for a moment, surveying the scene. My bedroom window faced the back of the house…and was on the *second story*. How the hell did she expect me to get down? But as soon as I saw her eyeing the trellis adjacent to my window, a chill of understanding ran through me. She looked up at me and I could see the mischief sparkling in eyes even from 20 feet away.

"Isa, no. There's no way—" I refused.

"K, it's simple, just crawl out the window, scoot your butt over to this plant thingy and climb down slowly. We'll spot you," Isa instructed.

"I could seriously kill myself."

"No, you won't!"

"We'll catch you!" Lincoln egged on.

Nervous that all this commotion would wake up my parents, I did the only thing logical to my teenage brain. I had to silence them…by crawling out the window.

"Okay, okay. Just…shhh!!"

I fumbled with the latches to the window screen and after quite a bit of jiggling and maneuvering, I was finally able to slide the screen free and out of the frame. Holy cow. It was cold. I was barefoot and still in my *Guys and Dolls* cast tee and a thin pair of striped pajama bottoms.

"Just a second!" I called out the window.

"Hurry up!" Isa insisted

I scurried through my closet to find a jacket and grabbed a knit cap that was laying on my dresser. Shoes. I couldn't climb down the trellis barefoot. I would get frostbite and that thing was also covered in thorny vines. I pulled on my gym sneakers, which were the first pair of shoes within reach, and approached the windowsill. Gulping hard, I leaned over the edge and saw them waving eagerly. There was a roof right below my window so, theoretically, Isa was right—I could climb out of the window and scoot across the roof, but the scary part would be getting from the roof to the top of the trellis…

"I'll meet you halfway!" Lincoln offered when I didn't make a move.

With a running start, he jumped onto the trellis.

"Ah! These things have spikes!" he exclaimed, examining one pricked hand while holding on for dear life with the other.

"Shh!" Isa and I urged in unison.

Lincoln climbed a few feet, slowly and carefully placing his hands in danger-free zones. I managed to steadily lift one leg, then the other, over the windowsill and land soundlessly on the roof. Isa still seemed so far away. The journey to the cold, hard, ground below would definitely break my neck. I'd never be able to act again. I'd never get a *real* first kiss. I'd never—

"K!" Lincoln whispered, his head now level with the roof where I sat, frozen and paranoid. "Scoot over here. Just take it slow." When I didn't move, he pressed, "Just keep your eyes on me and don't look down."

So, I did. I kept constant contact with his hazel eyes as I scooted inch by inch across the roof.

"You're doing great!" he whispered and extended his hand. "Okay, now, when you get to the edge, you're going to put your right foot out. Stick it right here, next to my feet. And grab my hand."

I hesitated. Did I ever notice before now that I had an intense fear of heights? That seemed like something a person ought to know about themselves before they spontaneously decided to sneak out via a second story window…

"K, you're so close!" Isa cheered from below.

I grabbed Lincoln's hand, slowly stuck out my foot, and then…

"Shit shit shit!"

I didn't even hear Lincoln curse as I yelped. I slipped off the edge of the roof and my left foot flew out from under me.

In a whirlwind of terror, I was able to hook my left foot into the trellis, grab on with my left hand, and at the last fatal moment, Lincoln wrapped his free arm around my waist. So close that I inhaled his warm, frantic breath, we stared at each other, panic-stricken. I couldn't tell if it was his heart pounding or mine but suspended there at the tip-top of the trellis after almost dying (or at least, breaking a limb), we began to laugh.

"Hey! Stop dilly-dallying! Let's go!" Isa said, shaking the bottom of the trellis and causing it to squirm beneath us.

"Isa! Quit it!" Lincoln snapped. "Okay, just one foot at a time. Like a rock-climbing wall. You've done one of those before, right?" I shook my head. "That's fine. It's easy."

And, for the most part—if I ignored my thumping heart and didn't look down—it was. When we finally made it to the bottom, we jumped off the wall. Lincoln stumbled and fell onto the grass. I miraculously landed on my feet. No broken bones.

"Lincoln, you're a true American hero," Isa congratulated, semi-sarcastically. "Now let's get out of here!"

Lugging the stuffed pillowcase along, Isa and I dashed out of my parents' backyard and onto the street. Lincoln jumped on his bike and sped in front of us, leading the way.

"So, what are we doing?" I asked as I followed them to our undefined destination.

"You, my friend, are going to roll your first house tonight," Isa declared.

She stopped walking and opened the pillowcase to reveal dozens of toilet paper rolls.

"You mean, we're *vandalizing*?" I asked, mortified.

"No, no, no," Isa explained, "we're *decorating*."

I stopped. It seemed that every time I hung out with Isa, she threw me for a loop. Would she always and forever be challenging me to break the law? It was possible.

"Guys, we can't just wreck someone's house. We'll get in serious trouble."

"K, it's totally fine. It's not like it's spray paint or eggs or anything," Lincoln justified, circling me on his bike. "It's just toilet paper. It'll blow away or wash itself out of the trees as soon as it rains."

"Don't knock it till you try it!" Isa sang, now skipping through the streets.

One thing I knew for sure was that I was too chicken to attempt to climb back into my bedroom window alone, so I ran to catch up with them. Maybe it really was harmless. How much damage can a little toilet paper do anyway? But when we came upon a familiar house, my doubts resurfaced with more tenacity.

"*Blair's* house?" I asked, facing the pillared colonial, and neatly maintained lawn.

"Shh!" was all Isa said in reply.

"But she'll know it was us!" I whispered as Lincoln and Isa unloaded rolls from the pillowcase. "No way, guys. We can't do this."

"We get Blair every couple of months and her parents don't suspect a thing," Lincoln said, handing me a roll.

"And it's the perfect house for it. Just look at these trees!" Isa spun and leaped around the Ford's front yard, the roll of toilet paper in her hand flying behind her like a ribbon dancer's wand. "Come on, just throw one tiny roll. I bet you'll like it…"

At that, she shot the roll in her right hand into the nearest naked maple tree. It landed somewhere halfway to the top, stuck among the branches, and then zigzagged its way down to the ground. The effect was actually pretty artistic.

"Kinda looks like modern art," I observed.

"See?" Isa ran up to me. "We aren't vandalizing. We're *expressing*. We're making their house prettier. Giving it a creative edge."

Lincoln was now working on wrapping the pillars on the front porch—a foolish risk in my opinion. I was far too skittish to attempt getting that close to the house. Isa picked up the roll that landed in front of the maple and tossed it back up into the air. The street was so quiet that I was able to hear the zephyr-like rustling of the toilet paper as it zoomed upwards, unraveled, and draped over a branch so high I had to crane my neck to see it. After a beat, the roll plunged elegantly to the ground.

"Nice!" Lincoln whispered, giving Isa a thumbs up.

"You sure you don't want to give it a go?" Isa asked.

Looking down at the roll in my hand, I thought about how Blair had deliberately tried to sabotage my performance since day one of rehearsals. She could have chosen to be my friend, but she always had to focus her efforts on knocking me down a notch. I was new to town, new to school, new to theater…and she couldn't cut me a break. And we were supposed to be comrades in the play. Adelaide and Sarah were friends, not rivals. Why was it so hard for girls to support each other? Why did everything have to be a competition? I would have been grateful to have a friend if she had only been a decent human being.

My blood continued to boil as I remembered the night of the sleepover—the laughing and teasing. I saw her smug, wicked smile as she said, "Oh Jason, can you carry these flowers for me?" And then I saw myself throwing the toilet paper into the trees. It was as easy as that. And what would it hurt, really? It was just paper. Like Lincoln said, it would wash away… And was this little act of deviance not better—more civilized—than humiliating her in front of her cast? In front of *Jason*?

So, I threw the roll. A dove of peace flying through the darkness, I convinced myself that this was my way of surrender. This was me waving my white flag in the face of teenage drama. I wasn't going to get sucked into it; instead, I would just let out my angst in a harmless "artistic" way.

Say what you want, Blair, I thought. *I have my friends and I don't need you.*

It turned out that once you started rolling someone's house, it was very hard to stop. I threw not one, but five or six toilet paper rolls into the Ford's trees and decorated the shrubs as well. By the time we were finished, Blair's house looked like the crime scene of a fleet of combusted ghosts.

We were wired on an adrenaline rush that was better than all the caffeine in a Chubbie's latte. Isa and I ran through the streets and Lincoln weaved between us on his bike. We arrived at the elementary school between our neighborhoods and finally paused to catch our breath as we sat on the playground swings.

"I would do that again," I said, which made Isa and Lincoln crack up.

"K's got a taste of sweet, sweet revenge. And she likes it!" Isa announced, pushing herself higher on her swing.

"No, not *revenge*. It was just fun," I admitted.

"Uh huh. Sureeee," Lincoln teased. He jumped off the swing and walked up the slide.

We were lost in our own thoughts for several minutes, our breath easing back to a normal rhythm, and the chill of the night cooling the heat our bodies created in our jumping, running, and generalized insanity. It was nice to just *be*. Crickets were chirping and fireflies danced. The neighborhood was settling back into a peaceful snooze after we had disturbed it with our teenage tomfoolery.

"Hey, about our mom…" Isa began. Her voice was a bit of a shock, pulling me out of the silence. "So…she's a trainwreck, to state the obvious. That's why I didn't want you to meet her."

"No, it's totally fi—"

"No, it isn't," she interrupted. "It isn't fine. Moms shouldn't act like that. But she wasn't always the World's Shittest Mom."

Lincoln, who had been laying on the slide and staring at the sky, sat up. "Mom is bipolar," he said delicately.

"Bipolar and mostly unmedicated because sometimes it doesn't strike her fancy to take her prescriptions," Isa added without attempting to mask her disapproval.

"We don't know that for sure," Lincoln said.

"Yeah, well, I know you're not supposed to mix that stuff with alcohol. Read the labels," Isa retorted.

Unsure of how to proceed from there, I did the best I could by offering a bit of my own family's baggage to the table.

"Really," I started. "It doesn't matter. My parents aren't perfect either. Like…I told you guys that we don't speak to my mom's side? Well, that's because my mom's family hates my dad and my parents just eloped without telling anyone."

"Dude, that sounds like a movie," Lincoln said, impressed.

"I don't think it was all that romantic… I mean, my mom got pregnant with me when she was 19. It was an accident. And then they got married and my mom dropped out of college so she could stay home with me."

"So what?" Isa said. "You don't have to be married to have a kid. It's not a crime to drop out of college. I don't even know if I *want* to go to college."

"Well, that's not everything," I continued. "My mom was supposed to have an arranged marriage. Her parents had the whole thing set up for years."

"No way! People still do that?" Lincoln asked. I could sense the wheels turning in his brain. Perhaps he was already working my family drama into his next play, or whatever he wrote in that notebook of his.

"Yeah, it's still really common in Pakistan and some families want to keep those traditions alive even after moving to the U.S. It's a religious and cultural thing… It's just what some people do," I tried to explain, even though I really didn't have the answers myself. I was so disconnected from that side of my history. "So anyway, my grandparents basically cut my mom out of the family when they found out she was having me. I only met them a few times when I was really little—just a toddler. And then we left Chicago and I haven't heard from them since. They don't want anything to do with us."

"Do you miss them?" Lincoln asked after a pause.

"No," I said without thinking. "You can't miss what you don't remember. And…I don't know…I feel like…*they're* the grandparents. They should want a relationship with *me*. And if…well, if they aren't going to be the first ones to make contact…then they might as well be dead to me. I've never met them, but I know I have cousins. My mom's sisters and brothers have kids and I know they all still live in Chicago. I'm sure my grandparents see *them* all the time. I'm sure they love them like they're supposed to."

I had been kicking the ground beneath the swing as I told my story, but then, I looked up. Isa and Lincoln were watching me. I had their complete undivided attention and, while I should have expected that as I was the one talking, that simple fact made me feel a bit odd. Happy, but exposed. Safe, but vulnerable. I guess I wasn't exactly used to being listened to.

"Sorry," I said quickly. "That was an over-share."

"No, it wasn't," Lincoln said seriously.

"Our grandparents died a couple of years ago," Isa said. "Mom's gone downhill ever since."

"Gramps had a heart attack," Lincoln said. "And Mimi…she…"

"She committed suicide three weeks after the funeral," Isa finished.

She sat there on the swing, playing with her bracelets. I tried not expose my shock.

"I'm…I'm really sorry," I said, looking first at Isa and then at Lincoln.

"We're okay," Isa confirmed, nodding her head, and beginning to pump her legs again, drifting higher into the sky. "We're tough, Abe and I."

"DeLuca's have thick skin," Lincoln said with a smile.

"And our dad. He can handle it. We lucked out with him," said Isa.

"Isa's a daddy's girl," Lincoln teased, coasting down the slide.

"I'm *nobody's* girl!" she proclaimed and jumped from the swing. "I'm a free-range woman!"

She cartwheeled across the AstroTurf and then started to gallop through the soccer field. Lincoln and I raced after her, heading back to my house to face the dreaded climb back up the trellis. Isa sprinting, twirling, skipping along as Lincoln sped atop smooth black pavement. I sat on Lincoln's handlebars.

"Fly, fly! Fly, little bird!" Isa hollered at me.

I closed my eyes and let out a hoot of sheer delight.

"I'm flyingggg!" I screamed and thrust one hand into the air.

"Hold on, crazy!" Lincoln laughed.

Only artists understand how profoundly you can entangle yourself with another artist when you embark on a creative venture. For us, it was a high school musical. It wasn't profound in and of itself—the show was problematic and dated for a modern audience's sensibilities. But the show made us bond in the way that is only possible when you're young, impressionable, and every single moment is a moment that matters. We spent hours together creating—creating something incredibly hokey? Yes. But creating, nonetheless. And that formed a connection that forged a chasmic distance between me and anyone else that wasn't them.

Within two months, my world was orbiting around my new identity as an artist and as Isa's new best friend.

7.

All I Want for Christmas

"What time do you think you'll be home tonight?" Mom asked, attempting to sound casual, as she dusted the mantle.

    She tended to clean before and after Mitsey's Thursday visits. "Well, I don't want her to come in here and think we're a bunch of *slobs*," she'd say when my dad and I pestered her about it. And "Mitsey does a lovely job, but I'm just getting a *few* spots that she missed," was her rationale for whipping out the Clorox wipes the moment Mitsey's car backed out the
driveway.

    "I'm not sure," I said as I examined my appearance in the foyer mirror, rethinking my entire ensemble.

    It used to be that the DeLuca Christmas party was a formal affair—the lawyers from Tamara's firm were always dressed to the nines, and the sophomore year Christmas party was actually the only occasion where I could justify my sparkly gold 1950s Mary Jane slippers. I tried not to think too much about the memory of Isa accompanying me and her guitar while I sang "Rudolph the Red-Nosed Reindeer" that year. The picture in my mind of us shooting cheery glances at each other like we were a two-woman girl band was too bittersweet to contend with…

I had texted Lincoln earlier in the day and asked what to wear, but all he said was, "whatever you want!" How completely unhelpful. I'm sure it didn't matter to him anyway, he was a flannel and jeans kind of guy no matter the occasion, no matter the weather. So, left in the dark with no direction whatsoever, I opted for a middle-of-the-road approach—I went for my black and emerald tartan jumper with a black turtleneck underneath, sheer black stockings, and (skipping the glitter this time) my basic Mary Janes. Throwing on a red headband at the last minute to shield my face from the curtain of curls, I was festively dressy-casual. But now, staring at myself in the mirror, I wasn't just doubting my outfit, but my decision to go to this party altogether.

It had been a couple of days since I last saw Lincoln and life remained unchanged, except for the new and welcome addition of now having someone to check in with throughout the day. I only rarely communicated with art history friends outside of class, and when I did, we usually kept conversation to school-related topics. So, it was rather nice to have someone to message when my mom tried to force a pair of reindeer antlers on F. Scott. It made me smile whenever I heard that tiny "*ding!*" and read that Whitney was still blasting "I Saw Mommy Kissing Santa Claus," or that Ella had eaten a popcorn chain meant for the tree.

Still, I questioned whether it was too soon to go to the DeLuca home. I definitely didn't want to be triggered into some sort of episode. The last time our friendship was in the fragile mending stages, I completely blew it. I didn't know whether I wanted us to go back to "normal," or as close to it as possible, or…were there other options? I didn't know. But I knew that I didn't want things to disintegrate like last time. I believed him when he said he forgave me, but how many times can you push your luck? You don't often get a second chance and I didn't feel like I deserved a third.

So maybe it would be best to skip tonight, just in case? It dawned on me then that I would be seeing Mr. DeLuca for the first time since the funeral if I did go…

"I doubt I'll be there longer than an hour," I told my mom. I wouldn't disappoint Lincoln, so I would go. But I'd just do a quick hello, eat an hors d'oeuvre, admire Whitney's decorations, and then I'd be on my way. If I didn't stay long, I wasn't risking much.

"Oh, but don't rush back on our account, honey," Mom replied, now Windexing the mirror where I was primping. "Daddy and I are probably just going to watch a Christmas movie and cuddle on the couch."

"Gross."

She laughed. She loved to talk about cuddling and kissing my dad. For some reason, my wrinkled nose and look of disgust at the mention of parental PDA always tickled her. My parents were cute. Gross, but cute. I guess it was a good sign that they still liked each other. So many of my friends' parents were divorced, including, of course, Lincoln's.

"Don't worry, we'll save *It's a Wonderful Life* for when you're home."

"Okay, you better."

I wasn't big on Christmas. It made me kind of sad, actually. "Seasonal blues are completely normal," Dr. McPherson reminded me every year as soon as the grocery stores started stocking candy canes and ornaments (by mid-October…), but it was more than that. It was a time devoted to reflection on family, life, years past, and years to come. It was a time when most people gathered with heaps of loved ones and, for my nuclear family, we just had the three of us. I didn't know what was worse—the loneliness on the odd years when Aunt Tiffany and Uncle Mark *weren't* there, or the claustrophobic even years when they *were*.

Either way, I felt lacking. There was always the unspoken reality that there was an entire side of the family that we didn't speak to. That we didn't even know. I had no idea if they even celebrated Christmas, for that matter. But moreover, the holidays were one of those times when you were expected to be perpetually cheerful just *because*. And I resented any occasion that expected anything out of me emotionally.

And yet, I was unabashedly fond of *It's a Wonderful Life*. It wasn't just that I couldn't resist a black and white film…I was a sucker for Jimmy Stewart.

"K, honey."

Mom paused from cleaning and turned to face me. The look she gave me—one of concern and forced enthusiasm—had become a popular go-to since Isa died. I knew I was in for a "mom moment."

"I just wanted you to know that I'm so happy you're reconnecting with Lincoln," she said.

"Uh…thanks."

"Please give Tony our best, okay?" she said, smoothing one of my stray curls into place. "And stay as *long* as you want!"

Not wanting to linger a second longer for fear that she might turn all Dr. Phil on me, (in addition to reading self-help articles, she also began to DVR programs like that as soon as she became a mother to a "troubled child.") I turned to rush out the door.

"Wait! Don't forget…" Mom called after me. She dashed over to the kitchen counter, retrieved the Tupperware container of sugar cookies, and placed it in my hands. "Please tell them if they're interested in the cookie cutters, we're offering a 75% off sale starting December 26th."

She winked at me, and I noticed that her Pampered Chef business card was taped to the lid of the container.

The five-minute drive to Lincoln's didn't give me nearly enough time for a decent pep talk and my car's radio blasting holiday cheer only added to my edginess. Unpopular opinion—I despise most Christmas songs, but particularly the god-awful contemporary ones like "Jingle Bell Rock" and don't even get me started on Mariah Carey's "All I Want for Christmas Is You." I parked several houses down from Lincoln's as there were tons of cars lining the street and took a long, deep breath.

I can do this for Lincoln. I can be a normal person. I know how to socialize. Just for an hour.

Grabbing Mom's sensationally frosted sugar santas and reindeer, I exited my anxiety cocoon, and walked up to the house.

Approaching the front door, I could already see that Whitney had gone above and beyond. Holly outlined the door, a gigantic authentic pine wreath complete with snow-dusted sugar plums hung heavily in the center, and even the doormat was cheery—shouting in intricate cursive lettering, "All who enter shall have a VERY merry Christmas!" Just as I debated whether or not to ring the doorbell, (I never knew what the rules were for parties of this size… Do you just walk in?) the door swung open. Lincoln's enormous grin was right in line with the jolly ambiance that awaited me inside, but it took me a second to register that he wasn't in his typical garb.

"K! Come in!" he said, beaming.

"Lincoln, you look…"

"Oh yeah, Whitney made me dress up a little," he said, referring to his ironed button down and crisp navy slacks.

He even had…was that *gel* in his hair? Complete with his new glasses, (or, new since we were in high school) I wouldn't have recognized him if it weren't for his dorky smile.

Once inside, I reached out to examine his necktie.

"Are these little reindeers?" I asked, amused. "Well, that's adorable."

Finally, someone other than me was blushing.

"K, is that you?"

Whitney emerged from a crowd of party guests in a floor-length velvet skirt and a sparkly sweater featuring the entire cast of the nativity—donkeys, wisemen, and all. The star of Bethlehem earrings that dangled weightily from her earlobes swayed as she walked. She went in for a hug without warning or consent.

"I can't believe it. After all this time!" Every word was drawn out as if she could park in one phrase for a week. "I always say, He's got a plan. He'll bring those back to us that matter most. All in good time. We just have to maintain faith!"

I smiled awkwardly and noticed that Lincoln, just as uncomfortable, was straightening his tie. Whitney was still very much the Whitney I remembered.

"Well, sweet girl, we are so thrilled to have you. There's cranberry punch—of course, *alcohol-free,* and just as yummy. Tons of baked goods and appetizers in the kitchen. My friend, Roberta from church—" Whitney paused to wave at a rather round black woman in a white fur collared sweater. "She made the pigs-in-a-blankets. They are *divine.*" The last word was pronounced as if it had ten thousand "e's."

"Um. Thanks, Whitney. It's, uh, good to see you too," I managed. The temptation to pick at my cuticles had already reared its ugly head, but luckily, I was holding onto my mom's Tupperware container. "Oh, these are for you. My mom made them." I handed Whitney the cookies.

"Isn't she a doll! Now, I know Tony will want to see you," she started again. "Let's see…now where did that man run off to?"

She inspected the bustling house but was interrupted when a woman with teased hair and a thick strand of pearls tapped her on the shoulder.

"Whit," the woman said. "Pardon me for interruptin', but it looks like we're all outta those pecan pralines. Didn't you say you had a backup batch? I wanted Lenard to try one. Could I trouble you for 'em?"

"Oh goodness, you know I do, Cheryl! Wouldn't be a Christmas party without two tons of pecan pralines, now would it?" she said. Both women laughed heartily. "Now, K, if you'll excuse me. I want to hear all about what you've been up to just as soon as I sort things out in the kitchen!"

Thankful that Whitney had taken her leave, I was finally able to soak in my surroundings. The house was completely transformed. Tamara's sterile showroom furniture had been replaced with oversized and patterned country farmhouse charm. But what was more, every square inch was layered with Christmas decor—tinsel, holly, twinkly lights, porcelain santas in all shapes and sizes. The Christmas tree, which was two stories high, stood majestically in the center of the living room and was absolutely drenched in ornaments.

"Did she, like...get help with all this?" I asked Lincoln, who was now leading me through the crowd to the punchbowl.

"Nope. This is what she lives for. She started November 1st."

Lincoln poured me a cup of artificially dyed bright red punch and I snagged a snowflake-shaped cookie from a nearby platter.

"So, we're the only ones under 40," Lincoln said as he balanced a brownie and two truffles in his punch-less hand. "I asked Jon to come, but his family's in California for break."

"Wait. Jon Seong?" I nearly coughed up my punch—both at the mention of a familiar name from high school and the fact that it was sickeningly sweet.

"Yeah, crazy right?" Lincoln said after a bite of brownie. "We lost touch when I went back to New York after, well, you know. But then, I moved back and he was working at Kroger part-time for the summer. He was my cashier. He's graduating in the spring, too. He's still at MTSU. Switched to Political Science though."

"Wow, good for him. He could totally be president."

"Oh, hell yeah. I've already called being his Speech Writer and Campaign Manager. But I'm sure we can squeeze you in somewhere." He winked.

Jon Seong blossomed after his big flop as Nathan Detroit in *Guys and Dolls*. He joined the speech and debate club, eventually ran the whole thing himself by senior year, and got cast as every male lead until we graduated. I remember he was on the pre-med track when I last saw him. Three years ago. At the funeral.

"Well, if it isn't Miss K Statham!"

Mr. DeLuca sauntered over to the punch table with a wide, warm smile. He was now completely gray and had more defined lines on his forehead and around his eyes. Though he appeared to be cheerful in the present moment, it was unmistakable to the naked eye that he had aged considerably. He was a man that had been pulled from the flames of heartache, devastation, and betrayal and lived to tell the tale. Knowing that he went through a messy divorce and the death of his daughter all while keeping his remaining child alive and stable, I found it remarkable that he was as relaxed as he was. Nothing at all like the broken man I had last laid eyes on.

Now, being pulled into a congenial side-hug, I couldn't shake the image of Mr. DeLuca weeping openly in the lobby of the church. He had seen me as soon as I walked in and crumbled. Whitney hovered over him as I walked up to say something, anything. What are you supposed to say to your dead best friend's dad on the day of her funeral? "I'm sorry I wasn't there for her"?

He had held me and wept into my shoulder.

"You were so special to her," he cried. "She loved you so much."

I had just stood there, patting his back, and staring at Whitney who looked on sadly.

"Come by the house and look through her things. Take whatever you want," he encouraged me.

But I never did.

"K, are you ready to graduate? How are your parents?" he asked.

His smile was a harsh contrast to the memory that I was struggling to push from my mind's eye.

"Yes, I think so. Getting there," I chuckled nervously. I had become increasingly insecure that each time I answered that question, it was more obvious that I hadn't a clue in hell what I intended to do come May 3rd. "And they're good. They wanted me to tell you hi."

"Well, it's just great to see you. And please—let Whitney and I know when your next play is. We miss our favorite actress!"

He clinked his punch cup against mine and disappeared into the kitchen.

"Hey," Lincoln began, always so obnoxiously observant. You couldn't hide anything from him, when you tried. "You wanna go downstairs? Get away from all the noise?"

"And the questions."

"Yeah," he agreed. "That. Let's go."

Taking my hand, he shepherded me through the clumps of chatty church women and their husbands, only pausing to politely acknowledge a few particularly nosey ones. I could finally let out a restrained exhale as we walked down the staircase and into the basement. The party disintegrated into a faint hubbub overhead and I shook the tension off my shoulders. The basement was the only part of the house that had been preserved from childhood. Ella was napping on the same old leather couch. There was the same coffee table that we used to litter with bags of junk food. The same flat screen tv, the same family photos on the walls, even. Lincoln was saying something about watching a movie and rummaging through the DVD collection, but I couldn't hear him.

I picked up a framed photo from the tv stand. Lincoln, Tony, Tamara, and Isa. They were in Times Square, smiling at the camera. I remembered Isa showing me pictures from this trip. They had gone the summer before their grandpa died and saw *Chicago*. Isa said, "One day, I wanna play Velma Kelly. You can be my Roxie," when she showed off the Playbill that hung on her bedroom wall. From this photo alone, you would have guessed that they were a perfectly ordinary family. No dark secrets. Nothing catastrophic waiting to shatter them all. Tamara's bleached white smile in the photo took me back to the funeral again.

Tamara stood by Isa's coffin the entire time. Her face was blank, her eyes were dry. She wore no makeup. Before and after the service, she simply stared at Isa. I had told myself that I wasn't going to look in the open casket. I tried to maintain my focus on Tamara, but when she spoke to accept condolences, she spoke only to Isa. I couldn't prevent my eyes from wandering and I saw her. Isa. Lying in a bed of silky white. She could have been dreaming. But Isa slept with her mouth partly open and on her stomach. I knew this. And I knew she wasn't dreaming.

They had put her in her light blue daisy print dress and kept her barefoot. Blonde waves draped over her chest. Lips that would never speak again, closed, and silent. Hands that would never move; never wave at me from across the hallways at school, never flail in the air as she danced, folded over her stomach. She had never been so fragile. I thought if I touched her, the shell that remained would shatter. People always say of the dead, "They're at peace," but Isa didn't seem to be at peace. She didn't seem real. None of it seemed real.

They forgot her bracelets, I thought at the time. *Damn them. They forgot her bracelets!*

"K? Are you—" Lincoln came up behind me and I quickly placed the frame back on the tv stand.

"I think maybe I should go," I said softly.

He glanced down at the photo.

"Would it be better if we, I don't know…left?"

Then he touched my arm gently. I shrugged it off. My breathing was starting to pick up speed.

Calm down. You're okay. You're okay. You're okay.

I shook my head. "Sorry, sorry… It's just. This is hard."

"Being here? The house?" he pressed.

"No. I mean, yes. But you. *This.* It's hard."

Calm down. You're okay. You're okay. You're okay.

"I know. But…stay. Please," Lincoln tried.

"Lincoln, I'm sorry."

"No, don't be sorry," he said.

He took a step away from me, which I appreciated. I needed some space. He crossed to the other side of the room and for a second, I thought he was going to go upstairs, leave me here in the basement alone with my memories. With her ghost. Then he turned.

"I don't want you to be sorry. But K…this is my life. This is my every day. I can't escape it."

Calm down. You're okay. You're okay. You're okay.

I sat on the couch and stared at my lap, memorizing the pattern of my jumper. Green, black, white, green, black, white. Lincoln sighed heavily and then sat down next to me.

"Hey, look. I didn't mean to make it sound like it's all been worse for me," he apologized.

"It's the same," I started. "It's the exact same for me. Every day. I think about her. I dream about her. I—I can't escape it either. I can't escape my own mind."

Any second now tears were going to force their way out. How was I going to make it all the way upstairs, through the party, down the street, and into my car without anyone noticing my blotchy face?

You've really done it now. You think you can be friends with him? Who are you kidding? You can't do anything anymore. You aren't normal anymore. No. No. NO! Calm down. You're okay. You're okay. You're okay.

"K, listen. I—" But he sighed. "What I'm trying to…poorly, it seems, explain is that…I don't know. Friendship with me…if that's what you…want…I mean, I *hope* it's what you…"

At a loss, he stared at me, and I stared back. Communicating through the fog was torture. I hadn't properly tried to do it with anyone in a truly meaningful way outside of Dr. McPherson's office and having only the other night on the swings as practice certainly didn't make either of us experts.

"Okay, I'm going to start again." He took a deep breath. "Friendship with me will be complicated. Because she made it that way. It's not easy for me either. To be around you… Not that I don't *want* to be around you. Okay?"

I began to pick my cuticles. He grabbed my hands. Did he know this was a nervous tick? I swore at myself for being so transparent.

"I do. I really do," he emphasized. Want to be around you. But. Sometimes it…K, look, I'm sorry… I don't even know what I'm trying to say anymore."

He let go of me and put his head in his hands, elbows resting on his knees, and slouched over. I understood perfectly. Being around each other was an effort and I still had a knee-jerk reaction telling me that this effort was *bad*. For a long time, I thought that meant that I should avoid him—erase him from my life so I would never have to confront my grief with the one person that knew my suffering all too well. It's uncomfortable to open up to strangers but mourning in front of someone you love is excruciating. Feeling your heart break then watching theirs break and then break again for you—it makes you feel as if you have nothing left. You want to be strong for them because they're hurting—you can see they're hurting because they're bleeding out right before your eyes—but you're too distracted by licking your own wounds to be the rock that they need you to be.

So, I guess, that's how two best friends came to give up on each other at the one time when they needed each other the most. When the link that bound us together was lost, neither one of us had the strength to make the effort.

I thought back to the other night. The moment under the streetlamp. After we said the hard things. We felt good. I felt it deep in my bones that it was right. So…maybe I needed to *let it be right*. Hard doesn't mean bad. That was it—hard doesn't mean bad.

You're okay. You're okay. You're okay. Hard doesn't mean bad. Hard doesn't mea—

"I understand," I said to him. "I think I can be ready now. I'm going to try. Abe, hard doesn't mean bad."

"You haven't called me that in a long time," he said.

The hint of a smile formed, and I could breathe again, knowing that, miraculously, we had pushed through the hard stuff. Again. Somehow.

"Well, you were being so damn honest with your feelings, it felt right." I teased and shoved him.

He fell sideways onto the couch.

"Feelings are for freaks."

And even though he quoted Isa, I didn't mind.

"You know what—I don't think so. I think I felt like more of a freak when I was blocking shit out," I confessed.

Lincoln stood and went back to the bookcase full of DVDs.

"I think we need to take our minds off of our own melodrama and..." He suddenly whipped out a copy of *Pride and Prejudice* and shook it in front of my face. "...take some notes from the Edwardians."

I laughed and grabbed the DVD case from him.

"Okay, it's the good one."

Everyone knew that the Kiera Knightley and Matthew Macfadyen 2005 version was far superior.

"I know how to make you stay," Lincoln laughed. I rolled my eyes. "And it just so happens that Whitney is also an Austenite. Which is why we own this."

"Hmmm," I said, impressed. "Whitney and I have a shared interest. A true Christmas miracle."

Lincoln inserted the disc into the DVD player and as he joined me back on the couch, I really did feel like I was going to be okay. We sat there, watching the sweeping opening shots of the Bennett home and idyllic English countryside. I was immediately engrossed, as I always was when it came to that film, but Lincoln was irritatingly reckless. Finally, 15 minutes in, I couldn't take it anymore and turned to him.

"Are you even paying attention?"

"No, yeah. Love it so far."

I raised an eyebrow but turned back to the screen.

"That's, uh, the guy's house, right? Darcy's?" he asked. "Why is she going there?"

"No, that's the Bingley house. She's going over to visit her sister because she's sick and can't—Wait. You're not even watching," I accused.

"Sorry," he said, stiffly. "Okay, it's just. I wanted to...do something and I think I missed my..."

"Lincoln. Spit it ou—"

"Can I do something I've been wanting to do for a long time?" he asked hurriedly.

"I don't know. What is it?"

"This," he said, leaning in and nearly closing the gap between us.

Elizabeth Bennett was in the midst of a verbal sparring match with Caroline Bingley on screen, but I wasn't watching. Lincoln and I stared at each other for a long time. He was so close that I could see the ring of gold in his hazel eyes. He was so close that I thought I was going to fall in; dive through those gold rings, and maybe never come out.

"Where did you steal this pick-up line from?" I whispered.

Then I burst out in an uncontrollable fit of laughter. It was the only way I knew how to handle the situation. If what I thought was happening was actually happening, this was completely foreign territory. Not completely *unthought of* or *unimagined*. If I were to be candid with myself, which I rarely was, I had been there before. I kept this hypothetical scenario in my filing cabinet, nestled in the folder labeled: "All the Things That Could Have Been." But that's what that folder was for—hypotheticals. Daydreams. These things wouldn't, *couldn't* happen in real life.

"Damnit, K. I rehearsed it and everything," he was saying now. I could only phantom the embarrassment, but I could not for the life of me stop laughing. "I go in ninety and you go in ten—"

And then I did it. I went the full one hundred. I kissed Lincoln DeLuca. It wasn't the first time, but I decided long ago that stage kisses didn't count. This one did. This one was real. We stared at each other. Then back at the tv. I held my breath.

What did I just do?

And then he cupped my face in his hands and turned my head to his. He smiled that big, goofy smile. That classic Lincoln smile. I'd always known what that smile did to me, but accepted its power only then—God, I *loved* that smile.

"Is this…okay?" he whispered.

"This is okay," I replied. And then, because it was still Lincoln and I was still me and our history hadn't changed, I teased, "Took you long enough."

My nose touched his and slowly, inch by inch this time, we met in the middle. We kissed again.

I hoped with every fiber of my being that I was right—that hard didn't mean bad. I also hoped that by crossing this line, I wasn't going to end up blowing it again. Like I said, I was lucky to get a second chance. And I knew I didn't deserve a third chance.

Twenty-four hours later, I found myself on a different doorstep holding another Tupperware container of Mom's sugar cookies. This time, I was five minutes from campus at the turn of the century bungalow that Dr. Mirza shared with her husband, Ben. It was a much cozier neighborhood with huge, ancient oaks lining the streets and friendly stray cats roaming about. The homes were refurbished beauties, maintaining original quirks from a hundred years before. In drastic contrast to the subdivisions on the side of town where my parents resided, there was not a McMansion in sight. Although my family had only lived in brand-new builds since leaving Chicago, I found the history and lived-in environment of Dr. Mirza's neighborhood more agreeable to my tastes.

Having developed a close-knit mentor-mentee relationship during my time in the art history department, Dr. Mirza had asked me to house-sit a few times when she and Ben were traveling. I always looked forward to an opportunity to imagine what it would be like to live in a home that was truly loved and not waiting to be put back on the market. I lavished the thought of finally reaching a stage in my life when I could own a home of my own. I would get a nice old place with a screened-in wraparound veranda for F. Scott. I would formally frame my artwork on walls that featured original crown molding. How I dreamt of built-in bookcases and never having to put together a "this will do for now" contraption from a Walmart box again. My books deserved better than cheap plywood.

I was carefully examining the coveted contents of the "Maybe One Day" folder (a folder I actually didn't mind frequenting) when Julia walked up, saving me from the ever perplexing "do I ring the doorbell or just walk in?" question.

"Ugh, I *knew* you would go homemade," Julia said as she approached me, carrying a store-bought package of red and green frosted cupcakes.

Julia Visser was, I guess you could say, my closest friend in the art history department. We met spring semester freshman year in Greek and Roman Art. When we were paired to work together on an Aegean sculpture analysis project, she sat next to me and asked, "Is that a daisy?"

True to socially awkward form, I looked down at my blouse—a breezy button-down with Monet's *Water Lilies* printed on it. I had dug it from a bin of clothes at an estate sale. For only $3.00, I thought Monet's calming blues and seafoam greens would give me the dose of courage I needed to tackle my first day of classes in my new major.

"No, it's uh…water…lilies…"

Frankly, I couldn't help but judge Julia at that moment. Was this girl a complete moron? Art history major or not, didn't everyone know the water-lily series?

"Oh, no!" she said, laughing. "Yeah, I know Monet! But I was talking about your tattoo! It's like, a minimalist daisy? I love it. Is that your own design?" She pointed at my exposed right forearm.

Of course. My tattoo. Now *I* was the moron.

"Uh, yeah, sorry," I said, rolling my sleeve up even further for Julia to get a better look. "It's supposed to be a daisy. I drew it but, um…the tattoo artist didn't get to finish it. That's why there isn't a lot of detail."

"I'm obsessed. It looks totally intentional to me," Julia complimented.

And because she didn't press for more backstory, I knew that she would make for suitable company. Julia was often too focused on her strife to achieve perfection to inquire beyond the surface when it came to the personal lives of others. It wasn't that Julia was purposefully conceited, more so that between all the information stored in her brain with her double major, internship, and two part-time jobs, she just didn't have the capacity for more. I didn't take it personally. In fact, I preferred to be relatively anonymous to most people. Besides, Julia even struggled to remember her girlfriend's go-to Chubbie's order—a small decaf cappuccino—and they had been in a steady relationship, visiting Chubbie's on most Wednesday nights when I worked every week for two years.

Julia took the liberty of opening Dr. Mirza's front door, and we were immediately greeted by the fragrant aromas of home cooked Iranian cuisine. Dr. Mirza was an outstanding cook and her holiday parties with warm barbari bread and savory Aush Reshteh put all my mom's Pampered Chef get-togethers to shame. This was why, I reminded myself as I maneuvered through the living room crowded with my professors and peers, I was socializing for a second day in a row—for the food. I wasn't too keen on debriefing about finals or speculating as to how grad school interviews might go, but I knew I'd get at least some facetime with Dr. Mirza and…well, I'd already spent too many unproductive hours replaying the events of the previous night in my head.

I still hadn't spoken to Lincoln, although he texted me that morning to say, "Morning! Fruity Pebbles or Cocoa Puffs?" and later in the afternoon he sent a Buzzfeed quiz that determined, "once and for all" as he said, that his Austen heartthrob personality indeed aligned with Mr. Knightley. I wanted to text back, "Ditch the cereal and get a bagel" and, "Told you" (maybe even throw in a winky face emoji), but I was too paralyzed by the weight of appearing completely and totally normal, so I opted to say nothing at all.

Two missed texts. I was a coward. He probably thought I regretted last night, but that wasn't even close. It was just that there would never again be a time when I *hadn't* kissed Lincoln DeLuca—for real, offstage kissed Lincoln DeLuca. All those years spent wondering, and now there I was, too wracked with fear to move forward. What if that time spent in the not knowing phase was safer?

"K? Earth to K?" Julia said, waving her hand in front of my face.

I had to stop staring into space and harping over my personal dilemmas, at least in public places. I did that too often.

"I was saying," she continued, "BU's deadline is January 1st. Did you start your app? I'm still editing my essay and, I don't know…you don't think my emphasis on my semester in Munich is too cheesy, do you? I'm sure everyone that applies studied abroad. And probably longer than a semester."

Suddenly, a faint *"ding!"* and my heart leapt. Sure enough, the name "Lincoln DeLuca" popped onto my screen when I pulled my phone out of my peacoat pocket.

"So, what do you think?" Julia asked. Then she eyed my phone. "What are you smiling about? Are you *talking* to someone?" She let out a yelp of excitement. "Who is it?"

I shoved my phone back into my pocket.

"I think you should use the Berlin stuff. There's no way you're not going to get in," I said, proceeding into the kitchen to deposit my sugary contribution to the food table and search for a plate.

I needed to stuff my face with rice pilaf before I said anything stupid.

Julia was at my heels. "You know what? You're right. I know Berlin. That's my thing. I should just stick to what I know."

She continued to rant about the tediousness of the application and fret about how she was going to find time to take Natasha out for a birthday date and put in some more hours at the gallery she was interning at. I was distracted by the food—piling my plate high with steamy, spicy goodness—but it wasn't just grilled pork kabobs that lulled me into a state of tranquility. I had a message waiting for me. Someone wanted to talk to me. I didn't exactly know what to do about it, but I enjoyed carrying around this pleasantness in my chest as I coasted from room to room, munching on appetizers, nodding agreeably along with conversation.

Unphased by Julia's incessant chatter and oddly not in the least triggered by all this talk about grad school, (Julia had moved on to discuss her indecision about Niagara University. She had an aunt that lived upstate, but did she really think that program would be challenging enough for her?) I spaced again; it was becoming impossible not to smile dumbly at memories that the rest of the room couldn't see.

"K!" Dr. Mirza popped into my line of sight, her arm linked with Ben's.

They were, by my standards at least, a perfect couple. Ben was a striking black man with shoulder-length dreadlocks who towered over Dr. Mirza. But they matched each other with their creativity; he was a photojournalist, which was one reason why they traveled out of the country so frequently.

"Hi, Dr. Mirza," I said, smiling wide (and praying that I didn't have spinach stuck in my teeth). "How's your break been?"

"Oh, you mean these past two days?" she laughed and threw her hands up. "A whirlwind, yes? Never enough time."

The smile she gave her husband would give any skeptic hope that true love really did exist.

"She's been in the kitchen from sunup till sundown, this one," Ben chuckled and gave his wife's arm a squeeze. "I try to help her, but she shoos me away."

"You will set the alarm off again!"

"Okay, *once* I set the smoke detector off. She'll never let me live it down."

"But two days has been time enough for you, yes? I see a great improvement in your eyes," Dr. Mirza said, leaning closer to me. "Have you gotten good rest? Or good news, I hope! I completed your recommendations."

Blushing, I struggled to think of an appropriate reply.

"Um. No," I laughed awkwardly, "I've just, uh…just had a lot of time to nap."

"Oh, well naps are good! We could all use more naps!" she said cheerily. "Ben, can you refill my glass for me, love?"

Ben swept Dr. Mirza's wine glass out of her hand and headed for the kitchen. Dr. Mirza took my arm and led me to the back porch. Her garden was mysteriously lush and green all year round. An artist, scholar, and chef who also had a talented green thumb—she did it all.

"K, my pet," she began, her voice lilting above the trickling of her many water fountains. "I am so pleased to see you smiling. I've been watching you from across the room since you got here. You glow."

"I'm just…" I couldn't hide my smile. "Okay, I guess I'm feeling a little lighter these days." Then quickly, "But it's really nothing."

"Ahh," she said, pointing at me. "You can't expect good things if you aren't willing to receive them, yes?"

I nodded, concealing another smile.

"You keep your secret. That is fine by me," she continued, good-naturedly. "But I don't want to see you dismissing your joy. When life is good, we embrace! Now, did you research Zubeida Agha like I said?"

Dr. Mirza had a superpower for seeing directly into your soul and churning out one-liners that would make for an ideal bumper sticker. After a couple semesters of having her as my advisor, I'd learned that her fierce quiet strength had been forged through fire. She told me during one of our meetings that she came to the United States from Iran by way of arranged marriage at the age of 18. That was her first husband, not Ben. Her first husband died at 22.

"I've reinvented myself many times. There are more women in us than we think. You're unsure how you can move on, but I know—there is more to come for you yet," she said one rainy late-April afternoon in her office.

We were attempting to arrange the jigsaw puzzle that was my sophomore year fall semester schedule. She'd asked how I was acclimating to the art history department, and I was fairly blunt—an unattractive habit I would sometimes fall into when others pried about my "progress."

"It's pretty isolating when everyone around you is thinking about who they're going to sleep with or how to pass their exams, but you're stuck grappling with questions about mortality and the afterlife," I said at the time.

She studied me through trained, wise eyes. "I don't know who you lost, but I know that look. I'm no stranger to loss. I lost someone too. But I am still standing, yes?"

I still wasn't sure if she knew what had happened to me during my first semester. I had no idea if professors from other departments talked and, if they did, were they allowed to share confidential information about their students?

"Whoever you lost must have loved you very much. Or the absence wouldn't feel so great."

I never told her the details. I never even gave her a name. She didn't ask. In lieu of a solved mystery, she gave me an artist to investigate.

"Independent study," she proposed. "You research and then we chat. Over tea if you'd like."

She assigned me artists that wrestled in a way that was familiar and eerily comforting to me. Degas, O'Keeffe, Munch. Each with their own distinct and devastating depictions of what it felt like to be a human trapped and misunderstood. Lately, we'd moved on to artists with whom we shared a cultural connection. Expanding my worldview to embrace artists that felt like me and artists that looked like me was more therapeutic than I could have imagined. But while I might have been caught off-guard, I think Dr. Mirza always knew exactly what she was doing.

"Okay," I told her on her back porch. "I won't dismiss it. I'll try anyway."

"And Agha?"

Zubeida Agha, the Pakistani modernist, was one of my favorites so far.

"Every one of her paintings is a rebellion."

Lincoln DeLuca [Saturday 7:47pm]: You free next Saturday? Dad and Whit have Rockettes tickets, and I need a date, or I'll be miserable. You in for a kickin' good time?

Almost an entire week later, I still hadn't replied to the text Lincoln sent when I was at Dr. Mirza's. Was it out of the ordinary for Lincoln to invite me to a show? Absolutely not. The three of us had "Act Too'ed" almost everything that toured through town, and we always got a kick out of sizing up the competition when other high schools put on productions. But that was then…

Now, it was the strange new word "date" that gave me a debilitating pause. I reread the text too many times to count over the next several days, attempting to decipher meaning. An irrational part of me believed that if I just stared at the little blue text bubble on my screen for long enough, the definition and parameters of our relationship would manifest, and it would all become clear. But no such luck.

As I wiped down the barista counter at Chubbie's, I replayed those last few days—which included the arduous visit from my aunt, uncle, and cousins. Predictably, Mom and Aunt Tiffany shared several choice words about parenting, decor, and housekeeping that Mom read into much too deeply and Aunt Tiffany let slide. Uncle Mark and my dad spent any free minute that wasn't occupied by eating or unwrapping presents either playing golf or discussing golf.

Paisley recruited me as her personal photographer. "If I don't post daily, I'll lose my followers," she had explained to me with severity. She was currently at 2,457 ("and counting"). The last time I checked, before deleting my Instagram account, I think I had maybe 40? The vast majority of my photos were of F. Scott...maybe if I "considered my audience" and "claimed a personal brand" like Paisley, I would have been an influencer by now. Alas... To Paisley's credit, she did gift me a mug decorated with colorful Shakespearean insults. "Because you like nerdy things like that," she said, extremely pleased with herself.

I had learned much more about Kinsley's reproductive system and sex life than I ever cared to during the visit. She was intensely focused on starting a family, but the trouble was that her husband was consistently out of town for work. It seemed that business could only be conducted while she was ovulating and for that, she despised Landon's managers. "It's so stressful. You have no idea, K," she told me one morning before downing three types of prenatal supplements. "There's a *very* small timeline when a woman can actually conceive. And most of the time Landon is gone. So, whenever he's home, we *have* to do it. I just wish I knew for sure that he was eating what he's supposed to while he's out of town. Diet impacts sperm too, you know. Quinoa is going to be the ticket to getting me pregnant, you just wait."

As was their custom, my cousins tried to engage me in a conversation about my "prospects."

"Have you been on any dates lately?" Kinsley asked.

"We can set you up with a dating profile," Paisley offered. "I was listening to a podcast episode the other day that said the profile picture is all about cultivating that balance of chill and put-together. Guys don't like girls they think are too high maintenance."

I didn't say a word about Lincoln and, as I always did, refused their expert advice on the online dating scene. But try as I might to delay the necessity of responding to his texts, sharing such close proximity with my relatives only highlighted the fact that Lincoln was one of the only people in my life that I could hold a conversation with.

While I woke up dreading having to make small talk with Aunt Tiffany at the breakfast table, I actually imagined myself looking forward to the potential of this Saturday "date."

But it couldn't be a real date if his dad and stepmom were tagging along, could it? I wasn't the most experienced in the courtship department by a long shot, but even *I* knew that at 22 years of age, you don't need a chaperone to be alone with a member of the opposite sex. It was 2013, not 1813. So maybe Lincoln was just being a dork and making a joke? But I couldn't decide if that conclusion gave me relief or more agony. What did I want it to be?

It's not going to be anything if you don't text him back, I thought miserably.

I locked up the cash register and unplugged the Christmas lights above the espresso machine, just as I heard Lenny lumbering down the stairs. Even though he typically finished for the day hours earlier, he would always make the small trip down from his upstairs apartment to walk me to my car after I clocked out. "Can never be too careful. Young lady out here on her own," he would say. "Now that I don't have my security guard, I gotta do double-duty to make sure we're all safe around here!"

It was true that the shop lacked a certain something after Chubbie had passed from feline leukemia our junior year of high school. Lenny would always and forever top his lattes with paw print or cat face designs, and he had no intention of rebranding.

"She was a good girl," he said that day he broke the news to us.

We knew right away that something wasn't right when we pulled up and Chubbie wasn't rolling around on the front porch, but we somberly entered anyway, privately hoping that our assumptions were incorrect.

"She lived a good, long life. Fat and happy. Never met a customer she didn't like. Blessed to have her. I'm just sorry to see her go."

When I started working there, years later, I asked him if he'd ever consider getting a new pet. "I don't think so, K," he said, reflecting. "Sometimes you have a connection with an animal that is so special, it can't be replaced. But one day, maybe I'll be ready. The time has to be right."

I never pushed the issue again, but, in Chubbie's honor, I made it my goal to be able to execute flawless cat-themed latte art within my first month of employment.

"K, you ready to hit the road?" Lenny asked, tapping the barista counter.

"Yup, just have to put my apron up."

I dashed into the "break room" that was actually just a large closet and hung my apron on my usual hook on the wall. My phone buzzed.

Paisley Wright [9:05pm]: Hey cuz! Let me know when you want to chat dating profiles!

I deflated. Not only because I didn't want Paisley bugging me about dating profiles, but because I knew then that I was hoping the message had been from Lincoln. Although, how self-absorbed could I be to expect him to keep reaching out when I'd been ghosting him for six days? I stood there, dumbly facing the wall of the storage closet/break room. Then it dawned on me…

It was Isa.

Isa was the problem. Not that I was unsure about Lincoln. I knew how I felt about Lincoln. I knew I wanted to see what could be with Lincoln and that was good enough, right? But the problem was Isa. And maybe it always would be. I never in a million years would have seriously entertained the idea of dating my best friend's brother back when my best friend was *alive*. And taking into account that after eight years of knowing I existed and never making a definite move, I assumed that the same could be said for Lincoln. It would have destroyed everything about our dynamic as a trio if Lincoln and I had dated back in high school. But then again, by junior year, our "trio," as it were, was already destroyed.

Still. *What would Isa have thought?*

But did it really and truly matter what Isa thought? Isa wasn't here anymore. I shouldn't have let her run my life when she *was* here, but I damn sure wasn't going to let her do it now. Not anymore at least. Not now that I'm actually *visibly* happy, according to Dr. Mirza. I cleared the three messages from Paisley containing screenshots of the "ideal cool girl aesthetic" and composed a message.

Me [9:07pm]: swings in forty?

It was time that I got what I wanted. It was time that I was happy. "When life is good, we embrace!" Dr. Mirza said days ago.

Okay, I thought. *This is me embracing.*

"She lives!" Lincoln exclaimed as I crossed the soccer field to the playground.

"Ha. Ha. I know, I'm an asshole." I plopped down on the swing next to him. "I'm sorry."

"You have my forgiveness," he said. "But only because it's Christmas."

"It's Dec. 29th. Christmas is over."

"Well, because I want to then. So…" He kicked off and began swinging. "You summoned me here to remind me what day it is or—"

"—we need to—" I blurted, overlapping him. "Sorry, you go first."

"No, you," he said, gesturing for me to take the floor.

I fidgeted with the pom poms that dangled from my knit cap. On the car ride over, I rehearsed my speech aloud. Imagining the traffic lights were Lincoln's hazel eyes, I word vomited everything that I had wanted to say—every uncomfortable, awkward, embarrassing confession that had been brewing inside over that last week (and perhaps much longer). It was exhilarating to say out loud, "Lincoln, I want to try this." To admit to my empty car, "I have feelings for Lincoln DeLuca! I like someone! I *want* someone! Who's going to stop me?" I felt reckless. Out of my mind. Giddy.

I had rolled down my windows, indulging in the crisp, night air and I blasted my radio. "All I Want for Christmas Is You" was playing. I didn't care. I sang along. Damnit, I knew every. Freaking. Line. Somewhere deep in my subconscious, I had memorized and hidden these lyrics; all along I had been waiting for my grand opportunity to belt them out. "I just want you for my own…More than you could ever know…Make my wish come true…" When was the last time I sang? I couldn't remember, but I was incapable of feeling shame. I was happy. Stupidly, absurdly happy. Which was why, sitting on the swings, I was bold enough to say exactly what I had rehearsed.

"I think we should kiss again."

Lincoln came to a dead halt on his swing and faced me.

"I thought you were going to tell me that we should never kiss again. I mean when a girl doesn't text you for a week and then sends you a cryptic message asking you to meet up, usually that means…"

I had totally blown it. I waited too long to make up my mind.

"Uh, yeah, well—"

"But I'm glad you didn't say that," Lincoln interrupted. "Because I think we should definitely… I want to, I mean… Oh hell—"

It was like we flipped a switch. In one swift motion, he grabbed the chains of my swing, pulled me close to him, and we were kissing. It was a longer, more passionate kiss than the timid kisses from before. It was the kind of kiss that lasts at least a couple full cycles of inhales and exhales. The kind of kiss that made you forget it was below 40 degrees.

Afterwards, we came up for air and stared at each other. His face was still so close to mine that my vision blurred. He had not two, but three hazel eyes drinking me in. Contrary to all those years I spent avoiding intimacy, it was all entirely natural. The smell of him. The feel of his eyelashes faintly fluttering against my cheek. His warm breath. It was all familiar and it was all mine. I wanted it all.

"Okay," I breathed, coming to at last.

"Okay as in okay *good*?"

"Okay, good."

There was the cheesy, signature grin. I smiled back and he put his hand on my cheek.

"But we need to talk about thi—" I started.

"No, yeah," he affirmed. He placed his hands in his lap and cleared his throat. "Definitely. So, what do you—"

He was so cute sitting there, sheepishly waiting for me to set the pace. I just couldn't watch him with longing. Not now that we'd flipped the switch and the lights were shining on the one thing I'd wanted more than anything over the last eight years. I took the collar of his coat in both hands and pulled him back to me, kissing him long and hard. A beat, then I released him.

"Okay," I said. His eyes were still closed, and his lips still puckered. I couldn't help but laugh. "Now we can talk."

"Right," he said, opening his eyes. "Yes, so. K." He shifted his weight in the swing and sat up a little taller. "I—You're—I want to date you."

He paused. I smiled. He laughed. So, this was really happening.

"I want to take you on dates," he continued, scratching the back of his neck. "In a public way."

"In a public way?" I repeated through giggles.

This was just too ridiculously adorable to bear witness. Lincoln DeLuca just said he wanted to date me. Was I about to throw up butterflies?

He ignored my teasing and continued, "...and call you without thinking that maybe I'm annoying you. And tell you finally that you're beautiful and I want to kiss you again. I want to kiss you again right now."

"I thought you were going to say that we should never date," I said before he could lean in for another go.

"Why would you think that?"

"I don't know. I'm dumb."

"It's okay. I'm dumb too," he said, and we laughed. "I don't know how to do this."

"Yes, you do."

We kissed again. He took the back of my head in his hand and placed the other on my waist. I put my hand on his cheek, stroking the stubble that wasn't there when we were in high school. This was so new and crazy and amazing. I was outside of my own body, floating above the swing set. I was soaring up to the stars. I was on the moon.

"But we have to set some ground rules," Lincoln said, pulling away finally.

"Go on."

"Well, first, you can't make fun of me if I hold the door open for you or something," he said completely straight-faced.

I snorted. "Lincoln, I've been entering and exiting buildings just fine on my own all these years. I think I can—"

"No, I want to really date you, K."

He was so damn earnest. I fought my desire to attack his face again because I sensed that this must have been a part of *his* rehearsed speech.

"But just so you know," he said awkwardly. "We'll have to do some cheap dates sometimes. Our parents might be rich, but we're—"

"Poor college kids," I finished. My dad loved to remind me of this fact.

"Exactly. And we have to be honest with each other. We were best friends first. So, if either one of us doesn't want to do this anymore, we have to say something."

"Okay. I can do that."

"We can't disappear…"

Ouch. But he had a point.

"You're right. Okay."

"Hard doesn't mean bad, remember? Like you said?" he said, taking my hands in his. "Because it might be hard. If things aren't always like…*this* awesome." He squeezed my hands and we laughed again, a little nervously but mostly with excitement. "But…I'm pretty sure kissing you is always going to be awesome."

We kissed again. Each time we were learning more about the other. The texture of his lips and the sensation of his tongue colliding with mine—I collected all the little details, storing them in my filing cabinet for safe keeping.

"Okay, okay," I probed when we broke apart. "But what else? We need to make a list. We have to get this right. This is too important to screw up."

"Right, so, I've been thinking…we need to fill in the 'Gap Years.'"

"The what?"

"The years when we weren't friends. I want you to know everything."

I was silent for a long time after that. I studied his eyes, which left no room for doubts. Whatever this was, it wasn't going to be like what I had experienced before. This was *Lincoln*. He pushed his glasses up the bridge of his nose. They had slid down when we last kissed. Just that simple, dorky gesture made a puddle of me.

"I can do that," I committed finally.

"Not all at once," he assured. "But I think that's important. I want to know everything about you, and…we're different people now." He stood then and halfheartedly began to hang on the monkey bars. He had always been too tall for the child-size jungle gym. "For one, you should know that I don't drink anymore. I don't drink. I don't smoke. I don't do any of it."

I had assumed this was the case. It used to be a rare occasion when we'd hang out without the presence of alcohol.

"That's not a bad thing. We drank like fish in high school. It was actually pretty nuts," I replied, but I knew I was downplaying it.

By the look on his face, he shared the same opinion. He let out a sarcastic snort as he climbed to the top of the monkey bars—his preferred spot.

"It was *very* nuts, K. I didn't realize how bad I was until after I got back to New York. I told you that I holed up in my dorm? Well, I completely lost my ever-loving mind. I stopped going to class and totally abandoned all my friends there. I started mixing Sailor Jerry's in my coffee first thing in the morning and then kept going. I was shitfaced all day. I'm actually kind of glad that you…you dropped off the face of the earth. Because…I would have been ashamed for you to see me. Like *that*."

I tried to conjure an image of the ever-optimistic Lincoln whose can-do attitude I relied on whenever I felt low in high school. With his sunshiny demeanor and devotion to candor, I found it heartbreaking to combine the person I knew with the mental picture he painted.

"I just want to be honest with you," he continued. "It makes me look like a real grade A loser, I know. But I swear, K, I'm not like that anymore. I started blacking out and when I'd sober up, I had no idea what I did in those lost hours. At first, I'd just wake up in my dorm. Maybe the place would be a wreck, or I realized that I must have drunk-ordered Dominos or something stupid. I know I definitely called your number more than once…"

I did remember that. The tormented voicemails that said so little (normally just, "K, where are you?") but so much. Stuck in my own fog, it became routine for me to delete them without listening.

"But this one night," he said, staring at his hands which were folded in his lap. "This one night I woke up and I was on the train heading to Newark."

"What?"

"See! I don't know. I have no freaking idea what I was doing. I don't know anyone in Newark," he said, lines of worry forming on his forehead. "And I didn't have my wallet—someone probably stole it off me. And the worst part was that I had this gash—this *huge* cut on my left cheek."

Bringing his hand up to his cheek now in remembrance of the episode, it dawned on me that maybe that was one reason why he had let his facial hair grow.

"I'll always have this scar and I have no idea how it got there. It—it scared me straight."

Suddenly overcome by a gust of cold air, I stuck my hands in my coat pockets and stared down at my boots for a moment. I considered briefly all the stories I could tell him to help fill in those gaps. But the trouble was, there had always been gaps. Dating back to high school. He just didn't know about them.

✳✳✳

"I won't let you control me!" Tamara screamed from behind the locked door of the master bedroom.

Mr. DeLuca hurried into the living room, closing the bedroom door behind him. His eyes were swollen and red, but he managed to turn the corners of his mouth upward as he pivoted to face the small crowd of onlookers. Only a few of us had arrived at the Christmas party so far, but it didn't take much for gossip to circulate. Blair and her parents stood shell shocked by the Christmas tree, Jon Seong had paused from playing "O Holy Night" on the baby grand, and a cluster of Tamara's colleagues were whispering in the kitchen. I was just grateful that my parents had opted to go to my dad's work party instead…my mom already had such a low opinion of Tamara DeLuca. In the lull of background noise, Tamara's hysterical sobs ricocheted off the walls.

"Go ahead, Jon," Mr. DeLuca encouraged. "How about something more upbeat?"

"'We Wish You a Merry Christmas'?" Lincoln offered.

Jon looked quizzically from Lincoln to Mr. DeLuca and then his eyes darted to the master bedroom—the source of the wailing. He resumed playing and slowly the party returned to a state of relative normality. Isa, who seemed to regain her voice an hour or so after Tamara's outburst, was betting me as to how many jalapeño poppers Lincoln could eat in a row without crying. Just as Lincoln inserted a fifth fried bundle into his mouth, I saw Tamara exit the master bedroom and stride through the living room. Although one could argue that she always appeared slightly unhinged, she didn't seem out of the ordinary with a full face of makeup, flat-ironed hair, and a skin-tight red dress. From the corner of my eye, I observed her chatting up party guests with her distinguishing air of flamboyance—waving her hands to emphasize key points in whatever story she was engaged in. And then she wandered into the hallway bathroom.

Not 20 minutes later, Isa and I were standing at the piano trying to convince Jon to play something outrageous just to see if anyone would notice—my vote was for "Hit Me Baby One More Time" but Isa was pulling for "Smells Like Teen Spirit"—when we noticed Blair tapping Mr. DeLuca's shoulder. We couldn't hear what Blair was saying but saw her point to the hallway bathroom and Mr. DeLuca walked off in a rush. Everything happened very quickly from there— Mr. DeLuca emerged from the bathroom, eyes glaring furiously at Tamara. Taking her arm, he pulled her away from the group of lawyers she was entertaining, and they began to have a hushed argument. In an instant, we weren't watching an argument, but Tamara shoving her husband who stumbled backward into Lanette Ford.

"What I put in my body is my business!" Tamara hollered, no longer hiding under any pretense. "I flushed them. So what? I'm an adult, Tony!"

Spit flew from her mouth as the party once again came to a screeching halt and all eyes were on Mr. and Mrs. DeLuca. Lincoln sprung into his role as the peacemaker, leaping off the couch in an attempt to get in between his parents.

"Mom, mom! What's wrong?" Lincoln said, but Tamara ignored him.

"You've always treated me like a child!" Tamara yelled.

"Tamara, plea—" Mr. DeLuca tried.

Isa grabbed my hand and squeezed. I felt like I was going to be sick, but that was likely nothing close to the mortification that Isa was experiencing.

In the calamity, Lincoln must have investigated the source of the commotion because he walked out of the bathroom asking, "Mom, is that your medicine in the toilet?"

The sarcastic chuckle that erupted from Isa, she later told me, was unavoidable. This information confirmed what she had suspected all along—Tamara was not taking her Lithobid. Without hesitation, Tamara strode over to the piano and smacked Isa across the face.

"Tamara!" Mr. DeLuca yelled.

Isa fell into me. People were gasping, others were shouting at Tamara, a few rushed over to Isa. Lincoln was still standing in the doorway of the hallway bathroom, frozen. I put my arms around Isa and led her into the basement, away from the chaos.

An unidentified amount of time had passed when Lincoln and Jon met us in the basement. Isa's head was in my lap. She had been crying and all I could think to do was stroke her head. Her thin white-blonde hair felt like silk running through my fingers. Her tears soaked my pleated skirt. My best friend—my Aphrodite, my goddess in the flesh. She was the strong one. The one who didn't let society tell her who to be or how to act. She, the one who gave me courage, was reduced to a crumpled heap. She was a broken little girl and I—who was I if I couldn't fix this for her?

I silently lamented my worthlessness as a friend when Lincoln said, "Pretty much everyone is gone."

I nodded. Isa was silent.

"I gotta jet soon…I told my dad I'd be back before midnight…" Jon said.

I met Lincoln's eyes. Isa was supposed to drive Jon home.

"Uh," Lincoln began. He was still in shock, but when I shook my head, he at least had the wherewithal to understand. "Let's, uh…let's go see if my dad can give you a ride. Are you guys going to be…okay here or should I, uh…"

"Yeah, we're fine," I said.

We spent several more minutes in silence. There were still traces of company upstairs—the muted shuffling of heels across the floor, light laughter, and the clatter of dishes cleared from tables.

"Should we go to bed now?" I asked.

Isa sat up and stared at me.

"Why didn't she do it in the master bathroom?" she mumbled in reply.

"What?"

"She wanted to make a scene," Isa said.

Her eyes were pleading, helpless. And while I was so incredibly gutted for her, I also thought, *She is so beautiful.* Because she was. It was the first and only time I'd ever seen her cry. Tears deepened the blue of her eyes and the tracks of wetness down her face sparkled. The blonde waves that clung messily to her forehead and cheeks could have been a halo. She was an angel. A very sad, beautiful angel; sorrow in its purest form. I was furious that someone had hurt her, a creature so winsome and wonderful.

We journeyed up the stairs but paused when we heard Tamara humming in the kitchen. She was tidying up and spritely as ever. But there was also another voice. A male voice.

"Tammy, where do you want these?"

One of Tamara's work friends was still there. He was visible from the basement door, standing at the kitchen table and holding two empty wine glasses.

"Ooo, I like it when we play house," Tamara giggled.

She crossed to him, now in our line of sight, and wrapped her arms around his neck. The man smiled a smile that only meant one thing. He set the glasses down on the table behind him, squeezed Tamara's butt firmly with both hands, and the two began to kiss. By the looks of it, it was one of many kisses that had come before. Isa wore a look of sheer repulsion. I pulled her silently upstairs and into her room.

Lincoln knocked on Isa's door when he arrived home from dropping off Jon with his dad.

"Isa? Are you awake? You wanna talk?" he asked in a gentle voice. "K?"

But we ignored him, pretending to be asleep.

***

I wanted to fill the gaps for Lincoln. I did. But, jumping off the swing now to meet him at the monkey bars, I decided that I would start by telling him only what wouldn't hurt him. Was I already failing before this new relationship had barely begun?

No. I will tell him everything. Eventually. I will. I'll have to.

Making this pact with myself was the only way I could move forward without crippling guilt. I *would* tell him everything, but for now…I climbed a few rungs up the ladder. High enough that I was able to reach him, I touched his left cheek.

"Is it here?" I asked.

He nodded.

On my tiptoes, I leaned closer and gave him a long kiss on that same cheek.

"I'm glad you told me," I said. He took my hand and kissed it. "And I don't do that stuff anymore either. After *Hamlet*, I was done."

"Sober buddies then?"

"Sober buddies," I confirmed.

We hopped off the monkey bars and began walking to my car.

"K," he said, stopping suddenly. I turned to face him. "I have wanted things to change for a long time. But I don't want you to change. I don't want anything about you to change."

"You just want me to kiss you again, don't you?" I teased. But only because if I didn't make a joke, I would have cried.

"You got me," Lincoln said softly, leaning towards me.

We kissed goodnight and I trotted the few feet remaining to my car.

"Oh! And about the Rockettes," I called back as I opened the door to my car. "It's a date."

I shut the car door, watched Lincoln walk in the direction of his house—was he almost *skipping?* —and started the car. I already knew I would for sure be belting Christmas classics on the short drive home. But when I turned on the radio, my mood plummeted. "Dry and High" by Radiohead. Isa. Oh god. Isa. What about Isa? What would Isa think about me and Lincoln? Isa. Isa. Isa. This was the Christmas station.

How was this playing? I hit the radio dial, but it wouldn't turn off. I hit the dashboard again and again and again. The mournful chorus reverberated through the car and pulsated in my bloodstream. Familiar lyrics that I hadn't thought of in years had taken on a newfound grimness by announcing her arrival. She was here.

Finally, I pulled the keys out of the ignition and silenced the music, but I couldn't silence my racing thoughts. She was here. She knew. She wanted to take this from me. How could I have forgotten about her? No. No. That wasn't true. I didn't forget about her. I had decided that I didn't care what she wouldn't have thought. It didn't matter.

Isa is dead, I thought, hitting my forehead with my palms.

Dead. Dead. Dead. You couldn't do things to please dead people. You couldn't live a life when you spent it being afraid of dead people.

Isa is dead. You're okay. You're okay. You're okay.

In my mania to turn off the radio, I had mistakenly activated the windshield wipers. I watched them move—

Left, right. Left, right. You're okay. You're okay.

I breathed in, let out a shaky exhale, then started the car once again. No music from the radio this time, but I didn't dare touch the dial.

When I got home, I ran upstairs, slammed my bedroom door, and without even taking off my boots and coat, I retrieved my painting supplies. I ripped a fresh canvas from its plastic packaging and thought, *Isa is gone. You're okay. You're okay.*

I could embrace. I *would* embrace.

I began to mix colors together on my palate—midnight blue, dark crimson, white, pink, gold. Selecting a thick brush, I swirled the paint around and around, allowing the repetitive motion to anchor my thoughts. Blue, black, purple, gray—the sky that was above Lincoln and I whenever we met at the swings. Baby pink, white, coral—the tickle of Lincoln's tongue. Yellow, burnt orange, crimson—the fire in my chest when I anticipated his touch. Each stroke, each turn of the brush released more and more of what was holding me back. I had to rid myself of her. Dip, swirl, stroke, release.

I would paint until I knew for sure that my voice was the only voice in my head. I thought of Zubeida Agha and her explosion of color. How each color and shape held something infinitely meaningful, something complex, something that demanded to be seen and heard. I took a step back from what I had regurgitated onto the canvas. It was painful and hopeful.

This is my rebellion.

8.

Sombrero of Truth

I like to burrow myself in the tranquil memories of the summer between freshman and sophomore year of high school. Thinking back on those never-ending days—the rain in the middle of an otherwise sunny afternoon, bare feet in the grass, icy tequila and Kool-Aid concoctions sliding down my throat—I know that I will ever again be so naive. Those were the last few months of carefree childhood bliss.

Nearly every day, I'd walk the short distance to Isa and Lincoln's house. Their parents were rarely around, so their 4,000 square foot family home became our ostentatious clubhouse. I introduced them to my old Hollywood favorites—*The Philadelphia Story, Rear Window, All About Eve*. We spent lazy afternoons loitering at Chubbie's, impersonating hip college students on break from the liberal arts college down the road. Isa taught me yoga in their backyard.

"It's best with your feet in the grass. Wiggle your toes in the dirt. Really dig them in there. That's how you get to be one with the earth," she had said as I tried to remember to tighten my core, count my breaths, and do all the other things she had instructed while balancing on one leg.

Lincoln preferred to jump on the trampoline while keeping a tally of how many times I had fallen over.

That was also the summer that I began my love affair with vintage fashion. Isa and I had wandered into a thrift store a block away from Chubbie's and we spent the better part of the day trying on billowing swing skirts, beaded flapper dresses, hats, glasses, and gloves of all varieties. After only a few weeks of throwing my allowance earnings directly at Secondhand Sandie's Vintage Thrift, I was hooked.

"This looks like you," Isa said, holding up a pair of straight-legged trousers that could have been snagged from Katherine Hepburn's closet.

"I think that's a reproduction, actually," I said after examining the tag. "See, it's from the Limited." I snatched a tweed blazer from the rack beside me. "But this—see how it has the name of the boutique and the address on the tag? It just says 237 Fifth Ave Brooklyn, NY. No zip code. Zip codes weren't a thing until the early sixties, so this is the real deal."

"Ooo you've turned into a little clothing snob," Isa said, impressed. But when color bloomed on my cheeks she couldn't miss a teachable moment, "Like what you like—own it. Recycled clothing is more sustainable anyway."

That cheered me; I lifted the corners of the polka dot wrap dress I was trying on to do a dramatic curtsey in front of the mirror.

"And you look freaking hot. K Statham—taking down one landfill at a time *and* turning heads."

"Do you think it's too low?"

"Show a little cleavage! Let's give these babies their moment in the spotlight!"

She came up behind me and tugged the dress down further, exposing more of my barely-there chest to the floor-length mirror.

"Isa!"

She grabbed my arms and rested her head on my shoulders, meeting my eyes in the mirror.

"You're gorgeous, darling."

Isa was always that way—pushing the boundaries. And that summer, I reveled in having permission to expand. I liked to think that I was broadening her horizons too, like the time I suggested that we all go to the art museum downtown and check out the Egyptian exhibit.

"The Quest for Immortality: Treasures of Ancient Egypt," Lincoln read from the museum's website.

"There's over a hundred artifacts literally straight from Cairo. They even have a legit replica of the burial chamber of Thutmose III. Doesn't that sound fascinating?" I asked.

"If you like dead things…" Lincoln said, now skeptically scrolling through pictures of sarcophagi.

"Come on, Abe," Isa pushed. "Let's go say hi to old man Thutmose."

Although, when we arrived at the museum, there was a banner hanging across the grand entrance: "Closed for Opening Gala."

"Just follow my lead," Isa coached as we joined the line of elderly patrons waiting at the door. "Lincoln, *don't say a word*," she hissed.

She tapped the shoulder of the woman standing in front of us and began to strike up a conversation. The line moved forward at a snail's pace, but Isa maintained a steady back and forth with the woman, who we learned was named Margie. Isa entranced Margie with the same horse and pony show she put on for every older adult. By the time we reached the doorman at the front of the line, we knew that Margie's late husband was an Egyptologist, her son had married a "tart," and that she was about to go on vacation to West Palm Beach with "a few gals from bridge club."

"It was a treat to meet such fine young people," Margie said before handing her ticket to the doorman. She was only a few feet ahead of us inside the museum when we were asked to show our tickets.

"We're with our grandma," Isa said through a smile as sweet as pie. She wiggled her fingers in the air, signaling to Margie. Margie waved in reply. The doorman, likely a bored college student and none the wiser, let us through and directed his attention to the next in line.

The wine that was served freely in the lobby was my inaugural taste of alcohol. It was blueberry Moscato—sweeter than anything I'd come to prefer later in life—but just the poison to work as my unknowing gateway drug. Lincoln and I snuck two glasses each. Both lightweights and first-time wine connoisseurs, we staggered through the galleries, me all but salivating at the richness of history right before our eyes and Lincoln continuously hiccupping while asking, "where are the mummies?" Isa, effortlessly more sophisticated, jokingly called us insufferable while she took controlled sips.

"To our new pastime as art aficionados!" Lincoln said, holding up his glass of wine. "What a *marvelous* idea, K."

"To being alive! Sorry, Thutmose. We love ya, bud," I said, snorting with laughter and trying not to choke up my wine.

Isa, who had to have the last word, lifted her glass. "That's right! To *not* being *dead*!"

Too unblemished then to be triggered by the word, we all said, "Hear, hear!"

While Lincoln was away at Governor's School for the Arts, Isa and I developed a symbiotic relationship to combat what she referred to as the "abandoned child syndrome." It was the first time that Isa had truly been alone, having always relied on Lincoln for company. I, on the other hand, was well-versed in fending for myself as an only child to two workaholics and it was new for me to have someone to share most of my waking hours with. And on the nights when she wasn't sure where her mom was and her dad was out of town for business, I also stayed over.

We did everything together from splitting a bagel for breakfast to sharing a bed at night. I once spent four straight days at Isa's before my mom said I needed to come home and "take a breather." Isa always turned on the charm around my parents, so my dad was smitten with her. But my mom started to suspect that Isa and I were turning into something more than friends. This budding infatuation, that she hypothesized, was out of her depths.

"What do you do together when you hang out at Isa's?" she asked me, stopping me in my tracks one morning as I headed for the door.

"I don't know…We talk and watch movies. You know, just hang out."

"Is there anything you want to…tell me? About you and Isa?"

I grimaced. "What are you even talking about?"

"Nothing, nothing. Just…come home tonight, okay? Let's go to the pho place for dinner. Just the three of us," she said.

And that was the end of that particularly awkward line of questioning. As much as my mother strived to be "in with the times," abreast of all the latest trends, and assimilate into whichever community we happened to be living in, she still clung onto some old-fashioned beliefs from her upbringing. We never discussed it—Mom didn't find it appropriate to talk about "the intimate lives of others"—but her intolerance, or maybe it was simply fear of what she didn't understand, was right below the surface. It was as if her Islamic fundamentalist parents still hovered over her shoulders, invisibly.

"I think my mom thinks we're carrying on a secret lesbian relationship," I joked to Isa when I arrived at her house that morning.

She was like a feral fairy nymph perched atop the kitchen counter. Her white-blonde waves, effervescent in the morning sun, hung in disarray all the way down to her waist. She wore only her underwear, a Radiohead t-shirt, and her stack of bracelets (which she never took off, even to shower) as she ate peanut butter with a spoon directly from the jar.

"So, what if we were? Is Azrah a homophobe or something?" she asked, gravely.

I wasn't sure how to take her humorlessness. I thought we'd be splitting our sides by now while writing this off as another instance of my mom being totally clueless.

"Um…no. I just—" I fumbled. "I think it's just, like, weird, for her. Because I guess my grandparents were—are—really, you know. Old school."

Isa shrugged indifferently, licked her spoon, then sealed the lid back on the peanut butter jar.

"The world would be a much better place if we could admit that we're all attracted to *people*, not gender. It's so limiting otherwise, don't you think?"

"Um. Yeah. I mean, I haven't really thought about it," I confessed.

"I want to show you something," she said, hopping down from the counter and leading the way to her room.

We spent the rest of the morning pouring into the poetry collections she had stuffed in her bookcase. Sylvia Plath, Anne Sexton, Virginia Woolf—all feminist writers that Isa admired for pushing the boundaries of femininity and female sexuality.

"I love how fluid her perspective is," Isa said after she read Anne Sexton's "Song for a Lady" aloud.

The final line— "as you knead me and I rise like bread"—made me squirm in my cross-legged position on the floor.

"I'm more of a Jane Austen fan," I laughed to hide my discomfort. "Her stuff is more…tame."

Or was discomfort the appropriate way to describe my feelings? I wasn't sure. I'd never read anything like these poems before. These women were so…*othered.* Not in a way that was bad or wrong, but in a way that challenged me to think beyond the restraints of my mind that I didn't even know were there until those words jumped off the page. Depression, sex, love, lust, loss. Nothing was out of bounds.

"Jane Austen is a total badass too," Isa affirmed. "See?" She rose from her spot on the floor and reached up to the top shelf of her bookcase, retrieving a worn paperback copy of *Pride and Prejudice*. "Assigned reading last year. She was a pioneer for womankind."

I took the book and thumbed through the pages. Making a mental note of Isa's highlights, underlines, and annotations made me smile. There was nothing so bonding as sharing an appreciation for beautiful words.

"Any woman creating art, especially in the times these gals were living in, is an act of feminism. An act of bravery, really," she determined.

I didn't have many people in my life putting femininity on a pedestal. Since my father grew up Catholic and my mother's family was Muslim, we had tried various churches and mosques over the years. Each time, I felt a disconnect and, evidently, nothing resonated on my parents' quest for eternal meaning because neither of them claimed to be religious presently. But one element that did stick with me over the years—a throughline in many of the teachings I had been exposed to in my young life—was that to be a woman was to exist as a second-class citizen. I always understood that I was to apologize for myself, blend in, and try not to draw attention.

In the back of my mind, I maintained a small burning candle of resentment from the time Lindsay Fargetti, a classmate in my second grade Catholic Sunday school, announced, "Do you know why girls have to bleed every month? It's because Eve was *bad*." And watching my mother rip off her hijab after the one and only time we observed Ramadan was an image forever ingrained in my mind symbolizing oppression and family disappointment. I guess you could say that I wasn't exactly proud to be a female. I wasn't ashamed, but I never saw it as a privilege. But what if that was wrong? What if femininity could be powerful? We have the capacity to create, don't we?

"Let's get some fresh air." Isa pulled something from the depths of her bedside drawer, opened her bedroom window, and began to crawl outside onto the roof below. "Come on!" she beckoned.

My fear of heights was waning after having snuck out of my own bedroom window on multiple occasions by this point. We often sat on her roof to look at the stars and sometimes Isa would play her guitar—strumming the melancholic notes of her favorite Radiohead songs, it was a private concert for a neighborhood that would rather be asleep. But this was the first time she introduced the little drawstring bag with the stars and moon print.

"Don't tell Lincoln," she said when I joined her. "He's such a nag about this stuff."

She pulled out a little baggie containing a yellowish green leafy blob, a pair of chopsticks, a small wooden tray that was probably originally intended to serve sushi rolls, some sort of plastic disc, and small, thin strips of white paper. It wasn't until she started sprinkling the leafy stuff into the plastic thing and performing a grinding motion that it hit me.

"Is that *marijuana*?"

"My innocent little dove," Isa said, pausing from her task to stroke my cheek. "Just give me one second and…I'm going to give you wings."

The very first hit sent me into a cough attack. I thought this was the end—I would die a druggie on Isa's roof. It was as if I had inhaled a hot coal and now a trail of scorching flames was crawling down my windpipes. Why was I crying? While I envisioned what my parents would put on my tombstone, Isa assured me that everything I was experiencing was to be expected. She started laughing—a hearty cackle that seemed as though it had surfaced from the depths of the earth. A wave of *something*—was it sun rays? Can the sun push you over? —bent me backwards. Or was it just Isa's arm pushing me down to a reclined position? The clouds were fat and puffy. I wanted to reach out and touch them—grab a piece of fluff and bring it to my mouth. It would be sweet like sugar. Then I remembered that cotton candy existed.

"Fluff," I said. "Is fluff a word? We should go to the circus and get some fluff."

Isa laughed, which made me laugh. I couldn't stop. Maybe I was going to choke again. Or maybe I was going to pee myself. My legs were tingling.

"When am I supposed to feel something?"

Isa responded with more laughter.

"What if I have, like, an opposite reaction? What if I go berserk and jump off the roof or something?"

Ignoring me, she crawled back into her room. Alone on the roof, I closed my eyes. I concentrated on the heat of the sun on my face, the scratchy asphalt shingles against my palms, and the splotchy red and blue formations that danced on my eyelids. It was as if the world around me had evaporated and this dank, smoky air was cradling me into a state of deep calm. Isa returned to her spot beside me, but I kept my eyes closed. She started playing with my hair, a habit of hers that normally annoyed me, but I couldn't be bothered to swat her away.

"Can I show you something secret?" she said.

I sat up immediately. I lived for moments like these. "Absolutely."

She pulled a turquoise Moleskine journal from behind her and placed it carefully in my lap. It could have been as precious as a baby chick with the amount of delicacy that she used. With reverence, I opened the cover. A few dried daisies fell out as I skimmed the first page.

Songs by Isabel Claire DeLuca

I traced my fingers over the crevices made by handwritten letters and doodles. There was ink of all colors—blue, pink, red—floating off the page and popping in neon bubbles as it drifted up into the clouds.

"These are actual songs? You wrote the music and everything?" I marveled.

All this time I took Isa for a novice at the guitar, not a legitimate singer-songwriter.

"I want you to read them," she whispered directly into my ear, rustling the baby hairs around my temples. Then swiftly, she snatched the notebook from my hands. "One day."

"Ugh, not fair! Can you just play one?" I protested. "Go get your guitar!"

"Nooooo," she laughed, dangling the little blue book of secrets in front of me like a carrot on a stick. "All of my power is in here. It's not meant for anyone to see. Lincoln's the writer in the family anyway."

"But don't you want to be a pioneer? What about Sylvia and Jane?" I urged.

Was I shouting? It was hard to tell.

Isa's laugh was more crow than human. She threw herself backwards, hugging the notebook to her chest.

"One day," she mused, "I'll make a mint playing my songs on the streets of Geneva and then I'll take my treasure and buy us a boat and we'll sail up and down the Rhône and the beautiful people on land will wave at us and throw flowers. And we'll wave back and say, 'We can't stop. We have other places to see.'" Turning on her side and staring me with fever behind her eyes, she said, "Oh, K! You'll come with me, right? We'll backpack through Switzerland and eat all the chocolate we want? We'll fall in love and shout things from the top of the Alps, and no one will tell us to come home. Ever. We can be brave, right?"

"Isa," I said slowly. I was flicking my wrists in the air and the beige of my flesh seemed to swirl with the vibrant cyan of the sky above. "Are we high now?"

She interlaced her fingers with mine, her collection of bracelets glittering against a golden June sun. For a fleeting second, we were one being on that rooftop.

"Yes, little bird. We're flying."

At my mother's insistence, I spent the longest two hours of my life socializing with Blair Ford that summer. It was the first and only time that Blair and I spent time together, just the two of us, but within only fifteen minutes it became abundantly clear that we shared a mutual understanding—despite the closeness of our mothers, we didn't click.

The neighborhood luau was an annual event put on by the HOA every June, usually the Sunday before the fourth of July. Lanette Ford had, on numerous occasions, complained to my mother over speaker phone that she was fed up with the "old biddies" on the decorating committee who couldn't agree on a theme.

"It's a jumbled mess every year. They had red, white, and blue leis last year, Azrah. Can you imagine?" Lanette wailed. "And the playlist was a disaster. No one wants to listen to Bruce Springsteen while they're drinking from a coconut! We need that Hawaiian singer that does 'Somewhere Over the Rainbow'—I can't pronounce his name, but you know what I'm talking about, right?"

My mother, eager to climb the social ladder and remain in Lanette Ford's good graces, saw the neighborhood luau as an opportunity. She assured Lanette that she could single-handedly steer the sinking ship into respectably decorated dry land—providing diligent guidance over the old biddies on the decorating committee and ensuring that the party reached Lanette's desired level of cultural appropriation. I was, of course, recruited to "help."

"Tasteful" was not the word I would use to describe the hula dancer costumes that my mom bought for me and Blair. As if it weren't aggravating enough to be wrangled into serving mocktails and announcing the winners of the "Best Tropical Dessert" contest, our moms gushed over how endearing Blair and I would be as "little hula girls."

"Mom, do you realize how embarrassing this is?" I asked her, refusing to emerge from the HOA's clubhouse restroom.

The strings securing the coconut bra were flimsy and the grass skirt showed quite a bit of bare thigh if it swished in the wrong direction.

"You have just the tiny little body to make it work. Now get out here before we open up the tiki bar!" Mom urged.

Mom commenting on my figure always sent a wave of hatred rushing through me. It was humiliating, even if she thought she was being complimentary. Moments like these made me want to wrap myself in thick layers from head to toe just to spite her. But I knew I was fighting a losing battle. The best I could do was drape no less than five leis around my neck to better conceal my chest.

"*Seriously*? You're already Polynesian or whatever, so of course *you* don't look totally ridiculous." Was the first thing Blair said to me when I joined her behind the bar. "You're like Princess Jasmine and I look like a total retard."

There were so many things wrong with those statements that I didn't know which battle to pick, so I settled on, "Um…I'm Pakistani, actually…"

"Whatever," Blair rolled her eyes, pulling the gigantic plastic plumeria hair clip out of her strawberry blonde locks. "Got a bobby pin? This stupid thing keeps falling."

I pulled one loose from my own hair which was thick enough to withstand the absence of one pin and still maintain its shape. "Here, take this." I handed it to her. "And you look…great."

And that was how the event took shape—with Blair telling me what to do and me going along to get along. I mixed most of the drinks, Blair contributed by lazily throwing in tiny brightly colored umbrellas. I counted the votes for the best tropical dessert, Blair assigned herself as the announcer (and decided that she had to sample all of the entries while I had to pump air back into the deflated palm trees that flanked the pool). But keeping busy at least avoided conversation, for the most part.

"I'm assuming you're going to audition for *West Side Story*?" Blair asked pointedly as I chopped up more pineapple for the buffet table.

I wouldn't have missed auditioning for *West Side Story* even if I had contracted strep throat. Playing Maria filled my daydreams since Ms. Morris announced our fall musical back in May. I had grown up watching the movie starring Natalie Wood and singing "I Feel Pretty" in the shower. It was no secret to my parents that I was gunning for the lead. On the odd occasions when I was actually home long enough to strike up a conversation, my dad would snap his fingers like the Jets and the Sharks to make me laugh.

"Sweetie, you should see if Ms. Morris can use Daddy in the chorus," Mom would joke.

"Look out, Broadway!" Dad exclaimed after I talked for ten minutes straight about my plan to prepare for the audition. He pinched my cheek. "K, you don't need to do all that. You've been singing those songs since you were born."

It wasn't a lie; I had gone as Maria for Halloween when I was just four years old even though my mom tried to persuade me otherwise, saying that no one would get the reference. In my adolescent brain, I thought everyone knew that a white dress with a red belt screamed, "Maria from *West Side Story*." Instead, most of the adults that dumped candy in my pillowcase that year asked, "Now who are you supposed to be?" I usually downplayed my interests and deepest wishes, but every fiber of my beginning was devoted to playing this dream role. Leonard Bernstein's score was just so enchanting, and I wanted to sing those soaring soprano notes so badly; it was impossible to hide my eagerness, even from Blair.

"I've always wanted to be in that show," I replied, much too enthusiastically for her liking. "It's my favorite."

She smiled in the way that a snake would smile if reptiles were capable of such a thing.

"Well, Ms. Morris will have a tough time casting. I know she'll probably want me as Maria. But then again, I don't think we have anyone else with a strong enough dance background to cover Anita…"

I focused on the sound of my knife hitting the cutting board and creating equally sized cubes in an attempt to drown her out.

"I've been taking private voice lessons all summer," she claimed. "My instructor was actually the 'Somewhere' soloist in *West Side* on the UK tour."

That bit of information gave me pause. I had never had a formal voice lesson in my life, as I highly doubted that children's choir at age eight counted for anything.

"I just have no idea who she'll use as Tony now that Jason's in college," she continued, now plopping a bit of pineapple upside down cake into her mouth. "Will Isa audition, do you think?"

"Of course. She does every year."

"Good. She can dance at least. Not much of a singer, but we need dancers for this show."

She was really irritating me now, but I didn't know what to say to shut her up. Blair stirred the pot. If I managed to make her like me even less, I wasn't sure who else she could sway to turn against me. Most of the girls in the drama club idolized her.

"I know you're friends with her and all. But…" She paused, bit her lip, then shook her head. "Never mind, I really shouldn't say."

"What?" I asked. Now finished with my task, I plated the pineapple and hoisted myself onto a barstool beside her.

"Well…" she began. "Do you really want to know the truth about Isa?" The more she talked, the harder it was for me to shake the analogy of Blair as snake from my mind. She took a sip of the virgin pina colada I had made for her and gave me a sly smile. "You know we used to be best friends, right? All through middle school and our freshman year?"

She may as well have tossed the slushy coconut mixture straight into my face or pulled my hula skirt down to my ankles—I was so thrown for a loop.

Recognizing my look of utter confusion, she went on. "Yeah, I didn't think so. We stopped hanging out because…Well, maybe you don't know. But Isa is…" She stirred her drink with her tiny bright green umbrella then leaned in close enough for me to hear her whisper, "she's a *slut*."

I shook my head. "*What?* Isa doesn't even have a boyfriend. I would know. We hang out all the time."

Blair raised her eyebrows. "Hmm…Interesting," she said, coolly. "When we were friends, she was sleeping around. Older guys that didn't go to our school. I think she lost her virginity when she was 13 or something crazy like that. I just didn't want to go swimming with her or borrow clothes or anything like that with her being *sexually active*. She could have STDs for all I know."

"That can't be true. We never even talk about guys." I was getting heated now.

She shrugged and took a long sip. "She's a druggie too. But I guess that's not really a surprise because, well…look at her mom."

"You don't know what you're talking about," I said, standing and returning to my post behind the bar.

But before I could launch into a deeper debate on Isa's morality, my mom and Mrs. Ford hurriedly approached us.

"We can't have Sharon McDonald winning the dessert contest. She should have been disqualified," Mrs. Ford said to me. The level of urgency was like I had proposed Mrs. McDonald as a candidate to perform spontaneous brain surgery.

"She's been in trouble with *the board*," my mother whispered.

"But I counted the votes and she…" I began, retrieving the coconut filled with little folded strips of paper.

"Well, I'm just glad we caught this before you girls made the announcement. We had to fine Sharon because she had her 'Santa Land Here' doormat out until April. *April*," Lanette explained.

My mother shook her head. "Unbelievable," she agreed.

"We were planning the Easter egg hunt and here this woman thinks it's still Christmas!" Lanette threw her hands in the air. "So, we're going to go with Patsy Markle. Her mango sherbet was good. Wouldn't you say, Azrah?"

I watched my mom bob her head then scoured the room for a clock, a phone, someone's watch—anything to tell me how many hours of torture I had left before I could finally shed this scratchy grass skirt and flee to Isa's. Blair was a liar. She had to be.

Lincoln was due to return home from his creative writing camp two weeks before we all had to go back to school. Isa and I wanted to surprise him with some kind of welcome home present, but after an unfruitful hour of brainstorming, we gave up and decided to smoke on her roof (an activity that had quickly turned into an afternoon ritual…unless her dad was home). While soaring higher than kites, we came up with the idea to wrap every object in Lincoln's room in wrapping paper. His entire room would be a greedy child's fantasy birthday party. This grand plan manifested after Isa offhandedly said, "He already has everything. What else does he need?" Our eyes simultaneously grew round as saucers and we burst into explosive laughter, which turned into coughing fits, then more laughter.

Mr. DeLuca didn't ask questions when we returned from a Dollar Tree shopping spree with five bags full of loudly patterned wrapping paper, ribbons, bows, and Scotch tape. He also didn't care that we spent the entire night in Lincoln's bedroom whispering and occasionally forgetting ourselves to exclaim, "Ooo that looks really good!" or "He's going to flip!" I thought Mr. DeLuca was the coolest parent alive because he gave Isa and Lincoln so much freedom. In hindsight, it's plain that he was simply too concerned with his crumbling marriage to supervise his teenagers and their friends.

"What if we wrapped…" I paused for dramatic effect, "the light switch plate?"

"Bloody brilliant, darling!" Isa exclaimed as she chewed on a peach ring.

She preferred to eat the gummies by placing them on all of her ten fingers and chewing away like they were sugar coated kabobs. When I laughed at her, she was dumbfounded. "Doesn't everybody eat peach rings like this?" she had asked.

After two hours of work, the major focal points of the room—the bed, headboard, computer, and desk—were wrapped and we were now concentrating on adding a bit of finesse. We were also fairly tipsy from the Absolut Isa snuck while her dad was in the shower. We mixed it with our Monster energy drinks because we had to stay up all night to get this done; Lincoln would be there at 9:00 am the next morning.

"Oh! Let's also do his underwear drawer," Isa said, jumping up to dig through his dresser.

I turned to pick up the open bag of sour gummy worms so she wouldn't see my face flaring red.

"I don't know. Won't he be really pissed?" I asked.

"This is half present, half prank," Isa justified. "Just imagine the look on his face when he opens this drawer!"

"Okay, well," I said, now pulling off a piece of tape to secure my handiwork around the light switch. "*You* can be in charge of that then."

She let out a maniacal laugh and then, in a sing-song voice said, "He's gonna dieeeee!"

I did begin to wonder if this idea made more sense when we were high, but we were too deep into it now to turn back. By 2:00 am we had every video game and book on his bookcase individually wrapped, his keyboard, mouse, and desk lamp, as well as his swivel chair. His posters of literature quotes, Broadway shows, and the map of Middle Earth (what a dork) wasn't neglected either—we taped sparkling ribbons in the dead centers atop of loud yellow "It's a Happy Day!" wrapping paper. Even the pencil holder—and all the pencils, pens, and highlighters that it contained—were wrapped.

Laying on the floor of Lincoln's room, dizzy from the Absolut and concerning levels of sugar with all the candies and Monsters, we marveled at our work. My back ached from hunching over his Star Wars action figures (again, Lincoln couldn't be nerdier) and meticulously covering their lightsabers.

"This will go down as my finest accomplishment," Isa said dreamily.

I snorted. "Put this on your resume for college."

"Ha. Yeah right."

She sat up and her smile drooped, maintaining not a trace of the playfulness from seconds before.

I had no idea what her grades were like, but I got the sense that they weren't great. When Lincoln and I would moan about homework, she appeared unburdened. Not because she didn't have any of her own, I think she just chose not to do it. For this reason, I wanted to change the subject. But the Absolut made me tactless. I clumsily blurted out what had been on my mind since the HOA luau.

"Have you ever had sex?"

She sat up straighter and a mischievous smile crept onto her face. "The birdie wants to talk about the bees, does she?"

Should I tell her what Blair said?

But I laughed her off, "Very funny." And trying to divert attention off my own inexperience, I insisted, "Well? Have you?"

"I have, indeed," she said in a put-on proper way.

She grabbed the bottle of Absolut. At some point we stopped mixing, opting for a more direct route to inebriation. She took a long, luxurious sip. I don't know how she stomached it, but she didn't give even the faintest wince after pulling the bottle from her lips.

"Just with one fellow…"

Resting back on her hands, she looked up at the ceiling like an ingénue waiting for a prince to rescue her from her tower. I threw a green and orange gummy worm, nailing her right in the nose.

"Be serious," I demanded.

She dusted the sour powder off her nose, placed the worm between her teeth, and pulled until it snapped in two.

"I *am,* but a *lady* doesn't kiss and tell."

I stood, fed up with her games and started collecting empty cans to toss out but she grabbed my hand.

"Okay, okay," she placated, pulling me back down to the floor. "Don't get your panties in a wad." As we leaned against Lincoln's bed, the wrapping paper crunched beneath us. "So, I lost it last summer. His name was Tate. And he was my Pre-Algebra tutor."

"*What?*" I was mystified. "A *teacher?*"

"No, a *tutor*," she explained. "He was only twenty or something. Not an actual teacher. He went to MTSU."

"Holy hell! He was *twenty*! And you were…15? 16? Isa oh my—"

"Shhh!" She gestured to the door. "Age is just a number. That part's irrelevant."

"Can't he go to jail for that?"

"Look, do you want to hear the story or not?"

"Okay, fine," I relented. "How did it…you know…happen?"

"I failed Pre-Algebra; you know that." I didn't but wasn't entirely shocked, so I nodded along. "So, Tamara's coworker, Derek, had a son that tutored on the side. She hired him. And after a few sessions, we just hooked up. But things fell apart because Dad thought Tate smelled like weed, so he fired him. I'm pretty sure Tate still deals to Tamara though."

Stunned, I tried to get her story straight, "Okay…so, you hooked up with the son of your mom's coworker. And this guy also so happens to be your mom's dealer?"

"K, how do you think I got the pot? It's Tamara's." When I stared blank-faced, she continued, "She hasn't noticed that it's missing, if that's what you're worried about."

But getting caught wasn't what I was worried about, even if it should have been. No, it was the fact that Blair wasn't an all and out liar that bothered me. Isa continued to be a mystery, even after spending every moment of my summer stuck to her side like a conjoined twin. I glanced at her, nibbling away at the peach ring positioned on her index finger. How much of my best friend was still secret to me?

"Trust me—we're *fine*," she said while I half-listened, still trying to wipe the memory of Blair's insidious grin from my mind. "Tamara would never confront me or Lincoln because she doesn't want us to know she smokes. She probably thinks Dad's hiding it because he tried to pour out her liquor a few months ago. They really got into it after that."

She proceeded to say that while she never had a sexual experience with a woman, she certainly wasn't opposed to it.

"Tate was just—eh, I won't bore you with the details. But think about it—who knows better about how everything works down there than another woman? Don't get me wrong, I'm more than open to trying it again with a man. I think we should all be open. How stupid would I be if I missed out on something amazing just because the first few times were so-so? You know?"

"Why didn't you tell me?"

"You never asked." Was her response, as if it really was that easy to glean a person's most intimate history. "I pride myself on being an open book. It's the only way to live."

She knew so much more of the world than I thought. Marijuana seemed like child's play compared to being properly sexually active. My parents never had "the talk" with me; all I knew about reproduction was from what we were told in 7th grade PE: "Don't have sex. You can get pregnant or get an STD. You could even die. Also don't do drugs."

With my limited understanding, sex intrigued me. I would daydream sometimes about a wedding and, along with what sort of dress I would wear and what my future husband would say in his vows, I imagined a sacred, blissful wedding *night*. Although I wanted to believe that my brief stint as a Catholic didn't continue to have a hold on my conscience, I thought I was supposed to wait until marriage. But religious influences aside, I knew that I wanted my first time to be with the "right guy"—whatever that meant. I supposed that it wouldn't be such a forbidden thing if you waited for what society deemed to be the right moments. But equal to my curiosity, was my fear.

When I got my first period, my mom cried, and I wondered if I had done something wrong just by growing up. My dad told me at 11 years old to stay away from boys, which probably explained why I had never been kissed offstage and in real life. Surely, the only reason my dad was comfortable with me hanging out with Lincoln was because he was Isa's brother, and she was with us all the time. Plus, you don't go around harboring a crush on your best friend's brother. Everyone knows that…

I considered all this, and I considered the reaction I would get if I went to my parents for guidance. Would they help me sort these things out? Likely, they would tell me the same textbook spiel that the PE teacher gave us. Maybe it was because my parents, who became parents accidentally and very young, hoped that by sheltering me I wouldn't repeat the same mistakes. Whatever their rationale, it bothered me that no one told me the truth. But Isa… All I had to do was ask and she would tell me.

"Tell me everything," I said. "The details. I want to know what it's like."

And she did. She told me everything.

Sophomore year I was equipped with two best friends, a passion, and a better sense of the space I occupied in my high school. My locker was, again, smacked in the middle of the "S" section—Megan, Todd, Enrique, and Cassandra remained dumb as ever, unchanged by a few months' maturity—but I was elated to have Geometry and AP European History with Lincoln. Isa, now a Junior, had a different lunch schedule and was supposed to eat in the Junior/Senior courtyard. But, as was her way, she'd frequently skip gym to visit Lincoln, Jon Seong, and I during our lunch period.

"How are you always able to get a hall pass?" Jon inquired once.

"I just tell Coach Jennings that I'm on the rag and need to go to the nurse," she explained, shrugging, and helping herself to a fry from my tray.

"What you *need* is to go to the emergency room if you've been bleeding for two straight months," I retorted.

"Guys," Lincoln interjected. "I'm *eating*?"

He pushed away his cafeteria spaghetti with red sauce. Jon, also disturbed, shivered. Isa and I cackled.

Day-to-day was largely uneventful until *West Side Story* auditions were upon us. Lincoln had already secured a position as Ms. Morris' assistant director, which was a notable step up in his book because he would get to help with auditions and block a few scenes.

"Now, I'll actually be able to tell Blair that her expressions are upstaging everyone," he joked; although, we all knew that no discerning eye could convince Blair to dial it back, even if it was Stephen Sondheim himself.

To everyone's surprise, my own included, I approached auditions with a sense of serenity. I had done everything within my power to prepare by watching the movie on repeat to singing along with the cast recording and actually memorizing lines from the script. My favorite scene was the "How many bullets, Chino! Enough for me?" bit at the end. Playing Sarah Brown was fun, but I yearned for a role with more depth—something meatier that I could sink my teeth into and flex my acting muscles.

With Isa, Lincoln, and my parents cheering me on (and Isa's jade stone in my pocket, which she said gave good luck), I somehow adopted a perspective that allowed me to get through the audition and callback without desperation pouring from every orifice. I viewed the audition as my mini solo performance in my dream role. If the casting ultimately went in Blair's favor, then at least I got my 16 bars and an opportunity to read sides in front of an audience…even if that audience was only Ms. Morris and Lincoln.

The Monday morning when the cast list went up was the first time it had ever been necessary for me to hold both the emotions of joy and hurt at the same time. Isa, who drove Lincoln and I to school every morning, magically hit all green lights and secured a primo spot in the senior parking lot (she told us it was unmonitored, so what was stopping her from parking there?). I was walking on air as we approached the double doors of the side entrance that was directly in front of the auditorium. It seemed that we were the first to arrive. And the first to read the cast list, as Ms. Morris even made Lincoln wait through the weekend. As soon as I caught a glimpse of the white paper against the maroon of the auditorium doors, my heart skipped. In my gut, I knew I was about to get the news I had been waiting for. Good news.

RHS Drama Club's 2007 Production of West Side Story
Please initial to accept your role

Tony — Jon Seong
Maria — K Statham
Anita — Savannah Albright
Bernardo — Lewis García

"K! I told you!" Lincoln beamed then swooped me into a bear hug, lifting me off my feet.

"Congratulations, dove!" Isa said, kissing my cheeks like an Italian grandma.

"I have to call my parents!" I said through happy tears.

Isa and Lincoln stood surveying the rest of the cast list as I stepped outside for better reception. I saw Blair and Mrs. Ford crossing the parking lot, heading directly to the double doors. As suddenly as my joy ballooned in my chest, it popped. I couldn't be there when Blair and her mom saw the list. Now thinking about it, I had seen my name then burst into hysterics. I didn't bother to check which part Blair had been cast in. Before they could see me, I dashed to the side of the building to call my parents. I could only imagine the gravity of this impending meltdown of the century but as much as I impishly wanted a front row seat, I also didn't want any of Blair's venom shot in my direction.

My parents and I hollered and giggled until the first bell rang. Just as we made plans to go out for sushi to celebrate and said our goodbyes, Lincoln and Isa walked up. Their faces—a mixture of shellshock and delight—said everything I needed to know.

"Holy shiiiit," Isa began. "You missed one hell of a show."

"What happened?"

"Allow me to give you a ten second reenactment," Lincoln offered.

He backed up several feet and began strutting towards us while sassily flipping invisible locks—his overdramatized impression of Blair. Then, he stopped, gasped, fainted, seemed to revive for a brief moment, then collapsed again to the ground. He hopped to his feet and bowed.

"In conclusion," he said. "She died. She is literally deceased. The funeral is scheduled for tomorrow during study hall."

Through a fit of giggles that I knew were wrong, I asked, "But what part did she get?"

"Velma. One of the Jet girls," Isa said.

I was astonished. *Blair* in the ensemble?

"Is she dance captain or something? Singing the 'Somewhere' solo? Anything?"

"Nope. You're looking at your Graziella and dance captain," Isa said, framing her face with two open palms and tilting her head. "And some senior got the solo."

"Oh my god! Isa! That's awesome!" Then I fumbled. "For you, I mean. Not awesome that Blair didn't—"

But Isa held up a hand to silence me. "It *is* a little awesome that Blair's finally been served some humble pie, you gotta admit."

As we made our way to our classes, I remembered that I forgot my biology textbook…which also contained my homework from Friday stuffed inside. I pulled out my phone to text my mom, but in the process bumped into Mrs. Santiago who was passing me on the right.

She grumbled, "Cellphone, Miss Statham. Put it away and watch where you're going!"

Verbal warnings from authority figures held a crippling power over me, so I decided to duck into the front office and use that phone to call my mom. Even if it meant a tardy, I could at least get in touch with my mom and have her drop off my homework before second period. As caught up in my dilemma as I was, it didn't even register that going into the front office meant facing Mrs. Ford, who was still the school secretary. But the scene of a crying Blair slumped over the counter jolted my memory as soon as I opened the door.

"You know she only got it because she's ethnic!" Blair wailed, without noticing that I had the door ajar and could hear her clear as day.

Mrs. Ford, who was behind the desk, patting Blair's hand, looked over at me with eyes wide. She coughed—a signal for Blair to cease her blathering.

"K, good morning!" She plastered on a tense smile. "Can I help you with something?"

"No, um, never mind."

As quickly as my feet would carry me, I turned to leave the office. But the venom had been injected; Blair had the satisfaction of seeing the tears in my eyes and I never stopped doubting that I actually deserved the role.

"Lincoln, just give her one itsy little chip!" I pleaded.

Ella's enormous brown eyes looked pathetically at the open bag of Tostitos that Lincoln was hoarding. She was sitting in my lap, letting me pet and cuddle her to my heart's content. Ella was an "unofficial emotional support dog," as Isa said. And emotional support was exactly why I was there, in the DeLuca's backyard that Friday night. All three of us were sprawled on the trampoline in a nest of sleeping bags, pillows, and blankets. It was going to be a clear, pleasant evening and Isa said, "sleeping under the stars revives the soul." We had Isa's now famous tequila and Kool-Aid "margaritas" in hand and were devouring a tub of queso with corn chips. The beloved Sombrero of Truth rested in the middle of our huddle. It was Lincoln's turn next.

After Blair's comment in the front office, I had been alternating between giddiness and utter defeat. One minute I would get butterflies in my stomach at the thought of finally wearing the white Maria dress with the red belt. *Finally* singing the "Tonight" duet. Those exquisite lyrics that I had adored since childhood—*I* was going to be the one to bring them to life. Then, Blair's voice in my head— "You know she only got it because she's ethnic!"—would pollute my daydreams and send me crashing down to an uncertain reality. What delusion had I been living in? Maria was Puerto Rican and in my white-washed affluent public high school, my wheatish skin was the boldest crayon in the box. I hadn't secured the role on my own merits; it was purely because of the color of my skin. And if that was the case, did I have any real talent at all?

Isa and Lincoln had been trying to get me to rally all week; assuring me that Ms. Morris wouldn't have cast me if she didn't think I could handle the role and imploring me to as Isa put it, "For the millionth time, don't dwell on the words of jealous twits." When I hadn't shown much sign of improvement by Friday at lunch, the plan for a Mental Health Sleepover and Sombrero of Truth Session was devised. "If you won't listen to reason, then let's at least get sloppy," Isa declared.

"Nooo, Ella. Human food. Not for you," Lincoln said, raising the chip bag over his head.

Isa picked up the sombrero and tossed it at him, exclaiming, "Enough stalling! Your turn."

"Alright, alright," he began, adjusting the sombrero over his head. "So…in third grade…I *may* have had a crush on Jon's sister. But I totally don't anymore so wipe that look off your face, Isa!"

Isa fell backwards, laughing and nearly snorting up her margarita.

"You dope," she said, coming up for air. "I've *always* known that."

Sulking, Lincoln took off the hat and tossed it at her.

"I didn't know Jon had a sister," I said.

"She's older. A junior at MTSU," Lincoln stated plainly.

"Her name's Gloria. She's totally his type…super nerd just like him," Isa chimed in then reached over to tousle Lincoln's shaggy hair. "You need a haircut, dude," she added.

"I told you. I don't have a thing for her anymore. It was only when we were kids," Lincoln said, then took a swig of his drink. "Your turn. And it better be good."

Isa lifted the sombrero and lightly situated it over her head. Today she wore a long side braid with wildflowers entangled throughout. Her pajamas, a boldly patterned jinbei-style set, was a gift from her dad when he went on a business trip to Japan. Even without the sombrero, she looked like a party.

"Hmm…let me see…" Scanning the area, her eyes fell onto Ella, still curled up in my lap. "Oh! Well…I actually named Ella. After Cinderella. When I was in elementary school, I had an obsession with Disney princesses."

"Seriously?" I asked, baffled.

Isa, the ultra-feminist free spirit, once idolized a character who longed for a handsome prince to take her far, far away and live happily ever after? But Lincoln was unphased.

"That's lame!" he said, "I already knew that! K, she used to dress up in the gowns and everything."

Isa rolled her eyes, but conceded, "Fine, okay…" She thought for a moment, dipped a chip in the queso, and brought it to her mouth. "Okay. I have one. So…Abe, remember when Tamara had a cow a few months back because she couldn't find her sapphire necklace?"

He nodded grimly and from the look on his face, I imagined that "had a cow" was likely an understatement.

"Well, I have it."

He actually performed a spit take. Until then, I assumed that only happened in movies.

"Ugh, Lincoln! Gross!" I squealed, shielding myself from flying spittle and margarita mixture.

"You took it? *Isa*. You have to give it back. Mom and Dad fired Laverne over that!" Lincoln protested.

"It's not my fault they fired Laverne. Tamara should clean her own house anyway," Isa shrugged, showing not a stitch of remorse.

"Okay, back up," I butted in. "What's the story here?"

"Mom had this sapphire necklace. Dad got it for her for some anniversary or whatever and Isa was super into it," Lincoln started.

"When I got older, I thought it looked like the Heart of the Ocean. But I've always loved it," Isa justified, bringing another chip to her mouth.

"Excuse me? The Heart of what?"

"From *Titanic*?"

"Never seen it."

"Serious gap in your film knowledge, K. We have to fix this ASAP," Isa said.

She was as authentically disappointed in me as I was, once again, baffled by her. Isa—Disney zealot *and Titanic* fangirl? Not to mention, it was odd for her to covet fine jewelry. She always said, "Nature is the best accessory," opting for daisy chains rather than the Tiffany's chokers that were popular with other girls in our school. How many former personalities had this girl embodied?

"Anyway," Lincoln continued, throwing an annoyed glance at Isa. "It went missing and my dad was convinced that the lady from Merry Maids took it. If we had known it was *Isa*…"

"Before you throw me any more shade, Lincoln, I had my reasons," she said as she crossed her arms.

"Be my guest. We're all waiting," he said with an air of sarcasm.

"Mom—Tamara—let me wear it a few times when I was little," Isa said, swirling her margarita. "I would dance around in it, and she'd say, 'Isabel, you're such a pretty girl.'" Letting out a small chuckle, she looked up at the sky and I knew that she was reliving that exact memory—a movie that she alone could see. "But once I was playing with it—I was three or four, I guess. And it slipped out of my fingers. I was a kid. It was an *accident*." She emphasized that word with an icy coldness. From the glow of the DeLuca's back porch lights, I saw not a mistiness in her eyes, but a void. "And she spanked me for it. It was the only time I remember being spanked. And it was hard. Aggressive. Like she was mad about something that—something that was bigger than me."

An image of an open flat palm coming down hard on bare, baby soft skin filled my mind. I winced. I had never been spanked, so I had not even the faintest frame of reference for what it might feel like when a parent inflicted violence onto their child. But Lincoln… If he was shocked at all, his face told a different story; his eyes were downcast, and he broke a corn chip into a million tiny pieces. He knew of a dynamic to which I was mostly unaware.

"But I still wore the necklace from time to time," Isa confessed. "Only when I was having a bad day or something. It made me feel better to feel pretty and important. I'd sneak into her room, open up her jewelry box, and just stare at myself in the mirror." At that point, Isa's eyes met mine. She was expressionless when she said, "Everyone wants to be someone else sometimes."

If you're Isa, why would you want to be anyone else?

"And a few months ago, she—" Isa continued, but paused to take a sip. "She asked me if this year was going to be 'a better year for me.' 'Are you going to get your grades up finally or am I going to have to hunt for another tutor?' she said. 'Other kids your age are looking at colleges now,' she said. And that night—when she was gone who knows where—I thought it would make me feel better to try on the necklace. Just for a minute. I had it around my neck, and I thought, 'Why shouldn't I keep it?' So that's it. I did. I kept it."

Lincoln and I sat in silence. The tension was only broken when Ella leapt off the trampoline and trotted to the backdoor. She barked a couple of times before Mr. DeLuca opened the door and let her in.

"You kids okay out there? Need anything?" he called.

"We're fine. Thank you, Mr. DeLuca!" I replied because Lincoln and Isa seemed to be in the midst of a stare-off.

Lincoln was the first to speak. "Isa. I think you should give it back."

"But I don't want to." Was all she said in her defense. "I want it. It makes me feel pretty."

I wasn't quite sure why, but I thought I might weep.

"K. It's your turn," Isa said, removing the sombrero from her head and handing it to me.

Possibly because the tequila made me sappy, or possibly because I didn't want Isa to feel alone in her vulnerability, I decided to tell a real secret. The reason why comments like the one Blair said couldn't be shaken but cut so deeply.

"When I was younger, my parents and I went to this Catholic church for a couple years. It was after they tried out Islam—my mom wanted to get back to her roots or whatever, but that didn't work out so well…" I said this nonchalantly, although the memories of how tense things were between my parents at that time still unnerved me.

Flashbacks of my mom praying on the floors of our home; crying, begging, asking to feel something, *anything*. The arguments when my dad would say, "I'm doing everything I can, Azrah. What else can I do? I can't make them accept me. Or us." Somehow, I knew their strife had something to do with me. I was the reason my mom's parents hated her. And try as she might to be a good Muslim wife and mother, they wouldn't forget how I got here or how my parents' marriage came to be.

"So, yeah," I went on, "My dad grew up Catholic, so I guess they thought, 'Let's give this a try.' Well, you have to take all these classes to be a real Catholic. My dad already did all that stuff when he was a kid, but my mom and I had to go to classes. She was with the adults, and I did Sunday school with the kids. I had to have a first communion, which was a super big deal. I got this frilly white dress. It was fun to dress up back then, but now it seems kind of…weird. We were like little brides.

"And part of the whole ceremony is to take a sip of this grape juice—they said it was wine, but it was really Welch's—and eat this little wafer thing. They said it represented the body of Christ and his blood."

Isa and Lincoln, who were now settled into their respective sleeping bags, were completely captivated. Propping their heads up with their elbows, they stared at me, unblinking.

"And I know this is…dumb, but…I was so nervous. I had to walk up in front of the whole church and drink this wine and eat this wafer. I thought I was going to spill the wine on my dress or trip or…I don't know. I didn't want to do it. But I did. And when it was my turn, I just…I couldn't swallow the wafer. My mouth was so dry, and I was scared. Everyone was looking at me. I spit it out into my hand. I thought no one would notice, but a lot of people in the pews gasped. It was like I had done this terrible, awful thing. And I've always wondered, 'What if I am?'"

"What if you are *what*?" Lincoln asked.

"What if I *am* this terrible, awful person? You know? Because of that. Because I couldn't do what everyone else was doing. I couldn't just swallow the damn wafer. What if…I don't deserve… What if I'm fundamentally, like…*flawed*. Does that make sense?"

"K…" Lincoln reached out and placed a sympathetic hand on my knee.

I was sitting crisscross applesauce, as they used to say in elementary school, in the center of the trampoline. With the sombrero on my head and my heart on my sleeve, I realized all at once how stupid I must have looked. Why did I constantly fall into this trap of empathizing with others, over-sharing, then getting caught in a web of vulnerability. I was a fly, squirming and twisting but I alone was responsible for the trap. I'd spun it for myself.

"Hey K, don't talk about my friend like that." Isa sat up and scooted closer to me. "You are my dearest one, little bird. I can see not a single flaw." An odd and whimsical statement that was only made genuine because it was so genuinely *her*.

She embraced me and something very small, but very heavy lifted from my gut, traveled through my throat, sighed out my lips, and floated into that clear, pleasant evening. It wasn't all of the ugliness or all of the doubt, but just knowing that *some* of it could be released gave me hope.

"Now, lights out I say!" Isa shook her fist curmudgeonly at the waxing moon.

"You weirdo," Lincoln said, throwing a pillow at her.

Isa fell asleep within minutes, like she always did—laying on her belly with her mouth slightly open. I laid awake, cocooned in my sleeping bag, and staring up at the stars.

"K?" Lincoln whispered after a long silence.

I rolled to my side to face him. "I thought you were asleep."

"Can't."

"Yeah, me neither," I confessed. "I just keep thinking about things."

"Bad things or good things?" he asked.

It was only then, with him lying next to me in his own sleeping bag, the moonlight overhead, and the nocturnal creatures humming and chirping in the background, that I realized how intimate this moment was; how intimate sharing a bed was. I'd shared a bed with Isa all summer, practically, and didn't realize how much trust you instill in another person when you allow yourself to fall asleep in their presence.

I'd never been this intimate with Lincoln before. Not that it was a big deal—he was *Isa's brother*, after all. Even still, looking into his eyes—which were only about two feet away from mine—caused tiny sparks to pop and fizz inside my stomach. I told myself that it was just because he was a boy, and we were horizontal. I had so little experience with guys.

"Good things. I think. Maybe both," I said without further explanation.

"Let's keep playing until we fall asleep. So, we stop thinking so much," he suggested.

He sat up, looking for the sombrero, but when he realized that it was under Isa's exposed left arm, he laid back down.

"Forget it," he decided. "We don't need the sombrero. I'll go first…" He paused to think of a secret. I tried to think of mine while I waited. "Okay, so once I…no. It's bad."

"Lincoln, really? You can't just start a secret and then stop."

"Ugh…okay. Once—when I was only like five and totally didn't know better and I would never do something like this again—I stole some Bubble Tape from CVS." He buried his head in his pillow.

"Oh. My. God!" I whisper-yelled. "Lincoln. We have to turn you in!"

He laughed, which made Isa stir.

"K, seriously. You have no idea how bad I feel about it."

"I know, which is why you have to come clean to the authorities. I'm sure you'll get a fair trial and everything. I'll even come visit you in prison if you want," I joked. This was too good to ever let him live down and also kind of precious that a childish misdemeanor actually seemed to bother him ten years later. "Did you eat the Bubble Tape?"

"…yes. All of it. I didn't even share with Isa."

I gasped dramatically. "Even *worse*. You're looking at 25 to life."

"Alright, alright, your turn," he insisted.

"Well…what I'm thinking of is really embarrassing…" I began, shifting around in my sleeping bag to get more comfortable. I finally flipped to my stomach and propped myself up on my elbows so I could see him more clearly.

"It's supposed to be," he pointed out.

"Yeah, I guess…okay, so…*sometimes*…I pick my nose." I covered my face with my hands.

He laughed again and this time Isa grunted in her sleep, which made me laugh too.

"Shhh!" Lincoln said, suppressing laughter of his own. "That's not a secret."

Mortified, my eyes widened like they might pop out of my head. "What are you talk—"

He gave in to his laugh attack. "Your face!"

"Shh! Lincoln, what are you—"

"I've *seen* you pick your nose, K."

I whacked him with my pillow. "Shut up. No, you haven't."

"Yes, I totally have. But it's *fine*. Everyone does it," he said as his laughter died down.

Appalled as I was, I did see the humor in the situation. "We're acting like babies."

"Oh, you want serious secrets?" he teased. "I thought we had enough serious for one night." When I glared at him, he shifted gears. "Not that serious is a bad thing. Jeesh. Just saying—it's good to lighten the mood. Better to fall asleep smiling than brooding over…whatever."

He had a point.

"I'll tell you a serious secret though," he said. "If you want… Well, it's more of a question I guess."

"Shoot."

"If Isa didn't claim you first, then would you think of me?"

"Is this a riddle?"

He flipped onto his back, hands behind his head, and said the next bit to the abyss. "Well, would you ever think of me as something other than Isa's brother?"

I took a second to absorb the question. I still wasn't exactly sure what he was asking. Would I have chosen to be friends with him even if I hadn't become friends with Isa first?

"Of course…" I said slowly. His eyes shifted over to me. "Abe, *you're* my best friend too."

He sighed and fixed his gaze back at the sky. "I've never liked that nickname, you know. Isa started it when we were kids. I tattled on her all the time, and she made fun of me for being so honest."

"Oh. I didn't know," I responded, taken aback. "I won't call you that anymore."

"No," he rolled to his side to face me. "It's okay. I like it when you say it."

He smiled and the sparks in my stomach went off again. I reminded myself that he gave everyone that same blindly bright toothy grin, it wasn't a look uniquely designated for me.

"K, what's your real name?"

I fidgeted again, tucked a loose curl behind my ear, and tried to form the words. Words that wouldn't make me sound like an idiot, but also give him the honest answer that he deserved—that I knew he would value.

"It's Katie. Just—Katie."

"Short for—"

"Nope. Not Katherine or Kathleen. Just Katie."

Picking up on my unease, he ever so gently pressed for more. "What's…what's wrong with 'just Katie'?"

What's wrong with "Just Katie"? Where would I begin? What *wasn't* wrong with "Just Katie"? I sighed then sat up to face him dead-on. And I told him the whole story. I told him about how we had moved so many times for my dad's job; every time my dad got a promotion—and he did every two to four years because my dad was really smart and really good at his job—we moved. I would change schools. I would be the new girl again and there would always, *always* be at least two other Katies. I told him about how I grew to loath my name because it made me feel anonymous; I was just "one of the Katies" or worse—the "New Katie." "Katie" in itself wasn't even a name that I felt proud of. It wasn't unique. It didn't have a meaning or story behind it. Knowing what I know of my mother, I suspected that she chose it because it sounded basic and thoroughly American. She wanted to erase my culture from me like she wanted to erase it for herself. And in a way that I couldn't put words to, I told him, that rattled me.

"I would have rather been at least a 'Katherine.' I just didn't want to be another 'Katie.' So, I made myself 'K.' I wanted there to be only one of me."

After my monologue, Lincoln smiled again and nudged my arm. "You're the only Katie I know."

"You're lying."

He put up his right hand. "I don't lie, remember? Swear to God—I literally can't think of another Katie in my classes or anything. I mean, sure, yeah, I've met other Katies in my *lifetime*. But you're the only one I hang out with. The only one that matters. You're the only Katie Statham." He took the cue of my raised eyebrow. "But I'll call you 'K.' If that's what you want."

"Thank you," I said.

"Your secret is safe with me."

He winked and extended his pinkie finger. I linked it with mine and knowing that he would keep his promise, I smiled.

"Hey," he said, staring curiously at my face.

"What?" I put my hands to my cheeks. "Is there something on my—"

"You have dimples!" he said like he just found a basket of fluffy baby bunnies hiding under the trampoline.

"Shut up." I shoved him. But then a moment of clarity overcame me. "Okay, but…" I began. I knew then that I wouldn't be able to go to sleep unless I got this thought off my chest. "Can I just confess one last thing?"

"Two secrets for the price of one?"

"It's not a secret because everyone already knows it. *I* just need to say it… Blair's a…a bitch."

I clapped my hands to my mouth. Never in my life had I ever used that word to describe another person. I tried to keep mean-spirited thoughts at bay and avoid letting them run rampant in the natural world.

Lincoln's jaw dropped.

"But she is, isn't she? She's a *bitch.*"

He snorted, then clapped—too entertained to fret about waking his sleeping sister. "Yes! She really is. She really, really is. Blair's a bitch."

"Blair's a bitch," I said again, more matter of fact.

"Blair's a *bitch*!" he yelled.

Isa rolled to her back and blinked her eyes open. I stood on the trampoline.

"Blair's a bitch!" I screamed into the darkness.

Lincoln stood with me, and we both threw our arms in the air, bellowing, "BLAIR'S A BITCH!"

"Hear, hear!" Isa exclaimed, drowsily.

And we ended the night just like Lincoln said—no brooding, just smiles.

9.

Aloo Gosht and Ashes

Lincoln grabbed Dr. Mirza's handwritten recipe out of my hand.

"Okay, this isn't so bad," he said, skimming the ingredients list and her methodical step-by-by instructions (she knew I was no chef and she had to spell it out like she was relaying information to a toddler). "You start with the onions. I'll do the potatoes. And then we'll worry about sauteing the beef. Easy!"

I sighed and threw him a vintage lady's half apron with red and white polka dots.

"Sorry. Was that mansplaining?" He shot me a look of grave concern.

We had two modes—the Friendship Mode and the Dating Mode. Friendship mode was like it had always been; when we weren't concentrating on "filling in the Gap Years," and just watched an old movie or went for a walk, it felt like no time had passed. But when we were in Dating Mode, things could go array at the drop of a dime. One second we'd be teasing each other about a booger that was hanging out of my nose or one of Lincoln's intentionally abrasive post-soda burps, and next second we'd be on my apartment futon making out. Coasting from Friendship Mode to Dating Mode took almost no effort at all—perhaps because this newfangled land had always been living just beneath the surface of our day-to-day interactions for several years, waiting to be explored. But once we were in Dating Mode, neither one of us seemed to be able to compartmentalize our anxious thoughts.

I found myself privately debating the questions, "Did I just say something wrong?" and "Does jabbing him under the armpits mean something else now? Does it say, 'Hey, I think you're hot and I want your tongue in my mouth,' or, 'You're an idiot' like it used to?"

"No, dork," I responded, tying my own apron behind my waist. "How many times do I have to tell you to talk to me like a human? Like *me*."

"I'll stop overthinking when you stop wearing lipstick when I come over," Lincoln said, batting his eyes in jest.

I chucked an onion at him.

"You do the onions. I want to see you cry."

He guffawed before spraying me with the sink hose. Friendship Mode. I put my hands over my face to shield myself and didn't see when he hooked his arm around my waist to pull me in close. When I looked up at him, he placed a long, firm kiss on my—yes, lip-sticked for the occasion—lips. Dating Mode.

"Hmm, that shade looks good on you," I said afterwards, referencing the traces of Forbidden Fuchsia by Mary Kay on his lips.

He wiped his mouth with the back of his hand. "Worth it," he confirmed.

"Hey! Chop chop. Get to work on those onions."

With the first week of our final semester under our belts, we decided to celebrate by cooking a traditional Pakistani dish, Aloo Gosht, at my apartment. Aloo Gosht is basically a warming winter beef stew. It's made of all the good stuff you want in your belly when it's cold outside—potato, cardamom, cinnamon, red chili powder, turmeric… But while a spicy stew seemed like the perfect addition to a wet and wintery January night, my culinary skills were limited to spreading peanut butter on toast.

Lately, however, I was inspired to lean into my roots—first through art and now through food—and I knew that would necessitate dipping my toes outside my comfort zone. My independent study with

Dr. Mirza had piqued my curiosity in learning more about the richness of culture that I had been denied for 22 years. Dr. Mirza, connoisseur of Middle Eastern cuisine, was all too eager to assist me in my endeavors.

Not knowing much at all about my mother's childhood, I suppose it's unfair of me to pass judgment on her insistence to leave her heritage in the dust. She might have traumatic memories associated with Pakistan if she actually remembered living there with her parents and three siblings. Maybe she had a relationship with her mom and dad that was so horribly abusive that she was grateful to be rid of them when they evicted her from the family tree. Or perhaps Azrah just wanted to do what Azrah wanted to do. She wanted to date American boys, wear American clothes, *be* an American. Not a Pakistani woman who grew up in America. Not a Pakistani-American. She wanted no trace of who she used to be before she took my dad's name.

And all that is fine and well for her, but I had started to feel as though I had been robbed; there was an entire half of my ethnic background that I had never been properly exposed to. Half of what made me *me* was untouchable and unspoken of. When the world is so quick to categorize, there are two options— "white" and "not white." I was both. I was, as they say in improv theater, the personification of "yes and." *Yes*, I'm white. *And* I'm…something else. I'm Pakistani, I guess. But could I claim that identity if I knew nothing about it? Thus, I began to seek out opportunities to slowly and quietly investigate this buried sense of self. Here in my tiny studio apartment, with only F. Scott and Lincoln as my witnesses, I could cook a bad pot of Aloo Gosht, and I could feel free in my failure. One micro step closer to solving the puzzle that was me.

Lincoln tossed the beef cubes in a pan already popping with hot olive oil while I scoured my pantry for seasonings.

"Perfecto!" he exclaimed. "Now we're cookin'! That's what I call a healthy sizzle."

I rolled my eyes and chuckled, reaching for the cutting board.

"I like learning new things with you," I observed, now dicing garlic. "You're more entertaining than F. Scott, at least."

F. Scott, who was still quite skeptical of Lincoln, was curled in a tight ball on my bed. He'd open one suspicious eye every now and then just to make sure things were still under control, stand to stretch authoritatively, and melt back into his ball. He didn't approve of noise or raucous or anything that was out of the ordinary. And hosting visitors definitely deviated from our normal routine of solitude.

"It helps to have a bit of eye candy in the kitchen," Lincoln said, flexing a flannel-clad arm.

"Charming," I said sarcastically. "Here's the garlic, Narcissus." I handed him the cutting board of freshly chopped garlic to add to the pan.

"I'll take a comparison to a Greek god as a compliment, thank you very much," Lincoln decided. Snide remarks never could steal his sunshine.

Once we had all the ingredients chopped and simmering in the pot, we retired to my futon for a breather. I figured that anything requiring an hour of incubation must wind up tasting semi-decent. At least the effort was there.

"I know we're supposed to relax tonight, but can I bounce a few ideas off you? For the play?" Lincoln asked as we nestled into a now-comfortable cuddling position. (The first few attempts he made at putting his arm around me on that futon ended in an immature giggle fit on my part and exasperation on his.)

"What's up?"

He leaned forward to grab his backpack, shift through the contents, then reveal a small, black notebook. His writer's notebook. It looked identical to the one he carried around in high school.

"I wrote down some ideas."

The page that he flipped to was titled, "The Isa Project" in bold and underlined in the top center location. He caught me staring.

"Fitting, don't you think?" he asked.

All I could do was smirk and grab at something to change the subject. "How many of those do you have?"

I imagined a bookshelf full of interchangeable pocket-sized black notebooks. A shelf with the all-important function of bearing one man's genius.

"Oh, this is my…I don't know. Tenth?"

"You should buy them in bulk at Costco."

I smiled and scooted closer to him. I was attracted to his brain just as much as I was attracted to those hazel eyes and that obnoxious grin. I always was, but now I didn't have to hide it.

"Soooo…I was thinking," he said, flipping through the pages to find his most recent ruminations. "We need to rally the troops. We need to build a cast."

"Who did you have in mind?"

"*That's* what I wanted your opinion on. What if we started by hand-picking people in the community that we know? Non-actors. People that we know have lost something, someone. It can be anything. It just has to be real stories from real people," he explained.

"Okay, what's the pitch?" I asked. He raised an eyebrow. "I mean, what's in it for them?"

He thought for a minute. "Well," he began, "aside from helping a budding literary genius and theater practitioner extraordinaire with his capstone project… Hmmm…you're right, Statham. You're right… We need an angle. There's communal catharsis, but what else?"

"It's also part memorial. You know, for all of those that are lost. Maybe some of these people didn't even have proper…you know…ceremonies or acknowledgements for their loved ones. Maybe that'd drive them to share?" I offered.

"Lovely. I like that," he said, frantically jotting down notes. "And just, plain old fellowship." I smirked. "No, K, I'm not trying to work *Lord of the Rings* in here somehow…"

I couldn't help but derail his train of thought with laughter.

"Anyway," he said pointedly, "we keep the rehearsal schedule to a minimum because we don't want to take up too much of peoples' time, but it could be kind of awesome…don't you think? To share a space devoted to remembrance with these strangers that will, I *hope*, turn into a united cast."

"We're just going to have to find the right people," I said. "Open people."

We were both silent for a moment, racking our recent memory for possible candidates.

"They have to be truly awake," I heard her say. "Lincoln is the only one who's really awake."

But Isa wasn't here. And I wasn't with her in the neighborhood pool. I was here. With Lincoln. On my futon.

"What about Lenny?" I blurted, mostly to silence the voice in my head. Lincoln raised an eyebrow again. "Okay, so I know he lost his *pet*, not a *person*. But that's still a loss. We shouldn't discriminate. Chubbie was family to him."

"No, yeah. You're right," Lincoln wrote Lenny's name in his notebook. "And Lenny's a soulful guy. We need that. Oh—I could also ask Jon!"

"Oh no," I started. "His…grandma?"

Back in high school, Jon's grandma had lived with his parents because she was too sickly to be alone.

"Not yet," Lincoln explained. "But she's gotten a lot worse. She's in hospice now. She doesn't even recognize them anymore. That's definitely a loss."

"Definitely. That…sucks." My vocabulary was so ill-equipped to discuss painful topics.

I watched him add Jon's name to the list when it hit me. Dr. Mirza. Of *course*. She was the most open and collaborative person I knew. And she was no stranger to loss. She said it herself two years ago in her office.

"Dr. Mirza," I said. "She's a born storyteller. And she lost her first husband. I think she might be willing to share about it if I explain what we're trying to do."

Lincoln put down his pen and closed his notebook.

"That's a start, for sure," he said happily.

He beamed at me and leaned in for a kiss. Sometimes I was absolutely used to this—it was as familiar a sign of affection as F. Scott rubbing himself against my legs to greet me at the door. But other times, the butterflies in my stomach took flight. It was like it was the first time all over again. When would I ever get used to it? I didn't know who I was talking to, but it made me want to pray.

Please, God. Don't ever let me get used to this.

"I'll think of someone else to ask…" he said as we broke apart. "And you can take Lenny and Dr. Mirza. But wait—are you sure you don't mind helping with all of this? I know you've got grad school stuff—"

"Please," I said, "this is a lot more exciting than filling out applications."

"How's that going, by the way?" he asked, then instant regret spread across his face. "Sorry, no more school talk."

"No, it's fine," I started. "It's going…"

The truth was that it wasn't going anywhere. Not really. I let the Boston University deadline come and go. I knew it was a long shot anyway. That program required proficiency in at least one other language, and I barely made it out of high school Spanish alive. It was perfect for Julia, though. There was still Tufts and Hunters College. I started the application for University of Washington but gave up after a conversation with an admissions rep about the cost of tuition.

"To be honest," I said, fixating on picking a dried speck of curry from my apron. "I got an email reminder from one of the schools yesterday and looking at it, I just didn't feel excited. I felt…I don't know. Tired. Just not, 'Yes! I can't wait to see if I'll get in.' I mean, I should feel that, right? Especially if I'm going to take out a ridiculous loan to go to one of these places… And I don't even know what I *want* when I get there, you know?"

He was hanging on every word I said, giving me the permission to purge all the indecision that had been mounting in me for the whole of last semester.

"Like, my friend, Julia—she wants to be a curator and live abroad, and I know she'll do it. But that track just doesn't really like me. There's the professor route; I could be like Dr. Mirza. I mean, that woman is, like, an icon. And she's so enthralled in her work. In cultivating these young minds. I thought I wanted to be just like her. If I just copycatted her path, then maybe I'd grow up to have that same air of…I don't know…unfaltering confidence. A *purpose*. But now that it's down to the wire; now that it's actually time to choose, I just feel sort of lackluster about it all. Does that even make sense?"

Lincoln nodded. "You make perfect sense," he affirmed.

I shrugged. "Well, while I'm spilling my guts, here's a Gap Years filler for ya—I see a therapist. And now that I'm thinking about it…this is all stuff that I should be bringing to him. At least he gets paid to listen to my rambling."

***

"Before we begin, I wanted to, hopefully, ease your mind by saying that we don't have to discuss the event that brought you in to see me. Not today. If you don't feel comfortable doing so."

Dr. McPherson looked too young to be a doctor. But he was too well-spoken to be too young. He had the degrees on the wall to prove that he earned his keep as a psychiatrist and his card read:

Dr. Daniel Leroy McPherson
Clinical Psychiatrist
CBT & EMDR Certified
Medication Management

I had no idea what half of those words meant. But I knew I had to be there—that was the deal I struck with my parents. They would pick me up from the hospital and keep me enrolled in school, so long as I lived at their house and went to therapy. The "incident was too scary not to take every precaution" they said, although I knew I would never try it again. I didn't want to go back to Vanderbilt. When you're about to turn 19 they don't put you in the teen psych ward. They put you in with the adults. I was the youngest one there; the only one to celebrate their 19th birthday while in hospital-issue pajamas.

"I'm not going back to the hospital," I told him bluntly. "That's why I'm here."

He nodded and wrote something down on his legal pad.

"You were only there for…what was it…" he shifted through the papers that were contained in the file folder on his lap. A file folder especially devoted to "Patient Katie 'K' Elizabeth Statham." "A week? In mid-December?"

I nodded and he went back to his legal pad, adding to his notes. I took the halt in conversation as an opportunity to observe his office. Music City Psychiatric Associates was located in the gentrified part of midtown. I was comforted by the fact that the office was simply an old Tudor converted into cozy, bright offices rather than a sad looking gray building void of sunlight. Dr. McPherson had a bay window offering a view of a café, record store, and bike shop below. As it was now springtime, dogwood trees bloomed along the street where the office resided, offering patients a bit of whimsy before tackling their demons.

On his floor to ceiling built-in bookcases, he had volume upon volume of expensive, important looking medical books. The DSM-IV sat thickly on a shelf directly behind his mahogany desk, which made me wonder what brand of messed up I was and if all the answers were within those pages. But what allowed me to relax—slightly—was the evidence that a real human with a personality, a life, and a history inhabited the office. I saw an empty Starbucks cup in the wire trash can beside his desk, framed photos of himself smiling broadly with a handsome Asian man, and multicolored crystals lining the windowsill.

"Do you believe those have any, like, real metaphysical powers?"

Dr. McPherson shifted his gaze to his windowsill then leaned forward to grab one of the stones. Examining it in his hand, he chuckled lightly and replied, "Ah, no. My husband just knows that I like to collect. I'm not even sure what each of them are called, truth be told."

"That one is rose quartz," I said.

It was the same soft pink as the rose quartz Isa used to keep in the center of her collection. Rose quartz attracts love. It improves self-esteem. It aids in forgiveness.

"Is metaphysics something that interests you?" he asked.

"No."

I began to pick at my cuticles. He noticed.

"Here," he said, handing me the rose quartz. "Sometimes giving your hands a job can alleviate restlessness."

I took note of the rose quartz's ridges and grooves. Smooth in places but rough in others.

"They don't want you back either, you know," he said, studying me as he leaned back in his chair. "The hospital. It's uncomfortable on purpose. They don't want you to be dependent. The goal of the mental health professional, myself included, K, is to help the patient arrive at a place of stability."

A flash of the ice-cold seats on the prison-style toilets danced across my vision. Little blue pills in small, white paper cups. The sensation of eyes on me at all times. The dreaded afternoon community circle: the group therapy session where I never said a word. The fact that the Natalie Wood biography my parents bought me for my birthday had to be unwrapped by the guards and cleared of any potentially harmful objects hidden inside. Although, in a sick way, the idea of death by bookmark still amuses me.

"I thought you said we didn't have to talk about it," I said lamely, flipping the rose quartz around and around in my hand.

"Absolutely." He nodded. "Let's switch gears, then. Can you tell me about your family? What is your relationship like with your parents?"

"We're not really close," I said automatically. "They aren't artist-types, so they think I'm on another planet most of the time."

"Is this something they've expressed to you in the past? This inability to relate?"

"No," I admitted. "But they just…they have a pretty limited worldview."

"Can you elaborate?"

"Well…"

I shifted my weight in the oversized armchair that faced Dr. McPherson's desk. I always found it impossible to put words to a dynamic that had always simply *been* there. I thought about the gigantic teddy bear my dad brought to the opening night of *Guys and Dolls*. I remembered how my parents both showed up at the hospital every single day during visiting hours…and how most days, I was the only patient to receive a visitor at all. Maybe I was being hard on them. I really didn't have a *bad* childhood, just two parents with whom I shared a disconnected relationship. But doesn't every kid feel the same way? I knew it could be a lot worse. There were people living without one or both of their parents. There were kids like Lincoln and Isa. Isa…

"I don't know…" I tried again. "It's just, like, for instance—my mom thinks that my 'suicide ideation' is a product of reading Sylvia Plath. But words on a page had nothing to do with…you know…what I did. Those words just made me feel close to…my…um…"

"Your friend? The one who passed?" Dr. McPherson nudged.

I nodded and considered pulling on the hangnail that dangled from my right thumb but knew I wouldn't get away with it with him watching.

Yes, my friend who "passed"—the person that I pushed away. So far away that I may have pushed her out of her own life.

But I didn't say that.

I had no desire to follow in the footsteps of the deranged artists of the past. I just wanted to rebuild a bond. To Isa. To myself. I wanted words for the budding black hole in the pit of my chest.

"And anyway," I said. "I don't strictly read authors that died in some tragic way. Jane Austen is my favorite. And she's completely different, stylistically. If my mom ever took the time to *ask* me what I'm reading, she'd know that."

"How does it feel to move back in with your parents?" he prodded.

"It's suffocating," I said flatly. "But I don't want to be back in the dorms. I don't want a roommate."

"Would you prefer to live alone?"

"Ideally, yes. But after... My parents would never go for it."

He paused for a moment, carefully scrutinizing my mannerisms as if they told a story.

"It's not out of the realm of possibility," he said. "We start by meeting twice a week. You commit to showing up, *opening up*, like you have been today. Perhaps you—and your parents, with the backing of my recommendation—could consider having you live on your own in the upcoming school year."

At the suggestion of freedom, I smiled for the first time in months.

"I'd like to assign you some homework, if you don't mind," he said, now filling out an appointment reminder card with the date and time of our next visit.

Was he going to make me memorize the suicide help hotline or something? What kind of "homework" did therapists give out?

"Since you're a reader—and one that appreciates the classics, I take it—I'd love for you to take a stab at *Frankenstein* by Mary Shelley."

"*Frankenstein*?" I was flabbergasted.

"Society has spun this work into something you would find in a kitschy Halloween store. But at its core, *Frankenstein* is Shelley's examination on the human condition. She grapples with the dilemma of creation—who deserves the right to create, who doesn't. Who decides who or what lives or dies?" he explained.

I had a mantra— "I'll read anything that is recommended to me by a person who's smarter than me." Dr. McPherson definitely met the criteria.

"Why I'm prescribing it to you is because I believe you and Shelley are trying to answer some of the same questions. And I bet you, like most before they read the novel, assume that 'Frankenstein' is the name of the monster. It's not. Frankenstein is the scientist."

"So, who is the monster?" I asked.

"Precisely. That's the question."

A doctor that "prescribed" classic literature... Even if he later piled Zoloft on top of the script, I knew I liked Dr. McPherson after that.

***

"You don't have to do that," Lincoln said.

"What?"

"Be all apologetic for telling me things like that." He took my hand. "I *want* to know. Gap Years, remember? I'm not gonna freak out because you see a therapist. I've been to a therapist too."

I had forgotten, but that was right—Isa and Lincoln were dragged into family counseling prior to their parents' split as a sort of hail Mary.

"But would you be freaked out if I told you that I had to see this therapist because I...because I spent some time at Vanderbilt? What about if I said that I take pills now?" I muttered.

Only my parents and Dr. McPherson knew that fun fact.

"Vanderbilt?"

"I tried."

He nodded, understanding without a need for further detail. It was a grim sort of club for those that had experienced the fog. The idea of simply...*ending it* was never far from your mind.

"What kind of pills do you take?" he asked.

He was still holding my hand. *A good sign,* I thought.

"Zoloft. For depression. My therapist doesn't think I'll need it, like, for*ever*. But for now...it's kind of what I need to have a normal day," I said.

It felt good. It felt really, really good to just say it out loud: "I take Zoloft for depression" not because I *am* a depressive. I am not depression itself. I *have* depression. You aren't the flu when you catch it...

"Well, first, I'm not freaked out," Lincoln said, giving my hand an affirming squeeze. "And second, I think that's pretty cool...pretty *brave* of you to do something about it."

I shrugged. "Brave" and K Statham, in my book, never shared a sentence. Or even the same page for that matter.

"Look, K," Lincoln pushed, "I told you what my coping mechanisms were. It sounds like, to me anyway, that you're being a grown ass adult about this stuff. I wasted so much time self-destructing."

"I just thought that maybe it would be weird for you because of your mom..." I mentioned, holding my breath until I knew I hadn't overstepped.

"Nah." Lincoln rubbed the back of his neck and looked up at the ceiling. He sighed. "My mom...she's irresponsible with her...uh...medicines. You're not like that. It's not even a fair comparison."

We looked at each other for a second. After years of bottling everything up, I was almost on a high. Maybe I would be really reckless and just spill everything—lay it all out on the table—tonight. There was no time like the present, right? But I dismissed that idea almost as soon as it popped into my head. Sharing all my cards seemed like a masochistic scheme to test how quickly he'd run for the door.

"What does it feel like?" he asked after a beat.

"The Zoloft?"

Lincoln nodded and pushed his glasses further up the bridge of his nose. I loved when he did that.

"Well, it's like...you've always needed glasses, right?"

"Right."

"And when you finally tried on a pair, was it like the whole world opened up?"

"I can see the leaves now. Every single one. I didn't even know what I was looking at before," he explained.

"Exactly. It's the details. You can see the thing for what it is. That's what it's like—your world opens up."

"It's more clear."

"It's more clear," I repeated.

"That's what it's like being with you," he said softly, taking my hand again.

We leaned in towards each other, but I couldn't stuff my sarcasm down long enough to make contact.

"I'm an antidepressant? How romantic."

"It could be worse!" he justified. "I could have compared you to a laxative."

"You provoke me to move…just like the gentle nudge my bowels get from MiraLAX."

We both cry-laughed for way too long. Even if I did thoroughly enjoy his soft lips and the feel of his fingers through my hair, there was nothing as sweet as Friendship Mode.

Later, with stomachs full of a fairly component attempt at Aloo Gosht and playing cards scattered all over my kitchen-table-in-a-box from Walmart, we found ourselves circling back to the capstone project. I thought I was depleted of brain power after Lincoln insisted he teach me how to play Gin Rummy, (I pleaded with him to settle for Go Fish—I'm hopeless at card games) but my vigor for this project shocked me. Maybe I actually did miss theater?

"So, everyone will write about their own experiences, and we'll kind of talk through what we've all written during the first rehearsal?" I asked.

"Yup, exactly," Lincoln agreed. "I just want raw material before we shape it into anything."

"And you're going to write something too?"

"Yeah, I was planning on it. But I won't steal your moment in the spotlight if that's what you're thinking," he teased.

I gave him a deadpan stare.

"No, that's not what I'm worried about. I'm just wondering… We're both going to talk about Isa?"

He looked down at the table, seemingly trying to find his response mixed in with the Queen of Hearts and the Ace.

"We have different perspectives, so—"

"No, I know," I interrupted. "What I'm getting at is—we're both going to be bringing up the same…tough stuff. And if we're opening up these wounds again…"

I couldn't believe I was even tossing this idea around in my own mind, let alone voicing it. Lincoln could do that; he could pull out in you the sorts of thoughts and imaginings that you once believed were completely ludicrous. He could make you believe they were possible, and you were ready.

"Well, if we're going to talk about it all again," I continued, "then maybe it's time to find out what really happened to Isa."

I glanced down at his hands. He was still holding his deck of cards. It was barely visible if you didn't know what you were looking for, but I could see the black inked daisy peeking out from under his sleeve.

"I was hoping you'd say that."

***

"K? Can you talk?"

It was the first time we had spoken since he left for Columbia University back in September. Five full months with no more than a text or two passed between us. Who's fault was it? We simply lost touch. It's completely normal for friends to fade from your life when one or the other goes away to college. But that wasn't it—there was always more than meets the eye between me and Lincoln.

"K, there's been an…accident," he said when I asked him why he'd reached out—why after five months—he was calling me at 10:00 pm on a Sunday night.

Surely it wasn't to randomly wish me a happy Thanksgiving. Thanksgiving was four days ago. And I knew he wasn't back in town. He said all those months ago that he wouldn't come back to Tennessee until right before Christmas. Did he want to talk about Blair? He must have heard.

"It's Isa," he continued in a dry, tortured voice, "She…relapsed and they found her… She's… Oh god, K."

He started weeping uncontrollably. I sank down to the floor of my dorm. I knew before he uttered the words. The words that set everything into motion:

"She's dead."

That was it. The verdict was final. Isa would never get married. She would never graduate college. She would never have children or buy a house or travel the world or learn another language. She wouldn't tell fortunes or teach anyone else how to hold tree pose. She would never write another song or play her guitar. Isa would never go to Switzerland. Isa would never even turn 21.

I sat like a statue in the pew next to Lincoln a week later. We were in the front row where the family was supposed to be seated. Lincoln hadn't said a word, but wordlessly took my hand and wouldn't let me go since he first saw me arrive at the church. Dad was solemn in the pew behind us. Mom wasn't there. She chose the other funeral that Sunday. I couldn't even feel the impact of Lincoln's palm pressed against mine. It didn't occur to me how weird it was to be so physically close to him after losing contact for almost half a year. I was numb and the fog had set in after that phone call.

The service was a blur—I tried not to think about what was in the casket as it was lifted and carried away. I tried to shut down any urge I had to cry. I didn't deserve to mourn like the rest of them. I made my choice last year before any of this ever happened, and I had chosen to forget about her. Maybe if I had made a different choice, maybe none of us would have been there. But I tried not to think about that too—I just tried not to think.

Afterwards, Lincoln finally spoke.

"Do you want to go back to the house? There's food."

I shook my head.

"Can I see you later?" he asked.

I nodded.

Dad and I drove home. I didn't cry. I didn't say a word. He must have known that I was in no mood to talk, but he sniffled and wiped his eyes the whole way home. I envied him for being able to express authentic emotion. He had no blame to share.

We met on the swings later that night and this time *I* brought the ice cream. Lincoln brought a flask.

"They're cremating her tomorrow," he said flatly after taking a swig and passing me the flask.

I took it but stared into my mostly untouched and melting pint of mint chocolate chip.

"I thought she was going to be…"

"My parents couldn't agree. Mom wanted her in the family plot with Gramps and Mimi. Me and Dad knew that she would rather be scattered. A viewing followed by cremation was the expensive compromise. Oh yes—" he said when he saw my look of disbelief, "they're *still* arguing about money."

We were both still in our funeral blacks. It infuriated me that Tamara had apparently taken charge of organizing the funeral, insisting on a traditional service with traditional attire. Isa hated black. Rainbow was her favorite color.

"I think that's best," I said. "I don't know where she is, but she wasn't in that…box."

"Yeah."

"How are you?" I asked suddenly. "Can I ask that? I mean, we haven't talked in—"

"I know. I—"

"Why haven't you called?" I blurted.

I didn't realize how hurt I was by our lack of communication until we were back on the swings. I never thought I would live to see the day when I would *miss* high school, but…

"Why haven't *you*?" he shot back.

It was one of the only times I'd ever sensed even a fraction of irritation in his voice. Irritation and, undoubtedly, hurt. And it was directed at me.

Recognizing my shock, he took a deep breath then started again, "I'm sorry. I—I'm just. I'm sorry."

"That's okay." I took a drink then began to swing lightly. "Do you like New York?"

"Not really." I nodded and waited for him to continue. "It's tough," he offered. "Living in the city. It's a lot different than the suburbs. Sometimes it's too much. At first it was great. But, that magic…I guess…is…short-lived."

"Do you see Broadway shows all the time?" I asked, attempting, but failing, to sound light and form a faint smile.

"Sometimes we get comps."

If this was a conversation we were having a year ago, we would both be fangirling over everything he'd seen, what show he thought was going to win a Tony, and who he met at the backstage door. But this was a conversation we were having in our funeral blacks and Isa was gone.

"Do you have friends there?"

I noticed that, aside from Jon Seong and myself, there was no one there for him at the funeral. Where were his Columbia people?

"I have a girlfriend. Her name's Samantha."

It was as though the wind had been knocked out of me. I stopped swinging and began to stir my soupy ice cream. A *girlfriend*? I'd never known Lincoln to have a girlfriend. Of course, it was none of my business but. It was. *Odd*. I felt lightheaded and for a second, imagined that I might pass out. I had taken my iron pills that morning. I should be fine. So why did I feel so strange?

"She didn't come, obviously," he added.

"Wh—why? Why not?" I stuttered, trying to act as calm as possible.

Don't pass out. Don't pass out. This is not about you. Don't make this about you. Don't pass out.

"She didn't know. That I…*had*…a sister," he admitted. His tone was thick with pain. "No one in New York knows. I told them all…I told them all that I was an only child. I was…*embarrassed* by her."

I let him sob and said nothing. I didn't touch him—I didn't even pat him on the back. I stared at the AstroTurf, wishing I could feel. Wishing I could rewind the clock. This had to be a mistake. This entire day—this entire week. There was a mistake. Isa couldn't be dead. She was only *20 years old*. How can someone be alive one second and gone the next? It wasn't fair; it wasn't supposed to be this way. I wanted a second chance. I wanted to give Lincoln a second chance too. How had we screwed up so badly? How had we all failed her? How did it come to this?

Lincoln finally recovered and wiped his nose on his shirt sleeve.

"I have to make it up to her," he said, grimly. "I want to spread the ashes. Will you help me?"

I knew if anyone owed Isa anything, it was me. How could I say no? So, I nodded.

"Where?" I whispered, still fixating on the AstroTurf.

"Where else?"

I knew exactly what he meant—Switzerland.

"I'll go," I promised, meeting his eyes for the first time in a long time.

"I can't do it alone," he said.

The look he gave me—so full of unmasked sorrow—nearly provoked tears in my eerily dry eyes, but most certainly broke whatever was left of my heart.

"I know."

He took the flask from me, downed a large gulp, wiped his mouth, then after only a slight pause went back for another.

"Whoa, slow down," I said, but he ignored me.

"Can I tell you…what…happened?" he asked, seriously.

I knew it was an overdose and that she was found at some random apartment complex, but I didn't know the details. I assumed she was visiting, or maybe living, with one of her old friends from TCC. It was handled like an accident—that was what Lincoln had said over the phone. What more was there to say? Still, I nodded knowing that this was the role I was required to play—Lincoln's confidant.

"She was at some apartment complex. She was in the pool. The maintenance guy found her and…she was completely naked."

Skinny dipping was the first phrase that popped into my mind. Of course, she was skinny dipping.

"But she wasn't alone," he went on. "The leasing agent there said that she'd seen Isa before. She went there to visit this guy… Some actor in town. Steve Nowak."

The playground was spinning. Steve Nowak. *Steve Nowak. What?* How was that possible? Did he have something to do with it? A single dangling cross earring still embedded into my mind's eye. Steve, leaning against the doorframe— "Slow your roll, doll." Did Steve *hurt* her?

No no no no no no, I thought. *No no no no. No, Steve couldn't have been the last person to see her. To talk to her before she…*

It wasn't right. It couldn't—it *shouldn't* have ended this way. There must be a mistake.

"The police are questioning him," Lincoln said as I tried to breathe. "All we know now is that he was there, but he said he left before…anything happened. He said they were swimming, and they had an argument and he left. They found heroin, cocaine, alcohol, and Xanax in her system. There was no way she was going to make it. He said all they did was cocaine. I just want to know."

I vomited all over the AstroTurf.

"K, oh my god! I'm sorry, I shouldn't have told you. That was selfish of me. I'm so sorry," Lincoln repeated over and over again for the next 30 minutes.

I was in a complete sweat, but at least the ground seemed solid again. We sat on the slide, Lincoln's arm was around me and my head was in his lap. I was still too weak to stand.

"Do you want me to drive you home?" he asked, concerned.

I slowly sat up and shook my head. The last thing I wanted to do was face my parents—my mom in particular. We hadn't exchanged a civil word since we learned of the news. I put my head on Lincoln's shoulder and he rubbed my back.

"Just breathe," he instructed. "I'm so sorry."

He wasn't the one that should be apologizing, but how could I tell him that? I shut my eyes to block out the flurry of memories carouseling through my brain—me soaring over the dinner theater's proscenium, Isa kissing me cheek before I went backstage, and *Steve*—God, picturing his face provoked another wave of nausea to course through me—waltzing around in his Captain Hook mustache. What a cocky bastard. What a sick piece of garbage. I *hated* him almost as much as I hated myself.

It was a long time before either of us spoke again, but eventually, a plan was born. We needed to leave the playground and *do* something, but neither of us wanted to go home. I found myself walking to my car. Then, still in a daze, I was following Lincoln in that familiar forest green Subaru to the tattoo parlor. I should have paid more attention to the fact that the flask was empty by the time we left the swings—Lincoln had finished basically the entire thing by himself. But as he seemed more or less sober, I didn't think twice about it. I was in no state to look for warning signs.

"You draw something," Lincoln said, handing me his black notebook, open to a blank page. We sat in the lobby, waiting for our turn. I didn't stop to think about what we were doing. I just wanted to feel something. And I wanted it to hurt. I deserved for it to hurt. So, I drew a daisy. She loved daisies, and I would forever wear a daisy on my wrist because she would never be able to smell the daisies again.

"You ready?"

A large, hairy man with two sleeves of colorful tattoos beckoned Lincoln to take the chair first. Lincoln didn't flinch as the artist bore the needle into his wrist. Perhaps he was meditating or praying as he stared up at the ceiling, but he did not appear to be present in the room, much less occupying space in the chair. Seated across the small lobby were a group of guys. I didn't recognize them, but one was wearing a TCC sweatshirt. They were laughing over some video one of them had pulled up on his iPhone. I thought about how Isa went to TCC, before she dropped out anyway, and that made me wonder what it would take for me to ever laugh again.

When Lincoln was done, the hairy artist bandaged him up and sent him back to wait in the lobby.

"It wasn't that bad," was all he said when I took his place in the chair.

"Same thing?" the hairy artist, who's name I immediately forgot, asked.

I nodded and stuck out my arm.

The needle made contact with my skin but rather than acknowledging the deep, gnawing sting, I thought about how my wrist would never be the same again. It would always be marked. And of course, if I were in my sober mind, I would have known that I had a choice in this matter. I knew my mother would call it "self-mutilation" because she didn't approve of tattoos. I didn't care. That night, sitting in the tattoo parlor, it didn't feel like I had a choice. Just like we don't have a choice when it comes to the marks and scars that people leave behind when they leave us. Isa had marked me. I never stood a chance at remaining the same after she had stepped into my life. Why did I even try to pretend otherwise?

"Almost done," the unnamed tattoo artist said encouragingly. "You're doing great for your first time."

The guys in the far corner of the tattoo parlor were gawking loudly at something else now. The guy in the TCC sweatshirt grabbed the iPhone out of his friend's hand and began to scroll for himself.

"Dude. Shit. No way!" TCC sweatshirt said, eyes bulging out of his head.

"What? Dude, gimme my phone!"

The owner of the iPhone swung for the phone, but missed when sweatshirt guy backed away, still engrossed in whatever he was reading.

"Have you been on Facebook today?" he asked.

The others looked at each other, confused.

"Bro," sweatshirt continued, "that chick that we got that—" whatever he said, he said it in a low, inaudible voice. "—from.

Remember? It was just like, what—three weeks ago? At Andre's party?"

The cluster of guys bobbed their heads.

"That girl is *dead*," sweatshirt finished, holding the phone's screen up for the others to examine.

"Brooooo, shit. You know I banged her, right? Chick was *dirtyyyy*," one of the guys, a muscular jock with a Budweiser baseball cap, said.

The rest of them hooted with laughter, play-fighting in that obnoxious way that even fully grown men do.

"Dude, you screwed a dead chick!" one of them said.

"No, bro! Obviously, she wasn't *dead* when she blew me."

The comment sparked another chorus of whoops and hollers. From my vantage point in the tattoo artist's chair, I couldn't get a good look at what happened next, but I heard Lincoln ask with unearthly calmness, "Hey, who are you guys talking about?"

Budweiser cap said, "Oh, shit, do you know this girl too? Isa or Elsa or something like that?"

"You go to TCC, man?" Sweatshirt asked.

"No, no, I don't. But 'that chick' is my sister."

And then they weren't play-fighting anymore. Lincoln had, presumably, thrown a punch right in Budweiser's face. The garish redness oozing out of his nose was all I could see.

"Whoa! Whoa!" the tattoo artist shouted, turning suddenly away from his focus on my wrist. The tattoo pen was still buzzing in his hand.

I leapt from the chair and ran over to Lincoln, reaching him just after one of the guys gave him a rough shove.

"Lincoln! What the hell!" I yelled.

The group of guys were shouting profanities at us, and one said, "You're sis's a druggie!"

The tattoo artist demanded that all of us get out of his shop before he called the police. I pulled Lincoln out of the door, and we turned sharply around the side of the building before the guys could see where we went. We stood silent and breathing heavily against the brick of the tattoo shop as we heard the guys burst out of the front door and head across the street for their car.

"That guy was a little pussy!" Budweiser said to his friends before they piled into the car and sped off.

"Abe," I breathed, "what were you *thinking*? Those guys! They could have really messed you up!"

He sank to the ground and put his head in his hands.

"The things they were saying about her…" he said, choking back sobs.

I joined him on the asphalt. I'd left my peacoat in the tattoo parlor, along with my purse and my cell phone. I was freezing and I had no idea what time it was. A tiny trail of bright red blood trickled down my arm. My tattoo was left unfinished. I stared at the curvy black lines, so alien against my otherwise unblemished skin. It was an abstract flower, to say the least, but it would have to do. It would never fade away or bleed off in the shower. That imperfect daisy, slightly wilted looking, had taken up permanent residence on my wrist.

Finally, after several minutes of listening to Lincoln cry, I started to shiver violently, and I knew I had to go back in to gather my belongings. The tattoo artist was not pleased to see me but handed me my purse and peacoat without a fuss.

"Put some Vaseline on that," he said gruffly, not offering to finish it or even bandage it up.

"Lincoln, let's go," I said when I returned, standing over his crumpled form.

We walked silently to our cars and embraced before parting.

"Text me when you get home," he said weakly.

"Okay," I agreed.

But when I got home, I realized that my phone was gone. It wasn't in my purse. It wasn't in my peacoat pocket.

Damnit, I thought when it hit me—my phone was still at the tattoo parlor. I had left it out on the coffee table while I waited on Lincoln in the lobby.

I was far too tired to think about driving back—the shop was probably closed by then anyway. I fell into a fitful sleep, on top of my comforter with all my clothes on and was only awoken by my mom pounding on the bedroom door the next morning.

"What? What?" I asked, groggily rubbing sleep from my eyes.

"Lincoln's here to see you!" my mom said through the door. "And it's 11:00 am. Time to get up!"

"Okay, *okay*! I'll be down in a minute!" I called back.

Ignoring the now crusty, dried trail of blood from my half-finished tattoo, I pulled my funeral dress over my head and flung open my dresser in search of something to throw on. I grabbed my dad's old University of Chicago hoodie, a pair of sweatpants, quickly dressed, then headed down the stairs. Lincoln was standing outside on the front porch, pacing, and running his hands through his shaggy hair. He looked utterly deranged.

"Linc—" I began when I stepped outside, but he pulled me into a smothering embrace.

It was clear that he had been crying and possibly didn't sleep. His eyes were red.

"Why didn't you text when you got home? I thought you were—I thought you were—"

He held me and wept into my shoulder.

"Please don't fucking do that ever again, K. Please. I thought you were…dead."

I put my arms around him and glanced back at the front door. My mom was watching us from inside. She knew she'd been caught, so she scurried away. It was all too overwhelming.

"I left my phone at the tattoo place," I admitted. "I'm sorry. I didn't think."

Lincoln broke our hug then stepped away and sat on the front stoop. I sat next to him, but we didn't touch. We didn't even look at each other—just focused on the rustling oaks in my parents' front yard. It was too beautiful of a day for these big emotions. Did the world not get the memo? Isa was dead.

"I love you," he said, still not meeting my eyes.

"I...love you too," I said simply.

What did he mean? What did *I* mean? I don't know. Maybe he didn't either. In any case, we just let it be.

"I don't remember the last time I said that to Isa," he confessed and wiped his face with the sleeve of his coat.

"I don't think I ever said it," I replied.

Birds were chirping and zooming from tree to tree. The sound of someone starting up their lawnmower in the distance. A frosty breeze sent a chill through me, and I pulled the sleeves of my dad's hoodie over my hands.

"I think I'm gonna go now," he said, standing. "I'll call you when I'm back in New York."

"Okay," I said.

I don't remember meeting his eyes before he left, just watching him walk down the driveway. He climbed onto his bike, and he drove off.

He did call me when he got back to New York, but we didn't speak again for three years.

✳✳✳

Lincoln pulled out the black notebook once again.

"Where do we start?" I asked.

"In her bedroom," he said, as if he had been mulling this over for quite some time and had been waiting to be asked.

"At your mom's or your dad's?"

"Dad's. He hasn't touched it since she died. That's why Dad won't move. Whitney's been nagging him about a new place since they got married, but he doesn't want to go through Isa's stuff."

I couldn't blame Mr. DeLuca. But Whitney had a point too—I wouldn't want to be the new wife living in the house with all those ghosts from the past. Isa's bedroom was like a memorial right across from the second story landing and I'm sure Whitney had to put up artwork to cover the various holes that Tamara created in the walls over the years...she was known to throw things.

"Have you even been in there?"

"No." He hesitated. "Well, once. To get the guitar. I don't *want* to, but there might be something in there that could help us. A diary or something. If she even kept a diary. Do you know?"

The turquoise moleskin. She didn't keep a diary, but she had her songs.

"All of my power is in here," she said.

"She had a notebook," I told him, although it felt like a transgression. "She wrote song lyrics."

"What? Really?"

I nodded.

"Did she ever play them for you? I had no idea she did that," Lincoln said.

I couldn't tell if he was impressed or upset that there was something, along with the never-ending list of other unknowns, that he didn't know about his sister. Perhaps it was both. Whenever I found out something new about Isa, it was usually both.

"No," I said, "But I read one once. A long time ago, obviously."

He didn't ask for details, for which I was grateful.

"You know what we could do..." he began. "It might be a shot in the dark, but we could visit what's-her-name."

Immediately, I knew who he was referring to. "Shot in the dark" was the giveaway.

"Is she still in business?"

"What, do I look like I'm a frequent visitor of Sisters of the Moon?"

Sisters of the Moon was a metaphysical bookstore owned by "Empress" Leonora Pearl. It was the city's one-stop shop for crystals and any book you could ever want if you had a question about past life regeneration or the phases of the moon. Leonora also provided Reiki healing, palm readings, tarot, and chakra balancing services...in addition to hosting bachelorette parties. Because, I guess, every business in this city was required to these days. Lincoln and I knew Leonora through Isa, our resident self-proclaimed "mentalist."

"I guess there's no harm in trying," I thought out loud.

Lincoln jotted "search bedroom" and "talk to the psychic lady" down in his notebook. Something about seeing a bullet point list devoted to unpacking the way in which my former best friend met her demise made me dizzy. I stood uneasily and announced that I had to go to the bathroom. Shutting the door behind me, I let out a long exhale.

In for five. Out for five. In for five. Out for five.

My heart rate steadied as I counted my breaths. This wasn't going to be easy, but this had to be done. How were Lincoln and I ever going to have a shot at a decent relationship if this massive unanswered question stood between us? How would *I* ever be able to truly—once and for all—move on with my life in general if I didn't at least try? Three years. It had been three years.

I can handle this, I thought as I opened my medicine cabinet to dig for my iron pills. I splashed some water on my face and stared at myself in the small, oval mirror above the sink.

"You can handle this. Hard doesn't mean bad," I whispered to my reflection.

Noticing that my curls were particularly crazed on the left side of my head, I reached for my hairbrush to smooth them down. But when I did, I gasped and dropped the brush. It clattered loudly onto the tiled floor.

"You okay in there?" Lincoln called.

"F—Fine."

Trembling, I knelt down to pick up the brush. It was no mistake—there were strands of long, wavy white-blonde hairs protruding from the bristles. But Isa had never used that brush. Isa had never been in my apartment. Isa was dead. I squeezed my eyes shut.

In for five. Out for five. In for five. Out for five. You're okay. You're okay.

When I opened my eyes, I threw the brush in the trash. I would get a new one.

Mistaking my ashen complexion for weariness, Lincoln said when I emerged from the bathroom, "I should probably head back to the bachelor pad. I know you've got to be up bright and early to enable the caffeine addicts of this community."

He drew me into his arms, and only then did I notice that I was still shaking.

"Are you cold? Where's your thermostat? Let's turn up the heat."

I wasn't cold, I was petrified, and I wanted him to stay. I clung to him even more tightly and being that he was essentially an entire foot taller than me, he kissed the top of my head.

"You know, there's something else we have to work on," he said, and I glanced up at him, questioning. "We have to work on dating."

I smiled and allowed the fear to melt away as I gave myself permission to bask in those hazel eyes. That grin that he wore—that grin was for *me*.

"Next week, I'm taking you on a *real* date," he promised.

Without a doubt, I would eventually have to tell Lincoln my part in all of this. It was all going to come out, sooner or later. I just hoped he would forgive me.

10.

The Whole Entire Rainbow

"**It'll do you good** to interact with the plebeians," Lincoln teased as we scoped out the Junior/Senior courtyard for a table. "Stardom is getting to your head."

Earlier that day, Ms. Morris posted the cast list for the fall 2008 production of *The Sound of Music*. I had been cast as a secondary character, Liesl—the "Sixteen Going on Seventeen" Von Trapp, while Jon was Captain Von Trapp and Blair, resuming her reign as Queen Bee of the Drama Club, landed the lead.

"She's not even the caliber of a poor man's Julie Andrews," Isa decreed when she saw the list. "I'm sure Ms. Morris just doesn't want to miss out on the funding from Blair's dad. Cheer up, little bird. Politics are a part of life. You're still a star."

When Blair was put in the ensemble for *West Side Story* the year before, she promptly dropped out of the play, citing that she was too busy auditioning for film agencies to commit to rehearsals. Consequently, the $2,000 check that her dad usually signed for the drama club's Comedy O'clock fundraiser was MIA as well. This was by no means a negative for me—without Blair's superiority complex dominating the rehearsal room, I was able to flourish as Maria. Although perhaps not-so-great a consequence in the long-term was that without facing Blair's comment head-on, I was able keep kicking the can with the question of, "Who am I and what part does my ethnicity play in the theater world?"

As for Isa, she opted to skip auditions for the first time since sixth grade. She claimed *The Sound of Music* was hands-down the biggest "snooze fest" of all Golden Age musicals and she'd rather "gouge her eyes out with a nail file than play a nun." When Lincoln encouraged her to at least help out with hair and makeup as it was our final opportunity to be in a high school musical together, she declined. Insisting that she needed to start taking her future seriously, she said she couldn't waste her senior year playing make-believe. And her idea of taking the future seriously was "apprenticing" at Sisters of the Moon.

"K, you have to check out this psychic shop," Isa had begged me the entire summer before my junior year. That summer wasn't like the preceding summer. Lincoln was accepted into the Sewanee Young Writers Conference and my parents enrolled me in ACT prep classes that met twice weekly. I also began babysitting for the neighborhood kids to save up for gas money in anticipation of finally getting my license and inheriting my dad's old BMW. Meanwhile, Isa was left to her own devices. We didn't see much of each other and when we did hang out, she talked of nothing but Sisters of the Moon and her new friends—a group of college kids she had met at an indie music festival.

"Friends" seemed like a loose term to me; they were more like random people with whom she could smoke with, listen to music, and get free booze from without breaking into her parents' liquor cabinet. I guess I would've had a clearer idea of what they were like, had I accepted her invitation to go to that music festival in the park...but I had to babysit. So, I spent the majority of my free time regretting that I didn't have the guts to bail on Mrs. Greer and her twin toddlers and join her. Maybe if I did, I wouldn't have had to grapple with the jealousy that impaired me every time Isa would talk about the parties she attended without me.

My parents sensed my discontent, but my mom's only method of comfort was to repeat, "You and Isa are on different tracks in life." Interpretation: Mom thought Isa wouldn't get accepted into college and

I would; I was on the path to success while Isa was likely to wind up flipping burgers. Admittedly, it'd be a true feat to be accepted into college if one didn't even attempt an application…

"Mr. DeLuca?"

Ms. Morris stood at the end of our picnic table and Lincoln, who was in the process of bringing a turkey sandwich to his mouth, froze.

"Ms. M?"

"I need to speak with you. About the play?"

Isa and I exchanged looks then watched Lincoln trot after Ms. Morris as she walked briskly back to her office.

"What's that all about, do you think?" I asked.

Ms. Morris rarely left the arts and humanities wing of the school—calling the rest of the building the "savage wild west."

"Probably some top-secret director-assistant director banter," Isa speculated before popping the can of her Dr. Diet Pepper.

A typical lunch for Isa consisted of a Dr. Diet Pepper, scraps of whatever she picked from my or Lincoln's trays, and the occasional Snickers bar. This was because she had gotten into the habit of ditching school a few minutes into lunch so she could meet up with her new friends. We said nothing. Lincoln rarely interfered with Isa's life choices, knowing full well how headstrong she was. And I didn't want to be accused of nagging.

I never took her up on her offer to come with, fearful that an unexcused absence would send my GPA into a downward spiral at the most critical time in my educational career—but I always wished I'd said yes after the fact. I could sense her fading away and that scared me.

Lincoln's shoulders were uncharacteristically hunched when he plodded back to our table. Jon Seong—who rarely had time to actually eat a sit-down lunch those days with all his extracurriculars and the daunting task of applying to pre-med programs—clapped him on the back.

"Ms. Morris told me! Congrats!" he said and walked off.

But Lincoln seemed far from a celebratory mood—by the looks of it, he'd either just seen a ghost or had been expelled.

"Whelp..." he began when he slumped into his seat, "I'm now playing Rolf."

"*What*?" I gawked.

Isa laughed that husky laugh of hers, her eyes crinkling at the edges with nefarious amusement.

"Abe takes the stage at long last!" she announced, standing on her side of the bench, and raising her Diet Dr. Pepper in the air—an action that, to Lincoln's mortification, provoked many an unwelcome gaze.

"That new kid declined the role," Lincoln explained, evidently referring to Kyle Dumfries, the original name next to Rolf on this morning's cast list. "I have to *sing*. I haven't had to do that since middle school. And even then, it was a one-line solo."

"Hey, at least you'll have all your scenes with me," I said, grasping at straws to cheer him up. "You can look at me the whole time. Pretend like it's just us hanging out."

"Hanging out on a stage with the whole school watching," Lincoln said miserably and laid his head on the table, tufts of his shaggy hair landing dangerously close to his green beans.

"Wait a second," Isa said. "She wants you to be *Rolf*? That's K's love interest, right? The 'Sixteen Going on Seventeen' dude?" She let out a jubilant hoot. "You'll have to *kiss*?! Does Ms. M realize that's basically *incest*? She's really off her rocker now!"

Whose face turned a brighter shade of red—mine or Lincoln's—was anyone's guess.

"It's not that big of a deal, Isa," I muttered.

"What was it that Mr. Denny used to say in middle school drama?" Isa continued, barreling over my comment. "In *The Music Man*, remember? He said, 'I give up! Everyone just harmonize with whatever note Lincoln picks.'"

Lincoln rose from the table, dumped his uneaten lunch in the garbage, and walked back inside the building. We still had over twenty minutes left in our lunch period.

"You just made it worse."

"What?" Isa feigned innocence. "I was just messing with him. He's the college-bound talent of the family. So, he can't carry a tune? Boohoo."

Even though I'd heard her talk trash about Jason, Blair, and their respective cronies—hell, I'd even assisted her in rolling Blair's house on multiple occasions—that was the first time I got a taste of how cruel she could be. This was different because Lincoln did nothing to provoke nastiness. And we were supposed to be a trio, a team. Why drive a wedge between us? I didn't understand. Lincoln's sluggishness in AP English and Spanish 3 only added to my confusion. He didn't gush with me about MacBeth and when we got our Spanish quiz back, he didn't want to compare grades like we normally did. Isa had hurt his feelings. But why?

"I'm going to pass out," I told Isa as we huddled on top of a toilet seat in the girl's bathroom.

"Did you take your iron pill?" she whispered.

After several instances of vertigo at rehearsal, I had recently been diagnosed with anemia. I didn't know who loved reminding me to take my pills more—Isa or my mother. It aggravated me no matter whose mouth the question came from.

"Yes," I hissed. "I'm just freaking out a little because we're *supposed to be in eighth period, remember?*"

"Okay then, you'll be fine. Nerves are fake."

Lincoln and I were two months into *The Sound of Music* rehearsals and Isa was, on most days, nowhere to be found. She skipped lunch more frequently, which was the only opportunity the three of us had to hang out with rehearsals and piles of homework bogging us down (for me and Lincoln anyway). The first few weeks of rehearsals were rough; it was like pulling teeth to get Lincoln acclimated to his new function in the production. I'd never seen him so out of his element—stiff when we were blocked to be dancing, sweating when he had to hold a note without the backing of the track, and monotone when he delivered lines.

I took it upon myself to save the production from certain disaster—Lincoln was my best friend, after all. If Isa had the power to wreck his self-esteem, then I wanted to claim the ability to boost it back up. And I didn't want to embarrass myself up there either. I started having nightmares of Lincoln missing his cues because he was shaking in the wings, leaving me onstage to sing a flirtatious duet with an invisible Rolf. So, we started doing the handshake before every rehearsal.

"Break a leg. Don't make me beg… Drop a line and they'll whine…" we'd chant while incorporating the simplistic choreography. The rest of the cast thought we were weirdos, but I couldn't have cared less. Whatever would drag Lincoln out of his head and focused on basic human-to-human interaction was what I was determined to do. If that meant joining him in miming what was happening onstage like it was a telenovela while we waited for our scenes, then so be. We also secretly rewrote the lyrics to everyone else's songs:

> "Dead roses and dogs that are flea-bitten
> Broken kettles and moth-eaten mittens
> Brown paper packages containing G-strings
> These are a few of my favorite things"

By October, Lincoln and I were cutting up both onstage and off. We'd even essentially mastered the "traveling basket" lift in "Sixteen Going on Seventeen"—a complicated move that involved Lincoln swinging me in circles for several dizzying seconds and ended in a cradling position similar to carrying a bride over the threshold. We were having so much fun that I forgot to be annoyed that I had an objectively better Maria audition than Blair, and Lincoln forgot to be nervous. Even

Blair's patronizing "Look how cuuuuute they are," comments from the sidelines didn't deter us.

But I missed Isa. I missed her when she wasn't there to witness the first time we nailed the duet, causing Ms. Morris to jump out of her director's chair and yell, "THAT'S the kind of energy this play NEEDS!" We had been inseparable for so long that I physically felt her absence. The sound of Lincoln's laughter was missing something—it was missing Isa's husky notes to harmonize.

This was how I found myself skipping eighth period. I didn't want to lose her. I considered myself easily replaceable—any day now she would give up on asking me to hang out if I kept declining. So, I knew I had to say "sure" when I got the text:

Isa DeLuca [2:05pm]: Meet me in the bathroom. I'm taking you to meet the sisters of the Moon!

We heard the clack of heels against tile entering the bathroom and Isa plugged my nose to silence my conspicuous breaths. It had to be a teacher. What kid wore heels to school? We listened carefully as the woman turned on the facet, washed her hands, then pressed the button that brought the hand dryer roaring to life. A few click-clacks later, and she was gone.

"It's probably safe now," Isa said, standing so she could peek over the stall. "Yup, the coast is clear."

Clambering out of the stall clearing designed for one occupant, I caught a glimpse of myself in the mirror. In my sweater vest and antique barrette, I did not fit the typical mold of a school-skipping juvenile delinquent. Was I willing to risk ruining my squeaky-clean school record just to hang out with Isa? Yes. Just like I was prepared to do anything to give Lincoln back his confidence, I was prepared to do anything to maintain my friendship with Isa.

"We'll walk straight out the double doors and get into my car. I'm parked in the third row. Just don't hesitate," Isa instructed.

"It'll seem a little suspicious if we're both walking together without a hall pass," I acknowledged. "What do we say if someone sees us?"

"Nothing. Because they won't. Not if we go now."

She grabbed my hand, pulled me out of the bathroom, and down the hall before I could let out another protest. We speed walked with tunnel vision directed at the double doors straight ahead. A few feet from freedom, the door to the band room creaked open. By the grace of the harvest moon/the universe/whatever Isa worshiped, we were able to dive out the double doors with a second to spare. We had just walked right out of the school, and no one stopped us. As we casually drove out of the parking lot like it was perfectly acceptable, I was grateful that Lincoln and I didn't share eighth period. He would know for sure where I had gone, and he wouldn't have approved.

We were singing along to Radiohead's Kid A album ("severely underrated," according to Isa), when she paused to ask, "Hey, remember Jason?"

I snorted. I hadn't thought about Jason in years. "Jason Calbots? Sky Masterson Jason?"

"Yeah," Isa said nonchalantly.

"Umm…duh I remember him. Why?"

"No reason, really," she said, speeding through a green light. "I've just seen him around at a few house parties lately. He's at MTSU, you know. But he has a ton of friends at TCC."

I didn't know. And I didn't care.

"Please tell me he's got, like, a beer gut since it's probably too early for him to have a dad bod," I joked.

"Actually, he's kind of cool now."

"Psssh. Since when has 'neanderthal' ever been synonymous with 'cool'?"

Was an Isa imposter driving the Subaru? Was the real Isa tied up and locked in a closet somewhere?

"People change, K. You should be more open-minded," Isa lectured. "He wants to study environmental law now and he's super chill."

Super chill? What the hell did that mean?

"Anyway," she continued. "I think I want to make him my third."

"Huh?"

Now she was really speaking in code.

"My *third*. You know, the third penis on my list."

I was unaware that such a list existed.

"You mean a list of…guys that you've *slept* with?" I asked, completely unable to suppress my shock.

"Don't be such a prude, K. Yes, my Sexcapade List. But it's a list of *people*. I don't limit myself to masculine energy exclusively."

"So, wait, how many people are on your list? And—*what*? —I thought you said you've only been with what's-his-name? Tanner the tutor?"

"Tate," she corrected.

She merged into the other lane, cutting off the Honda Civic to our right and sped through a yellow just in time.

"And K, I keep telling you to come with me to these TCC parties! I stand corrected—I really thought there was no one in this town that got me, but I was wrong. I just needed an older crowd. I'm an old soul, anyway."

While that comment stung, I couldn't feel the depth of the hurt because my virtuous young mind was still fixated on The List.

"…who are the others?" I asked.

"Oh, just Farrah and Cam. Farrah and I were on shrooms so that was—oh K, it was poetry. Cam was just ehh…which is why I'm still on the hunt."

"SHROOMS? Like, *drugs*? How did you get shrooms?"

I pressed pause on her iPod. I needed answers, but I also felt like jumping out of the car. Maybe I would have considered it if we weren't on the freeway and miles away from school at that point.

"Relax, relax," Isa said with an air of condescension. "Do I need to remind you, young lady, that *weed* is a drug too? And *alcohol*? Hmmm? Raise your hand if you're 21 in this car…"

I hated to admit it, but she had a point.

"Okay, but, shrooms just seems…hardcore."

She snorted. "Please, K. It's really not. Trust me. It's a very tame, peaceful high. It's not a 'gateway' or 'addictive' or anything."

She said the words "gateway" and "addictive" like they were myths. Like people couldn't actually become drug addicts—it was all just some tall tale our parents and teachers had fabricated.

"Were you in…or do you *want* to be in a…relationship? With anyone on the…list?"

Now Isa was the one who was confused.

"*Relationship*? I mean, I am. In a spiritual sense. I feel a spiritual connection with everyone I've exchanged fluids with—"

I thought I was going to have to roll the window door and barf. "Fluids"?

"But I'm not going to *marry* anybody if that's what you mean. Jesus, real life isn't a musical where you end up engaged after one dance. And you don't need a label to have an experience with someone. In fact, I've found that all the conventional stuff complicates things. I don't love in a Hallmark way, K. You of all people should know that."

Why me of all people? I thought no one but your college friends get you now.

"Long story short—I have a good feeling about Jason. I feel like he'll be a real *considerate* lay. Not a jackhammer like Tate or basically asleep like Cam. He did cry afterwards—Cam. That was kind of nice. I think."

At that, she pressed play on her iPod, blasting "In Limbo."

"Are you at least using, um…protection or…?"

It was one thing if she was going to have multiple sexual partners—who was I to judge? —but I at least wanted the reassurance that she wasn't being stupid.

"Really, K? What are you, my mom?"

That's rich, coming from someone that asks if I've taken my iron pills forty times a day.

"Seriously, Isa. I'm just looking out for y—"

"*Yes,* you kill joy. I'm on the pill."

"Okay but, what ab—"

"Maybe I shouldn't have told you," she snapped.

"No, Isa—" I didn't know where to go from there. "I think it's…cool that you're having these experiences. I just…just want to make sure you're—"

"Safe. Yeah, I get it. Thanks."

We drove in silence for a moment, and I tried to concentrate on the lyrics of the song rather than the sting behind my eyes. I didn't even know what I was feeling, which only furthered my irritation; I hated being so emotionally incompetent.

"K, once you let go of your 'holier than thou' attitude, you'll be a lot freer."

I wasn't trying to put on any sort of attitude. Isa and I simply wanted different things. We saw certain matters—like homework and sex, it seemed—in a different way. That was becoming clearer. But I also couldn't dismiss the unsettling voice of doubt that said, "Maybe she's right. You think you're better than her, but you're just scared to leave your perfect little bubble."

"Don't be mad at me, please?" she begged dramatically, reaching over to stroke my hair. "We're on an adventure! And I'll get you a Chubbie's on the way back. What about a chaiiiii? You know you want one…"

"I have to go straight back for rehearsal. Remember? I told you," I said, batting her away.

"Tomorrow, then."

"Okay, fine," I relented. "But I want a large. And a pistachio muffin."

"Done."

And we were back to normal.

"I want Jason," she said, in a sing-song voice. "And I'm gonna get him."

As usual, her world was full of green lights. We hit not a single red, not even a stop sign. When Isa had a mission, she always succeeded. Taking in the somber-looking weeping willows as we turned into Sisters of the Moon's gravel parking lot, I knew it was only a matter of time before Jason became her third.

Sisters of the Moon was housed in a circular yurt-like structure overlooking the Cumberland. Stepping onto the front porch was like taking a front row seat at the symphony—windchimes of all different varieties were reverberating gaily against the breeze.

The door swung open before we could touch it.

"Ah, I was expecting you closer to noon," a woman with a deep, mournful voice said by way of greeting. "My third eye chakra is imbalanced today. Ah well, nothing a touch of sun gazing, and lemon oil cannot fix. Come in, come in!"

"K, this is—" Isa started.

"Empress Leonora Pearl, mystic. Pleasure."

Rather than shake my extended hand, Leonora clutched it with both of hers, held on tightly, and closed her eyes. I glanced at Isa who didn't appear off-put in the least.

"She's an indigo, right?" Isa asked expectantly.

Leonora opened her eyes, furrowed her brows, and squinted as she unabashedly starred directly into my face. My hand was starting to ache. I didn't like being put on display. I thought of the baby pig we dissected last year and how we labeled every one of its embalmed parts. I could almost smell the formaldehyde.

"Clever mind, Isa," Leonora affirmed, breaking her hold on me.

I almost asked what being "an indigo" meant but was too distracted by the hut of enchantments we had walked into. Every type of crystal known to man sat along windowsills and some were purposefully placed in surprising nooks and crannies. Dreamcatchers hung from the ceiling like stalactites. Books collecting dust were stacked not only in bookcases with price tags but used as end tables. There was a fireplace burning a collection of well-used candles rather than embers. Charts depicting complex astrology were tacked on walls draped with lush, deep purple fabric. The strong aroma of burning sage wafted throughout the space and intertwined with the notes of Tibetan singing bowls that blasted through an unseen stereo.

Leonora herself was equally arresting; her lavender hair was cropped into a shockingly asymmetrical bob, she wore layers of beaded strands around her neck, and a handmade earth-toned shawl. It was impossible to guess how old she was. With a thick layer of glittery magenta eyeshadow, dark plum lipstick, and the gauge in her right ear, one might take her for an edgy 40-something. But her leathery hands and the way in which she carried herself—a slightly labored stride and hunched posture—told another story.

"Are we interested in a reading today?" Leonora asked me.

Her eyes were the exact shade of dark gray that I remembered from when it would storm over Lake Michigan, and they held a gloom that was disconcerting. I didn't believe in psychic abilities, but I found myself teetering on the edge of skepticism from the all-knowing gaze she couldn't seem to turn off.

"Um…I don't kn—"

"Isa, gem, you start her off and Cressida and I will assist if anything becomes murky," Leonora offered, and Isa lit up like the rising run.

As we were the only three in the shop, I didn't recognize anyone that could possibly be this Cressida character but didn't probe.

"Isa is in training. I never charge a customer for a reading with an apprentice," Leonora whispered in my ear as she guided me to an elaborately carved oak chair that faced a small matching table.

Isa sat across from me, but the candelabra in the center of the table obscured my view of her as she opened up a deck of cards.

"Ah ah ah," Leonora interrupted just as Isa was about to hand the deck to me. "What do we need to do first?"

"Oh my god. Cleanse the deck!" Isa said, as if she were an idiot for nearly neglecting such an obvious, rudimentary step.

"And what crystal do we use?"

"Clear quartz," Isa recited.

Leonora handed Isa a see-through stone and Isa placed it on top of the deck. I didn't know what we were waiting for but stared at the unmoving pile of bizarre cards.

"Now would be a good time to think of a question to ask the cards," Leonora advised me.

"What kind of question?"

"A little nervous, are we?" she asked.

But I didn't consider that observation as a mark of her psychic abilities—I'm sure anyone would have been about to detect my trepidation from a mile away. She placed her hands on my shoulders to give me a deep rub. I flinched. Dang, that woman had a firm grip.

"Try to relax," she insisted. "Tarot does not tell us the future, so you need not fret. It simply presents what might happen, and more importantly, how you should show up for it. For the next 15 minutes, your only task is to remain open to your intuition and where it guides you."

"Ask an open-ended question," Isa added. "Not a 'Will I…fill in the blank' kind because that'll set you up for taking a passive stance in your own future."

"So, not 'where will I go to college'?" I asked.

They shook their heads.

"What about: Am I headed in the right direction?" I modified.

Isa glanced at Leonora for approval, and she nodded, stating, "That will do."

I assumed that the deck was sufficiently "cleansed" when Isa handed it over and asked me to shuffle while meditating on my question. I couldn't help but marvel at the gold-trimmed cards and their ornamental Art Nouveau style drawings. What did these tiny swords, wands, and cups mean? I was slightly scared to find out. What if they told some terribly embarrassing truth? There were some things that Isa and I didn't talk about. The fact that I was very much looking forward to kissing Lincoln onstage was likely the biggest of those unmentionables…but I didn't even dare acknowledge that secret to myself.

Isa then instructed me to cut the deck into threes. From there, she flipped over the top card from each small pile.

"All Major Arcana," Leonora mused. "Curious."

She was crotched next to Isa, so closely that, at first glance, it looked like Isa had two heads. She was apparently a full-time mystic and part-time ninja because I didn't notice that she had moved from behind my chair.

"What does that mean?" I ventured, uneasily.

"Basically, you're going through a life-changing event. Also, there's probably an important lesson that you have to learn so you can progress further in your spiritual quest."

Quest? This was starting to sound like one of those nerdy video games Lincoln played—Final Fantasy or The Legend of Zelda. I looked down at the cards to examine them more closely. There was an upside-down sorceress holding a lantern labeled as "The Hermit," (not much of a shocker) a colorful jester called "The Fool," (were these cards trying to call me dumb?) but most alarming was the dancing skeleton surrounded by tombstones simply named, "Death."

"What is this?" I asked, pointing at the Death card which was the focal point of the spread.

Maybe there was going to be an accident. Maybe on the way back to the school. Maybe we were going to crash.

Leonora held a finger to her lips to shh me. "Isa, go ahead."

"Alright, so, you have a powerful spread, K," Isa began.

Powerful? More like tragic. I was going to die. I mean, obviously we were all going to die, but…

"These cards, in this position, represent the past, present, and future."

As if it couldn't get worse! The Death card was in the "present" position.

"Don't freak out about this guy," Isa continued, realizing that my eyes hadn't moved from the skeleton. "We'll get to that in a minute."

This is not real. This is just pretend witchcraft stuff. Just calm down

"This card, your past, is 'The Hermit.' She's upside down, or reversed, which means that it holds the opposite meaning," she explained.

"Which is…"

"Well, first off, a reversal means that you're out of balance in some way. I guess since this is the past, though, you *used* to be out of balance. You were probably once hiding from the world; not reflecting deeply enough about your inner self or leaning into your destiny."

"And what else?" Leonora nudged.

Rather than floating between us and hovering over our shoulders, she had taken an armchair at the table. She studied every move Isa made—her stormy eyes eerily lingering on each precise point of the finger or lift of the card.

"It could also mean loneliness. Maybe someone lied to you, or you felt abandoned," Isa expanded.

"Very good, very good," Leonora said.

But it wasn't "very good." It made me think of moving across the country, starting new schools in the middle of the year, and our disjointed family. My parents praised me for being adaptable whenever we drove off in a U-Haul, en route to the next location. They said I was resourceful because I didn't need a sibling or other kids my age—I always played alone. But what if there was loneliness sprinkled in with the adaptability and resourcefulness? Or maybe adaptability and resourcefulness was just what my parents wanted to see?

"Now, this baby." Isa directed her attention to the dreaded Death card. "It's really not scary. It just means 'end of a cycle.' Have you had a period from hell lately?"

She met my eyes and snorted, but Leonora cleared her throat and Isa immediately switched back into serious mode. Evidently, she respected this strange woman.

"It represents a change or metamorphosis, right?" She turned to Leonora for guidance.

"In the present position, this card does in fact suggest a monumental change. And great duress—that much is certain," Leonora assisted.

Oh, fabulous—great duress is certain.

Leonora closed her eyes and pressed her fingers to her temples. She began to hum or moan or...croak? I wasn't sure *what* noise was coming from her body. I met Isa's eyes and tilted my head in Leonora's direction.

"Do we need to help her?" I mouthed.

She shook her head. "Cressida," she mouthed back.

But right as I was about to ask who Cressida was, Leonora regained consciousness.

"Cressida wonders if you are perhaps worried about the stability of your job? Do you ever feel out of touch with the world around you as obsessions about the economy become your preoccupation? What about personal property loss? You are a victim of a recent foreclosure, is that right?"

Rather than explain that I was only a 16-year-old living with my parents and did not have a job aside from inconsistent babysitting on the weekends, or that I'd never before considered the state of the economy (my dad worried about that enough for my mom, me, and him combined), I asked, "Sorry, but—who's Cressida?"

"My twin. She died in utero, but I inherited her life force. She guides my visions. Cressida *is* my conscience," she said with a completely straight face.

Two things were running through my mind: First, was this woman a psycho rather than a psychic? And second, Cressida was definitely not a reliable compass for the future.

"The Death card is impossible to ward off," Leonora continued without waiting for a response. "You will do well to accept the fate that is at hand and seek to work within it today for a happier tomorrow."

"Wow," Isa sighed. "That's good."

"When Death and Hermit cards appear together, your feelings of frustration center on the end of a *good* time in your life. These feelings are compounded because you have previously been left alone and unable to properly cope with overwhelming transitions. Does that sound familiar?"

I didn't *want* it to sound familiar, but I couldn't deny that she—or Cressida—was somewhat on track.

"Um...maybe," I said.

"Let us move on, shall we? Isa? Take us to the future, my gem."

"You pulled The Fool. This is a good one—in the upright position he represents new beginnings, innocence, taking a leap of faith, spontaneity...things like that," Isa said, clearly regurgitating from a textbook that she must have studied from while she should have been taking the PSAT. "The Fool is the spiciest card in the deck. It's the only one without a Roman numeral."

I glanced down at the card for a better look. There was a tiny zero in the corner of the card with a vine of roses wrapped around it.

"It starts with nothingness but has the potential to reach into infinity," Isa said.

She smirked and her eyes literally twinkled. So, this was Isa fully in her element. Even if I thought all this psychic stuff was a bunch of hoopla, it was lovely to witness. I could tell that she was empowered and carried a heightened sense of importance when she spoke about the cards. Granted, she always acted like she knew what she was talking about and what she was doing...but sitting across from her in that weird little shop, I recognized the difference between her faking it and actually owning her space.

"Looks like little birdie's gonna get herself a new life," Isa said, pleased that her reading ended with a positive outcome.

"Okay...so I guess the answer to the question is...yes? I'm headed in the right direction but there's going to be a rocky patch? And I'm in the rocky part right now?" I tried.

"Let me take a look here," Leonora said, reaching for The Fool.

She picked up the card, gave me a once over, and shut her eyes. There was more of the peculiar moaning and finally she said, "Cressida wants to remind us of The Fool's second meaning. There will be a coming love interest who is not ordinary by any stretch of the imagination."

I knew then that she was phony. A love interest? That was likely what she told every sucker that walked through her door.

"Cressida predicted when Earl came into my life those 15 summers ago," she explained. "I drew that very card. Of course, the following year I pulled The Empress, and he joined the spirit realm shortly after. Carnival accident. I used to travel with a troupe, and he was the lion tamer. Alas... He is still here though... He inhabits that pipe. I take it everywhere I go."

We all shifted our gazes to the fireplace. Sure enough, there was an old-fashioned tobacco pipe resting atop the mantel. I wasn't exactly sure what she meant by "inhabit," but I knew that I had no interest at all in touching that pipe or even going within six feet of it.

"Never loved again," she said as she stood and crossed to the windowsill cluttered with crystals. "Whoever is chosen by The Fool is most likely your soul mate. Oh yes, those exist," she added.

She selected a smooth, muted coral and black stone, rubbed it across her forehead and the bridge of her nose, then dropped it in her pocket.

"Rhodonite. What is that for, my gem?"

"A gentle release for suffering," Isa said proudly.

"Very good, very good."

At that, thunder cracked above the Tibetan singing bowl recording. The sky had progressed into a threatening shade of navy and next there would be rain.

"Isa, we better go. If it's raining, the traffic's going to be terrible. I really can't be late for rehearsal," I suggested.

"Alright, alright," she agreed, "But before we go, I have to return these to you, Leo."

She hoisted her satchel onto the tarot table and pulled out two thick books—*How the Stars Came to Be* and *Twelve Faces of a Goddess*.

"Enjoyable?"

"Oh yeah, totally blew my mind," Isa confirmed. "Also, could you do a quickie aura check-up on me? I've been feeling kind of off."

"Did you charge your crystals?" Leonora asked.

"Yeah, and I've been drinking the moon milk. I'm still all funky…"

Leonora approached Isa and took her palms in her hands. I glanced out the window. Yup, it was definitely raining. And everyone forgot how to drive in this city when the least bit of precipitation crept into the forecast. I was going to be late for rehearsal and then Lincoln would know that I skipped eighth period. I hated to side with Isa and rag on him, but if he pulled his "honest Abe" crap, I might even find myself pressured into writing Mrs. Hollins a letter of confession and apology for ditching her class. Fortunately, the examination was over almost as soon as it had begun.

"My dear gem," Leonora gasped. "Evergreen. Evergreen for *envy*. We must cleanse. That toxicity is blocking your sacral chakra."

Isa flashed a worried glance at me.

"Don't have time. I'll cleanse at home. Thanks, Leo!"

She quickly retrieved her satchel and grabbed my arm, directing us to the door. I turned to wave goodbye and noticed that Leonora bore a look of perturbation.

Isa shoved me into the pouring rain, and we sprinted the short distance to the car.

"Whoa, what's with your sacred chakra or whatever? Did we upset her?" I asked when we were safely inside the car.

"*Sacral* chakra," she clarified, as if I knew the difference. "No, she just probably hoped we'd stay for tea. And, for the record, she wasn't her best today. Her third eye was off, so she probably wasn't spot-on about the evergreen aura."

I wrung rainwater from my curls while I listened to her spout off metaphysical gibberish. Something had embarrassed her. It wasn't an emotion that I was used to witnessing in Isa. I was no "aura reader," but her scattered energy undoubtedly led me to suspect that she was trying to conceal something.

"What are you spazzing about? What's evergreen even mean?"

"Nothing," she said. "It doesn't mean anything."

To my secret disappointment, Ms. Morris blocked the kiss between Liesl and Rolf as a brief, childish peck. Knowing that Rolf ends up betraying the Von Trapp family and joining the Nazi party in act two, she was aiming to highlight the "jarring juxtaposition between young love and the loss of innocence when political persuasions interfere." I suppose this direction was better for all involved because if it had been a prolonged moment of passion, I may have been the one in need of confidence coaching.

As it happened, the first time we ran the kiss after "Sixteen Going on Seventeen," Lincoln came at me headfirst while I also approached him… With both of us going the full one hundred, we banged foreheads. Any tingling of butterflies had dissipated instantly and was replaced with a pounding migraine. Each and every time thereafter, we found a way to accidentally stumble into each other, sometimes missing the lips entirely and landing on an "Eskimo kiss" of sorts. Completely unintentional as this was, Ms. Morris was thrilled by the comedy.

"This is genius!" she told us after we missed each other's faces by a full six inches (we both had our eyes closed and leaned in…the wrong direction). "Let's make this a bit! You two have more of a friendship chemistry and we should capitalize on what's *organic*."

I almost thought that Isa wouldn't show, but she was there for opening night. To my delight, she even snuck backstage to do our handshake.

"This is the last time we do this before you both leave the nest!" she said, imitating a proud southern mom. "I'm so proud of y'all, I'm gonna take out a full-page ad in the yearbook just for my babies!"

"You're the one graduating," Lincoln reminded her before Ms. Morris shooed her out of the greenroom.

I liked to think that Isa had missed us and perhaps attending opening night of *The Sound of Music* reminded her of the memories we all could have made. But I also knew that most of her college friends had left town for winter break… Either way, I was overjoyed that she seemed to come back to us that December.

Ms. Morris cornered the three of us and all but begged us to help out with Dickens of a Christmas. And even if we begrudged the polyester petticoats and suffocating neckerchiefs of the Victorian age, we ended up having a blast. There was something so satisfying in researching curse words that would have been used in Dickens' time and implementing them into conversation with festival attendees. By all measures, life was sweet again. It was as if the collective chakras of our trio had been balanced…or something like that. I never did devote myself to comprehending the terminology of Isa's metaphysical world.

And then the DeLuca Christmas party happened. As much as I was saddened for Isa, there was a part of me that was prideful at being the one to take care of her through it all—not her new friends, certainly no one from her Sexcapade List—it was me. It was me that listened when she ranted about how enduring another Christmas with Tamara would be impossible now that she was harboring the knowledge of her dirty betrayal. It was me that she came to when her dad nagged her about signing up community college courses in the fall. It was me that Googled "Excursions in the Alps" with her when she wanted to block out the sense of time passing us by. And it was me that was laying beside her when she found out that her parents were officially separating.

    The Friday after we returned to school, I spent the night at Isa's. Our plans were to veg out by watching my beloved Jimmy Stewart in *You Can't Take It with You* and gorge ourselves with popcorn mixed with peanut M&M's. Times like these were my favorite—with no fears of getting caught for sneaking out or partaking in forbidden substances, I could genuinely relax. I knew that with too much of this routine Isa would begin to deem it boring, so I just savored the quiet company while it lasted. I had begun to notice that, for me at least, the thrill of danger and adventure didn't hold a candle to comfort and security.

    Lincoln was out with Jon at the Schermerhorn that night, (a concert featuring the music from *Star Wars* the only thing that motivated him to put on dress pants and a collared shirt) so he wasn't there when Tamara stumbled into Isa's room at midnight.

    My back was facing the door, but I could tell it was Tamara when the door creaked and she whispered, "Isaaaaa. My pretty girl. Are you sleeping?"

    I shut my eyes and pretended to be asleep. I didn't want to interact with Tamara, especially when she reeked of booze. She sat on Isa's side of the bed, and I heard her kick her heels off.

    "What? We're trying to sleep," Isa whispered.

    "I just wanted to say goodnight," Tamara slurred.

    "Stop touching me," Isa said, and I felt the rustle of the covers as Isa supposedly swatted her mom's hand away.

    "You used to love it when I stroked your head until you fell asleep," Tamara said. "You used to say, 'Mommy, can you pat my head so I can dream?' Remember that? Remember Isa? Remember when you used to call me 'Mommy' and we would talk and talk and talk? You'd ask me, 'Why is the sky blue, Mommy? It would be prettier if it was purple.' Remember? And you gave me daisies for Mother's Day every year. Every single year..."

Isa said nothing.

"I remember everything," Tamara continued. "You used to want to wear those princess dresses and you would dance around. Isa?"

Isa was so still that I wondered if she had fallen asleep. Tamara began to whimper.

"Isa? I remember one night, I was tucking you in and I asked you, 'What's your favorite color, Isabel?' and you said...you said... You looked up at me and your eyes were so big. You said, 'Mommy, I love the whole entire rainbow. It's not fair to choose.' The whole entire rainbow. I never forgot that. Oh Isa...I've been...I know I haven't been...the best..."

Tamara sniffed. I suspected she was fully crying now.

"You've always been my favorite, you know," she whispered. "I always wanted a little girl. And you were such a pretty little girl."

"Please. Go," Isa said flatly.

There was a long pause. I didn't hear Tamara get up and could still feel her weight on the bed, but I almost thought she had disappeared.

Finally, she spoke, "Your father and I are getting a divorce. I'm moving out Monday. I'm sure you're happy. There. You got what you wanted. Me out of your life. Goodnight, Isa. Goodnight, Blair."

She stood, strode across the room, and slammed the door on her way out. Isa was silent for a long while. I knew this was my cue to jump in and offer advice, condolences, or whatever you're supposed to do when your friend finds out that her parents are divorcing, but I couldn't get my voice to work. I was stuck on Tamara calling me "Blair" and the fact that there must have been a time when Blair was known to spend the night. This bothered me just as much as it had bothered me when Blair claimed authority on all things Isa at the HOA luau two summers ago. Then, Isa kicked my foot underneath the covers.

"Are you awake?"

"Do you think she'll hear the garage door?" I whispered as we were about to tiptoe out of Isa's bedroom.

"What does it matter?"

We had debated for 20 minutes about sneaking out of the house to attend a party at Jason's. I was insistent on staying in bed—we were nearly asleep before Tamara barged in and ruined the night—but Isa was determined to shake off pent-up aggression.

"We could do some yoga? Or what about your stones or…the cards? Can you do a tarot reading on yourself?" I offered—anything to get out of being dragged to Jason Calbot's in the middle of the night.

"I bailed on this party because you wanted to watch a movie. Now, I want to go. If you want to stay—stay. I'll be back before you wake up."

"I thought you wanted a movie night too," I said, hurt.

"Well now I want to go out. Are you coming or not?" she said curtly while zipping her jeans. "Can you hand me that tank top?"

I picked up the "Good Vibes Only" tank top that was haphazardly thrown over her vanity mirror. Cartoon mushrooms with smiling faces stared up at me as I held it in my hands. A college party with older kids and definitely booze and maybe (okay, *probably*) drugs… It occurred to me to wake up Tamara or call Mr. DeLuca, who was away on a business trip. Maybe one of them could stop her. But if I prevented her from going to this party, I might lose her forever.

I had an ominous feeling in my stomach. I knew this party was going to be out of my comfort zone, but not in a way where I would look back on and think, "I'm so glad I did that." On the other hand, Isa had apparently been to dozens of parties like this. She had managed to take care of herself thus far, so maybe I was just being chicken.

In the end, there was no way I would be able to peacefully go back to sleep—not with knowing that Isa was out partying with strangers and potentially driving home intoxicated; not with knowing that she was slipping through my fingers. She was clearly distraught about her parents, and this was her way of coping. I wanted to be a part of that. I *needed* to be a part of that.

"Okay but, will you promise to stick with me?" I asked. "Don't ditch me to hook up with Jason or…whoever."

"Yeah, of course. You're safe with me. Now get dressed!" she hissed urgently.

I put on the polka dot tights and black dress with the white peter pan collar that I wore to school that day.

"Come here," Isa said, undoing my braid and combing her fingers through my hair. "We can't show up with you looking like Wednesday Adams."

She unbuttoned the first two buttons of my dress.

"There, that's better."

We were almost out the door when she whispered, "You took your iron pill, right? I don't want you passing out on me."

I dashed back upstairs to dig for it in my overnight bag, but in the process saw that I left my phone on Isa's bed.

"K, come on!" Isa whisper-yelled from the bottom of the staircase.

I grabbed the phone and left. The iron pill in the little Friday box of my medicine holder remained untouched.

The party was further away than Isa claimed—almost a 40-minute drive. As soon as we pulled up to the shared worn-down duplex where Jason lived, my stomach sank. The street was full of cars and crawling with the Friday night college scene. With the level of blatant inebriation and the volume of the music from Jason's place, it was clear that no one was afraid if the cops were called.

"Just, try to have a good time, alright?" Isa said as we approached the front door and a girl in a tube top puked in the grass. "These people are *nice*. I promise."

The cacophony hit my eardrums like a wrecking ball when we stepped inside. There was a group playing beer pong in the entryway, a Drake music video up on a gigantic flat screen tv, people congregating in the kitchen, and others dancing anywhere there was a place to stand. Solo cups littered the floor and the strobe lighting made it hard to tell what exactly you were stepping on. It was thoroughly filthy and thoroughly bachelor pad. It was like every frat party sequence from the teen movies of the 2000s had thrown up in Jason's house. Exciting for some—a waking nightmare for me.

"Isa! Eyyyy!!!"

"Look what the cat dragged in!"

"There she is! You said you weren't coming!"

People flocked to her like she was a celebrity coming to grace them with her presence. I recognized Jason, but no one else. Isa introduced me as her "Future Fellow Swiss Explorer" and got us Blue Moons from the fridge. We made our home base the kitchen as she seamlessly plugged right into the ongoing conversation. I leaned against the fridge like a wallflower and ended up passing drinks to strangers as a result of my unfortunate location.

Isa clung onto Jason, laughing at everything that came out of his mouth and kept finding excuses to touch him. She playfully slapped his cheeks, declaring that he would look better with a beard and traced her finger over his chest to read aloud, "Alpha Sigma Phi."

"Do your boy scout friends know that you used to sing and dance?" Isa teased.

He was just as all over her—grabbing her waist and whispering dirty jokes into her ear. Every time I heard her husky cackle, I felt a ping of second-hand embarrassment. It was like I was observing a private moment that should be taking place behind closed doors. I'd never seen Isa flirt, but assumed she'd have more subtlety than my locker neighbors, Cassandra and Megan. As was becoming the trend with my assumptions of Isa—I was wrong.

"They need to just screw and get it over with, am I right?" the guy that was standing next to me said in a low voice.

I laughed halfheartedly. This guy, with a black sweatshirt that ironically (I supposed) simply said "College," downed two IPAs like they were water. He had a booming laugh and greeted everyone by name as they squeezed in and out of the kitchen. I assumed he must have been popular. Maybe in a fraternity or on a sports team. And though I didn't think I went for sporty, fratty college guys, I had warmed up to his ridiculously long eyelashes and his habit of calling anything interesting "dope." He had a stain on the collar of his sweatshirt that looked like mustard. Normally, I would have found that repulsive; I've always been a neat freak. But he was kind of funny and the only person that seemed to acknowledge my existence, seeing that Isa was indisposed by her aggressive pursuit. I let the mustard stain slide.

"Dope earrings," the guy said, pointing at my dangling Victorian bees.

They were a recent birthday gift from my parents, and I'd worn them almost every day since I unwrapped them. An astute find on my dad's part from an antique sale where he got my mom's new wardrobe, they were a bit tarnished until I polished them. Now they gleamed a warm golden hue, just like honey.

"Oh, thanks," I said, feeling heat rise in my cheeks. "These are…um…the Victorians were really into naturalism in design and fashion. Bees were super popular back then. They symbolize wisdom."

"Dope," he said and handed me a fresh Blue Moon.

"Who wants to go out on the deck?" Jason eventually asked the kitchen squad.

Isa was following Jason out of the kitchen, and I grabbed her hand before she could abandon me.

"Loosen up, kid," she whispered. "Just going out to smoke. Come. He has some good stuff."

She winked at me then led me through the jungle of party people and out the backdoor. Jason's back deck had only a dirty grill and a few mismatched lawn chairs to create ambiance, but at least there was less garbage at my feet and the comfort of the night air. Because there weren't enough chairs for everyone, Isa sat on Jason's lap, and I stood awkwardly in the periphery of the circle. Someone started passing around a bong. I'd never used one before, so I declined when Mustard Stain offered it.

Since apparently my naivety was written all over my face, he said, "Here, I'll show you."

He placed the colorful glass contraption in my hands.

"Here, grab onto the base and put your mouth right here on the tip," he instructed.

"Yo! You teaching her how to give a BJ? There are empty rooms upstairs, dude!" Jason shouted.

To my shame, Isa snickered with the rest of the group.

When she saw the look on my face, she inserted, "Hey now, leave her alone."

But still. She laughed. And I was trapped. Isa was my ride home, so I couldn't storm out. I couldn't just stand there either. I didn't want to put a target on my back as the lame easily offended high schooler. So, I took a long, powerful pull from the bong and held it in.

"Atta girl! Pretty dope, right?"

I nodded, though, truth be told, it was way too intense. Seconds after the inhale, a powerful force rushed directly to my head, and I had to concentrate so I wouldn't further embarrass myself by coughing or stumbling backwards. Although, if I had stumbled, I wouldn't have been the only one. Just then, a very intoxicated guy with a ponytail fell headfirst into Mustard Stain.

"Whoa, whoa! Kenny what the hell, man!" someone shouted.

Kenny spilt his drink all over Mustard Stain's mustard stained "College" sweatshirt. The whole of the back deck roared with laughter, and some even applauded.

"Dude, Kenny, let's get you inside," someone else said, guiding Kenny back into the house.

"S—So—Sorry, bro!" Kenny yelled as he was carted away.

Mustard Stain stripped down to his undershirt and tossed his soiled sweatshirt at Jason, who threw it like garbage onto the floor. I couldn't *not* notice that Mustard Stain—who was *still* Mustard Stain in my mind with or without the sweatshirt—had quite the trim physique. He was broad shouldered, his arms looked like those of a pro athlete, and he had a large tribal tattoo on the right bicep.

"What's your tattoo?" I asked, mostly just to appear occupied.

"Ah yeah," he said, flexing a bit to show it off. "It's a wolf. A few buddies and I have the same thing. It's our spirit animal."

"Oh, cool," I said, trying to sound authentically interested. I always worried that I wasn't doing the right things with my face or incorporating the appropriate tone of voice in large group settings. "Is there any sort of special meaning behind it? Why a wolf?"

"Nah. Wolves are just the dopest creatures in the wild. And we're—me and my guys back home—we're like a pack. Get it?"

He sounded like a true simpleton, but I smiled and nodded anyway.

"I wanna get one on the other arm one day. A pink ribbon. For, uh, breast cancer? My mom—she's a survivor."

Now I felt terrible for privately categorizing him in the "good looking but brainless" box.

A tattoo in honor of his mom? That's pretty sweet.

"What about you?" he asked. "Do you have any?"

I didn't say that I wasn't legally old enough to have a tattoo but instead, "No. I'll probably never get one."

I took the final sip of my beer then glanced over at Isa. She and Jason were now blowing smoke into each other's mouths and, finding that completely grotesque, I wanted to get out of there. When Mustard Stain asked if I wanted another drink, I agreed. Then, with a fresh beer in my hand, he asked if I wanted to learn how to play beer pong. I agreed. I later agreed to a cranberry White Claw and by my second round of beer pong, realized that I was actually having fun.

"You're a BEAST!" Mustard Stain whooped when I slayed him for a second time.

"Beginner's luck," I laughed.

By the middle of the third round, we had attracted a crowd.

"Big Bee! Big Bee!" my fans chanted.

The nickname was bestowed on me after Mustard Stain pointed out to everyone that would listen that I had the "dopest style." I'd never gotten so many compliments on a pair of earrings, and I felt kind of…cool. It was odd. I was smiling, laughing, and shouting with the rest of them. I even did a few victory dances and high fived so many random people, I had lost count.

"The undefeated champion!" Mustard Stain said.

He hoisted me off the ground. My dress was hiking up and I yanked it down. It was when Mustard Stain put me down that I started to feel dizzy.

"I need to find Isa," I told him.

"What?" he shouted.

"Isa! Where is she?" I shouted back—the music was deafening.

He shrugged and I left him to scope out the back deck. Isa was still on top of Jason, but now they were making out. Her hands were all in his hair and his were sliding up and down her back. She wasn't keeping her promise. She had totally forgotten about me and was only concerned with getting into Jason's pants. But so, what? I didn't need her. I could clearly handle my own—I was the reigning beer pong champion now. I stumbled back into the living room and asked Mustard Stain where the bathroom was.

"Hey, you want another drink?" he asked.

"No, no. I'm good. Is there any, like, *food* around? I'm feeling kind of…um…"

"I think the last of the pizza is gone but let me see if I can find something. Bathroom's that way." He pointed down the hall.

In the bathroom I splashed some water on my face and stared at myself in the mirror. I was undoubtedly drunk as a skunk. There was also that weed… That wasn't like anything I'd had before. I was Big Bee, Queen of Beer Pong five minutes ago, but suddenly I was hitting rock bottom. Then I remembered—my iron pill.

You idiot.

No wonder I was out of whack. I forgot the damn iron pill. I needed some food and I needed Isa to take me back to her house. It must have been at least 2:00 am.

"Made ya peanut butter and pickle crackers," Mustard Stain said, holding out a paper plate when I reentered the living room.

"Peanut butter and *pickles*?"

"Try it. Nutty, creamy, and tangy. Super dope."

I was repulsed but needed to sober up somehow. We sat down on the couch, and I took a small nibble. It wasn't "dope", but it wasn't bad either.

"Annnd…I made you my world famous Cheerwine Surprise!"

He held out a solo cup that smelled exactly like Christmas. If Santa ever got hammered with Mrs. Claus, Cheerwine Surprise would have been his adult beverage of choice.

"No thanks," I said, pushing away the cup.

"Aww sad day…that was the last Cheerwine. You wouldn't let it go to waste, would you?" he asked, pouting his bottom lip and batting those obscenely long eyelashes. "It has a scoop of vanilla ice cream, some cinnamon, cranberry juice, and Fireball. Just a little sip?"

"Fine. I'll just taste it," I decided.

It pleased me to see him waiting on bated breath for my opinion as I brought the drink to my mouth.

"This. Is…*dope*," I said, surprising both of us.

We started giggling. I snorted accidentally and that inspired more laughter. I could wait out Isa's Sexcapade mission, I thought. I would just sit on this couch with Mustard Stain and sooner or later she'd come out and we'd go home. I took another sip. The ice cream was good for me, I reasoned. It was filling my stomach with sustenance. Maybe it even had some iron…? Before I knew it, the cup was empty.

"Can I ask you something personal?" I asked him, feeling silly.

"Anything."

"Are you wearing mascara?"

"Ahhh shit! You know how many chicks ask me that? What even *is* mascara? Like blush or something? Please, I need to know!" he blurted, grabbing my shoulders, and playfully shaking me.

My laughter combined with the shaking caused me to smear peanut butter on my left cheek.

"You got—" Mustard Stain said, pointing to my face.

He took the uneaten cracker out of my hand and set it on the coffee table. Then, with his finger, wiped the glob of peanut butter from my cheek. When we had started to occupy the same couch cushion, I couldn't say, but he held his hand on my cheek and pulled me closer. And just like that, I was kissing someone. It wasn't onstage. This was in real life. At a college party.

I couldn't wait to tell Isa.

The kissing grew steadily more intense, but before I could process what was happening and if I liked it or not, beads of sweat formed on my forehead.

Wait, this is not the person I want to be kissing, was the vague thought that floated through my mind. Out of the blue, a profound, unexpected sadness coursed through me. *This is not the person I wanted to kiss.*

He pressed his lips more forcefully against mine and when his tongue protruded into my mouth, I turned my head to side. The room was fuzzy. And there were only a few people left.

Where did everyone go?

"Who knows," Mustard Stain said, but I didn't think I said that out loud.

I was laying on my back when I felt weight on top of me. Was *he* on top of me? I was definitely sweating, and my stomach didn't feel right.

He's going to notice I'm sweaty.

"You're really beautiful. You know that, right? You have to. Pretty girls always know they're pretty."

There was a wetness on my neck and the uncomfortable tickle of a spider crawling up my thigh. But it was his mouth and his fingers. I had to get up. I had to go to the bathroom. I was going to throw up.

"Scoot, scoot, scoot!"

Isa had squeezed herself onto the couch. Now my head was in her lap, and she was stroking my hair.

"You used to love it when I stroked your head until you fell asleep," I remembered Tamara saying.

When did Tamara come into Isa's bedroom? Was that today? Or did she say that? Was that a dream? Smoke was everywhere.

"Not inside," someone said.

Isa blew smoke into my mouth. I was now sitting in Isa's lap. I was kissing Isa. No, Isa kissed me. No, I was kissing Mustard Stain. Long eyelashes like moths. Was I dreaming? I was dizzy. Really dizzy. Black blobs were skewing my vision. I rubbed my eyes to try to get them to go away. Isa was on the floor making out with Jason. Isa's tank top was missing, and her lime green bra was too bright for my eyes.

I must be high, I thought because her bra was glowing.

And then I was standing in the hallway in front of the bathroom.

"Listen," a voice said into my ear, "Jason and I will be right back."

"Isa, I need to—"

"Looks like Jason's friend is really into you…"

"Isa, just—"

I was standing in the hallway. Alone.

"Isa?"

Someone grabbed my hand, and I was crawling up a flight of stairs. I heard laughter. Isa's laughter. I fell on something soft. Isa's bed. We were back at Isa's house, and I could finally go back to sleep. No, no…this wasn't Isa's room. I didn't know whose room it was. The wetness on my neck again and a crushing weight. It was the guy. I remembered a sweatshirt with a stain. A tattoo. What was his name? *What was his name?* Did he ever tell me his name? His hands were everywhere all at once. The room was spinning. I shut my eyes. There was moaning. My bottom lip stung. He bit me.

"I don't—" I said or thought. I didn't know the difference.

And his shirt was off. It was so hot in there. Sweat was running down my face. No, tears. Was I crying? Why was I crying?

Oh god, they're all going to see me crying.

"It just hurts for a second."

Searing, deep pinching. Deep pinching. Deep pinching.

And then nothing.

When I came to, we were moving. I looked to my left—Isa was driving. I was in the passenger's seat with my seat belt on and it was nearly daylight outside.

"Isa?"

"Are you awake?" she asked, bemused.

I sat up and thought I was going to barf. The clock on her dash read 5:07 am. I pulled down the sun visor to look at myself in the mirror and that's when I noticed that one of my bee earrings was missing. I wanted to cry, but I also noticed from the dried flakes running down my cheeks, that I had already been crying.

"My—where is my earring?"

"You got sloppy, birdie," Isa said.

"I don't remember," I said slowly. "What happened? What did I do?"

"We've all been there before," she assured me as she pulled into her neighborhood. "But for real—you don't remember? You were talking to me right before we left. You fell asleep and when I woke you up, you were talking about going to Taco Bell. Remember? You said you needed food. And then you fell back asleep when we got in the car."

"Oh. Yeah, yeah."

But I didn't remember walking to the car. I remembered asking for food… I ate something, but what was it?

"We ate peanut butter and pickles," I said, the memory coming back to me as she parked the car in the empty driveway.

"*What?* Ew!" Isa burst into laughter. "All they had was pizza. You must have dreamt that. I get really weird dreams after I smoke sometimes. Now, let's get you to bed, drunkie. We'll go to Taco Bell later. But I need to crash first."

Isa got out of the car and slammed the driver's door, but I didn't trust my legs to follow her. I sat there, still staring at my reflection in the tiny square mirror. I wanted my earring back. I loved those earrings, and what would I say if my dad asked why I wasn't wearing them anymore?

"Are you waiting for me to open the door for you, princess?" Isa teased.

I was relieved that Lincoln had stayed over at Jon's. Not that he would be awake at five in the morning, but I didn't want to risk him asking us where we had been. It was hard for me to lie to him, especially since I knew he valued honesty so much. It was almost worse to lie to him than to my parents.

I went straight into the bathroom that Isa and Lincoln shared because I had the strangest feeling that I had wet myself. I swore to never drink that much again as I shut the door and made my way to the toilet. I wasn't a pee-your-pants type of drunk, or I didn't want to become one, anyway. But when I pulled down my underwear, I screamed.

"Isa! ISA!"

"What, what?" she asked when she swung open the bathroom door.

"There's—"

I looked down at the blood that soaked my panties. My polka dot tights were also ripped just below the crotch.

"You want a tampon?" she asked.

"No. Isa. I'm not—on my period. I'm not—supposed to—start yet!"

"Mine's always unpredictable. That's normal," she replied, not understanding my horror.

"NO. *Isa*. What—What happened? What—what—who was that guy? Did he give me something? Did you see? Do you know him?"

This wasn't happening. But *what* was happening? *What happened*?

"Shhh…Shhh…" Isa placed her hands on my shoulders and spoke gently, but I could see the doubt in her eyes. "You're okay."

She handed me a wad of toilet paper and left me to wipe as she started the shower.

Trembling and woozy, I stood, gradually removed my clothes, and took unsteady steps into the shower. The heat of the water beating down on my skin slowed my frantic heart beats. I closed my eyes and when I opened them, Isa was climbing into the shower with me. I wasn't embarrassed. We'd seen each other naked plenty of times, although never like this. Blood trickled down my thigh, onto my leg, and ran into the drain. I didn't care that she saw. We stared at each other in heavy, accusatory silence. Steam began to blanket us. The water was scalding but I wanted to stand there until my skin was raw. I wanted to burn off every inch of me that had been touched. Every part that was dirty. I didn't bother with soap. I would never be able to fully clean myself.

Staring at Isa, I saw that for the first time in her life perhaps, she didn't know what to do. Guilt was written all over her face. She had messed up. I remembered, then, that in biology when we talked of symbiotic relationships, they weren't always mutually beneficial. Isa was the leech. I was the bloodless host. And I hated her for it.

When we got out of the shower and toweled off, I followed her to bed. I didn't know his name. I didn't remember anything. I couldn't even be certain about what had been lost along with my bee earring. I didn't know if I had the right to claim that nothing had been *lost* but *stolen*.

When I woke up hours later to Ella's barking, I had a raging headache. I grabbed the small trash can by Isa's bed and immediately expelled my guts.

"I need to walk Ella," Isa said. "I don't think anyone else is home."

My eyes were fixed on the pile of vomit.

"Hey, look at me."

When I did, her face fell.

"You need some fresh air," she asserted. "Give me that."

I handed her my barf bucket, which she placed somewhere in the bathroom for the time being, so we didn't have to tolerate the smell. She walked over to my side of the bed, took my hands, and helped me into a standing position.

"Squeeze my hands," she ordered.

I thought of opening night of *Guys and Dolls*. I wanted more than anything to go back in time. To be backstage, about to transform into a different person. A tear trickled down my cheek.

"You're okay. Squeeze my hands."

I didn't want to touch her. I didn't even want to look at her. But on autopilot, I did as she said. Like I always did.

"Squeeze and release," she coached. "Breathe in. Now let it go."

I clamped my eyes shut, forcing several more tears out.

When I opened my eyes, Isa said, "See? Now you're back in control."

Control—what a funny word. I wasn't in control. I was never in control. And neither was she.

Ella barked and started pawing at the bedroom door. Isa opened it and we made the journey down the stairs to get the leash and take her for a walk. So much in a daze, I didn't bother to put on shoes or change out of the pajama boxer shorts that Isa let me borrow. Within a second of stepping outside, Ella bolted.

11.

When the Camellias Are in Bloom

"I said to my mom, 'Hang on—if we're going to Nǎinai's I have get on my comfy pants.'" Jon paused so his enraptured audience could softly giggle. "Nǎinai's house meant fun. My parents are stereotypical Chinese parents—they're strict, they're traditional, they put their heads down and they work hard. We had a chore chart that was color-coded. We got grounded if we got B's. That sort of thing. They did it because they wanted us to succeed. Nǎinai also wanted us to succeed, but her measurement was: 'You laugh today?' We'd say, 'Nǎinai, what's for dinner?' and she'd say, 'Whatever will make you smile—we have that.' That's what I miss the most—wearing my comfy pants and going over to Nǎinai's for hours of cartoons and good food. It was the only place me and my sister could be kids."

As our meager cast of five—or the "budding rebel alliance," as Lincoln nicknamed us—hung on to his every word, I stole a glance at Lincoln. He had the "artist mode" glint in his eyes, which deepened my smile. I could tell that this first rehearsal was going better than he expected.

"Nǎinai doesn't recognize us anymore," Jon continued. "When we visit her, she usually calls me 'Haoyu,' which was the name of our grandpa. And she calls my sister, 'Qinyang'—that's our mom. My sister cries a lot. My mom copes by keeping busy—she's the same drill sergeant she's always been, but now she's also keeping the hospital staff in line. On bad days, I wonder, 'Does she remember us coming over for Saturday morning cartoons and youtiao? Does she have any memory of us at all?'

"But then I think about how Grandpa Haoyu was the love of her life. She told us so many stories about him; he was my Superman. Grandpa Haoyu could slay dragons if he was put to the test. If she's going to see anyone in me, I'm glad it's him. I can stand in for Haoyu until she gets to be with the real deal. After all she's done for me, I can bite my tongue. When I stand at her bedside and she says, 'I love you, Haoyu,' I don't say, 'No, Nǎinai, it's Jon. Your grandson.' I say, 'Wǒ yě ài nǐ.' I love you too."

Jon refolded his story back into a neat square, dropped his hands to his lap, and looked around the circle. Most of us had tears in our eyes. Lenny was the first to clap and, stunned out of our contemplation, the rest of us followed suit.

"Thank you for sharing your Nǎinai," Dr. Mirza said, her warm smile radiating the sincerest of gratitude.

We had gathered in the theater department's Blackbox space, which was in the basement of one of the original residence halls. This space, lovingly referred to as simply "The Box," was what you'd expect from a Blackbox theater—a versatile ground-level playing space with endless options for seating arrangements. Although, The Box was a tinge creepy given the fact that it was underground and almost certainly had a ghost haunting the bathrooms. When I was a major, toilet paper mysteriously went missing at the most inopportune times and the lights liked to flicker when you were alone in the building taking a pee. According to Lincoln, Charles the Mischievous, was still up to his old tricks.

Our cast consisted of me, Lincoln, Lenny, Jon, Dr. Mirza, and, in a surprising turn of events, a woman from Whitney's Bible study—Deja. Whitney was invested in Lincoln's capstone to a degree that was helpful, albeit over-the-top; she offered to host a bake sale to fundraise, promised a packed house with all her church friends, and repeatedly asked if we needed help running lines, although we explained that it wasn't exactly that kind of play...there was no script. Yet.

"She's, like, the opposite of the Evil Stepmom. She's Super Stepmom," I observed while popping a bit of her freshly baked banana nut muffins into my mouth.

"I think she's just stoked to have a pseudo-kid," Lincoln explained. "Dad said she and her first husband tried for kids for ten years and they ended up splitting over it."

"Well, her heart's in the right place," I said. "And she's a damn good baker, so she can stay." I stuffed two more muffins into my purse before heading home that night.

As overbearing as she could be, Whitney had come in clutch when it came to Deja. After explaining to the Bible study what her stepson was up to, Deja, unprompted, walked up to Whitney and volunteered to participate. Deja called herself a "birth mom," meaning that she had placed her baby for adoption. Going to Whitney's Bible study had been therapeutic for her in coming to terms with the decision she made for her son when she was just 16, and she was eager for an opportunity to share her story of loss. From what she shared already in rehearsal, it was incontestable that she was made of pure courage.

"Before we wrap up, let's go over the logistics," Lincoln announced, tapping fully into his director voice—slightly lower and more authoritative than his usual breezy casualness. "Capstone performances are a one-night gig. I'm assigned to April 26th, the Saturday before graduation. We'll meet here, in The Box, once a week on Thursdays nights. We can start by working on our written pieces, giving each other feedback, and brainstorming the ways we want to present. And then maybe incorporate some Viewpoints work and definitely Patsy Rodenburg's circles of energy theory." Lincoln paused at the confused exchanges around the circle. "Sorry—I'm going to try not to use theater lingo. Please, if I say anything that sounds like hocus pocus, just call me out. I don't want theater mumbo-jumbo to hold anyone back."

I gave him a wink. He blushed. My heart danced.

"The most important thing I want everyone to walk away with tonight is the understanding that these rehearsals are a safe place to explore and fail. I'm open to every single off-the-wall idea that pops into your head. This is as much your piece as it is mine—that's what devised work is all about."

Like standing on the DeLuca's trampoline prepping for a tremendous gravity-defying bounce, I was ready to spring into action. And from the awe-struck looks of the rest of the cast, it seemed like they were all just as eager to dig their heels into something meaningful and innovative. I didn't picture my reentry into theater happening so soon, but when I realized that the dimple smile was permanently plastered to my face over the last two hours, I knew that this was how it was supposed to be.

"And we could probably use two to four more storytellers—do you guys like that word? 'Actor' and 'performer' don't feel expansive enough…"

We nodded, enthusiastically.

"'Storytellers' it is!" The goofy grin was still intact, even in director-mode. "Reach out to me or my *partner*…" He threw me a bashful sideways peep. "…if you have anyone in mind before we meet next week."

"Partner" was the title we had settled on the day before. Lincoln followed through on his promise for a "real date" by taking me to the historic district during their tribute to National Bagel Day. I had no idea that January 15th was an officially recognized holiday devoted to my carbo-loaded breakfast of choice. The event was a bagel history themed scavenger hunt that involved stopping by every shop in the town square to grab samples of gourmet bagels and cream cheeses. We argued over the superiority of the jalapeño versus the chipotle schmear but agreed that the honey lavender bagel was the perfect complement to our piping hot cups of black coffees.

Right after we learned that bagels were once given to women in Poland as a gift after childbirth, (bizarre, but if I told Lincoln with assurance that if I ever popped out a kid, that's exactly what I would request as my post-labor snack) I blurted, "How are you going to introduce me? At rehearsal."

"Most of them already know you. You're K Statham," Lincoln responded after swallowing a mouthful of sesame bagel with smoked salmon cream cheese.

Men could be so clueless. Paisley had warned me of this, so she demanded I define the terms of the relationship sooner rather than later.

"Don't just assume that because you're besties, you're on the same page," she had said after I told her that Lincoln and I were dating. "'Dating' and 'official *girlfriend*' are two different things."

"Abe, I'm trying to D-T-R with you. What should we call each other?" I said, teetering into a tone that Paisley would most likely deem too blunt to be palatable for the "emotionally underdeveloped male brain."

"DTR?"

"You know…" I forged ahead despite the heat rising in my cheeks. "'Define the relationship'? Am I your girlfriend or what?"

"Ohhhhhh," he said, finally comprehending. "Do you *want* to be my girlfriend?"

I raised an eyebrow. "Why do you think I'm asking?"

Paisley wasn't lying. Men could be thick when it came to matters of the heart.

"Just checking!" He laughed. "Well then, that settles it. You're my girlfriend."

"I'm your girlfriend. I guess that settles it. That was…*easy*!" I smiled so wide; I knew my cheeks would be sore for days. "But maybe for rehearsal we could say something more…professional. How about 'partner'?"

"'Partner' for professional settings. 'Girlfriend' in casual settings…and when we're alone, I'll just call you mine."

Even if I wasn't one for public displays of affection, I was perfectly content to let him wrap his arms around me and plant a wet kiss squarely on my lips right in front of the "1610 - New Baby, New Bagel" display.

"Is this what it feels like to a bagel on a plate full of onion rolls? Because everyone's looking at us," I joked.

"Huh?"

"*Funny Girl*! Are you a theater freak, or aren't you?"

I filed that moment in my "Happier Than I Deserve to Be" folder, which had been filling up quite rapidly those days.

After Lincoln locked up The Box, he grabbed my hand and gave me a twirl.

"That was AMAZING!" he exclaimed.

Unprepared for this impromptu ballroom stunt, I stepped on his foot, banged into his chest, and slipping on an unseen patch of ice, we both tumbled into a nearby garden of camellias. I landed on top of him and could feel the lively rise and fall of his stomach against mine.

"We've gotten rusty since *Sound of Music*," he laughed.

We debriefed at Chubbie's over peppermint "meow-chas." Lenny's nephew and our only other coworker, Elijah, had held down the fort while Lenny and I were at rehearsal and insisted on making our drinks even though I told him I could do it.

"You work too hard. You tryin' to show me up in front of my uncle?" Elijah said as he delivered our mugs to the bird table. He added extra whipped cream and mini candy canes were hooked to the side of the cups.

"I have to do something to compensate for your showstopping presentations," I lamented.

"Am I about to witness a Barista War?" Lincoln asked.

"Not tonight. But that *would* make for a great next play…as long as you write me in as the winner and Elijah as the sore loser. Which he is." I leaned in to whisper, "His presentations are no match for my innate ability to strike the perfect balance of milk to espresso."

Lincoln smirked. "I'll consider it."

Lapping in the success of rehearsal while watching Lincoln attempt to lick up his whipped cream mustache, I couldn't be more proud to be "his." I wanted to say as much but decided that commenting on the play would be a safer bet—I still skirted away from overly romantic gestures being that it was *still* Lincoln DeLuca, the formerly shaggy-headed dork who used to sign my yearbook with quotes from *Star Wars*.

"You know," I began, "you're the only person I know that's actually done the thing—stayed with theater and did what you said you were going to do. That's impressive, dude."

He took a long sip of his mocha and I wiped off the whipped cream that stuck to his nose.

"I can't do anything else," he said nonchalantly. "I have literally no other skills."

"Not true," I protested. "You were semi-decent at math. Better than me anyway."

"That's not saying much…" He laughed and I whacked his arm.

"Remember when you said you were going to name a character after me in your first Broadway play?"

Leaning back in his chair and looking out the stained-glass window beside us, he said, "That was the best summer."

"The summer before sophomore year. It really was."

"That was the night that Isa played for Raymond. What did she get? $200 or something insane like that?"

He was referring to the night that we snuck into the opening gala for The Quest for Immortality: Treasures of Ancient Egypt exhibit. After we left the museum, we walked along the river to sober up and came across a homeless man. He held up an "Anything Helps" sign made from a scrap piece of cardboard. All he said was, "How y'all doin' tonight?" but I immediately felt uneasy. I had always been told to avoid the homeless—don't make eye contact and just keep walking.

Isa, however, refused to abide by discriminatory social conventions. She told him all about the museum, asked for his name, and to my shock, even prodded into his personal life by interrogating, "How did you end up living off the land?"

He was a stranger for only a matter of minutes because once he got talking, he didn't stop. His name was Raymond, he was a disabled veteran, and he had no family to speak of. But he didn't just talk of his "down-and-out sob story"—his words. He also told us that he loved music, specifically rockabilly. It was his dream to tour Graceland. "Blue Suede Shoes" was what he used to sing to calm himself down before going out on the front lines. He said he had some connections in Memphis that might be able to help him get back on his feet, but he couldn't afford the Greyhound fare.

"I have my guitar in the car," Isa said. "What if we tried playing for money? You'd probably get more takers if we gave the people a little entertainment."

And that's what she did. She played while Raymond sang Elvis songs. After an hour and a half, Raymond had more than enough for his Greyhound ticket.

"Yeah," I confirmed to Lincoln as I pulled the candy cane from my mouth. "After, like, song number three or four we just started talking and let them do their thing."

"That's right…" he mused. "And you said, 'You can only use my name if the character is really special. No boring ingénues.' And I told you that you make whatever role you play something special. Because you *are* something special."

Almost eight years later and my insides still liquefied over the same line. I wondered if I was supposed to be "harder to get." Paisley would've probably thought so.

"Do you still think that?" I asked. "You know, now that you aren't wearing rose-colored glasses? I'm not who I was when we were 15."

"I have permanent rose-colored vision when I'm looking at you."

I didn't know if I liked that response, as romantic as he intended it to be.

"I'm not perfect, you know."

"I know. You still pick your nose."

"I'm serious," I exhorted.

He had no way of knowing that underneath the playful banter, I was still wrestling with the question of when I would come clean about…well, *everything*. But now was not the time. Not now while we were celebrating this first rehearsal triumph.

"*I'm* serious," he said, "You are and always will be—special. Not just to me. You need to believe it."

I scooted my chair closer to his and laid my head on his shoulder. There was still time and I wanted to savor the "Happier Than I Deserve to Be" file before I had to give it up.

"I wonder what ever happened to Raymond," Lincoln conjectured.

"I hope he's an Elvis impersonator," I replied.

"I hope he lives in a replica of Graceland. He deserves it."

"Our chats have been somewhat of an inspiration then, yes?"

It was confirmed—Dr. Mirza was a puppet master in the best possible way.

"Mildly so," I downplayed as we strolled through campus.

We were discussing my senior thesis and because it was unseasonably in the low 60s, she proclaimed that we would walk and talk rather than subject ourselves to her stuffy office.

"Any ideas for the title as of yet?" she asked as we passed the gazebo packed with lunching liberal art students.

"The Female Artists that Gave Birth to Modernism in Postcolonial Pakistan," I stated. "But if that's too wordy…"

"I think it's perfectly poetic and to the point," she praised. "Look at you, K. You no longer need an advisor—you are steering the ship!"

I laughed my evading-the-real-problem laugh. After three years as my advisor and mentor, Dr. Mirza knew what it meant.

"And may I inquire about…graduate studies?"

She took a seat on the edge of the water fountain that faced the quad and patted the cement beside her. I sat and took note of the camellias that were in bloom. It was like the campus itself was a blushing bride with the number of pink petals that sprung from the ground. This university was the Gardens of Versailles of college campuses. Most recognizable for the millions of dollars spent on springtime tulips, but I always preferred the camellias. The camellias were in bloom the January of my senior year when my dad and I toured the campus. Of course, I'd always admired the school from afar every time we passed it to go to Chubbie's, but I had never actually stepped foot on the grounds as a prospective student. It was magical. I didn't apply anywhere else and told Dad my intentions when we got back in the car. For me, it was Belmont or bust. I had always been a sucker for beautiful things.

"I'm considering taking a year off."

It came out as a confession, knowing that Dr. Mirza had previously expressed such high hopes for me at the commencement of my graduate school hunt.

"I had an inclination that perhaps you needed a bit more time to reflect," she said.

"I don't know what I'll do instead," I admitted. "But I'm pretty confident that I'm not ready. I want a master's, but…I feel like I don't have a good enough reason for wanting it."

"With that, I disagree. Sometimes, to want can be reason enough. But is there another path that you want *more*?"

I stared at the camellias. I had no idea what I wanted other than I didn't want to choose. I had been running from the burden of having to choose for longer than I could remember, at least, that's what Dr.

McPherson concluded. In one session, we discovered that the fear of choosing was one of the major motives that led to dropping my theater major—I didn't want to choose an identity.

***

"If you want to promote yourself for more ethnic roles, I would use your given name and maybe even your mother's maiden name on your resume," Professor Ralph Scott said one afternoon in Business of Show Business. "What's your full first name?"

"It's…just…Katie."

"*Katie?*" he asked, aghast. "I thought it'd be something from your native country."

"I was born in Hinsdale. It's a suburb of Chicago," I said flatly as the rest of the class stared.

"In that case, I'd stick with Katie Statham. Which is unfortunate because white females with dark hair are a dime a dozen. You'll have to work harder to prove you deserve to be in the room. But either way, you'd have to prove that directors should take a 'non-traditional casting' bent if your agent submits you for roles that are supposed to be played by white women," he explained and then directed his focus to the class at large. "In this business you need to know how to market yourself. You need to know your type and how you're likely to be cast. Pick a lane and stick to it."

The class snatched up his words like he was throwing out gold coins. He had been a replacement in *Biloxi Blues* on Broadway back in the 80s. To fame-thirsty young minds, he could do no wrong. While everyone else took notes, I excused myself to cry in The Box's bathroom. Predictably, Charles switched the lights off, leaving me to sob in the dark.

***

"I think I came here for my tour exactly four years ago this week," I said to Dr. Mirza.

The memory was melancholy because the college experience had once held so much promise. But in my three and a half years, it had let me down in a lot of ways. In others, though, I couldn't deny that it had been a refuge. The verdict was still out as to if I would miss it for what it was, or the wide-eyed 18-year-old that imagined herself blooming alongside the camellias—what it could have been.

"Ah, now I see it through your eyes," Dr. Mirza said. "When the camellias are in bloom, that is decision time, yes?"

"Put *that* on a bumper sticker," Lincoln snorted that night when I told him what Dr. Mirza said.

"Right? The woman is a fortune cookie personified," I said as I leaned forward to grab another slice of mushroom pizza. "That reminds me—we have an appointment with Leonora next week. Apparently, business is booming, and she doesn't take walk-ins anymore."

"Great! Although, I never met a physic yet that you could trust," he said, intentionally misquoting Arthur O'Connell's character.

We were sitting on the floor of my apartment, sharing a pizza, and watching *Anatomy of a Murder*, which was two hours and forty minutes of Jimmy Stewart brilliance.

"This is basically as long as the extended edition of *Return of the King*," Lincoln complained. "How many times have you seen this?"

"Not enough," I shot back. Then, I reluctantly committed myself to *The Matrix* when I said, "It's your pick next week."

"But, anyway," he said, wiping pizza grease from his mouth, "what *are* you going to do?"

"What are *you* going to do?"

"Have you thought about—and it's totally cool if you don't want to—but have you thought about…Switzerland?" His face suddenly turned serious against the glow of the tv.

I had; I thought about how Lincoln said just about a month ago, "Or you could come with…like you said you would…" I thought about that at least once a day, swore I'd bring it up, and then, like everything else, pushed it to the backburner.

"Of course," I said, setting my half-eaten slice down on my paper plate.

If we were about to have this conversation, then I wanted to do it without strings of mozzarella dangling from my mouth.

"Well, I have too…" Lincoln began, "And like I said, it's totally cool if—"

"Just say what you want to say."

"Okay. I've been thinking: What if we go this summer? Together."

He held my gaze, and I knew this was the moment where I could either step up to the plate, or I could run off the field screaming. The ball was in my court. I was up to bat. Insert whatever sports-related analogy fits—I never had an interest in such things, but I knew it was now or never. This could be my gap-year purpose. I had to choose eventually, and I could make this my choice. Following through on a long-ago promise was as noble a purpose as any.

"Yes," I said simply.

"Think about it—you're not sold on any of these programs, and I don't have concrete—Wait. Yes?"

"Yes," I said again.

"You'll go?"

"I'll go."

"This summer? After graduation?"

"Why not?" I asked. "We need to do this. And why not? We could even…"

My mind was spinning with possibilities. All at once this seemed like the best and most obvious next step. Why hadn't I thought of it before?

"…we could backpack all *over* Switzerland," I proposed. "That's the only way we can do this right; we can't just go there, do the…thing…and hop back on a plane. I want to know what it is that she wanted."

"We can research how to backpack without starving or getting lost in the Alps or whatever! We can YouTube it! There's got to be so much content out there," Lincoln said, excitedly. "And what if we didn't stop there—we could do a whole European tour, K! Why not?"

I laughed. "Why not?"

"*Why the hell no*t?!" he exclaimed, now standing on his knees.

"Okay, but what about money?" I asked. "I don't want to kill the mood but…"

"No, no, no. That's fair. Well…I didn't blow *all* of my grandparents' inheritance by being a screw-up alcoholic in New York," Lincoln thought aloud.

"Don't say that."

"Okay, 'being an irresponsible griever.'"

"That's…better," I laughed.

"And there's graduation money… I assume we'll both get graduation money?"

"I actually have a lot saved from Chubbie's and I can do some overtime too before we go," I offered.

"Do you think this is doable?"

"I mean, how much do you think it would cost?"

"You know what—I have no clue. But it's happening. We're doing this, K. We're going to Switzerland. We're going to find out exactly what happened to Isa and then we're going to put this all to rest. We're going to move on with our lives."

He embraced me and the relief that washed over me was like the first burst of sunshine after a year of dreary Januarys.

"This is what you want too, right?" he pulled away to look me directly in the eyes.

"Yes, more than anything." My eyes were brimming with the kind of tears that soak your face after you've finished a very hard and taxing feat. "This is what I want."

Pizzas forgotten on the floor, we fell into each other. We were kissing and grasping for each other. His fingers were tangled in my hair and my hands glided over his chest. Sighing, he grabbed my hips and rolled me on top of him. I took his face in my hands and plunged forward. His lips held a nectar made of sweetness and vitality and I couldn't get enough. We were moving in unison—a dance with unspoken choreography. I wanted closure. I wanted to move on. I also wanted *this*. I wanted *him*.

His chest rose and fell under me, and his lips tickled my neck. I placed one of his wandering hands at my side. He held me tighter, and I imagined melting into him. His hot, crushed red pepper breath filled my nostrils—I didn't care. It made me want him more. Pressing my cheek against his, the scratchiness of stubble reminded me that this was real and not a dream. I didn't know where my tongue ended and his began. We were completely stone cold sober, but I'd never been more intoxicated; the warmth of him sending me into delightful oblivion. And then his hand moved ever so slightly northward. With his fingers grazing the underside of my right breast, I became stiff.

He guided me to my back and now he was on top of me—his hands slipping under my cardigan and meeting bare skin, sighing my name.

"*Katie.*"

I couldn't move. I couldn't think anymore. The sweetness was gone. I turned my head to the side, breaking our kiss, but he seemed to take that as a cue to kiss my neck.

"I've wanted this for so long," he whispered. "I've always thought of you."

He felt too heavy. I squirmed underneath him, but he was too heavy. I was sweating. And he was so heavy. I couldn't move. My heart threatened to beat through my shirt and push Lincoln across the room. Stop. Stop. Stop. The heaviness held me in place. I gasped for air. Lincoln thought I was moaning with pleasure, and he didn't stop. His hips pressed into mine and his hand crept over my bra. Stop. Stop. Stop. I smelled the sickening sweet aroma of Cheerwine mixed with vanilla and when I closed my eyes, I saw a glob of mustard on the collar of a black sweatshirt. Without thinking twice, I used the voice that I once lost.

"STOP!" I yelled and rolled out from under him.

Instinctively, I curled into a ball, hugging my knees to my chest. The tears of relief had, unbeknownst to me, turned into tears of fear.

"K," Lincoln sat up, his face was white. "K?"

He reached for me, but I flinched.

You're okay, you're okay, you're okay. The pizza. Count the mushrooms on the pizza. One, two, three, four, five...

It wasn't working.

"Did I do something wrong?"

You're okay. Try rocking. Forward. Backward. Forward. Backward.

I still couldn't breathe. I heard a howling. Was that me? That couldn't be me?

"K? What can I do? I'm so sorry. I'm so sorry. What can I do?"

Lincoln reached for me again.

"Don't. Touch. Me. Don'ttouchmedonttouchmeddontouchmetouchme…"

"Okay, K," he said, calmly. "I'm going to stand up now. I'm going to go sit on the futon now, okay? I'm not going to touch you. I'm going to give you some space, okay? Is that okay?"

Barely deciphering his words above the out-of-body howls, I nodded.

"I'm on the futon now, K. You're safe. I promise. I won't touch you again, K. I promise. I'm so sorry."

You're okay, you're okay, you're okay. In for two. Hold. Out for two. In for two. Hold. out for two.

"Do you want me to count breaths with you, K? Will that help?"

I nodded.

"Okay, I can do that. You're safe, K. It's going to be okay. Breathe in…and let it go. That's one. Are you with me, K?"

I nodded.

"Good. Let's do that again. Breathe in…and let it go. That's two."

When we reached seven, the ringing in my ears stopped. At 13, I knew my heart was going to stay inside my chest. By 20, I could look at him again.

Fifteen minutes later, the credits to *Anatomy of a Murder* were rolling and F. Scott was licking my discarded slice of mushroom pizza. We sat in hollow silence, Lincoln hanging his head on the futon and me still in a ball on the floor.

"Is he allowed to eat that?" Lincoln finally broke the silence.

I shook my head.

"Hey, Scottie. Hey, give me that, buddy," Lincoln said, lifting the paper plate from the ground. F. Scott attempted to swat him. "Hey…that's not a very nice kitty. I just don't want your mommy to have to clean up diarrhea, okay?"

F. Scott meowed deeply and followed Lincoln as he crossed to the kitchen and dumped the plate in the trash. He was rubbing himself against Lincoln's legs, causing him to trip. F. Scott purred but when Lincoln stumbled into him, he hissed.

"Dude! You're making me trip. What do you want?"

I couldn't help but laugh a little. F. Scott was so finicky with new humans; one second, he'd accept belly rubs and the next second he'd nip your heels.

"He's hungry. I haven't given him dinner."

My voice was a fragile croak. I was about to stand to refill the cat bowl when Lincoln stopped me.

"No, it's okay. You sit. Is the food in the pantry?"

I nodded then found my way to the futon. After F. Scott had been fed, Lincoln cleaned up the rest of the pizza mess and joined me on the futon. He didn't sit as close to me as he normally would have. I wasn't sure if that made me sad or relieved.

"K, I'm—sorry. I get it. That was too much. I forget that we've only technically been 'together' for a few weeks because it feels like…I don't know. That's not an excuse."

"Lincoln," I said. Tonight was the night of now or nevers. "Can I tell you something?"

"You know you can."

I was crying again.

"Or," he piped up, "you don't have to tell me anything. K, it's my fau—"

"No," I interrupted him. "It's not your fault. It's som—someone else's."

And by the look on his face, I knew that he knew.

"You don't have to tell me—" he said quietly.

"Yes. I do. It's not a very nice story. But if we're ever going to do…that…again. If you ever want to after what I…what I just did…then I have to tell you. Will you listen?"

"I can listen."

I told him what he needed to know and what I could remember. I told him I didn't have a name and I told him that no one else knew apart from Isa and Dr. McPherson.

"So…that's why…" I finished. "It's not such a rose-colored reality."

I knew he'd have to be a narcissistic asshole to storm off and confirm what I secretly thought was true—that I was damaged goods. I knew that Lincoln wasn't like that—even if I was too messed up to be his girlfriend, he'd at least have the decency to treat me with respect. Even still, I was taken aback by what he said next.

"What happened to you... I don't see what…happened. I just see you. And K, I know this doesn't make it better but…I wish I had been there that night. Someone hurting you…it…I wish I would've been there. But you are unchanged to me. I'm not trying to diminish—"

"I know. Do you pro—"

But we spoke each other's language. He knew to say, "I promise. I wouldn't lie to you."

He tentatively reached out his pinky finger and I linked mine around it. Then he pulled my hand closer and kissed it gently.

"I never want to hurt you."

I nodded, took my hand back, and tucked my hair behind my ears.

"Can I tell *you* something?" he asked.

"Yes."

"I just—I want to be honest with you about my, uh, experiences…so everything is on the table. I really don't want to screw this up, K. You gotta believe me on that. Maybe this will screw everything up once I tell you, but you have a right to know everything—"

"Lincoln, it's okay."

He took a deep breath.

"Okay, well…you know I dated someone freshman year?"

"Samantha."

"Yeah, Samantha." He ran a hand through his hair and sighed again. "Okay, so…Samantha and I had sex. A few times."

I really did not want to hear this. I had hoped I'd never have to know these details.

"And twice was before, uh, before Isa…before the funeral. And then the last time was when I got back. I knew when I got back that I wanted to break up with her. I never *loved* her. I know that sounds bad, but it's true. I was so messed after the funeral, and I had just seen you and… It made me realize that Samantha… She was a—a placeholder, I guess. And how was I supposed to be this girl's boyfriend when I was thinking about you all the time and calling you in the middle of the night and leaving you all those drunk voicemails? It wasn't fair to her. But I did it anyway.

"We had sex again when I got back. And then I just stopped answering her texts and picking up her calls. I think she cared about me. I don't know why. I didn't deserve it. But I think she did. And I didn't even care enough to break it off like I should have. I really regret that, K. It was just regret on top of regret. Regret for all the things I maybe had the power to change but was too selfish to try. I don't know if it's appropriate at this point to say I'm sorry to Samantha. But…I want to say I'm sorry to you. For…treating a woman that way. I will never, ever do that again. You have my word on that. I'm sorry for tonight."

"Me too."

I knew his confession warranted more than two simple words, but I couldn't think of any other way to relay that I knew so profoundly and all too well what he meant.

"You too?"

"I have a lot of regrets."

"I don't want any more regrets. Not with you. I wouldn't be able to forgive myself."

There were a lot of things I could have said. There were certainly a lot of feelings pulsating through my mind and body, competing for attention. But I didn't think. I just said, "Then let's go."

"To Switzerland?"

"Yeah."

He nodded, rolled up his flannel sleeve, and revealed his daisy tattoo. I did the same. It was the first time either of us had acknowledged the mark that branded us since we'd reunited. Looking at the black lined designs side by side, they took on a new meaning—we had a mission, and we were going to fulfill it.

"I should get going," he said, standing. "Sorry this wasn't the night that we planned. I know what I just told you isn't exactly the kind of thing you want to hear from the guy you're bringing home to meet the parents."

"This isn't the 'hometown date' on *The Bachelorette*, Abe," I teased. "My parents already know you. It's just dinner."

"Yeah, but it's my first dinner as The Boyfriend. They're going to be assessing me with fresh eyes. And excuse me…are you watching *The Bachelorette* with Paisley now?" he asked as he put on his jacket.

"Say that again."

"Are you watching *The Bachelorette*?"

"No, the other thing."

He smiled a knowing smile.

"This is my first dinner as…" always a ham, he paused for dramatic effect. "The *Boyfriend*."

"I just like to hear you say it."

I stepped closer and stood on my tiptoes to reach him. He stood still, letting me take the lead and I met his lips with a soft kiss. Everything was as it once was.

"You know," I said, "My dad used to say that whoever was going to sweep me off my feet would be a guy that met me at one of my plays. He'd say, 'There's going to be some fine young man in the audience, and he is going to be *spellbound*.'"

We both chuckled at my poorly done Tim Statham impersonation.

"Well maybe I stand a chance," Lincoln said, leaning one arm against the front door, stalling like he always did when it was time to say goodnight. "Because I've seen every one of your plays."

"Not all of them. You didn't see—"

"Yeah, actually…I did." Fidgeting, he put both hands in his pockets. "I saw *Hamlet*. I should have told you. I came that Tuesday night. It was the day before I flew back to New York. I waited at the stage door, but you didn't come out. I didn't know that you had a panic attack onstage. I watched the whole damn play, K. And I thought you were…exquisite. It was real grief, and it was…I'm sorry I didn't say anything back on the swings. I didn't want you to be embarrassed."

"How did you know to come?" was all I could say as I tried to process this unexpected piece of information.

"In New York, I kept tabs on the school's theater site. For cast announcements? I wanted to know what you were up to, I guess. Is that crazy? That's crazy."

I shook my head.

"I did the same thing for Columbia. For a while," I admitted sheepishly.

"And I didn't know you switched majors," he went on, "I came to most of the shows here once I moved back, thinking I might see you. It wasn't until I started last semester that I realized you weren't in the department anymore."

"That's not why you transferred here, is it?"

"Not entirely. But I hoped. I was really hoping we could…start fresh. And I wanted a degree from somewhere that *wasn't* TCC."

We laughed.

"You know what's so stupid? We could've just called each other," I pointed out.

"Yeah, we could have. *If* someone didn't change her number…"

"Touché," I relented. "Okay, now, sir—I must bid you farewell. Stop stalling. It's past me and F. Scott's bedtime."

He bent down to give me one more kiss, but then something occurred to me.

"Wait," I said, "you didn't see *Peter Pan*. So, you've seen all but *one*."

"No, I was there. Closing night. Came halfway through act one and left right at curtain call. Not to bring up water under the bridge but…we weren't exactly the best of buds back then…"

He winked at me because we both knew that I was completely responsible for the animosity between us at the end of junior year and the awkwardness that continued through senior year—I was the one who bailed on his play after all.

"But that was graduation day," I said, accusatory. "There's no way—"

"I left as soon as I walked. I had to see you fly."

He left while my mouth still hung open. Out of all the confessions of the evening, this had to be the biggest bombshell. If Lincoln saw *Peter Pan*, Lincoln had seen Steve. There was a husky-tone laugh just then…so faint that it could have been my imagination. Of course, it had to be my imagination. The hair on my arms stood at attention. I knew that laugh.

"But of course," Leonora said, inspecting my empty cup of Earl Grey, "the water bird. Emotional creatures with psychic energy."

She held the cup out for my inspection. I saw a few squiggly mushy black blobs—definitely not a bird of any kind.

"Purification. And travel," Leonora stated.

I glanced at Lincoln, and he rolled his eyes. All Leonora saw at the bottom of his cup was the need for sleep and a possible B-12 deficiency.

"Um, thanks, Leonora," I said. "That sounds…good."

"Very good. Very good," Leonora confirmed as she stood to clear the table of the tea accouterments.

"When are we going to get on with it?" Lincoln whispered.

Leonora had already bamboozled us into a 35-minute aura check-in and tea leaf reading, claiming that these practices assisted in "raising the vibrations necessary for a clearer message." We had come to Sisters of the Moon for Leonora's "afterlife communication" service—her most popular after she published her recent guidebook, *How to Communicate with the Transitioned*. The dust jacket professed that there was no such thing as death, rather there is only a transition from a physical being to a spiritual being. Furthermore, anyone who seeks an answer from "the beyond" can find it with an open mind, sharp intuition, and $75.00 cash when booking an appointment with Sisters of the Moon.

The only reason we were entertaining this mind trip of an excursion was because we figured that Leonora had information that we weren't privy to; knowing how much Isa hero-worshiped her, it was a safe assumption that she would have been a confidant during the time when the three of us went our separate ways. Unsurprisingly, Leonora told me over the phone when I booked the appointment that she "speaks with her little gem often" and therefore she didn't require us to bring anything to use as an "aid." Wherever that meant…

"Do you use a Ouija board or something?" I asked, hoping to get the ball rolling.

"No, no, no, my dear," Leonora dismissed. "Goodness no."

She provided no further explanation. This was something I had grown accustomed to from my previous interactions with her, but it was a habit that inspired sighs of frustration from Lincoln.

"First we must silence all electronic devices," she instructed.

Lincoln snickered under his breath, "Is she also going to tell us where the emergency exits are? And that concessions are located in the lobby?"

I glared at him as Leonora dimmed the lights and hung up a sign on the front door reading, "Respect the Transitioned and do not disturb! Séance in progress!" When she rejoined us at the round table, she lit only three of the candles on the candelabra.

"Now, we will join hands," she said, reaching across the table for us. "We are creating a bond that cannot be broken throughout our time with our dear gem. You must not surrender your grip no matter what manifests during our session."

I found that instruction a bit eerie but nodded in agreement anyway.

"I will begin with a chant, and then I will invite dear Isabel to our table. Please, rest your eyes for the time being. You will know when the time is right to open them."

Without my sense of sight, the aroma of burning tea tree oil and the faint creaks in the corners of the room that was otherwise cloaked in silence became more pronounced. Leonora began chanting. At first, the noise was similar to the "om" noises Isa would make at the conclusion of a yoga flow, but after a while, it sounded as though two separate tones were lilting through the space. I squeezed Lincoln's hand but kept my eyes tightly shut. Leonora was just doing something freaky with her voice—that was all. Then I remembered Cressida, the twin. A shiver went up my spine.

"We are humbly reaching out to Isabel Claire DeLuca, resident of the beyond. Please join us in our circle tonight when you are ready," Leonora said.

After a beat of silence, the table shook. My eyes popped open.

Leonora released a pleasant laugh. "Why hello, gem," she cooed.

Lincoln's eyes were wide, and it was hard to maintain my grip on his hand when both our palms were sweating. How was this happening? I looked down at Leonora's lap. No part of her lower body was making contact with the underside of the table.

"Now, we have three flames before us. The right you will use for 'yes,' the left you will use to say, 'no,' and the center you can use to tell us that you do not know the answer to our question. If you understand, please flicker the right flame."

Instantly, the right candle went dark and then without striking a match, it blazed back to life. In the same instance, that specific husky laugh echoed through the space.

"What the fu—"

"Shh!" Leonora hissed at Lincoln. "She tells me that she attempted contact before with someone at this table. That someone has not been receptive to her visits."

The table shook again. I tried to avoid Leonora's stormy gaze, fearful that she would draw out the guilt from my subconscious.

"Gem, tell us—do you have a message?"

The right candle flickered.

"Does your message concern one of the physical beings present in the circle?"

The right candle flickered.

"Where is she? Is she in pain? What happened to her?" Lincoln blurted—clearly a skeptic no longer.

"Patient, patient," Leonora scolded. "One at a time."

Lincoln nodded then began again, more tentative this time. "Isa, are you in pain?"

The left candle flickered— "no."

Our sighs of relief almost extinguished all three candles.

"If you would like, dear," Leonora encouraged me, "you may ask a question."

I couldn't believe we were doing this. Were we really buying into this? But what was the logical explanation for the candle trick? The shaking table? The laugh... Then and there, I didn't care about having to explain myself to Lincoln or Leonora. I wasn't worried that admitting to these hallucinations or waking dreams—whatever they were—might grant me a one-way ticket back to Vanderbilt's psychiatric floor. I needed to know. So, I asked...

"Is—Isa?" I croaked. "Has it all been my imagination?"

The left candle went out. Smoke drifted towards the ceiling in swirling loops. It did not glow again.

"I fear that our gem is growing tired," Leonora observed. "We can ask but one more question."

Lincoln and I exchanged glances. I nodded, indicating that he could take the last one.

"Okay, um, Isa… Was it an…*accident*?"

A tiny orangish spark fizzled from the left candle but was gone within a second. The center candle went dark as well.

"What does that mean?" Lincoln frantically looked to Leonora. "Is that 'no'? Or 'I don't know'?"

Leonora simply nodded and shifted her gaze to me. Was she incriminating me? And there was the low-toned laughter again. I knew Lincoln heard it too because his eyes darted around the room, trying to locate the source of the noise.

My tongue tasted of metal and my throat burned—it was a sensation akin to swallowing a large pill without enough water to chase it down. An intense rush of nausea surged inside me, and I was for a second fearful that I was going to projectile vomit all over the table. I closed my eyes and saw Isa underwater. It was just like the time we went skinny dipping in the neighborhood pool. She appeared as a siren with a rhapsodic chlorine haze surrounding her silhouette. Her hair was wild—floating in all directions. Her eyes were crystal clear, and she was laughing. The delicate crinkles at the corners of her eyes made her so alive. I wanted to touch her. I had to pull her out of the water. I knew this, somehow. I reached for her, but she started to sink.

"She has a name," a voice in my mind whispered.

Her eyes were closed but she was not dreaming. She sunk, sunk, sunk. And then she was gone.

When I opened my eyes, all three candles were dead and there was water on the table. The distinct smell of chlorine overpowered Leonora's calming essential oils.

In the darkness, Leonora said, "I now accept all major credit cards."

"I know who *this* is…" Lincoln said playfully, pointing to the primary-colored feline on my bedroom wall. "Mr. F. Scott Fitzgerald himself. How'd you get him to hold still?"

After dinner, Lincoln begged to see some of my artwork so I was giving him the grand gallery tour—a half wall covered with the canvases that I had left each time I returned to school (and that my mom decided would look better in frames).

"But *this*," Lincoln stared closely at the smallest canvas.

In the center of the hodgepodge of color was the piece I completed in the hospital. Surrounded by the vivacious acrylics of the others, this was a lonely monochromatic grayscale watercolor.

"Is it a lake?" he asked, then squinted to discern the fine details. "Are those tiny birds flying over a lake? That's what it is, right?"

"It's not supposed to be anything," I explained, but then thought better of it. "I guess, if it's anything, it's my mind."

"That's sort of…heartbreaking."

"It can be. Mostly, it just is."

"K! Lincoln! Dessert's ready!" Dad called from the landing of the stairs.

We paid Leonora then rushed to my parents' house for the all-important Boyfriend Dinner without speaking a word. It was better that way—dinner with my parents forced us to press pause on analyzing the freakish events that had transpired before they could unravel us.

"Just act like yourself. They already like you, remember?" I coached him as I parked in the driveway of my parents' house.

"Yeah, yeah," he said, deflecting nervous energy by polishing his glasses repeatedly with an edge of his ironed buttoned up shirt. "I'm fine. This is no big deal. Are you sure this shirt is nice enough? I should've worn the navy…"

"You look like a quality suitor, even with the bristles," I teased and tickled his chin.

"I should have shaved…"

"Stop it. You're fine," I promised.

"Okay, yeah. Yeah, it's not like I'm asking your dad for your hand or anything. It's a completely casual dinner."

"Wait. You're not? But he's going to expect that." I gave him a disappointed stare and he blinked twice, clearly racking his brain for a response. "Kidding, you idiot!"

He groaned but replaced his look of vexation with his larger-than-life grin as soon as my mom opened the front door. As I predicted, dinner went off without a hitch.

"Well, whatever it is," Lincoln said, backing away from the gallery wall and following me back downstairs, "you're a genius and I like it."

"Baked apple strudel," Mom presented when we returned to the dining room table.

Like every other home in our neighborhood, my parents had a formal living room and a formal dining room—spaces that were only used approximately once a year and whose primary function was to collect dust.

"I bring this to all of my fall/winter Pampered Chef events—people *love* it. Please, Lincoln, get a bigger slice!" Mom said, adding an extra sliver of strudel to his china dessert plate—another extravagant feature in my parents' home that was rarely ever used.

With the vase of fresh flowers, the dining room table set like it was Thanksgiving, and food served on the wedding china, clearly my parents were also playing to impress. All of the above proved unnecessary because the conversation flowed easily and there were good spirits all around. Lincoln didn't possess the same talent for charming older adults as Isa; he was much more genuine in his quirky shyness and mild manners. It was adorable to watch him attempt sports jargon with my dad— "Oh yeah, I've been to a Titans game once. Loved the...hotdogs," and compliment my mom— "Ms. Azrah, this shepherd's pie is better than Cracker Barrel!"

"Well, I have to say," my dad said after we'd stuffed ourselves with strudel, "your play sounds incredible. Never heard of anything like that before. Not that I hear much about the arts in my line of work..." He chuckled. "Where do you kids come up with these ideas?"

"Um..." Lincoln gave me a look. "Well, my sister was the inspiration."

My parents nodded and for the first time that evening, conversation had hit an uncomfortable lull.

"That was great, mom," I said, breaking everyone's somber strudel crumb stares. "Lincoln, I didn't get to show you all the paintings."

"Oh, there's more?" he asked.

I kicked him under the table.

"Right, oh yeah. I didn't see the, uh, ones on the, uh, wall..."

I almost shut my bedroom door but, to my horror, my dad called up, "Hey, you two! Keep that door open, will ya?"

Lincoln looked at me, ready to explode into hysterical laughter and I pushed him away before my dad could get a glimpse of his mockery in the doorway.

"K, you got a sunburn or are you blushing?" he teased.

I backed him into my walk-in closet, shut *that* door, pushed him up against the summer clothes I had stored, and gave him a long, hard kiss.

"Who's blushing?" I said in my sultriest Vivien Leigh voice.

"Whoa. We should come to your parents' house more often."

I rolled my eyes, grabbed him by the collar, and led him back out into my room. No more playing around. Now it was time to come clean. I swore to myself that I would do this tonight and after what happened at Sisters of the Moon, there was simply no more putting it off. I sat on my window seat and beckoned him to come over.

"Have you ever tried to Google Steve?" I asked.

"No…" he replied, taken aback by the abrupt change of topic. "To be honest, I didn't want to. Until recently."

I nodded. "Well, I think we should, you know…look him up. That's the next thing we should do."

"I agree," he said. "We need something more concrete than that witch stuff…"

"Right. And if he's still in town, we should…or *I* can…talk to him."

"Why wouldn't we do it together?"

I sighed. *Now or never.* "I have to show you something."

I knelt down and pulled a shoebox from underneath my bed—my box of playbills. I kept all of them since *Guys and Dolls*—even the little brochures we made for the Comedy O'clock fundraisers. Mixed in with the playbills were other memorabilia—photos of Isa, Lincoln, and I with various castmates backstage, "break a leg" notes, thank you cards, even a pocket-sized Puerto Rican flag taken from the set of *West Side Story*… I avoided this physical record of bittersweet memories; I hadn't opened it since *Peter Pan*. I never even bothered to add the *Hamlet* playbill to the collection.

Lincoln had no idea what an act of bravery it was for me to lift the lid and take out the dinner theater's thick, glossy playbill. *Peter Pan* written in giant yellow script and underneath, a photo of Sherry

Lauderdale—our Peter—in her green tights along with Freddy, Lucas, and me as Michael, John, and Wendy—the Darling children.

"I never got one," Lincoln said, taking the playbill out of my hand. "Because I came late and left early."

"I figured," I said. "I wanted to show you…"

I flipped to the cast bios page.

"Look at little high school K," he teased, pointing to my headshot and bio.

"Lincoln, *this* is what I'm trying to show you," I interrupted.

I pointed to one of the actor headshots. It was a guy in his mid-20s. He was suave and slightly sinister looking, making him an ideally cast stage villain. His cocky side smile also gave the impression of being somewhat of a smart ass (which was accurate). Defying what was the industry standard for such things, he wore his silver cross earring even in his headshot. The graininess of the black and white ink dulled and flattened his eyes—the appearance of someone with a secret. Someone who possibly had the potential to hurt someone else.

The caption: Steve Nowak (Captain Hook)

"*Wait*, K…is this…"

"I introduced them."

12.

What Was Missing

"**Happy birthday!**" Isa sang when I opened the front door.

She held out a miniature tree in a small ceramic pot. Its twisty branches and plump green leaves gave it the appearance of the whimsical plants you'd find singing about destiny in a Disney movie.

"My birthday was December 16th…" I said, without moving to accept the gift or give her entry, "It's February 21st."

"Duh, I know *that*," she said, hoisting a duffle bag further up her shoulder. "But today is *better* because Neptune is in Sagittarius's third house. And I got you this bonsai. For luck!"

She may as well have been speaking Spanish. I wouldn't have known—I'd recently failed a Spanish exam. I'd recently given up on pretty much everything. I was dreadfully incorrect when I thought that I could carry on with life as normal after Jason's party. I guess I figured that if I acted like nothing happened, then maybe I could convince myself that it didn't. But every time I shut my eyes, I saw an oblong yellow glob atop a black backdrop. Every time I found myself alone, even sitting in complete silence, I would begin to hear the bass of raging party music ringing in my ears.

The worst part was when Dad asked me over breakfast one Sunday, "Hey, haven't seen your bees in a while. You still like them?"

I soiled my bagel with salty tears in response and made up a story about how I lost them—took them off during gym and they disappeared. I said I suspected someone stole them.

Stunned by my overblown reaction, he assured, "We'll get you something else. I know those were special, but we can find something similar. I'll do some digging for antique earrings on eBay."

I didn't have the guts to tell him that what was taken couldn't be replaced.

My mom, who was distracted with preparations for the HOA "Galantine's" Day ice cream social, was easily persuaded to let me stay home sick for two straight weeks. First, I feigned intense menstrual cramps, then I pretended to have a migraine. I had to stretch my acting abilities by the end—rushing to the bathroom whenever she was nearby, claiming I must have food poisoning. When it got to the point that she talked of making a doctor's appointment, I made a miraculous recovery and reluctantly went back to school.

I ignored most of Isa's phone calls and texts during that time. I barely spoke to Lincoln either, except to ask him what I had missed in our shared classes. So, when Isa showed up at my door, it was the first time I had seen her since the morning Ella briefly escaped. I'm not exactly sure what motivated me to let her in—surely not the house plant because I knew I'd forget to water it. Maybe it was the fact that misery likes company. Or, more likely, that I knew she wouldn't be turned away. I opened the door wider, stepped back, and let her through the threshold.

"Do you mind if I stay with you for a week or two?" she asked, handing me the bonsai, and setting her duffle bag down in the foyer. "I can't go back to Tamara's, and I don't want to give Tony the satisfaction of showing up on his doorstep, not yet anyway. I'll go back, eventually, but... Anyway, is that okay? I promise I'll make the bed and drive us to school and do my own laundry. It'll be fun! Like we're roommates! It'll be practice for when we're backpacking through the Alps!"

I knew she had moved into her mom's condo when I read (but didn't respond to) the text:

Isa DeLuca [Tuesday, January 27th 6:18pm]: Staying with Tamara. At least she doesn't pressure me about college. She's out so much anyway. She won't even realize I'm there. Tony can be such a dick.

I'd learned that she extracted titles of affection to distance herself; if she was now referring to her dad as "Tony," she was past the point of perturbation. But I also knew that there was no way she could stand to live under Tamara's roof for any length of time. Especially because I'd heard from Lincoln, when he stopped by to deliver me my missed assignments, that Tamara already had a live-in boyfriend. I supposed the separation gave her the freedom to finally cease her halfhearted efforts at covering up her affair. Whatever led Isa to my house that day with duffle bag and bonsai in tow, I didn't want to know. I had lost my reserve of energy for Isa's drama.

    She didn't wait for me to give consent. I followed her up the stairs and sat on the bed as I watched her unpack her duffle bag, push a spread of my clothes to the side, and hang hers up in the newly created closet space.

    "I should probably ask my parents," I said dully, staring at the plant that was still in my hands.

    "Your parents love me!" Isa said. "And I'll only be here for two weeks. Three—tops. And then I'll go back to Tony's. Mind if I set these out to charge?"

    She held up two handfuls of crystals. I shook my head, and she began to arrange them on my windowsill. Within minutes, my bedroom was Isa-fied—complete with a dreamcatcher over the bed and the smell of burning sage already "purifying" the space.

    "We have two guest bedrooms," I asserted after tripping over her guitar case.

"I sleep better with a bedmate. If I start hogging the covers or snoring after a few days, just tell me and I'll move downstairs."

Later, as I watered the bonsai and Isa plopped onto the bed, opening a copy of *Badass Women Manifest: A Guide to Manifestation Meditation*, I caved.

"What happened at Tamara's?"

Isa groaned but didn't look up from her book.

"It's a long story, but basically—*as we already knew*—Tamara is jealous of me. She views me as a rival and can't compete with my energy. She kicked me out."

"Can you be more specific?" I asked, taking a seat on the edge of the bed.

"Ugh, if you really want to know…" She sighed, sat up, and discarded the book. "So, Devlin—you know, her 'boyfriend' or whatever—has a thing for me. And why shouldn't he? It's not like she owns him."

"Devlin isn't the—"

She sighed again. "The dude from the Christmas party? Yeah, I thought you'd ask that."

"Isa! That guy was, like, 40-something! Wasn't he? He's old enough to be your mom's boyfriend anyway. He could be your *dad*! That's seriously disgusting."

"Whoa whoa whoa—calm down. He's 37. Too young for her, actually."

"Thirty-SEVEN?"

I was no good at math, but even I knew that the gap between 18 and 37 was essentially equal to that of the Grand Canyon.

"I'm 18, K! *Jesus*. You know what your problem is? You're so hung up on the little things that don't matter—age and numbers and 'getting caught' and all that stupid shit. None of that is going to mean anything years from now," she said, getting testy.

I didn't want to argue with her. Not now especially, given that there was no escaping her. What was I going to do? Drag my stuff to one of the spare bedrooms? How would I explain those sleeping arrangements to my parents?

"Yeah, well," I began, rolling my eyes to the ceiling, "did he try anything with you?"

Her look of defiance faltered just a bit. I had a distinct inclination that what she was about to tell me was a lie.

"Not really. I mean—just—Tamara walked in and he… Well, we were in the kitchen making lunch and she spanked me. That's all."

"*He spanked you*? Isa, that's creepy! Can you not see how creepy that is?"

"It was just a *joke*! He was making a sandwich and I was hogging the mayo."

"So, Tamara threw *you* out because *he* was being a pervert? That doesn't make sense."

"When has Tamara ever made sense?"

I couldn't argue with that. And even if I maintained a nagging feeling that she wasn't telling me the full truth, I let it go. After all, she was a legal adult. I had to realize at some point that Isa's disaster of a love life was none of my business—but moreover, not my problem to fix. I had enough to worry about without adding responsibility for Isa's life choices onto my plate. I had a GPA to repair, colleges to research, and I was supposed to help Lincoln with the Comedy O'clock fundraiser. I had to pull myself out of this pit and make it through the rest of junior year. So, head down, mouth shut, I didn't mention Devlin—or any of Isa's other misgivings—for as long as I could, anyway.

If we stuck to safe topics of conversation—movies, books, music—having Isa for a "roommate" was, at times, more enjoyable than it was divisive. She made an effort to tidy up after herself, deviating from her usual unkept and borderline sloppy habits; she drove us to school, never cut class, and never asked me for gas money; she even went as far as making dinners to prove her amicability.

"You can stay as long as you want if you keep making these delicious meals!" my dad decided after eating two servings of her spicy tofu pad Thai

Mom was less enthused, frequently dropping hints and inquiring about her departure.

"I bet your dad and brother miss having you around. You know men can't hold a household together by themselves…" she'd say.

"I doubt it," Isa would reply, flippantly. "And they're grown men. They can pick up after themselves."

From what I could tell, Lincoln was doing just fine—better than fine, actually.

"You're joking! A full-length play?" I asked for the second time.

"Quiet!" Mrs. Templeton, the school librarian, hushed.

We met in the library during study hall to discuss the plans for the drama club fundraiser, but Ms. Morris wanted to do something new this year—something we had been begging for since we were freshmen.

"Goodbye clumsy cabaret and stupid sketches!" Lincoln whispered excitedly.

"Your sketches weren't stupid," I protested.

"You're just saying that," he said. "But never mind. The days of Comedy O'clock are over! Hello high drama, bloodshed, and witchcraft!"

"For the last time!" Mrs. Templeton hissed.

"She's going to chew our heads off and spit out the bones if we don't shut up," I whispered.

"Hey, we could use that bloodlust for the play," Lincoln laughed.

By some miracle, Lincoln had convinced Ms. Morris to let him direct a fresh, modernized version of *MacBeth* in lieu of the usual comedic sketches and musical acts.

"The drama club needs revitalizing and you, my protégé, will assist me in leading us into this new frontier!" she had told him.

"So…will you be my Lady M?" Lincoln asked, now serious.

"Really? Don't you want me to audition?"

"What? No! You read the part in class every day for the last month. I know you can do it. You want to, right?"

We had just wrapped our Shakespeare unit in English and Lady MacBeth had become a bucket list role. She balanced so many complex emotions and was a total departure from any character I'd played before. I thought it'd be the thrill of a lifetime to take on someone with a wicked streak. And the "Out! Damned spot!" monologue in act five—just reading the words on the page made me swoon.

"Yes!" I shrieked. "And I promise I'll be so dazzling that you won't regret pre-casting me!"

Mrs. Templeton lowered her glasses and pointed to the door.

We murmured a series of "sorrys" as we gathered our things and hurriedly exited the library.

"Let's brainstorm later?" Lincoln asked before we parted ways.

"Swings? Around six?"

"See you then!"

And so, I began leaving Isa alone to hang out in my room or watch America's Got Talent with my parents as I met Lincoln a few nights a week for our "Mackers and Ice Cream Chats" on the swings. Over mint chocolate chip and butter pecan, we discussed who he should include in the rest of the cast, gabbed about subtext, and I listened as he verbally processed ideas for his directorial vision. Rehearsals would begin the second Wednesday in March and we'd have to cram in a lot of them because the fundraiser was scheduled for the end of April. With the addition of a new role and a new roommate/permanent sleepover guest, my life was suddenly far too busy to dwell on the things that I was trying to forget.

On the way to school the morning of our first rehearsal, I reminded Isa that she didn't have to drive me home. I also made a final attempt at convincing her to join the cast (Lincoln offered her Lady

MacDuff, but she said "dead white guy plays" weren't her thing... We didn't point out that 95% of the musicals she had been in were also written by deceased white gentlemen...). Isa barely acknowledged me. She had been suspiciously quiet over breakfast and hadn't eaten a thing. Not even five minutes outside of my neighborhood, she pulled over on the side of the road without warning.

"Isa? What are doi—"

She answered by kicking the driver's side door open, heaving her body out of the car, and retching. The smell was foul.

"Isa? Are you alri—"

"Fine," she said, wiping her mouth and slamming the door.

But she wasn't—she'd been keeping me up all week. I'd feel her get out of bed in the middle of the night and hear muffled gagging sounds coming from the bathroom.

"You're clearly not," I reasoned. "Do you think you have some kind of bug?"

She shook her head and concentrated on merging back onto the road.

"Maybe you should stay at the house? I can drive myself. Or you should at least go to the nurse when we get to school."

"Yeah, okay."

I knew she wouldn't listen.

In eighth period she texted me:

Isa DeLuca [2:08pm]: Can you drive me back? I feel like shit. Please, K?

Finding Lincoln outside the double doors of the auditorium, I explained that I had to bail on rehearsal.

"I think Isa is seriously sick or something," I said. "I'll just drive her back to my place and I'll be back before you can say, 'Double, double toil and trouble!'"

"All good, Miss Statham. No attendance fines will be charged this time," he joked.

When I met Isa at the car, she looked like she'd been hit by a bus.

Pale, sweaty, and lethargic, she tossed me the keys and asked, "And can we stop at Walgreens?"

When we parked, I offered to run in for her. "What do you need? Some ginger ale? Pepto-Bismol?"

"No, I'll go in. You just wait."

She returned to the car with a plastic bag in one hand and a box of already opened animal crackers in the other.

"Never mind…" she said after swallowing a second cracker, "I can't eat these."

She stuffed the box into her shopping bag, and we were silent for the rest of the drive. She shot up the stairs and locked herself in the bathroom with her Walgreens bag as soon as I unlocked the front door.

"Isa? Are you okay? Do you want me to stay for a bit before I head back?" I asked.

A few minutes went by. I pulled out my phone to text Lincoln and tell him I'd be on my way shortly when I heard a scream.

"Isa?! Let me in!"

I pounded on the bathroom door.

"Shit shit shit shit shit motherfucking *shit*!"

"Isa! What's wrong?"

The lock popped and she opened the bathroom door a crack. I slowly pushed my way in and saw her sitting on the toilet holding a small white stick.

"What's that…" I began, although I already knew. I had a feeling since she pulled over that morning.

"What do you think?!" she shouted and shoved the stick in front of me.

I saw the two fat pink lines that marked the end of Isa's life as we knew it.

All I could offer was, "Take another one."

Two tests later, Isa announced, "I'm out of pee," and we sat on the floor of my bathroom, gaping at the three positive tests that laid on the tile before us. And we cried.

"When did you have your last period? Are you *pregnant*, pregnant? Or, like, a little pregnant? What do we do?"

"There is no such thing as being a 'little pregnant,'" she snapped. "And I don't know. I don't remember when I last had it. I don't keep track of that stuff. It just comes when it wants to come."

"Is it…Jason's…?"

"Maybe," she said softly, hugging her knees to her chest. "But he wasn't the last person I…"

Understanding overcame me and I let out a long, hopeless sigh of disbelief.

"Did you sleep with Devlin?"

She dropped her head to her knees and buried her face with her arms.

"…yes…"

"Isa! Oh my god. *Oh my god*! What are we going to *do*? He's so *old*!"

"Stop judging me!" she wailed. "That's all you ever do. You and Lincoln think you're so perfect! I know what you guys think of me. I'm not stupid."

"Isa—what? No. What are you—We've *missed* you!"

"Yeah, like I believe that. You have your plays and your little meetings… I know you talk about me…"

"Isa, we've invited you *every single time*. And who cares about who is hanging out with who right now? We need to talk about *this*," I said, picking up one of the positive tests and waving it in the air. "This is—this is—*fuck*."

I wasn't a frequent user of the eff-bomb, but there were no other words.

"I'm an adult and I can do what I want. Don't judge me for doing what I have every right to do!" she said through angry tears, now bold enough to look me in the eye.

"Well, *no*, Isa. Clearly you can't! You can't just do whatever the hell you want because *look what happens*! Isa, there's an actual baby inside you! What do we do now, Isa? Huh? What's your grand idea? This is serious! This is, like, as serious as it gets!"

Eyes wide and face pale, she stared at me like she was *afraid* of me. I guess I'd never yelled at her before. Come to think of it, I wasn't sure if I had yelled at anyone like that before. She started sniveling and the noise cut a jagged slit directly through my heart. As much as I loathed her for her selfish recklessness, the way she could be so condescending, and the decisions she made that was so clearly and obviously *stupid*—she was so stupid, damnit! I tried to tell her! —still, I loved Isa the way you love and also hate your own blood. She was the sister I never had and always wanted. She was messed up. God, she was so, so messed up—what used to be off-beat and entrancing was all just a guise for brokenness. That much was evident now. But…she was mine. She was my best friend. My sister. This mess was my mess too.

"We have to tell your parents, Isa." I spoke gently and put an arm around her shaking back.

"No," she sobbed into her knees. "They already think I'm a fuck-up."

Coming from the girl that didn't seem to hold any respect for her parents, I was stunned to hear the pain in her voice with this admission. My folks were busy, mostly unaware of my existence, and largely uninvolved, but I'd never thought for a moment that they regarded me as a failure.

"Okay…maybe my parents can help," I suggested. "They'll know what to do. Azrah will understand, I mean—she was only a year or two older than you when she had me."

Isa shook her head and continued to sob.

"No one can know."

"But Isa…people are going to find out…I mean…"

She sobbed even louder, and I heard the thunder of the garage door opening below us. Someone was home. And then I realized what time it must have been. Lincoln. The rehearsal. Damnit. Pulling my phone out of my jumper pocket, I quickly composed a text with one hand while rubbing Isa's back with the other.

Me [5:15pm]: Abe I'm SO sorry! Isa's having a hard time. Had to stay :(

"Shhh…Shhh…" I coaxed, "Isa, okay…okay…I won't tell anyone. Let's sleep on it, alright? You don't have to decide anything right now."

"But I—I already know what I need to do," she cried. "I think it's too late for anything else. I can't take a pill or anything. And I—I—I need to get rid of it."

"Isa, you should think about it. I mean, do you need to *tell* him or, or—?"

"What is he gonna do? Marry me?" she shot back, suddenly overcome with anger. "This is my problem. And I can't have a baby. Look at me. I can't do anything. I'm not even going to college."

She clung to me, soaking my jumper with snot and tears.

"We're going to fix this, okay?" I soothed, stroking her hair. "You don't have to tell anyone if you don't want to."

I had no idea if that was acceptable or morally correct. I had never been in this situation before—never even considered what one would do in a mess like this. But what was *right* didn't matter then. What mattered was fixing this for Isa.

"Will you take me?"

"Take you where?" I asked.

"To the clinic. To get it—get it—out."

"You mean, to get an ab—"

"*Yes*, K, you don't need to *say it*," she snapped before melting into a fresh puddle of tears. "I'm sorry. Just please…please help me…"

I held her, unable to silence the wails.

"K? Isa? Everything okay up there?" Dad called from downstairs.

"Fine! We're fine!" I responded with forced casualty.

"Okay, Isa, look." I held her face in my hands and pressed our foreheads together. "I'll do whatever you need me to do."

On Friday, we skipped school and I drove Isa to the clinic. She wanted to go the day after she found out or, preferably, that very Wednesday afternoon if they would let her in—but Friday was the earliest appointment. I knew she was suffering from the worst imaginable anxiety, but I was privately glad that she had to wait 24 more hours. This felt like a decision too big to be made by two teenagers. If she was going to resist my pleas for getting the parents involved, then I would have to hatch a scheme of my own that would fix everything before 9:40 am on Friday. I didn't go to Thursday's rehearsal. I told Lincoln that Isa was sick, and she felt uncomfortable having my parents wait on her. When he asked what exactly was wrong with her, I pretended to have forgotten a textbook in my locker and dashed off to avoid further inquiry.

While we were watching a documentary in Spanish, I imagined that Isa could continue to live with us, have the baby in secret, and my parents could raise it. That would still involve telling my parents, of course—which Isa wouldn't like—but it wasn't an entirely inconceivable idea. My parents were still young enough to have a baby. That reminded me that my parents were actually a year *younger* than the guy who likely got Isa into this situation, and I felt dizzy. I jumped when the girl who sat behind me, Patricia Figeria, tapped me on the back to pass me a note from Lincoln:

> Are you sure everything's okay with you? You've been weird. You coming to rehearsal tonight?

I tried my best to appear unburned in my reply:

I'll jump in next week? Busy babysitting your sick sister. When are you going to come take her home?

But the joke left me lightheaded and clutching the sides of my desk. *Baby*sitting. Babies. Isa was going to have a baby. Isa was going to…going to…abort her baby. I was going to help her. I was going to take her to the place where some doctor was going to go inside her and pull it out… It wasn't for political or religious reasons—I had no affiliation with either—it was the fact that *I* could have easily been one of those discarded babies that made me see this entire plan in a different light. And once I saw it that way, it became personal. *My* mom didn't plan to be pregnant, and her parents were so furious at her that they shunned her for it. What if *my* mom thought about doing the same thing Isa was about to do? What if she wanted to but couldn't? What if she wanted to but she didn't have the money or she waited too long or…? I asked for a hall pass and spent the rest of class dry heaving in the bathroom.

    That was how we ended up driving downtown to the beige building with the protesters barricading the entrance—because I couldn't think of another way. And because Isa was set on "getting it over with so everything could go back to normal." There was no plan that wouldn't involve the parents or ruining her life—if it wasn't already in shambles. There was no other way.

    At first, I thought I'd just wait in the car. The receptionist that booked the appointment for Isa told her the procedure would only take five to ten minutes, but that she'd need to do a brief consultation beforehand. In total, she estimated that she would be in and out of the clinic within 20 minutes or less if she didn't need to stay in the recovery room. I tried not to think about what would elicit a need for the recovery room.

"I really don't need you to come," she said calmly. "I'm okay. I just want to be done with it. Hell, I bet you I'm going to be *smiling* when I walk out of here. Trust me."

But I didn't want to wait in the parking lot, feet away from signs that read: ABORTION IS MURDER

We sat next to each other in the waiting room. I held her hand and tried not to make eye contact with anyone there. With my limited knowledge, I assumed everyone must have been there for the same reason and I didn't want to look more desperation in the face.

"Isabel DeLuca," a nurse said from the door that led to…I didn't know where.

Isa looked at me. The composure from before was replaced with a vacant look of confusion. I suppose I could have begged her not to follow that nurse, but she said she wanted to do this. I knew there was no telling Isa what to do. She was an adult. She had the right to choose. As she said late Wednesday night as we tried, unsuccessfully, to fall asleep, she was not going to be "forced into motherhood." So, I gave her a nod.

I said, "I'll be right here when it's over."

Then she walked away and disappeared behind the door. I waited for over an hour. When she came back out to the lobby, she was alone. She was not smiling. Now we both felt the absence of something lost. We would both always yearn for what was missing.

Isa spent the weekend as a shadow of herself; she rotated from the bed to the bathroom and never once changed out of her pajamas. My job was to bring her pads, hand her capsules of Midol, microwave her heating pad, and douse her forehead in lavender essential oils. My parents were oblivious, sending her dinner up to the bedroom without argument when I vaguely explained that she was under the weather.

Lincoln wanted to get together and fill me in on what I'd missed at the first three rehearsals. He sent me a few texts and left two voicemails. At first, I thought he was just antsy to get the show on its feet and annoyed that one of his key characters had been a no-show. But I knew he was concerned when he began to ask if Isa was feeling better, if I had caught whatever she had, and finally, did I know when Isa wanted to come home? I felt bad, but I put him off every time. I couldn't have him over when she was moaning about pelvic cramps, and I couldn't leave her—what if she bled out? Did that still happen? I was pretty sure that people used to die after abortions.

We didn't talk much; when she wasn't asleep, she complained of cramps.

"Do you think you should go back to the clinic? Or the doctor?" I asked repeatedly.

"Read the handout," she moaned, "they said it's normal. What are they gonna do?"

I spent most of the day in my room, watching her like a hawk. I'd read while she slept, catch up on homework, or research college theater programs. By Sunday evening, she was ready to finally take a shower, wash her hair, and change into a fresh pair of pajamas.

"I'm going to school tomorrow," she said when she stepped out of the shower, wrapped in a towel.

"Are you sure?" I asked. "I mean, no one's going to stop you from taking a few days off."

"I'm fine," she replied, although the sudden chipper attitude alarmed me.

"What about…I don't know. How do you feel?"

"*Fine*. I said—"

"No, I mean…do you think you should talk to someone? Like, maybe the, um…guidance counselor? You know…when you go back tomorrow?"

What was the protocol for a proper recovery in this situation? I had no idea. But I figured that tossing and turning throughout the night and waking covered in sweat at four in the morning wasn't exactly normal. Sometimes she'd scream in her sleep, and I had to coax her out of whatever nightmare she'd been trapped in before my parents barged in and demanded answers.

"Are you seriously suggesting that I tell Mrs. Ketchum that I just offed my baby?"

Her bluntness left me speechless.

"You…you don't have to put it…like *that*, Isa. That makes you sound like…I don't know. But that's not what you—"

"Yes, it is. That's what I did. And *I* made that choice, which means that *I'm fine*. I just want to go back to normal, okay? Besides, shrinks don't help. All they do is judge you and ask about your childhood. You know we all went to family counseling…and look at my family now."

"But it cou—" I tried.

"No, K. You're the only one that I can talk to about this. Okay? Seriously. Don't go telling people and try to save the day. I'm *fine*," she finished. It was a forgone conclusion—she knew what she wanted, and she made her choice. "But do you think you'd have time to maybe help me with something else?"

Dear God, what now? was the unfair thought that popped into my head.

"Could you, um…help me sign up for some classes? At TCC? For the fall?"

I paused for longer than I should have before saying, "I would love to."

At lunch on Monday, we were able to give Lincoln the shock of his life when we announced that Isa would be taking College Algebra, English Composition, and Personal Finance at TCC in the fall. Of course, I had my doubts that she would actually show up to the classes or change her mind before August… Or worse still, that this community college in particular would have her in close proximity with influences that would steer her back into trouble… But I tried not to think about the possible pitfalls. There had been too much heaviness and we both needed a sunny horizon to look forward to.

"When did you change your mind?" Lincoln interrogated while Isa sipped casually on her Diet Dr. Pepper.

"I don't know…I just don't want to be a screw-up anymore. I have an appointment with an admissions counselor on Thursday. Apparently, they help you map out a whole long-term plan," Isa said and bit into a carrot stick.

Lincoln, who sat across from us at our usual picnic table in the Junior/Senior courtyard, was nearly at a loss for words.

"You're a good influence, K," he said. "She spends a month at your house and now she's a changed woman. Do you have any ideas for a major?"

"Oh, I'm not completely sold on the whole college thing. I just want to take a few classes to start and have a back-up plan in the works. Leonora has a monopoly on the metaphysical scene here and it'll take me a bit to build my clientele," she continued. "I might even get a part-time job. I can save up while I wait on K to finish school."

Lincoln raised an eyebrow.

"Because we're going to Switzerland, dork! You know this!" Isa exclaimed.

Happily, she bounced from her seat to discard her tray.

"I've got to jet. I'm supposed to send my transcripts to TCC and I'm going to try to figure out the copier in the library before next period."

Once alone, Lincoln shook his head in confusion.

"I'm sorry, *what*? Isa's going to college. You're going to *Switzerland*? Since when has this been an actual plan? What about getting your bachelor's? Am I in the Twilight Zone?" he asked, waving his arms wildly—his Italian heritage fully activated.

"Shhh…I don't want her to hear you."

"What, is she *God*? She left," he said. "Tell me what's going on."

"Okay, okay, listen…" I started, lowering my voice unnecessarily and leaning across the table. "Of *course,* I'm still going to college, are you crazy?"

"That's not what Isa thinks—"

"Shh! I'm just going along with her whole Switzerland idea for now. Maybe I'll convince my parents into sending me there for a graduation present and she'll settle for a two-week trip. Or maybe by the time I'm graduating and getting ready for college, she'll be on to the next lunatic idea, and she'll completely forget all about it. But the thing is—I have to just go with it for now."

"But why?"

"Because..." I knew that it wasn't my secret to tell, so I did the best I could without lying to him. "Because Isa's been through...a lot...and look at her—she seems motivated now! I can't crush her hopes. She's too fragile, you know?"

"Psssh...*fragile*? I think you're just scared of her being mad at you when you don't do what she tells you to do," he challenged and nonchalantly took a bite of his hamburger.

"What is that supposed to mean? You think I do everything she tells me to do? Like what, I'm her plaything or something?"

"I mean...now that you say it...yeah, kind of. We barely hang out anymore and you never even text me back—you're just up Isa's butt *all the time*. You said you'd play Lady MacBeth but haven't shown up to a single rehearsal. Blair's been reading your part. *Blair*. This is my first shot at directing a play by myself and you know what a big deal that is. And where were you this weekend? Probably feeding her grapes and fanning her with palm leaves.

"Everyone caters to Isa. That's how it's always been—my whole life. Isa's the one that makes the messes. Isa's the brightest. Isa's the eccentric. Isa's the loudest. Isa's the one that everyone wants to please. When will everyone stop kissing Isa's ass? So, she's finally getting her act together and enrolling in what, three gen eds? Whoop dee-freaking-doo."

"Are you done?" I demanded as I rose from the table.

"No, one more thing," he said, also standing, "you said Isa's been going through a lot. Well, it was *my* parents that got a divorce too, you know. It was *my* mom that moved out. *My* dad that's never home.

And now *my* sister that has caused *my* best friend to drop off the face of the earth. Did you ever consider that while you guys are having a marathon sleepover, I'm home alone literally five nights out of the week?"

The fact was, no I didn't consider this. I should have, but I didn't. It was, just like it always had been, all about Isa.

"Lincoln. I—"

The bell rang signifying the end of lunch.

"See you in Spanish," he said and stormed off.

If by "see you in Spanish" he meant that he would deliberately look everywhere in the room but my desk, then yes, I did see him in Spanish. I knew I should apologize—he did make a lot of fair arguments. And I felt miserable for what he was going through. But that was the thing with Lincoln—he never let on that he was upset, or needed help, or was anything other than an upbeat, optimistic, good-natured goofball. How was I supposed to recognize the non-existent signs of his grief? I didn't know whether to dismiss his outburst as babyish, pity him, or throw my desk across the room... Did he really see me as Isa's "plaything"?

As we left Spanish, I tried to catch up to him, but he beelined for the door.

"Lincoln!" I yelled down the hallway.

He stopped and turned around. Until that moment, I didn't know if I called out to him to apologize or to continue our argument where we left off.

But then he asked, "So will I see you at rehearsal today or are you going to be too busy taking Isa back-to-school shopping?"

Pride made the decision for me.

"Just give the role to Blair," I said and sped past him to Geography.

I texted Isa that I was taking the bus home because I wanted to stay late and talk to Mrs. Santiago about extra credit. Really, I just wanted a moment of space. I'd always been a loner, an introvert, the shy only child, but for the last month I had someone breathing down my neck literally day and night. I was at the end of my rope. Isa kicked in her sleep, Isa used all the hot water, Isa played her guitar while I tried to do homework.

This was my bedroom, my parents' home, and Isa had just barged in, expecting me to clean up her mess. She even had a spare key. And now Lincoln was mad at me, and it wasn't even my fault. I was just trying to be a decent human being. I was just taking care of the sister that neither he or his mom or his dad could be bothered with. I resented her and her neediness and I resented the rest of them too—this was not my job. Where were *they* when Isa saw the results of that pregnancy test?

When I flung open my bedroom door, Isa was laying across the bed, strumming lazily like she didn't have a care in the world. I wanted to snatch the guitar and throw it out the window.

"Mind if you do that somewhere else? I have homework," I said.

"Whoa, need a Midol?" she laughed.

I spun on her and let my backpack drop to the floor.

"How can you make a joke like that after what just happened?" I demanded.

"What are you talk—"

"I'm talking about how for the last three days, I've been feeding *you* Midol and telling my parents I'm helping you through a bout of PMS, when really, I was cleaning up after your big mistake."

The words spewed from my mouth. I was a broken faucet that couldn't be turned off.

"K…"

"What? Did that hurt your feelings?"

"Feelings are for freaks," she muttered.

I could see her eyes growing red. She was so quick to tears these days and I knew why, but I didn't care. Lincoln lit a fire under me, and I had no idea how to extinguish it.

"You know what *your* problem is, Isa? You think I'm too worried about what people think, but *you're* completely out of touch with reality. And you have absolutely zero boundaries."

I'd never experienced this sort of rage. I was unrecognizable, even to myself. Was this a scene in a play? Had I always had this monologue in me and ready to perform? Had I been subconsciously writing it since the night at Jason's?

"That's not true," Isa said, tearfully. "I'm trying the best I can. What I do doesn't concern you."

"Doesn't concern me? Are you kidding? You drag me to wild parties, you throw me into the deep end… you show up at my doorstep and you say that what you do doesn't concern me?"

"You're jealous. You're just like Tamara. Worse—*Blair*. You wish you weren't so ordinary, but you are. You're jealous and I've always known it," she spat.

Never in my life have I laughed the way I did in that moment— it was sheer disgust and befuddlement mixed into one booming snarl.

"*Jealous*? Oh yeah sure, Isa. And you're so unique? You have *one* unique ability—to justify whatever screwed up delusion crosses your mind."

She scoffed.

"And speaking of Blair. How come you aren't friends anymore? Was it because you tried to use her as a plaything too and—let me guess—she got sick of being treated like a marionette?"

When she didn't respond, I continued. There was no stopping what had to be said.

"You get close to people just so you can control them. And when they don't like it any more you drop them? Is that what happened?"

"That's not true," she said quietly.

"I think you should go home now, Isa."

She hadn't moved from the bed since I first barreled in, and I was still frozen in my fighting stance by the door. Blinking away tears, she finally scooted off the bed and began packing her duffle bag. She grabbed her gems from the windowsill and plopped them into the bag, one by one. She walked into the closet and started pulling down the clothes she hung up weeks ago. She moved to the bathroom and collected toiletries. She removed the dreamcatcher, zipped her guitar back up in its case. She did all of this through tears and sniffles and I stood there dry-eyed, not saying a word.

"I know I've messed up," she said suddenly. "That's why I was trying to change. I didn't want to give up the… I want to be better. I didn't have a choice!"

She wilted, leaning on the dresser, and allowing her tears to run freely. But I couldn't find it in myself to empathize.

"Didn't have a choice? Wait, I'm sorry, did someone force you? I don't recall handcuffing you to the passenger's seat and forging your medical forms!"

"But you let me! *You didn't stop me*. You let me do it and now—now—now I'll never get her back. I'll never—ever—can't—undo—my baby—"

"I didn't do that, Isa. *You* did. And you made me watch."

"I nee—I needed you and now I can't take it back," she choked.

"Get out."

"I needed you to st—stop—stop me!"

"GET OUT," I bellowed. "You don't get to tell me that I wasn't there when you needed me. *I* needed *you*! I needed you to save me from that monster that ra—*hurt* me and *where were you*?"

At the almost slip of the tongue, I collapsed to the floor. Sobbing and hyperventilating, I couldn't believe I had almost said it.

No no no no no. It didn't happen. Nothing happened. It didn't happen. Nothing happened, you're okay.

But it was there. I almost said it—rape.

I sat there, on my bedroom floor, and sobbed for hours. Isa was long gone by the time my parents came home. When they came up to check on me, I simply told them that Isa and I had a fight, and she went home.

I fell asleep in my bed alone that night. I thought it would have been the best night's sleep in a month. But something was missing.

I threw out the shriveled-up bonsai tree before I drove to school the next morning. The whole day was a blur. The whole *week* was a blur. Junior year had transformed into a poorly done ABC Family original. Lincoln and I avoided eye contact in our classes, and I sat by myself at lunch, masking my outcast status with a few textbooks strewn across the picnic table. I wanted people to think I was studying, not banished from the table where I used to sit with my only friends. With Isa, I was untouchable. I was somebody. My presence meant something. Without Isa, I was nameless, faceless, taking up space.

    On Tuesday of the following week, I nearly dropped my grilled cheese and peas on the grass when I saw Isa sitting with Blair and her minions in the courtyard. Her guttural laughter danced through the open air as Blair told a story to the group. A phantom trace of the rage I had felt towards her on the day I kicked her out snuck up on me. It took an immense amount of willpower to not glare at her the entire lunch period, but even as I glued my eyes to my English textbook, I was entirely aware of her presence. I heard every snicker from that table.

    In Geography, I picked furiously at my cuticles as we discussed the rise in terrorism over the last decade. Blair and I shared this class and, up until then, I didn't mind; I felt satisfaction in assuming that she was probably there because she must have failed, seeing as that was a class composed of juniors. But today I couldn't stop wondering what she and Isa were talking about at lunch and I couldn't focus. I wanted to be anywhere other than sitting at a desk in the row opposite her.

    "You'll find on page 217 some examples of countries that support terrorism," Mr. Feheely droned on.

    I glanced down at my open textbook.

Examples:
- Libya
- Iraq
- Afghanistan
- Iran
- Pakistan

My eyes zeroed in on Pakistan. Obviously, I was no idiot and hadn't slept through years of history class. I also couldn't avoid the news as my dad always had it on in the background. This wasn't shocking information to me, but it always made me cringe. And that's when I heard giggling from across the aisle.

"You know K's family is from Pakistan," I heard Blair whisper to the girl who sat in front of her.

My face burned as they glanced at me. I slouched down in my chair, wishing with all my might that I had one of those invisibility cloaks from *Harry Potter*.

After the final bell, I tried to lose myself by playing *The Phantom of the Opera* on my iPod; something about the melodrama of a soprano and sketchy/arguably gorgeous, masked dude traveling by boat through the depths of a secret lair grounded me. Entirely zoned out, I didn't notice at first what my locker neighbors were gawking at as I made it down the crowded hallway to the "S" section.

"Dude! Cass! Didn't know what you were up to in your free time, but that's some dark shit! Stick to cheerleading," Enrique mocked.

"That's not even *my* locker, dumbass," Cassandra replied.

Taped to my locker was a piece of notebook paper. In black Sharpie lettering, the note read: TERRORIST!

Agape, I stood in the center of the hallway. Kids were shoving past me, knocking into my backpack, and nearly causing me to topple over but shame's almighty grip kept me in my place. Never had I been called that name before. It was an ugly, heinous title. It would destroy my mother if she found out. It was one of the reasons she tried so hard all the time—to avoid that very accusation.

I tore through the passersby and shoved Cassandra out of my way. Snatching the paper in my fist, I ripped the vulgarity off the locker and bolted for the parking lot before anyone could see the tears streaking down my disgraced, crimson face.

Blair. Blair made that comment in Geography. Blair put the note on my locker, but Isa knew where my locker was. Isa must have told her. They were lunch chums now—probably besties again already. Blair was the one who did it. That much was plain. But what my heart couldn't figure out was how Isa possessed the cruelty to help.

13.

Rose Quartz

"I introduced them."

Lincoln furrowed his brows. I was about to repeat myself when I saw the understanding wash over him. His eyes bulged.

"*You knew him?*"

Whelp. My first official relationship had lasted approximately three weeks and four days. What was I thinking—doing this in my parents' house? Now I was about to be broken up with and a nearby audience of two would probably hear every other word.

"He was in the play…" I said, stating the obvious.

"Yeah, I can see that. I remember him now. I could have shaken hands with this guy."

"Lincoln—"

"What do you mean you introduced them? Oh my god…K, you have to get him to talk. You have to call him. What are you waiting for? He might have lied to the police, but if you know him…then…K, maybe you could get him to confess if he had something to do with—"

"Knock, knock!" Mom said as she literally knocked on the open bedroom door. "Are you staying for America's Got Talent, Lincoln?"

"Um, actually, we're about to head out," I said, glancing uneasily at Lincoln. "We both have homework."

"Alright, well come in and say goodbye before you leave. Lincoln, please take some of that strudel with you!"

She joined my dad in the bonus room. The electronic intro music boomed as I grabbed Lincoln's hand and led him down the stairs and out the backdoor. I couldn't think with yodeling and tap dancing and whatever else would be featured, loudly, on this week's episode.

Once outside, Lincoln jumped in with 20 questions all over again.

"So, what's the plan? Where's your phone? Or should we think of a list of questions first? Maybe it would be better done in person?"

"Lincoln. Wait. Slow down. I don't know him anymore. I barely 'knew' him back then. I don't have his number. But I did…introduce them. When Isa came to see *Peter Pan*—"

"I didn't know she came," he interrupted.

"I know. I figured you didn't. But she did," I said, and because we were so still, the motion sensor lights blinked off. I crossed over to the glowing lights of my parents' pool and continued, "She showed up and met me outside the cast door. Steve was there and we were all talking but…Lincoln, don't you get it? *I* introduced them; I'm the reason they met. And I guess they—they must have started hanging out after that and—"

He came over to join me by the pool and sat in a nearby lounge chair.

"Yeah?"

I hated pools. I hadn't been swimming since Lincoln told me where Isa was found but, as punishment, I said my piece directly into the soft glow of blue-green underwater light.

"If it weren't for me, she wouldn't have been at his apartment. Maybe she wouldn't be dead…"

That was it. I had finally purged my vile secret. And all he did was look at me. I loved that sweet, stubbly face but the look currently plastered on it made me question if he was a moron. Why was he not storming off in a rage right now? Didn't he get it?

"How can you even stand to look at me?" I challenged, bracing for an argument.

"What are you talking about?"

"It's *my* fault."

"K, *what*?" he sprung from the lounge chair and stood next to me, placing his hands on my shoulders. "K, look at me."

I did.

"No," he said, giving me the most intense eye contact. "No, it's not. Maybe he gave her his number and they became friends but—"

"No, Lincoln. *Listen*! What Steve 'gave' her was an invitation to die. He was there when… He might have given her the drugs. I knew he was into hard stuff. I should have told her to stay away from him."

He released my shoulders, anxiously rubbed the back of his neck, and sighed. When he started nodding, I thought that this for sure would be the moment he'd cuss me out and tell me we were done.

"I see how you could think that."

"*Think*? I kn—"

"No, K," he stopped me. "You don't know for sure. We don't know that she got the drugs from him. We don't know that he was there the literal moment she…overdosed. We don't know any of it. And no matter what we find out… Even if he *watched* her… Even if he knew and didn't try to stop it or report it or…whatever's in your head… You need to stop imagining it because it's not your fault. It's not."

The water was so peaceful. It would be a calm, beautiful thing to see right before the end. I latched onto his words, "…it's not your fault. It's not," and turned them over in my mind. No one had ever told me that. Not directly, anyway.

"Does that mean that you don't want to break up?" I asked.

"*What*? Why? *No*. Why would I want to do that?"

"I thought you would think—"

He took my hands and looked me dead in the eye, determined to get his message across this time.

"It's not your fault. I will tell you that every day if that's what it takes. And you can say it to me too. It's a lot easier saying it to someone else than it is to say it to yourself, trust me."

"I've never thought you had anything to feel guilty about," I said, shaking my head. "Are you saying that you thought it was…? But you're the last person to blame. You didn't do anything."

"That's how I felt about *you*—you of all people. *I* left. I ran off to New York."

"Lincoln, you can't—I mean—you did all you could do," I said, squeezing his hands.

And I meant it.

"So did you."

We fell into an embrace. After a whirlwind of a day, nothing felt better than collapsing into his arms.

"We're in this together," he said, his face buried in my curls. "Let's go to my dad's next week. We'll look through her stuff. See if we can find Steve's contact information—anything that might give a hint about what kind of relationship they had. And then when we track him down, we'll have something. You and me. Okay? It's been just you and just me carrying all of this by ourselves for three years. Not anymore. You and me *together*. From now on."

I nodded and nuzzled myself against his chest. I realized then that it was kind of nice to be 5'1" and have a boyfriend who towered over you—you were already in prime snuggling position even while standing.

"Are you free right now?" Lincoln asked when I answered his call the following Wednesday.

I was scouring the university library before work, but he had called twice already.

Crouching low within the stacks, I whispered, "I'm trying to find thesis material. Spoiler—there is almost nothing here on feminist Pakistani art. I'm going to have to make up sources." But knowing that the joke wouldn't sit well with a compulsive truth-teller like Lincoln, I added, "Kidding. I'd never falsify a source."

"Soooo…I have a problem," he said, the potential breach of the academic honor code completely ignored. "How soon can you get to my apartment?"

When I arrived, he was standing outside waiting for me.

"They're in the back," he said, taking my hand and guiding me to the back courtyard.

"What's in the back? What's going on?"

"Shh…don't talk so loud. I don't want to scare them," he warned, holding a finger to his lips.

I was about to make a plea for more information, concerned as to what I'd walk into and slightly annoyed that I was required to give up valuable research time…but then, I saw them. Underneath a picnic table in the outdoor communal space, there was a variety snack box of Kirkland Signature mixed nuts. But there weren't almonds or walnuts inside…there was an old towel and the smallest kittens I'd ever laid eyes on .

"Oh my godddddd!" I squealed.

"I found them this morning," Lincoln explained. "They were behind the grill, just hanging out in the bushes. I got them this box, but it's so cold. We have to do something with them. The gray one doesn't look good."

There were three in total; a tortoiseshell, a cream with white paws, and the smallest was the gray kitten. Their eyes were all shut. But while the tortoiseshell and cream kitten were mewing with all their might, the gray kitty was much less vocal.

"Let's take them inside," I insisted, bending down to carefully pick up the cardboard box.

"We can't," Lincoln said, "I would have done that already, but Kanye and Sarah Jessica are in there."

Kanye Westie and Sarah Jessica Barker were the impeccably groomed West Highland terriers that belonged to Lincoln's roommate, Dave. While adorable at first glance, in reality, they were untrained lunatics. They barked incessantly, licked, jumped, peed all over the house… Dave was tasked with dog sitting for his parents while they were on a cruise. Since Kanye had literally eaten my Medieval Irish Art homework earlier that week, we'd stuck to hanging out exclusively at my apartment until Dave's parents returned from the Bahamas.

"Oh, right," I said, "Okay, well…I can't take them to my place. F. Scott would kill them in a heartbeat."

This was another valid dilemma—F. Scott did not play nicely with others. Though he'd been an indoor cat and only child since I'd taken him in, he always found a way to provoke the strays on our street. I'd catch him sitting on the windowsill hissing and squatting at the glass as cats retreated fearfully from our fire escape. F. Scott needed to be the alpha and since these kittens more closely resembled newborn mice than felines, I wouldn't be surprised if F. Scott decided to forgo his Fancy Feast and take a bite out of their fuzzy little heads.

"Have you seen a mama cat?" I asked.

"No, and I also asked the guys in the apartment across from us. They said they heard meowing last night but didn't investigate."

"*Seriously*? So, they might have been out here all night and all morning? Why didn't they do anything?"

Lincoln shrugged. "I don't know. Their trash can have also been out on the curb for two months so…they're not ones to take initiative."

I rolled my eyes, which were now starting to tear up from the combination of February chill and the sentimentality I always felt for animals. More than ever, I begrudged the consistently inconsistent Tennessee weather; it was in the low 60s two days ago and now it was 38 degrees.

"We need to get them to the humane society," Lincoln urged. "Could you…? I have class at 11:50 and the guys aren't home."

"I'm working a double for Lenny—he's been running himself ragged all week," I explained.

Elijah had the flu and Lenny had been busting his butt to cover most of the shifts while I was in class. Professor Russo, also out with the flu, couldn't find a sub for Advanced Ceramics, so I offered to pitch in and make some extra cash for Switzerland.

"But I could take them *with* me to Chubbie's!" I thought aloud. "Lenny wouldn't care. I'll put them in the breakroom—at least they'll be out of the cold. And when you get out of class you can pick them up and take them to the shelter."

"It's the best we can do for now," Lincoln agreed.

I had Lenny meet me at my car when I pulled into the Chubbie's parking lot. I figured it would be best to explain before I waltzed in with a box full of kittens, or he accidently trampled them if he needed to get something out of the supply closet.

"Oh my goodness! Oh my goodness!" he squealed, possibly in a higher pitch than me when I first laid eyes on the fluffy little things. "Oh, Miss K you get these babies in here right away."

Once inside and safely nestled by a space heater, it became obvious that something was definitely wrong with the gray kitten. The little guy was lethargic while his siblings continued to squeak.

"You hold down the fort and I'll take them to the animal hospital," Lenny said. "I don't want no fur babies suffering on my watch."

Chubbie's was so slammed with students and professors seeking an afternoon caffeine buzz that I didn't have time to text Lincoln. I'd almost forgotten about him and our plan A entirely as I was wrist-deep in espresso beans, then I saw a tall guy in plaid approach the barista counter from the corner of my eye.

"What can I get you to—Oh, *hi!*" I laughed at my own stupidity.

"I caught you in full-blown barista mode," he teased. "We could role play with me as the handsome stranger in need of a latte and you— the stunning barista that's struggling to make ends meet—but I have some kittens to rescue. That's sexy too, right? Me rescuing kittens?"

I snorted at his dorkiness then explained the situation.

"That's even better! Do you think Lenny will want to keep them?!"

"I doubt it," I said as I began to make him a caramel apple macchiato—it was out of season, but that was the perk Lincoln could enjoy by dating the barista. "He doesn't seem to want another cat. He had Chubbie for 17 years, you know? I think he needs more time."

As if summoned by the sound of his own name, Lenny lumbered through the backdoor with a cat carrier in hand and a deep frown on his face.

"How'd it go?" I asked, peering into the cat carrier.

I didn't expect him to bring them back, but thought he'd drop them off at the shelter once they were given a clean bill of health.

"The gray one…" Lenny began, setting the cat carrier on the counter and taking a seat at the bar, "poor little guy didn't make it."

I gasped and Lincoln patted Lenny's back. Knowing what he went through with Chubbie, I was ashamed that I had gotten him involved.

"Lenny…no…I'm sorry you had to be there."

"No, Miss K. I was glad to do it. Little man didn't have a chance. They saw that as soon as they took him back. They called it Fading Kitten Syndrome. Anyway, I was glad to be there with 'em."

"And the others?" Lincoln asked.

"I got them right here," Lenny said, tapping the cat carrier. "I done already named 'em both. It's a boy and a girl—Beans and Crema."

He smiled wide with this announcement, evidently proud of his coffee-themed creativity.

"Cute!" I exclaimed, looking in the carrier at the two kittens now sleeping in an inseparable ball of tortoiseshell and beige.

"Are you going to take them to the humane society? I'll drive if you want," Lincoln offered.

Lenny reached out to open the small, wired door of the carrier, stuck his hand in, and began to stroke the purring kittens—his large hand made them appear even tinier.

"These babies are gonna stay with me," he resolved. "They've been through enough—lost their mama and now their brother. They need somebody and that somebody might as well be me."

Standing inside Isa's room for the first time in over four years felt exactly like the inside of one of the tombs featured in The Quest for Immortality exhibit. I remembered reading that the Egyptians decorated their sacred burial spaces so the deceased could enjoy the afterlife; they believed that everyone had a right to an eternal home. I tried to find comfort in the idea that, to some—even if it was centuries ago, death was cause for celebration. Although, as I held Isa's beloved bracelets in my hands—discarded on a dusty vanity—I couldn't view death as anything other than an end. If death was the period at the conclusion of a person's life sentence, I was sure that Isa would have wanted to go out with an exclamation point. But to those of us that were left with nothing but a McMansion-style bedroom tomb in suburbia, we saw a question mark.

"Nothing in the dresser," Lincoln said, closing the bottom drawer.

"Nothing in the vanity either," I confirmed.

We had been investigating the room for over an hour, specifically hoping to uncover the turquoise moleskin or something that would form a direct line of connection to Steve. Though, the first 20 minutes were spent holding each other and coaxing away the pain that resurfaced from inhaling the air that still somehow smelled of her. Dried daisies hung in bunches above the window, an empty water glass that never made it to the dishwater was untouched on her bedside table, and there was a wrinkled tie-dye tee at the foot of the bed. I knew she did a lot of couch surfing at the end, so there was no way to tell when she had last inhabited the space. But, according to Lincoln, she always wound up back at Tony's for short stints when she got desperate. So, when I imagined that she might have slept in that tie-dye shirt—maybe she pulled it off when she woke up the morning she went to Steve's apartment—I couldn't breathe.

I didn't even know what I was looking at when I came across the ashes. It was a wooden box with engravings of a crescent moon and stars. A quote from Sylvia Plath in delicate script read:

"If the moon smiled, she would resemble you."

"That's Isa's…um…" Lincoln said, when I picked it up to examine. "That's…Isa."

I almost dropped the box on the floor. The blonde haired, husky voiced, larger than life Isa DeLuca—reduced to a 6″ x 4″ box.

"Oh, I didn't know," I said, placing it back on the dresser with care.

I knew the rest of that quote. It was from Plath's poem, "The Rival." I'd read it in the *Ariel* collection.

"…You leave the same impression
Of something beautiful but annihilating."

A shiver passed through me like a gust of brittle wind. Whoever decided on that quote couldn't have read the full poem. Whoever decided on that quote also couldn't have known how truly it encapsulated the resident of the wooden box it was carved on.

"I think this might be harming more than it's helping," I said after some time.

What good was it to pick through her belongings if they held no answers? I could no longer justify the invasion of privacy or keep my panic at bay—just the sight of the Hail to the Thief vinyl I got her for her 17th birthday provoked my heart rate to double. Lincoln, on the other hand, seemed to be able to put emotion to the side and tap into a private detective persona that I didn't know he possessed. Singularly focused on finding the missing pieces to the puzzle, he didn't shudder as I did when he tore through her shoe rack and held up a Ziplock containing multi-colored pills. He didn't know how to properly dispose of them, and I didn't want to touch them—the little smiley faces on the pills were more insidious than inviting—so back in their beaded moccasin hiding spot they went.

"Are you ready to leave?" Lincoln asked as he pulled the rainbow quilt back over the mattress.

In a shattering instance, I realized that the last time I slept in that room was the night we snuck out for Jason's party. I pushed open the bedroom door and walked out without explanation. I needed air or I was going to pass out. I'd barely gotten any sleep the night before because I was working on my thesis. I accidentally skipped lunch because I offered to check in on Lenny's new kittens while he was running errands for the shop. Overwhelm was beginning to kick in and, as it turned out, this was far from an impassive viewing of some ancient pharaoh's final resting place. This was my dead best friend's bedroom. This room had seen us bond; this room held our secrets; this room knew the dirty jokes we had laughed at and the tears that were shed late into the night. Those sheets were once stained with my own blood.

"K, let's get out of here," Lincoln said, rubbing my back as I leaned over the banister, staring at the formal living room below. "We're getting nowhere."

"Lincoln, the last time I spent the night. That was the night… The last time I woke up in that bed…"

Understanding, he pulled me into a tight hug and kissed the top of my head.

"I don't want to go back in there," I said.

"You don't have to."

On the ride back to campus, we talked of our upcoming rehearsal and begrudged the fact that rush hour traffic, in this city, started ridiculously at 3:00 pm. Conversation lulled as we merged onto I-65 but when I reached for the radio, Lincoln suddenly spoke again.

"Have you ever thought of reporting him?"

"Who? Steve? He was already questi—"

"No…the…guy. The guy from Jason's party."

Oh.

I focused on reading the states on passing license plates while I processed the question.

Tennessee, Tennessee, Alabama, Tennessee, Georgia, Arkansas, Maine—oh that one was interesting—Tennessee, Tennessee…

"K?"

"No," I said, forcing myself back into the present moment, "I can't. I don't have proof. I told you—I don't know his name."

"What if we could find out?" he asked. "It can't be that hard. We start by messaging Jason. Did you say this guy was his roommate?"

"I—I don't know if he lived there…"

"Even still, there's gotta be a way—"

"Why don't you focus on playing detective with one case at a time?" I snapped. "It was years ago. Do you think anyone is going to believe me?"

"Of course, people would believ—"

"Not when it's been this long, they won't. I should have said something back when…when…I don't know. When it was *relevant*."

"Relevant? It's always going to be relevant, K, it's your life. And guys like that—they can't just be allowed to get away wit—"

"Well, he did, okay? He got away with it. Because I never said anything. I even washed away every stitch of evidence the very same morning it happened. I *helped* him get away with it."

Lincoln took the next exit…which was not our exit. He turned into a deserted parking lot that looked like it had once belonged to a Spirit Halloween that had once belonged to a K-Mart.

Putting the car in park and silencing the engine, he looked at me and said, "You are in no way responsible for the actions of that scumbag. He *assaulted* you, K."

"Don't say that—"

"But we *should* say it. If we don't say it—if we dance around the issue—then that's—that's—K, you can't let him get away with it."

Less than a week after the tense Steve conversation, there we were *again* blundering clumsily through baggage that neither knew how to handle. Was it possible for us to have a healthy, normal dating life? I thought we were magnets—our physical chemistry combined with our years of friendship certainly lent itself to that belief. Maybe I was irritable because I was hungry and exhausted. But maybe I was wrong; maybe we were the ends of the magnet that repelled each other.

"I don't want to do anything about it," I said, raising my voice to a level that was not quite yelling, but by no means pleasant within the confines of the cramped car. "What happened, happened to *me*. You don't know it would feel to drudge this up again. Or how many times I'd have to possibly tell the details to strangers. You don't know and you can't know, so let *me* be the authority on what else happens to *me*, alright?"

"It just makes me so angry—"

"*You're* angry? Think about how angry I've been for the last five years! Why I've never had a boyfriend… Why I've never told anyone anything. Lincoln, it's like…sometimes I'm still…*I'm still so mad.*"

My phone buzzed. I glanced down to find a new email from Dr. Mirza. The subject line: Meeting today?

"Damnit!" I said, slamming the back of my head against the passengers' seat. "My thesis project meeting with Dr. Mirza. I was supposed to meet her 30 minutes ago."

"Hey, it's okay," he soothed, grabbing my hand. "You've got a lot on your plate. She's cool. She'll understand."

I sighed. While that was true, I hated making stupid mistakes. With my thesis, classes, working overtime, rehearsals, and now afternoons as an amateur detective, I was quickly drowning.

"You're right," Lincoln said, "about everything. I'm sorry I was pushy. I was out of line."

"Just promise me you won't try to track him down, okay? Please, Lincoln. I don't want to see his face again. I don't want to speak to him or go to the police. I want to forget it ever happened. Please."

I expected him to extend his pinky finger, but instead he took my face in his hands.

His thumbs grazed my cheeks as he said in almost a whisper, "I love you so much."

The golden rings dancing around his pupils were as beautiful and painful as gazing directly into the sun. Beautiful was the radiance of amber yellow when he laughed at me crashing into his face during "Sixteen Going on Seventeen." Painful was the dimness of them after he'd punched that stranger in the tattoo parlor. Those same knowing eyes had watched me win and lose. Had watched me strut through hallways in my most prized vintage dresses…and fling boogers out of car windows. Those eyes looked back at me and in them, I saw history. I saw love.

"I want to make this right because I love you."

"I love *you*," I replied without missing a beat.

I thought of sitting on my parents' front stoop, watching Lincoln walk down the driveway. Not seeing him again for three full years and filling the void by trying to interpret what he meant when he last used those words. I didn't need my dating coach cousins to tell me that the phrase we all long to hear had multiple meanings. This time I wanted to say what I meant to say. I was tired of not using my voice when I had a chance.

"I don't mean in a best friend way. I mean in *the* way. I am in love with you. Don't feel like you have to say it bac—"

"Katie," he interjected, "I've been in love with you since we were 14."

"Hey, don't call me—"

But the dimple smile couldn't be suppressed, and it only encouraged him.

"Katie Elizabeth Statham, I am *in* love with you."

The windows were comedically foggy by the time we left the parking lot. A Spirit Halloween/K-Mart graveyard might not have been the most romantic site for a make out session, it suited us just fine.

"It's a little sad to be done," Julia said while I scrolled through the university's online database for scholarly articles.

EBSCOHost, don't fail me now, I prayed, typing in the keywords "Pakistan," "female," and "modern art."

"Yeah, totally," I replied, although I didn't hear a word she said, I just knew that the endless stream of consciousness prattle had stopped and that meant it was my turn to respond.

"It's been nice to be absorbed in German art again. It made me crave another afternoon in Maxvorstadt. I might keep researching. Just for fun."

"Wait. Hold up. You're *done*?" I asked, suddenly comprehending.

"Uh, K, hello? That's what I've been saying," Julia nagged as she powered down her laptop. "Haven't you been listening?"

"Yeah, 'course…" I lied, tearing my eyes away from the blue light of my own laptop screen, "but do you mean *done* done? Already? We still have two months before it's due. How did you have time?"

"Like I said—my thesis basically wrote itself. It almost felt like cheating; honestly, it was so easy. The hardest part was condensing it, so I didn't go over the page count. Anyways, Natasha is taking me to that new wine bar to celebrate tomorrow! I heard a rumor that they have Gewürztraminer."

"I'm sorry, what?"

"That type of wine I was telling you about. You know, made from those German grapes? Like a Moscato."

I knew nothing of wine—only that it was red, white, and sometimes pink. Julia's pretension could really get on my nerves sometimes. And now, with only a few viable references in my stunted bibliography, this was one of those times.

"That's cool, Julia. Hey, maybe with all your free time, you can write mine?"

She laughed but, at that moment, I may have actually considered offering her my last three Chubbie's paychecks (tips included) if she would've obliged. The Burnout Monster was rearing her ugly head and when I succumbed to burnout, it was not a pretty sight. But it was impossible not to—I'd had too many sleepless nights either working on or worrying about this paper. On top of that, there was a budding relationship to maintain, an attention whore of a feline companion to care for, work, and the rest of my classes to not flunk out of while in the home stretch before graduation. Oh, and rehearsals. Lincoln's play, sadly, was low on the list of priorities. I still showed every Thursday night, but I hadn't written my piece yet…

"Natasha's waiting for me in the quad," Julia said, reading a text. "She's super excited about the play, by the way. It's all she talks about. She says it's *fun*. I'm like, 'How is talking about sad personal stories *fun*?'"

"If you'd join us, you'd know," I baited, although we all knew that the biggest loss Julia had ever endured was getting an A- in Contemporary Art and Design.

"I shall be an active participant…from the audience," she said. "Are you staying?"

"Yeah, you go. I'll see you tomorrow."

"Don't stay out too late," she warned, "Lincoln might start suspecting you're having an affair—with Lila D. Bunch."

Lila D. Bunch, the university library, and I were known to have many an overnight rendezvous, a privilege that Lincoln was denied…I wasn't ready for that, and I had no idea when I would be. But Julia didn't need to know. I laughed and allowed her to continue to think she was made of exceptional wit.

With Julia gone, I had sole possession of the second story reading room. I didn't consider myself a night owl, but I had a fondness for the library after dark. When you were there, it meant that you had a purpose. No matter what was going on in your life at the moment—it could wait because when you were at the library after 10:00 pm, whatever you were working on mattered more. The permission to think about just one thing at a time was a luxury.

At long last, I finally had a call number—a magic code—leading me to *Hanging Fire: Contemporary Modern Art from Pakistan* by Salima Hashmi. My confidence was rising as I skimmed the orderly spines in the art and criticism stack.

"There you are you sneaky minx!" I said to number N7310.7 .H37 2009 because if I was the only one there, no one could call me crazy.

My fingertips clutched the spine but when I pulled the book free, a dozen or so soft pink stones tumbled out from behind and bounced onto the carpeted floor. Stunned, I jumped backwards and ran into the stack behind me, disrupting other books in the process.

"What the—"

I couldn't believe what I was looking at, but it was unmistakable—rose quartz of all shapes and sizes, scattered all over the aisle. Who put them there? And *why*? Why behind this of all books? I was probably the only person all year to come into the Lila D. Bunch with such a specific and obscure research topic. Who else was hunting down modern Pakistani artists? To confirm that my mind wasn't playing tricks on me, I reached for the nearest stone. It was real—I could hold it in my hands. This wasn't a hallucination brought on by lack of sleep. I was alone. In the middle of the art and criticism section. And I was holding a real rose quartz stone. It was smooth and cold to the touch. Distinctly pink, but with cloudy white swirls trapped deeply below the surface. This was *real*.

My arms covered in goosebumps and my breath shallow, I thought of Leonora's words during the séance: "...someone has not been receptive to her visits."

"Isa?" I whispered to the emptiness.

Was she here? Was she trying to tell me something?

"What is it?" I asked.

Why did communication with the dead have to be so cryptic?

"What is it? What do you want?" I nearly shouted.

But the books didn't reply. And Isa, if she was there, did not give herself away. I was frightened enough that I imagined bolting out of the library. But I stayed stubbornly planted in my spot on the carpet, determined not to let Isa get the best of me—not now that I was moving on. Didn't I already conclude that she can't control me from the afterlife? What did she want? Why wouldn't she leave me alone? I was trying to figure things out, trying to bring closure to all of this…for everyone's sake. Was I not doing enough? *What did she want?*

Think, think, I told myself.

Say that, hypothetically, Leonora was right—Isa was trying to deliver a message and these creepy coincidences were her attempts at breaking through to me. Okay, if that was true, then what was Isa trying to say? I rolled the cold stone around in my palm. Rose quartz… Isa put so much stock in the meaning of these things. What did rose quartz mean?

Rose quartz attracts love. It improves self-esteem. It aids in forgiveness.

That still didn't make sense. Love? Certainly not. Self-esteem? No. Forgiveness? Did she want me to apologize? Was she trying to tell me that her death *was* in fact my fault and I needed to ask for forgiveness?

The fluorescent lights overhead flickered. Was a bulb burning out or was Isa trying to reply? Was she telling me I was on the right track or to go in a different direction?

Fully aware that what I was about to do possibly meant that I had entirely lost my marbles, I whispered, "Once for yes, twice for no."

Nothing happened. Utter stillness.

"Did I do something wrong? Something I need your forgiveness for?"

The lights flickered. Twice. Twice for no.

I woke the next morning to the robotic purging noises of paper shooting out of a printer. I had fallen asleep in the second story reading room, face down in a book entitled, *Gemstones and Their Hidden Meanings*. Abandoning my thesis paper, I had spent the better part of three hours researching the damned rose quartz that now filled the front pocket of my backpack. I rolled my head from side to side, massaged my neck, and realized that I had drooled all over a sentence that declared that gifting someone a gemstone offered a different meaning than when you bought a stone for yourself. It came back to me—the realization that I arrived at before submitting to the temptation of sleep. If I viewed the incident of the night before as Isa "gifting" me the stones, then *she* was trying to give *me* forgiveness…possibly. Apparently, rose quartz as a gift was a symbol of unconditional love. A discovery that only further stumped me.

As I closed the book, I happened to notice something written in pencil in the upper right-hand corner of my pillow page. I didn't put it there and I didn't remember seeing it last night… I clapped my hand to my mouth when the words sunk in:

She had a name

The same phrase that was whispered to me during the séance. But what was more, it was written in Isa's handwriting. Of that fact, I was one thousand percent certain. The loopy, fat "o" shape of the a's and the way she curled the upper half of her h's.

I didn't have time to analyze it; it was 6:50 am and my first class was at 7:15. It was not my intention to sleep over at the library and definitely not my plan to forgo my thesis research. I had to rush back to my apartment, feed F. Scott, and change into something that didn't accuse me of taking the walk of shame from the Lila. *Who* had a name? What was Isa trying to tell me? I didn't know and I didn't have time to find out. Not now.

Of course, it occurred to me to tell Lincoln everything. I almost called him at 11:00 pm last night and begged him to meet me at the library because I was so shaken up, but I decided against it. I couldn't give him one more thing to worry about. He had just as much on his plate as I did—maybe more now that Leonora was involved in the play. Trying to expand the cast, he'd asked if she'd consider participating in honor of her twin. She accepted, citing her past life as an Austrian opera singer as credibility. Unlike Natasha, our other new recruit, Leonora was harder to…contain. "I once gravitated to the stage," she told him when he tried to rein in her three-page single-spaced monologue.

I was a zombie moving through the motions for the remainder of the day, but somehow managed to stay awake for my classes. Although by the time Lincoln came over for our Friday night movie, I had to acknowledge my limitations.

"I'm going to fall asleep if we watch a movie," I told him as he threw a bag of popcorn into my microwave.

"Is this your way of saying that you're not thrilled by *The Hobbit*?" Lincoln asked.

"I mean…you knew that," I teased, "but for real—I didn't get good sleep last night. Can we do something else? Something to keep me awake?"

As much as I needed sleep, I didn't want him to go.

"We could look up Steve," he offered. "We can think of some questions and make a plan."

That wasn't what I had in mind. Friday nights were meant to detox from the responsibilities of the week. But this was a task that had to be done. Better to get it over with. Maybe then I'd be able to focus more clearly on my thesis, my piece for the play…Lincoln himself. I wanted to put all of this Isa stuff to bed. If we found the answers we needed, then she might leave me alone.

"Yeah, sure. But I'm still busting out the Twizzlers."

"Duh," he agreed. "I'm gonna run to the bathroom real quick. Don't do anything without me."

He placed the bowl of buttery popcorn on the kitchen table and walked off.

"I'll just get my laptop going," I called after him.

But when I tried the power button, the laptop wouldn't start. I realized then that not only was it dead, but that I had left my charging cable at the Lila. I groaned to myself, not looking forward to making a trip back to the library first thing tomorrow morning. Luckily, Lincoln brought his laptop with him everywhere he went—it was attached to his hip with super glue, just like his little black writer's notebook. I unzipped his backpack, pulled the laptop out, and opened it on the kitchen table. Lincoln's password for everything that required a password was 10.17.1991—his birthday.

"Hey, what are you using my laptop for?" Lincoln asked when he came out of the bathroom.

I didn't respond. I couldn't. I was too distracted by the face staring back at me from the screen. It was Mustard Stain. I was looking at his Facebook.

"K..." Lincoln said quietly as he approached me.

"What is this?" I asked, still in shock and unable to remove my eyes from the page.

I gasped when I scrolled down and recognized that people I knew were friends with him. People I had sat beside in classes, talked to in the Caf, recognized from high school. People that came to my plays and used to be my Facebook friends when I had a Facebook. These people were commenting on posts, liking photos... These people— *people I knew*—were friends with Connor Lathers. Connor Lathers...my rapist.

"I told you not to look him up!" I shouted as I spun around in my chair. "You promised me!"

"K, I'm sorry..." Lincoln started, "you weren't supposed to see that."

"It doesn't matter—you *promised* me you wouldn't! I asked you not to!"

"But I didn't—I didn't promise you. I told you that I wanted to make it right. I wasn't going to get you involved. I never wanted you to—"

I stood from the table and slammed his laptop shut. F. Scott, spooked by the abrupt noise, sprung from the counter, and darted under the futon.

"You didn't want me to know? What were you planning to do?" I yelled.

Connor Lathers. I had a name now. And that made it…*worse*…somehow. He wasn't a boogeyman, and it wasn't a nightmare. He was a real person living out an ordinary life without consequence. It was worse than not knowing. Seeing that…*it was worse*.

"I was going to handle it myself—meet up with him and—"

"And what? Knock his lights out like you did to that guy at the tattoo shop? Is that the kind of person you are? What good would that do? What *were* you going to do, exactly?"

"I hadn't really thought about it—"

"No *shit* you hadn't thought about it!"

Angry tears threatened to discredit me. I didn't want to cry. I didn't want to appear weak. I didn't need a savior.

"I didn't tell you what happened so you could swoop in here and be prince charming. I don't need you to save me."

"K, that's not what I was trying to do."

"Then what were you trying to do, Lincoln?"

"I was trying to help!" he said, finally breaking composure and meeting my frustration. "He needs to know the impact he had and what he's done!"

I was too tired for this, and I was growing paranoid. Paranoid that I didn't recognize the signs the first time and that I had unknowingly fallen into a similar trap. I should have known to keep my heart and my brain where my feet were, but I had gotten too swept up in idealizing this romance with Lincoln. Not the reality of what was in front of me—another person trying to control me. When would I ever be able to decipher what was good from what was bad? Who meant to harm and who I could trust?

"You think I'm weak," I accused. "I thought Isa was the one that played games, but you're doing the same thing. You said it yourself, remember? That I was Isa's plaything. Well, you're trying to use me in the same way. You're trying to control me and 'handle things' without my permission. You're trying to make me the damsel to inflate your own ego. What makes you any different from the other toxic males that just take and take and take?"

"No, Katie, I didn't mean it like that! How could you ever think that I would—"

"Don't call me that!" I yelled, tears rocketing out of my eyes. "Don't make me anonymous by calling me that name. That name everyone else has."

"You know what?" Lincoln said, reaching to pack up his belongings. "You're obsessed with this idea that you're flawed. That you're damaged beyond repair in some way, but no one else is allowed to try to fix it."

"I don't need you to fix anything."

"Yeah, I know. I see that. From where I'm sitting, I see a person who has everyone rooting for her but herself. Ms. Morris believed in you, your parents—they were at all your shows—*they* believed in you. *I* believed in you. And now this fancy university thinks you can do no wrong. The only person that doesn't believe in Katie Statham is Katie Statham. The only person that thinks Katie Statham is weak is *Katie Statham*.

"Isa didn't irrevocably damage you. You're stronger than that. You aren't fundamentally flawed because she couldn't swallow a communion wafer. This douchebag—this Connor—he didn't ruin you. Stop letting this narrative own you. It's so—it's so *pathetic* to watch. I think you *like* to be damaged. It's easier for you to be miserable than to face things and move on."

"I was wrong," I said quietly to the linoleum kitchen floor.

"What?"

"This isn't going to work out," I said, looking him directly in the eyes. "It was wrong to kiss you at the party. It was wrong to try and date you. It was a mistake, and we should stop while we're ahead."

He didn't say anything, which I understood to mean that he either agreed or didn't care enough to argue against it.

"If this is your idea of me and you *together*…then…Lincoln…I can't do it. It's too hard."

14.

Fly Little Bird

"Soooo...you heard about Blair, right?" Lincoln asked, from the swing beside me.

Having ended junior year in contemptible silence, it was the first time we'd been around each other in months. It wasn't my first time back at the swings, though. I visited them most days over the summer—I'd bring a book and read while subconsciously hoping I'd see a DeLuca walking across the soccer field. To be the first to apologize was out of the question; the words we exchanged in our final interactions still cut like knives every time I'd replay them in the shower. At first, my excuse was that I needed space. I needed to think, get my priorities back on track, and figure out who I was if I wasn't part of a trio. Without anyone else to fret about, I had to ask myself, "What did K want? What did K like?"

But then, the loneliness got...*lonelier*. It wasn't like before. Before, I didn't know what it felt like to have such intense soul ties. Even if I thought I had missed certain acquaintances when I changed schools, I had no idea what "missing" actually felt like until around mid-June. That was when I realized that Isa and Lincoln weren't coming back to me. No calls, no texts...no surprise appearances at the swings.

So, when I heard the news about Blair, I had no one to talk to. Until the Saturday morning before senior year. When I saw Lincoln walking Ella. My ache for companionship superseded my pride; I was the one to call out to him and wave him over. But I liked to think that he could have taken a different route to walk Ella...and he didn't. He chose the playground. Maybe he was looking for me too?

"Yeah, my mom told me," I replied.

Months ago, I would have laughed if someone told me that Blair would be the drive force behind Lincoln and I reconnecting. But months ago, Blair didn't have stage four melanoma.

"Honey, come sit with us," my mom said earlier that week.

She was sitting with my dad on the living room sofa and patted the center cushion. The last time we'd sat down like this, my dad announced that we were moving to Tennessee. I gulped and joined them in the rarely occupied formal living room. I didn't want to move again—couldn't my parents wait one more year? If they could just wait until I made it to college, they could move wherever they wanted, and I wouldn't care. But then again—who was I desperate to stay in town for at this point?

"K, we have some bad news," my dad started.

Okay, so this was obviously not about a move... Whenever we were moving, my dad always started the conversation with, "Wouldn't (insert new location) be a blast?!"

"Sweetie, your friend Blair—" my mom said, taking my hand.

"Blair's not my friend."

I didn't mean to say it; it slipped. I expected my parents to scold me for rudeness, but instead they looked irrationally horrified. As if I'd just put a curse on the entire Ford family.

"Blair has *cancer*, K," my dad said sternly. "She's very sick."

Bile slithered down my throat. I may as well have planted the cancer in her body myself.

"I didn't mean—"

"She was diagnosed in the spring and the Fords kept it quiet," Mom explained, "But it spread to her lymph nodes and now it's in her soft tissue. They're starting chemo this week."

"No…but…she's going to Oklahoma City…" I said in disbelief.

This couldn't be right. Blair was fine at the end of the year. In fact, she was more obnoxious than ever before after she found out she'd been accepted into Oklahoma City University's musical theater program. She boasted about how it was Kristen Chenoweth's alma mater and the training ground for future Glindas.

"She's not going to college, honey," my mom continued. "She's going to be in the hospital for a while. They might be taking her to St. Jude if she can qualify. Lanette is going to quit her job at the school, and I'll be taking over her HOA duties."

Azrah, who a week before didn't know how to accept a friend request, created, and managed a Facebook page devoted to Blair. "Bringing Hope to Blair Ford" featured pictures of Blair ranging from a freckled-faced strawberry blonde toddler to her high school glory days. Absolutely everyone from school—whether they knew her personally or not—commented daily, saying that she was continuously in their "thoughts and prayers." Within less than 24 hours, $40,000 was raised to help the family pay for Blair's medical treatments.

"It's surreal," I admitted to Lincoln as I slowly pumped my swing back and forth, "seeing those pictures of her in the hospital… She lost her hair. You can't even tell it's her, you know?"

Lincoln nodded. "Are you going to visit?"

"My mom's been taking care of things at their house and dropping in at the hospital."

"Yeah, but…are *you* gonna go?" he insisted.

"I don't know… She hates me. What am I going to say? It'd feel wrong to just show up with 'Feel Better' balloons when… She's not going to get better, Lincoln. My mom says it's really bad. The doctors said 11 to 22 *months*…"

"But she's young," Lincoln offered with forced optimism.

"But they caught it too late," I concluded.

"Yeah…"

"How's…um…Isa taking it?" I ventured cautiously.

I never confronted Blair or Isa about the note on my locker. Nothing happened after that other than whispers and stares from their lunch table. I took a cruel pleasure in assuming that Isa and Blair's rekindled friendship was no more than a tactic for getting under my skin and that once summer hit, Isa would likely cut her ties with Blair once again. But *what if* they'd stayed friends? What if all summer they were having sleepovers? What if Isa was in the hospital right now holding Blair's hand? The thought made me wretched with jealousy, even if I knew I didn't have a right to be. No one deserved cancer. And no one that had it ought to be alone… But I couldn't erase the image of that note from my mind. "TERRORIST!" it read. I couldn't step foot in the hospital or bring myself to write, "Thinking of you," on her Facebook page.

"Isa's…Isa's being Isa."

"What does that mean?" I asked, despising myself that I couldn't shake my curiosity.

"I've barely seen her all summer," Lincoln explained. "She only comes home to get clothes and stuff—I guess she's out with friends. She told my dad that she wanted to start her TCC classes in June to get a head start. He paid for them. She never went. I don't know what she used the money on…"

I wanted to say, "I'm not surprised," because I wasn't. But the tortured look on Lincoln's face prevented me from burdening him with my residual bitterness. I grabbed the chain of his swing, forcing him to a holt. When he looked at me, my stomach tightened. He hadn't looked me straight in the eyes since that day in the hallway when I said— "Just give the role to Blair." I never even showed up to the performance. It could have been a masterpiece or a complete flop—I'd never know, and I was too guilt-ridden to inquire.

Instead, I asked a question I should have asked a long time ago, "Lincoln, are you okay?"

"Yeah, things are...good. Ms. M's letting me direct *The King and I*. Dad took me to Brown last month and I'm gonna check out Columbia in September. I hope we can make it out to U of M, but Dad's got a lot of business trips coming up. I think I've got a good chance at getting into one of my top three—"

"I mean, that's great. But how are you? Not college applications. *You*."

He fidgeted with Ella's leash, avoiding the question.

"I'm worried, K," he said at last. "About Isa. She's...I think she's doing...I don't know. I really don't. I'm just speculating so—"

"What? What do you think she's doing?" I urged, ignoring Ella's wet nose sniffing my leg.

"Drugs. Maybe some...bad stuff. I saw her about two weeks ago—she's really skinny, K. She doesn't want to talk when she's home. She doesn't tell me where she's at or... I don't know, K. I was wondering if...if you might be willing to reach out to her?"

I sighed. Leaving my swing to shudder in my absence, I crossed to the edge of the AstroTurf and stared over the soccer field. Any minute Isa was going to leap across the dewy grass—white-blonde waves riding on the wind, her laugh provoking the birds in the trees to take flight. I pictured her in her blue daisy print sundress—the one that was arguably a little too short and too worn from overuse—but her favorite. The clatter of her bracelet collection as she bounced towards me. The feel of her arms when she threw them around my neck, exclaiming in her sing-song way, "Hello little bird!"

Isa, what have you done?

"I don't know what happened between you guys," Lincoln said, but my focus was on the Isa in my mind.

It hurt to imagine the Isa that he was describing.

"I know she can be mean when she wants to be. But I'm worried. Dad can't get in touch with her. Mom is...I don't even know. But she might listen to you. K? Would you at least think about it?"

"You want me to go ahead and put in an order for you, Miss K?" Lenny asked from behind the bar. "I hate to see you sittin' there twiddlin' your thumbs! You sure you don't at least want a cold brew? Mighty warm today."

"No thanks, Lenny," I replied, checking my phone for the third time. "I'll give her five more minutes and then I'll head out. I have my personal statement to work on anyway."

"Alrighty, then. Something must've come up, Miss K. But listen, you keep me posted on those colleges, you hear?"

"Thanks, Lenny. I will."

It wasn't until the lavender cold brew was back in season that I finally confirmed a date to meet up with Isa. That is to say, months went by before she responded to my unanswered texts, calls, and Facebook messages. Since we didn't have any classes together that year and we were both distracted by college prep, the only interactions Lincoln and I had were clipped, whispery conversations about Isa over lunch. I began to view myself as nothing more than a sounding board but accepted the role as the penance I deserved for not being there for him when he needed me the year before. The never-ending inquiry—"Have you heard anything yet?" "Did she text you back?"—drove me batty. I didn't go out of my way to hang out with him outside of school because being the unsuccessful middleman Monday-Friday was already enough.

Finally, on my birthday, I heard the distinctive ding of an incoming Facebook message in the middle of Chemistry.

> Hey. Lost my phone a while back. Happy birthday, birdie!

I didn't wait to alert Lincoln or even attempt discretion as I messaged her back in the middle of class.

Isa, can you meet up?

I heard nothing for two days and then I got:

When?

And that was the pattern we were stuck in for three months—I'd ask her to hang out, she'd ghost me for days, she'd accept the invite, I'd try to solidify concrete plans, and she'd ghost me for days. I asked her about her phone when she used the "Sorry, I don't check Facebook much!" excuse. Her phone was always not working, lost, or she couldn't remember her new number. She used the phrase, "Life's crazy! Raincheck?" so many times that I thought I'd make a collage out of those messages and mail to her out of spite. But that was the thing—*where did she live?* Lincoln claimed there was evidence of her at their house, but she never stayed for long. He'd catch her pulling out of the driveway as he came home from rehearsal or hear his dad arguing with her over the phone. I asked why he and his dad couldn't file a missing person's report or get the authorities involved in some way.

"It's not 'missing' if you don't want to be found. The police can't make a full-grown woman go back to her dad's house if she wants nothing to do with us," he said.

That was why I didn't tell Lincoln about our potential Chubbie's date that March afternoon. I didn't want to see the disappointment on his face when plans fell through, yet again. Swearing to myself and resolving that I was officially done waiting for her (possibly done with further attempts at communication once and for all) I started gathering my things.

"Where are you running off to?" she said, flinging open the door.

And there she was—there was Isa. I hadn't seen her face in almost exactly a year. "Where have you been?" and "Why are you thirty minutes late?"—the questions I'd thought I'd spew at her the moment she walked through the door (if she ever did), were lost to me now. I ran up to her, crocodile tears running embarrassingly down my cheeks, and squeezed her like I could trap her into never leaving me ever again.

"Isa!" I breathed.

"Aww, it warms my heart to see my two favorite ladies back together again!" Lenny said, too invested to pretend he wasn't eavesdropping.

Isa held me at arm's length, gave me a thorough head to toe examination with tired eyes, and took two curly strands of my hair into her hands.

"You look so *beautiful*, little bird! But why are you crying? Silly goose. You need a coffee. Lenny! Get this girl a double shot."

"Coming right up, Miss Isa!"

But Isa was the one in need of an extra shot of espresso. Purplish bags had taken occupancy under her eyes, her skin was sallow, and her long hair—even though it was pulled into an untidy bun—was visibly greasy. She still had her bracelets, but she was wearing an unrecognizable faded pair of jeans and a funny smelling long-sleeved pullover that was two sizes too big. Her deep, sultry voice boomed loud as ever as she chatted with Lenny and made herself comfortable at the bird table. Maybe her bubbly energy fooled him—the way she perched on the window seat cross-legged and how her bun bounced when she nodded enthusiastically at the offer of whipped cream atop her hazelnut Frappuccino. I wanted to see what Lenny saw, but the thinned face and sunken eyes distracted me from her giddy performance. I had no control over the waterworks.

"Come onnnnn," she cooed just like she used to. "What's this all about?"

She held one of my hands in both of hers. I wanted to say, "Isa, come live with us again. Isa, are you okay? Isa, can we go back to the way it used to be?" Instead, I was tongue-tied when I felt her once-smooth palms—she was notorious for using mango cocoa butter lotion before bed every night. Now, her hands were scabby and dry.

"I just—I've missed you," I mustered as Lenny delivered our drinks to the table.

"And I've missed *you*!"

She grabbed my head and brought it to her chest, embracing me. Her collarbone poked my eye. The smell of her—it was body odor masked by patchouli, tinged with vinegar.

"Now," she said, pulling away to take a sip of her frozen drink. "Tell me everything! What have you been up to? You're a sexy senior now!"

I wished I could match her euphoria. She was jiggling a leg and widening her eyes to punctuate every other word.

"Any *romance*?" she said, nudging me with her elbow and booming with laughter. "Please, *God*! Please tell me you've gotten some romance. You deserve to be romanced, birdie. You really do. If anyone does, it's you. What about plays? What's the next gig? Sign me up—I'll be there! I'll be there throwing roses to you from the audience! Encore, K! Encore!"

She stood, clapping wildly. Others were staring and my face began to burn.

"Shh…Isa, sit down."

She giggled but took her seat.

"I've been marvelous, darling. Thank you for asking." She stuck out her tongue like we were elementary schoolers taunting each other on the playground. "I've been traveling a lot—Atlanta, New Orleeeeeeans." She giggled again. "There are lotsa witchy things in New Orleans. We should go sometime!"

"Where are you staying?" I asked.

"Oh…here and there…with different friends. I'm a nomad. Never miss an opportunity that way," she said.

I couldn't let her get away with flippant responses. Not after all the time Lincoln and I had spent worrying about her. I cut straight to the chase.

"Where were you on Christmas?"

"What?" Perplexed, she started biting her straw.

"Lincoln and your dad. They couldn't find you on Christmas. You said you were going to be at the house…but you never showed? They tried calling and went out looking for you. You scared them, Isa. Abe came over that night and he was a mess."

Her face went slack. It was as if the mere mention of her forgotten family aged her by ten years. She roughly scratched her right arm and rubbed her face.

"I told Tony I was staying with friends for Christmas."

"Okay…but…why did he expect you to be at his house then?"

"Lenny? Can I have some water, pretty please? My mouth is super dry," she called, ignoring my question.

"*Isa*."

"Yes, *what*?" she snapped.

"Where were you?"

Lenny set a cup of water on the table and walked off before she replied, "Maybe my phone died. Maybe I told him I *might* stop by. I don't remember. I was with friends on Christmas. What's the big deal? Christmas was a million years ago. It's summer now!"

"Isa," I said and clutched her hand, "where are you living *now*? Do you have a job? Or—"

"What's…with the third degree, birdie?" she laughed. "Yes, I have a…*job*. I have loads of them. Thank you very much."

"Doing what? Where do you work?"

"Just…this and…that. Wherever and whatever I feel like doing, really. I don't want…to be tied down…I have a life…to live."

Either I was incredibly dull company, or she was on the verge of falling asleep because her speech grew slower and slower. Her eyes drooped and her neck appeared to be made of Jell-O as her head rolled from side to side.

Asking the question without really asking the question, I said awkwardly, "And you're taking care of yourself, then. Right?"

"Tell me about *you*. What about the…acting?"

"I got cast in a professional show," I admitted. "At the dinner theater. I'm, like, getting a check for it and everything."

As uncomfortable as I was becoming in Isa's presence, I couldn't suppress a bashful smile when revealing the news. I decided to forgo participating in drama club that year—I needed a change of scenery and, frankly, after the *MacBeth* incident, not many thespians at school liked me. I didn't think I stood a chance, but I worked up the nerve to audition for *Peter Pan* anyway. Auditioning for industry professionals that weren't my high school theater director would be a valuable experience before the do-or-die college theater department auditions. When I wasn't dismissed after the first cold read, I saw that as a win. When I was asked to read with three different Peters, I was shocked. When I was invited to callbacks, I literally pinched myself. And I lost my ever-loving mind when I got the email from the director with the subject: Can we call you Wendy Darling?

"When is it? I'm coming!" Isa said, brightening.

"Starts April 9th and runs until May 16th!" Lenny announced, pointing to the poster he allowed me to hang on his bulletin board. "I got my tickets already!"

"I'll be there!" she declared. "Let me guess—you're the pretty, little cute one. The girl. The girl that's…the big sister…her name was…"

"Wendy," I finished for her.

"That's right!" Leaning in, she whispered, "Do you get to fly?"

I nodded. Again, this was a topic that I couldn't pretend *not* to be ecstatic about.

"I've got my own special harness and they brought in this whole company—all they do is special effects stuff like this. We have 'flight call' every day before we rehearse, and they choreographed *everything*. It's like dancing on air. You're going to…" My animation abruptly stalled when reality sunk in. "You're going to…you *would* love it."

Despite her insistence, I knew she wouldn't be there. I also knew by the haunted look that had crept into her eyes that Lincoln's suspicions were correct…and I had absolutely no power to fix it.

When I recounted all of this to Lincoln, he became adamant about devising a plan to stage an intervention.

"Get her to hang out again. But try to get her to come to one of our houses—No, wait…she'll probably suspect something's up… Ask if you can meet her at…wherever she's staying…and me and Dad will meet you guys there. It's got to be a private location. We can't make a big deal in Chubbie's. What if we need to hold her down or block the exit or something?"

"Lincoln, *what*?"

The taste I had in my mouth since seeing Isa could only be described as battery acid. Every time I recalled her dingy clothes and the way her eyes shifted like hunted prey, I had to force myself to count breaths and grab onto whatever was nearby for stability. What happened to the sparks in her eyes? Or the forever young brightness of her complexion? We used to stay up all night and she'd still be fresh-faced and springy the next morning. It didn't make any sense…only, it did. If I thought of the potential cause, it made perfect sense.

"You saw her for yourself. We have to do something about it!" Lincoln insisted, leaning in closer to me.

His erratic whispers caused spittle to fly from his mouth and land on my nose. We were at lunch, now occupying the same side of the picnic table so we could conceal our conversation. Even out of doors, his proximity and urgency made me claustrophobic.

"Do you really think that's a smart idea? Tricking a—a—" I didn't want to slap an unfair label on the person I once thought could do no wrong, but there was no other word for it… "*druggie* into an intervention? Ambushing her when she's made it clear that she wants to be left alone? We don't know who she's hanging around. It could be dangerous, Lincoln."

"Exactly! That's why we have to get her out! She's in trouble."

I began to rip at the edges of my Styrofoam lunch tray. We were out of our depths. On tv they have camera crews and professional psychologists backing the families that intervene with their wayward loved ones. We were just two teenagers. Even if Mr. DeLuca got involved, the pressure of playing the bait that led her to the hook was too great.

"I can't have this all on me!" I hissed. "It took *six months* to arrange one 15-minute hang out. If she doesn't respond, what more can I do? Don't *you* ever reach out to her?"

"I try every day."

The bell rang, ending our conversation…and all conversations for a while. I was too absorbed in tech rehearsals to smooth things over and, stunned into paralysis, couldn't fathom the complexity and risk involved with rescuing Isa. Not a day went by that I didn't shame myself for giving up. Still, I was afraid and—if I'm being honest—selfish. I was days away from opening my first ever professional show and weeks out from graduation. I thought it could wait. But, of course, for years afterwards, I would wish that I had tried.

Hi, K! I know this is random. I hope it's not too weird for me to message you. I saw your posts about *Peter Pan*. Congrats, girl! Happy opening!!! And omg that's so cool that you're actually flying. :D

So, I wanted to say that I'm sorry for putting that nasty note on your locker last year and for being kinda bitchy to you. That's not the kind of person I want to be remembered as. I'm livin it up in the cancer unit rn. JK, I hate it and the food sux. :(LOL. I've had a lot of time to think, and I just wanted to apologize. You're a really good actor.

XO, Blair

What got to me the most was how immature she still seemed via Facebook Messenger. Not in a critical way, I found it heartbreaking that someone who used emojis and phrases like "LOL" was sitting in a hospital bed waiting for the end. She was too young to die. I tried to type a response at least five times before settling on:

Thanks! No worries!

What was I supposed to say? "I hope you feel better soon"? And even with the disturbing knowledge that this girl was most likely not going to make it out of the cancer unit, what disturbed me more was that I said, "No worries!" to a Facebook message apology for a public display of racism. Opening night of *Peter Pan* was the last interaction I ever had with Blair Ford.

  It was easy to forget the rest of the world while rehearsals dominated my existence. The cast became a tight knit family of misfits that would often go out to T.G.I.F's after rehearsal. Aside from Freddy, the 9th grader that played Michael and whose mom picked him up promptly at 11:00 pm, I was the youngest in the cast. But I was never treated like a high schooler; especially on nights when we'd hang out on the back porch leading to the dressing rooms and I was offered vodka cranberries and cigarettes like the rest of the actors.

  Though nowhere close to a replacement for Lincoln and Isa, I was content with my new band of theater freaks. Sherry Lauderdale, the brilliant out-of-town Equity actor that played Peter, and I were quick pals. She was 25 and a recent graduate from DePaul's MFA in Acting program. We talked at length about Chicago, her life on the road as a touring actor, and I soaked up every tip of the trade she threw my way.

  "I don't think I'd ever be brave enough to chop my hair off for a role," I admitted one night as we were getting fitted into our flight harnesses.

  "That's fair. You have to love your look when you're playing *you*. But it's worth it if the paycheck's right!" she joked. "Never change your appearance for a non-eq gig, though. I bleached my hair to play Elle Woods for a summer stock run. That stipend didn't come close to salvaging my roots. And don't be afraid to get a tattoo if you want one! I've got four. If the director wants you badly enough, there's makeup for that."

I enjoyed learning from our director, Kevin O'Brian, who introduced himself as the "Resident Queen of the dinner theater" at our first read through. He was hilariously blunt but always made sure to "watch out for his theater babies" (i.e., the younger members of the cast). He'd cuss like a sailor, then look to me and Freddy and say, "Pardon my language! Mama almost forgot about her theater babies." When we'd rehearse my final scene with Sherry—the one where Peter says goodbye to Wendy and Wendy resolves to grow-up—Kevin would scream, "Make me cry, y'all! Make me want to slit my *wrists*!" from the booth. As shocking as his commentary could sometimes be, I adored him. Knowing that I was missing my graduation to perform in our closing matinee, it was Kevin that proclaimed our cast party would serve joint purposes.

"We'll make it a graduation celebration! I'll bring a whole Costco sheet cake, sugar!" he promised.

And then there was Steve, who played Captain Hook. Steve was a local actor and a dinner theater favorite, but not without a reputation. He was a notorious flirt and from the moment I met him, I could tell he thought his resume spoke for itself. He casually broke just about every "rule" the rest of us followed; he always wore his personal jewelry—a single silver cross earring in his right ear—while onstage. He'd swagger into rehearsals consistently five minutes late, but usually brought a Starbucks latte for Kevin and split a pack of American Spirits with our stage manager, Nyasia, during break; his indiscretions were never called out. I wouldn't have been surprised if he actually thought he was a pirate—he certainly dressed and acted like one. I didn't like his cocky attitude or the way he wooed the woman who played Mrs. Darling. Alicia was her name…and she was married. Though, with the exception of a few off-color cracks here and there about my age— "Hey, Wendy.

You legal yet?"—he only talked to me onstage. Until I walked in on him in the backstage bathroom.

Bent over the sink, he snorted a line of white powder before he noticed me standing in the doorway.

"Sorry! I didn't know anyone was in here!" I said as I turned to retreat to the women's dressing room.

He placed his arm on the doorframe and leaned out, a crooked smile on his face. I had to give it to Kevin—there was no other actor in town more fit to play a twisted pirate with a nefarious agenda.

"Slow your roll, doll," he said. His voice oozed with the type of sweetness that turns suddenly sour. His silver cross dangled teasingly from his ear, mocking me. "Cute little nightie they got you in," he said, reaching out to fiddle with the lacey sleeves of my costume.

"Thanks," I said, stepping back. "I have to finish getting ready."

"Don't you have to go to the bathroom? It's all yours…"

"Um…yeah, actually. But it can—I can wait—"

"But they're doing mic check soon. Better go before they call us onstage," he urged.

"Yeah, um. Okay."

He didn't move. What was he expecting? For me to come into the bathroom with him, lift up my nightgown and pee with him watching? I took a step forward, hoping that would inspire him to dodge out of my way and leave me in peace. My bladder was full to bursting. He wrapped his fingers around my arm again and leaned in so close that I felt his lips graze my ear lobe.

"You saw nothing. Our little secret."

Thirty minutes before places, Nyasia said I had a visitor waiting on the back porch.

"Who is it? My parents?"

"No, some girl. You have a sister?" Nyasia asked. "I told her to greet the cast after the show, but she said you'd want to see her."

"Birdie!" she exclaimed and bolted into my arms.

It was Isa.

"It's me! I told you I'd be here!"

For a wonderful fleeting moment, she was just as I remembered. She was wearing her favorite daisy dress and her eyes seemed to have more life in them than before. A few wildflowers poked out of a loose braid and her bracelets rattled like maracas. But when I took a step back, I noticed bruising on her legs. Despite the rising temperatures, an oversized cardigan concealed her arms. I didn't ask why. I hoped it was because she anticipated a relentless AC in the theater.

"I—um—thanks for coming," I stuttered, trying to detect a cry for help in her eyes. Only they wouldn't stay still.

"*Thanks for coming?*" she taunted. "I wouldn't miss this! Tonight, you FLY!"

She jumped and spun in a circle, waving her arms madly. Taking my hands, she guided me through the same nonsensical twists and turns. My heart ached to throw my head back and laugh with her, but I couldn't. It occurred to me to have Nyasia hold the house while I called Lincoln and begged him to rush to the theater. He could bring his dad and they could take Isa home. The thought evaporated when Steve stepped out from behind the backstage door.

He was still in street clothes, preferring to wait until the last possible moment to get into costume, and he lit a cigarette. I waved the smoke away, fearing the fines I would incur if my costume smelt of tobacco.

"Lookie here, Wendy's got a fan club," Steve teased, leaning against the porch railings.

"Uh…Steve, this is Isa."

"Her sister," Isa said, jutting a hand in front of him.

"You don't look like sisters," he observed with a laugh.

"We have different dads," Isa said and tossed her braid over her shoulder.

Was she flirting?

"Isa, um…I have to go get ready, okay? I'll see you after?" I was all but pushing her to go take her seat and get away from Steve.

"Yeah," she agreed, eyeing Steve as he took another drag. "Hey, can you spare a smoke?"

"Sorry, where are my manners? Here's a cig for the pretty lady," Steve obliged and held a fresh cigarette out for Isa.

"You should really go find your seat," I insisted.

"Relax! You got some pre-show nerves?" she said in a sing-song voice. She tucked the cigarette behind her ear and shook me gently. "Loosen up! You're going to be spectacular!"

Grabbing my hand, she gave me a twirl. Her deep laugh filled every crevice of the back porch. I wanted to drag her to her seat. It was embarrassing to be fooling around like this with Steve leering just feet away. At the same time, I didn't want her to let me go. Perhaps in some inexplicable way, I already knew. This was the last time.

"Fly little bird," she said with assurance, staring deliberately into my eyes. "I give you my blessing."

She pecked me on the lips.

"Sisters, huh?" Steve snorted.

And then I disappeared backstage. Leaving Isa alone on the porch with Steve…to talk, to flirt, exchange numbers…whatever it was that they did—a moment of regret that I would think about every single day for years to come.

In early September, I met Lincoln at the swings. I'd already completed my first week of college classes and, overcome by a new environment and fresh faces, high school was already becoming a distant memory.

"How was your summer?" Lincoln asked—the kind of question you'd ask an acquaintance you run into at Kroger.

"It was…fine," I said. "Boring."

"What about London?"

The family trip to London was a graduation present from my parents, and the only event of note that summer. I didn't see Isa. I didn't see Lincoln. I didn't want to get involved with the mess. Isa was too far gone, and Lincoln was going to leave for New York. Knowing that he was about to move away and start a new life filled me with emotions too complicated to untangle. I was happy he got into Columbia, but I was devastated to see him go. Even if our friendship wasn't what it used to be, I had found solace in the fact that he lived right down the road. I could always walk to his house and ask for a do-over. But getting my feet to do the walking was the problem.

"I saw the photos. On Facebook. What did you think of Rachel Tucker's Elphaba?"

"Oh, yeah…um…London was good. And *Wicked*," I said. "Utah looked cool. I saw that too. On Facebook. It was just…just you and your dad?"

"Yup," he replied after swallowing a huge mouthful of butter pecan ice cream. "I'm shit at skiing though. Won't try that again."

He smiled, expecting my laughter to follow, but I fixated on breaking up a chocolate chunk with my spoon. If I saw that smile, I would cry.

"Are you excited for New York?" I asked, avoiding his eyes.

"Yeah. Nervous, but excited. I already met my roommate. He seems cool. He's from Jersey so he knows the city really well," Lincoln explained.

I brought a spoonful or two to my mouth before either of us said another word.

"Thanks for, uh…thanks for meeting me, K," he said. "It would feel weird to just…well…"

I finally met his eyes but bit the inside of my cheek to distract myself with a different sort of pain.

"It wouldn't feel right to leave town without seeing you first," he finished.

I went back to breaking up chocolate chunks.

"Do you like your school? Still glad you chose to stick around? It's not, I don't know…too close to the parents and stuff?" he asked, trying his best to power through the awkwardness.

"Nope, it's good. You know, I didn't feel like moving again... The campus is nice. Professors are nice... I can stop by Chubbie's in between classes."

"Ha! Now *that's* living the dream. Chubbie's within walking distance."

I smiled. "Yeah, I bet you'll be jealous of that when you're stuck in the Starbucks black hole."

"There's gotta be some cool indie coffee shops in New York. It's *New York*—they've got everything!"

"It won't be the same, though," I said in almost a whisper.

And then the tears. Damnit. I wasn't sure if it was a mistake to meet up with him or if the mistake had been avoiding him all summer. I should have known that the moment itself was unavoidable. He was leaving no matter if I acknowledged it or not.

"You'll miss it, right?"

"Yeah, sure," he said softly. "And I'll miss you. I already do a little bit. I know that's dumb."

I nodded and took another bite of ice cream. I'd finished half of my pint already. When we both had empty containers, would that be it? Would he say goodbye?

"Well, I'm sure you'll be busy. All those shows at your fingertips. And the museums. It'll get cold though. Do you even own a real winter coat?"

"What do you mean a *real* winter coat?"

"Nashville winter is not 'winter,' Abe. Trust me on this. It'll get brutal up there. I'm talking lips so chapped that they bleed."

"You've never lived in New York," he retorted.

"Philadelphia is just as cold, worse even. It's only a bus ride away."

"I promise to wear earmuffs and send you a picture when my lips start to bleed."

The thought of him in fuzzy earmuffs made me chuckle despite myself.

"There's one other thing, K," he said, his face now void of playfulness. "I, uh…I have something… Okay, well, first…we got Isa into rehab."

"*What?*"

It was bizarre to hear her name after so many months.

"Yeah, uh…that wasn't on Facebook…obviously," he attempted a laugh, but fell quiet when he saw the look on my face.

"Dad hired a private investigator and tracked her down. She was…messed up. And I think she was just out of it enough to agree to go with him. I didn't see it, but my dad said where she was staying…apparently it was just really…rough…scary."

"So, she's okay? She's safe?" I asked, barely able to contain myself to my swing. "Is she clean?"

"She's safe. I think she's gonna be okay. I haven't visited. Only my dad is allowed for right now. But, uh…she gave this to him."

He pulled a white envelope out of his back pocket and handed it to me. I stared at the envelope, not understanding.

"It's for you. She wanted him to give this to you."

I took the envelope and sure enough, "Birdie" was written in that familiar loopy script across the center. Months ago, I would have torn the letter open immediately, desperate for contact and clarity. But for reasons unknown, my adrenaline from seconds ago dissipated; I stared out the envelope with indifference. Isa likely needed something. Again. And even though she had access to trained professionals, she was coming to me. Again. Putting the burden of secret-keeper on me. Again.

What now?

I had almost successfully moved on; I was in college, I was meeting new people, learning new things, engrossing myself in my art and environment. And now this…Isa was reeling me back into her self-inflicted chaos.

"Don't feel like you have to, uh, read it in front of me or anything," he said uncomfortably.

"I'll look at it when I get home," I said.

He nodded. "You could write to me, you know…"

The sudden segue made me laugh.

"*Write* to you?"

"Yeah. While I'm in New York. I won't be back till Christmas."

"You're not, like, going off to war," I teased. "And we have phones."

"Fine. But will you call me and let me know how things are?" he said, his brows furrowing.

"Duh, you idiot," I said, punching his arm because I knew this was goodbye and if I didn't make it a joke, then I'd spend the rest of the day in tears.

"I'll call you too."

"Okay," I said.

He sighed. "So…talk soon, then?"

"Talk soon."

I drove back to campus with the envelope staring at me from the passenger's seat. Then I brought it into my dorm and set it on my nightstand. It stayed there, unopened, for two weeks. I'd pick it up, rip the tiniest bit of the corner, and then put it back down. Eventually, I shoved it into my dresser so I wouldn't have to look at it. I didn't hear from Lincoln. I didn't reach out myself. We didn't "talk soon" and that made me angry and hurt and ashamed of myself. The longer I delayed action, the easier it was to forget. Forgetting, I'd come to realize, was better than living with regret.

And then Lincoln called.

"K? Can you talk?" he said. "K, there's been an…accident."

When I hung up the phone, I lurched my dresser drawer open with such force that it came off its track. Digging through the mound of underwear and socks, I finally found the crumpled envelope. I tore it open, and I began to read:

August 30, 2010

Dear K,

I wrote this for you. I'll play it next time I see you. I have my own horse here! His name is Sunbeam. Miss you, little bird. You can write back. Please write back.

~Isa

G
Tell me something new
em
Tell me how to touch the moon
G   am
Tell me how to catch a star

C G C G
Tell me

G
Tell me what's on your mind
em
Tell me you've got the time
G   am
To sit and stay with me
C G C G
With me

F   C G
You're my best friend, my only friend
    F
The one that lights the sky
  C   B7
The one that dries my eyes
  em   G   A7   D
I know it, I've known it

```
G                          em
I want to chase the wind
G                  G7
I want to dance in the rain
   C            am
I want to run through the streets
   F    G
again


      E                      am  em
To go back to when we were younger
am   E       am   A7    D    D7
Stronger and brighter


     G
So Tell me something new
em
Tell me how to touch the moon
G            am
Tell me how to catch a star
C   G    C   G
Tell me


G
Tell me what's on your mind
em
Tell me you've got the time
    G        am
To sit and stay with me
C   G    C   G
With me
```

15.

She Had a Name

Steve was seated in a booth when I walked into the diner.

"Hello, Wendy," he said, setting his oily cup of coffee down on the table.

I'd thought his opening line would be something cringey. Maybe, "Wendy's all grown-up now," with that seductive undertone that didn't just border on suggestive, it was. His Facebook wasn't regularly updated, so I was shocked to see how much he'd changed. He had gained weight, cut his hair, and was clean shaven. If it weren't for catching a glimpse at the earring hole in his right ear, I wouldn't have recognized him. He was wearing a *suit*.

"You didn't have to suit up on my account," I said sarcastically, taking my seat at the booth.

Steve couldn't intimidate me anymore. I decided that when I messaged him on Facebook. I went through the trouble of creating a new account just so I'd be able to send a message and I waited over three years for this face-to-face conversation. He was guilty. I was not. I had the upper hand. But just in case, I told him to meet me at the diner. Since no one knew where I was—I didn't want to involve Lincoln; I had to do this alone—I needed witnesses.

"I work at a bank. I'm on lunch," he said.

A waitress swung by our table to take my order before I had the time to comment on his jarring shift in career.

"Just a coffee, please," I told her.

She walked off in a huff, probably assuming that with just two cups of coffee she wouldn't receive a stellar tip. Steve cleared his throat. Was *he* uncomfortable?

"Obviously you know why I wanted to meet," I said.

I could play the role of a badass detective—not a character I would typically be type-cast as, but if I thought of the next hour as an acting exercise, I could get through it.

"So, I'll just skip to the point," I continued, meeting his somber eyes—now that I was staring directly at him, I could tell he had aged. "I want to know everything about your involvement with Isa. That's why I'm here. To get answers. And you, Steve, owe it to her to be honest with me."

Hey, not bad. Maybe I should audition for Law and Order.

He sighed and drummed his thumbs against his coffee cup. The waitress returned with not only a mug for me, but an entire warm pot of coffee. She set them both on the table—I guess she figured it wouldn't be worth her time to continue to check in on us; we were capable of pouring our own refills.

"I'm assuming you know that I was questioned and cleared years ago," he said, with a tinge of sourness that I didn't like.

"I know that. But answering to an anonymous cop isn't the same as answering to her best friend."

"I'm clean," he justified, "I did my time and I lead a Narcotics Anonymous group Sunday nights. I'm engaged and I have a good job now."

"Good for you. Tell me about Isa," I said flatly.

He was playing a role too—the newly cleaned up turned-his-life-around character. I wasn't buying it. I never thought Steve was a convincing actor in the first place. He tried too hard.

"Honestly—swear to God—there isn't much to tell. We met. You were there when we met…"

"Tell me what I don't know," I insisted.

He picked up the coffee pot to pour himself some more of the vile, burnt-smelling liquid that disguised itself as coffee.

"We hung out a few times. Chased the dragon and whatnot—but I'm not into that stuff anymore, like I said." When I didn't give him a round of congratulatory applause, he continued, "Then I didn't see her for a few months. She was in rehab, I guess. And then around October…November…I don't remember…she turned back up again."

"Was she your girlfriend?"

"No, no. Nothing like that."

"Are you lying to me?" I asked—I wanted to leave this diner knowing that I didn't leave one stone unturned.

"We were having sex, yeah, if that's what you're getting at. She wasn't my girlfriend. But I told you—I'm not like tha—"

"Yeah, I get it. You have a fiancée now. I don't care about that. What happened at your apartment that night?"

"Look, I'll tell you what I told the police. She came over, we did some…stuff…but we didn't speedball, okay? She was holding out on me. All I had was the happy dust, I didn't kno—"

I put a hand up to silence him. "Talk to me like I'm not a drug addict. Definitions please."

He glanced around the diner then leaned in to say, "Coke. Cocaine. All we did was coke that night. I didn't know she had heroin. Or any of the other stuff they said were in the toxicology report."

He was squirrely, as if he thought that uttering the formal names of the poisons would send him back to jail on another possession charge.

"And then she wanted to swim," he continued. "When we were at the pool, we got into this massive fight. I don't even remember what it was about, but I didn't touch her—I swear. You can read the autopsy. It's public record here. *I'm cleared.* I didn't—"

"What was the fight about?"

His eyes darted to the side. He was lying. There was something there—I knew it.

"I don't—"

"You have to remember something."

"Really, I've got to get back to work soon and I'm telling you everything I remember—"

"You agreed to meet me here for a reason. Don't you want to put this behind you?" I asked, "Because if you don't tell me everything—and I mean everything—then I can assure you, Steve, that I won't back down. I found your fiancée on Facebook. I'll message her too."

"Vanessa knows. She knows I used to use and—"

"I bet she doesn't know the full story. Or your reputation at the dinner theater. So, tell me what the fight was about."

This badass detective role was starting to feel natural. Whether it be a momentary power trip or the purging of all the questions I had had for years, I wasn't sure. In either case, it was working.

"I was being a dick," he finally admitted. "We found this…I don't know…what do you call those things?"

I shrugged, annoyed. How could I possibly know what was in his mind?

"A um…pacifier. That's it. Those things you give to babies. We saw this pacifier in the cleaning vent of the pool. And she made some comment about how whoever let their baby swim in this pool—it was disgusting, by the way—was probably a terrible mom. And I said something like…"

"Like what?"

"I was high. I was a dick. I thought I was being funny. I didn't want to be a dad back then—"

"What did you say?"

"I said… 'Fuck babies. If I had a kid, I'd dump them at the pool too.' And she went ballistic. We got into this whole argument, and I asked her why she had a bug up her ass because she'd be the kind of mom you see on the news. The type to leave a kid in a hot car and forget about them. She was like that—she was a *drug addict*, Wendy, she was fucked up. Christ—she'd leave her *shoes* at my place and walk out barefoot. It was a *joke*."

His words alone would have led me to believe he thought he was innocent, but his face and the tormented look in his eyes spoke only of shame. He was here for a reason. I was so close to bringing that reason to the surface.

"So, you got in a fight and you…"

"I left. I went back to my apartment, got some stuff, and left. I went to my buddy's house. Eric—he was my, uh, dealer. *I left.* I don't know what happened after that. I wasn't there. Eric lived in the same complex, okay. It's on the security cameras. Me entering his apartment and everything.

"She was high—sure, I knew that. I watched her rub the coke on her gums. But she didn't seem… She must have done more when I left. That's the only explanation because I'm telling you—I wasn't there, and I didn't know. If I knew she was…if I knew, I wouldn't have left. I was a shithead and an addict, but I wasn't a monster. I'm *not* a monster."

I would have thought he'd relax after confessing what was supposedly all he knew, but something about the hunched shoulders and the perspiration on his hairline told me not to accept this as the end of the story.

Keep pushing.

"Is there anything else? Anything else that you might not want…Vanessa to know when I find out. Because I will find out, Steve. I've committed to this and I'm not going to quit."

He was silent for several beats, then wiped his forehead with a napkin and said, "When I went back to my apartment…I took her, uh…took her little book or whatever. Don't ask me why. I don't know. I just wanted to be a dick, I guess. I took it and I still have it…it's in the car. I brought it. I can't have it in my house anymore. If Vanessa finds it…I don't want to explain that to her."

"What book?"

"That blue book—notebook or diary or whatever it was. She had it with her all the time and she'd write in it and tell me I couldn't look at it. It was so damn annoying. I don't know what I was thinking—I just took it. But then…when the police told me what happened…I felt like shit. I've never opened it. I don't know what's in there. But I can't have it in my house. I brought it with me. In case you wanted it."

Isa. Your song book.

As if by way of response, the hanging light above our booth flickered.

"I want the book. Give it to me and I'll leave you alone."

We paid our bill then I followed him to his car. When I saw the little turquoise moleskin, I had to fight back tears. I couldn't—I *wouldn't*—cry in front of Steve.

He placed the journal in my hand and said, "Please, don't ever contact me again."

I unlocked my front door and in my frenzied rush, slammed it into the wall with a loud thud. I sped home because I had to read this song book, but I wanted to give it the ceremony it deserved; I couldn't do it in the parking lot of Country Kitchen. F. Scott sprung from the coffee table and gave me the evil eye as he almost overturned the dying pot of African violets Julia gave me. The pot said in jubilant orange lettering, "I Be-leaf in You!"

"To cheer you up!" Julia said.

What was it with people giving me houseplants? I kept meaning to throw it away—by day three it had already wilted from lack of water and after a month of neglect, it was nothing but a pot of dry soil. To her credit, she didn't pry into the details of my breakup with Lincoln, but simply allowed me to stuff my face with a box of Godiva chocolates and cry. I shoved the last Godiva into my mouth for courage before pulling the turquoise moleskin from my purse. I promptly spit the truffle into my hand—key lime.

Gross.

Placing my hands on the now-tattered cover of Isa's song book, I was transported back to that summer afternoon on her roof. "I'll play on the streets of Geneva," she said that day. I took a deep breath.

This is okay. Isa wants you to know the truth. You're not betraying her by reading this.

The multicolored scribblings on the front page broke me. Childish rainbows, doves, puffy clouds, and moons with cartoonish smiles. I was holding Isa's heart in my hands. I grabbed the nearby box of tissues—another gift from Julia—to prevent my tears from soiling this treasured artifact. I'd always wanted to read her lyrics. I begged her to play me just one song…but not like this. She'd written chords and words, but the melodies would forever remain a mystery.

April 4, 2007

Float away, let's get lost today
I want to ride on a ~~this wave~~ cloud with you
Out of this town, ~~into the deep blue~~ to find what is true

I had no idea who the anonymous "you" was that she was referring to page after page. It could be one person. It could be multiple people. Maybe they were lovers? Maybe it was me or Lincoln or her "friends" from TCC. Maybe it was Isa talking to herself? I yearned to ask, but I knew I couldn't.

March 19, 2009

Am F am F am C dm end on E
am F am F
am
You're a body of lies and
F
she couldn't grow

```
     am
with your heart of stone
        F
And nobody loves you at all
c                            dm
Nobody would love you if they knew about
c                                    E
No, nobody would love you if they knew
                    am
Because you took stole her away
          F
and you tossed her aside
am
threw her away
            E
with your heart of stone
      am                      F
No, nobody would love you if they knew
      c                       E
No, nobody would love you if they knew
Am    F    Am    E    am
```

Her handwriting was sometimes neat and sometimes chicken scratch. She never used a pencil but would cross out discarded lyrics and even tear out whole pages that didn't suit her. The more I read, the more I craved *just one more* conversation.

What does this mean, Isa? Tell me!

Her lyrics poured out regrets and longings that I didn't know she was carrying. She thought she was getting closer to freedom, but she found herself spinning out—moving further and further away from everything she wanted and everyone she loved. I used to privately shame her for the drama that seemed to follow her everywhere she went. But with her lyrics right in front of me, I wondered:

Did she know what I thought of her?

I remembered that terrible afternoon in the bathroom—Isa sobbing hysterically, holding the pregnancy test. She suspected that me and Lincoln thought we were better than her. And at the time, I denied it.

Of course, I don't think I'm better than her, I consoled myself, sitting on the bathroom floor and rubbing her back. *What kind of friend would I be if I did?*

But the truth was that I did. Not always. Certainly not a first. But at times, especially toward the end, I definitely did. Although what pained me more was wondering if she only saw that selfish, prideful, defensive side of me. Did she also know that as much as she exhausted me, she had also brought me to life? I guessed not. Evident in her words, she didn't think nearly has highly of herself as I thought.

October 24, 2009

dm
I've ruined myself today
    dm
But I was ~~in ruins~~ ruined anyway
g
You can take her
        F   dm
Take the girl I claimed to be
D
I don't want her
        D7   D
I don't need her, don't you see?
    D
I'll find freedom
I'll Find myself
   D7   D   am
I don't want her. Not anymore
Dm
Don't you see

  Dm
I'm not who I used to be?
    G
But where do I go?
   F   dm
Where do I go from here?

And where was I when she had these questions? I could have tried harder. Part of me wanted to show Lincoln every last one of her songs. I wanted him to cherish these words with me and help me decipher their meaning. But equally, I wanted the moment to myself. I wanted Isa to speak to me and me alone. I wanted to take back lost time. If I could do anything, I'd go back in time and respond to her letter. I'd ask her to play that song she wrote for me. Why didn't I write to her? I'll never know the melody. Even with an invaluable relic of Isa's creative spirit, I would still never have it all.

    I realized then that I had gotten lost in a sea of self-pity. This wasn't about me and my regrets. This journal was a tool to uncover the truth. I flipped through and located the final pages. What was her final entry and when did she write it? Did she say anything about Steve or that night? Would it even be feasible to write in the state of mind she was in when she was last with him? Even as unlikely as that was, there was still a chance.

    Isa, tell me why. Is there something Steve didn't tell me? Is there something more?

November 27, 2010

 E
She had a name
  A   E   A
A name that only I know
 E
She was a girl

```
   A                    E       A
A little fact that only I know
         c#m
They said she didn't feel
  f#m     B      E    A
A lie that only I know
            B
But for all that I thought I knew
       A              E      A
I didn't know she held the world


     D
I'm sorry, Gemma
    A
My precious stone
     D
I'm sorry, Gemma
  A        B
Mama didn't know
B7                E     A
   That you held the world


  E
My precious Gemma
    A          E
I'll never be complete
        c#m
Until I'm with you
 f#m      B7     E
This I'll always know
  A       E    A    E
   I'll always know
```

November 27th—that was two days after Blair died. Lincoln called me on the night of November 28th. November 27th had to have been *the* day. Isa overdosed on the evening of November 27th. When exactly did she write this? I would never know, but she had written it *that day*. "She had a name." That's what was on her mind on her last day. The living room spun. My Starry Night tapestry was blending into the tv, and the hardwood floor morphed into the beige of the wall. Everything was a twisted, swirling jumble of color. "She had a name." She did have a name. Her name was Gemma—Isa's child.

"Isa? Is this what you wanted me to know?"

I clutched the throw pillow that was nearest to me on the futon when right in front of my eyes the dead African violet sprung to life. But the deep purple hue wasn't reborn, fresh, and perky as the day Julia handed it to me. It wasn't an African violet at all. It was a daisy.

With a trembling hand, I reached for the flower. It was real. The petals were flimsy and soft as silk. Just as I acknowledged that silent tears were spilling onto the coffee table, I felt a sensation that could be nothing other than an invisible hand on top of mine.

"Isa?"

My floor lamp flickered.

"Once for yes, twice for no."

The lamp went dark, then came back to life. It was unbelievable. But it was happening. I wasn't scared. I was jubilant.

"Isa!" I shouted through tears. "Isa, I'm sorry! Isa please…do you forgive me?"

The lamp flickered once. Once for yes. I released an uncontrollable laugh.

"Isa, I've missed you!"

Another flicker. More laughter. We were *talking*. We were sharing the same space and I was…I was *happy*. Everything was forgotten.

"Isa, I forgive you," I said before I even knew what was coming out of my mouth.

It had to be said. And the moment I said it, I knew it was true.

"Isa, nothing that happened was your fault."

It was all spilling out now. Where were these revelations coming from? I had no idea, and I didn't want logical explanations. All I wanted was one last conversation.

"I'm sorry you lost her. I'm sorry you went through that."

"She had a name," I heard a faint, husky voice whisper in my ear.

"I know, Isa. *You named her Gemma.* I'm sorry you lost Gemma. Was she the reason why? Was she the reason why you…left?"

The lamp went dim then shone again, so bright that I thought the bulb would explode. That was once. Once for yes.

"Oh Isa," I cried. "Oh Isa, I wish it had all been different."

I finally had my answer, but the question of who did it and why was replaced with "what now?" What was I supposed to do now that I knew? I couldn't fix this. I couldn't bring her back. Then it hit me. I dug through the front pocket of my backpack and retrieved the rose quartz. No one had known of Gemma's existence apart from me. I placed the gemstones around the flowerpot, creating an altar of sorts. No one had known, but since I knew, I had a purpose.

"I'll remember her for you, Isa."

She said nothing after that. I wasn't sure if that meant that she was satisfied, but if she was, I hoped that what I was about to do would keep me in her good graces. I'd always maintained that it wasn't my secret to tell. But things had changed. If Isa's death was intentional and done by her own hands—out of repentance, out of sorrow and grief—Lincoln deserved to know. He had to know for certain that it wasn't his fault. It didn't matter if he was only speaking to me at rehearsals—our relationship was secondary to telling the truth. I grabbed a composition notebook from my backpack and flipped to a fresh sheet. I would write it down for him—every detail. I would stuff the letter in the Moleskine, and I would give it all to him after the play. Because he had to know. Isa would have wanted him to know who Gemma was and that she had a name.

"Knock, knock!" said the voice that I recognized as my mother's.

I put down my paintbrush and opened the front door. My mom would occasionally "pop by" for lunch if she happened to be throwing a party in the area, but she always insisted on meeting at one of the off-campus cafés. She rarely ever stepped foot in my apartment—I didn't have sparkling water or garden-fresh chopped salads.

"What's…is everything okay?" I asked when I saw her standing on my landing dressed head to toe in pastel florals.

She took off the enormous sunglasses that I thought made her look like a beetle. A very elegant beetle, but a beetle, nonetheless.

"Does a mother need a reason to pop in and say hello to her daughter?" She shoved a Starbucks cup into my hand. "I got us chais and these little cake pop things. You should sell these at your place! Really, Lenny could make a mint. They're precious."

She let herself into the studio—cluttered with textbooks and papers stacked atop every surface. I had been cramming hard on my thesis and rewriting my piece for the play. With so many commitments vying for my attention, I'd been able to push the breakup out of my mind—until I'd go to rehearsal. After rehearsal, I'd usually spend 30 minutes weeping into my pillows. Azrah had caught me on the upswing—after my allotted wallowing time, I'd take up my paintbrush and "paint it out," per Dr. McPherson's recommendation.

She took a stack of art criticism textbooks from the coffee table and plopped them onto the floor to create space for our spontaneous teatime.

"I got us both birthday cake. Cute, right? I could probably make these at home. Oh! Idea! Wouldn't these be darling dipped in white chocolate with little faces. Ghosts! For Halloween!"

She handed me a pink piece of cake balancing precariously on a lollipop stick.

"Thanks…"

It wasn't that I wasn't appreciative of the unexpected chai (and I never refused free dessert)—there was something forced about her upbeat perkiness.

"So, you were just in the neighborhood? Did you have a party, or…?"

"Nope! Just wanted to see you. And I thought we could chat…"

There it was. She wanted to have one of her Dr. Phil moments. I had almost gotten away with it, but not quite…

I had dinner with my parents last Friday, mainly to explain that Lincoln and I were no longer "an item" (Paisley and Kinsley's term) so that things wouldn't be awkward when they came to see the play the following week. But after I decided to change the direction of my piece, I felt that I owed them a content warning before allowing them to walk in blind. My original plan was to forbid them from coming, although my dad made it crystal clear that nothing would stop him from attending my "reentrance to the theater." Dr. McPherson advised that if I was ready to be open about my past, it was time to tell my parents. And better to tell them in the privacy of our kitchen than with a spotlight overhead as I read my story in The Box.

"Before you decide whether or not you're coming to the play, there's something I have to tell you," I started while my dad cleared the table.

"What do you mean 'decide?' Of course, we're coming! Saturday night. We'll be there—front row!" Dad chuckled.

"I want to make sure that you know…the play's not going to be like the musicals I used to do…or even *Hamlet*. It's going to be sad…"

"Oh honey, we watched you point a gun at that poor boy in *West Side Story*," my mom laughed as she carried a freshly baked lemon tart to the table. "We can handle a little drama."

"No, what I mean is…the stories in the play are real, personal stories. The actors wrote them," I continued. "I know Lincoln mentioned that, but I wanted to make sure you knew what you were getting into—"

"About Lincoln, honey, do you think there's any possibility you two can still work things out?" my dad inquired.

"Dad. No, just—I'm trying to tell you something."

My mom paused from cutting the tart. My dad put down his wine glass.

"Something happened to me in high school. Junior year…"

They had taken it "well," I supposed. They cried, held my hands, and swore up and down that they were going to track down the "rotten punk." I expected that and I was able to talk them off the ledge eventually.

"I've been working through it with Dr. McPherson. He told me that you might think you're to blame, but I need you to know that you aren't. That's not why I'm telling you…I'm telling you because…I'm ready to move past it. And…I have to handle this in my own way. I hope you'll respect that."

There was more crying and hugging, but by the time I drove home, a tremendous weight was lifted. I thought the awkwardness of over-sharing with my parents was over. They'd see the play and we would never speak of what happened again. But now, Mom was here. And she wanted to chat.

She took one of my hands. Her manicure was perfect.

She was the woman who never made a mistake, so it shocked me when she said, "K, honey, I know you said that…what happened to you…I know you told us that it wasn't our fault. And I appreciate you saying that, sweetie. But I've been thinking about it every day this week. Honey—" she paused to wipe the moisture from her eyes before it could ruin her flawlessly applied makeup. "My little girl. K, I'm so sorry I failed you."

"Mom, that's not—" I started, reaching for the box of tissues.

"I know, honey, I know. And I understand you had your reasons for not speaking up before, but K…I *wish* you had felt comfortable enough to talk to me. I hope that we can… We've had some hard times, me and you. But I hope that we can change how we relate to each other. I want that for us. I want us to have an open relationship."

I wanted that too. Of course, I did. Every daughter wants to be her mom's best friend. But she couldn't just barge in my apartment with a cake pop and think that now we could ride off into the sunset.

"I mean, yeah, mom…I'd want that, but…you don't want to listen to me half the time. So that's why I stopped talking. You're so busy. Constantly. You've always been."

"What—where did I go wro—" She paused and took a deep breath. Perhaps a tactics she had read about in an article on dealing with difficult children. "Okay, K. Okay. Now I'm here. *Now* I'm listening."

"You didn't even come to Isa's funeral, mom."

She looked down at her chai. It was getting cold, and I could tell she hadn't tasted it—there would have been red lip prints on the lid if she had. The unspoken grudge was out in the open. But it shouldn't have shocked her. She had to know that choosing Blair's funeral over Isa's would drive a wedge between us, but she did it anyway. Was it because she wanted to be BFFs with Lanette? Was it because she actually had a fondness for Blair? I didn't know, but I knew that *I* needed my mom.

I needed my mom to hold me when I showed up at the house the morning after Lincoln called me with the news. I needed her to tell me the things moms are supposed to say—that Isa was a lovely girl and now she's in a better place. Maybe she didn't believe that—maybe *I* didn't believe that—but it should have been said. Because that's what you do. That's what moms do. She should have told me it wasn't my fault. She should have listened.

"The way you ignored Isa's death—like it was shameful," I continued—apparently, if she wanted to listen then I was going to say it all. "You treated Blair like a saint and where does that leave Isa? Forgotten because she was sad and lost? She wasn't perfect. But neither was Blair. If you knew—"

I almost said, "If you knew that she called me a terrorist—" but I couldn't. I saw my mom's face and how she had resolved to let the mascara-diluted tears run freely down her cheeks… I knew that telling her would hurt her. I couldn't use that word to hurt anyone else.

"…if you knew…how much I loved Isa, then you'd have thought it was important enough to be there," I finished.

"Honey," Mom began, "I can't tell you how sorry I am that I let you down. I should have been there. I knew Isa was dear to you and I should have been there."

She let out a sigh and took a sip of her tea.

"I've always thought that the best thing I could do *for you* was to fit in. I was ostracized growing up. My siblings and I—we were the only kids at school that looked like us. I hated it. Kids made fun of us, and my mom didn't do anything about it. They made fun of the hair on my arms. I asked my mom if I could use Nair to get it off. She wouldn't let me. All I wanted was one of those short, sassy hairdos the girls in school had but my sisters and I started wearing hijabs to school when we got our ghaids. We'd get all these questions— 'Do you have to shower in that?' 'What happens if you take it off?' 'Are you bald under there?'

"My mom was adamant that we didn't change our traditions just because we were in the states. She packed our lunches with the Pakistani food we ate at home. Kids said it smelled. We couldn't go on dates or go to parties. I resented her for it. The moment I broke free, I…well you know the story. I met Daddy. And when I had you, I swore to myself that I wouldn't be the mother that stood in the way of you fitting in. I didn't want *my* heritage to hold you back."

"But what about when we used to go to the Islamic Center on Fridays? I remember you wearing a hijab then and no one was making you. Why did we stop going?"

"With all the moving, I thought religion would give me stability but…I had already shed so much of myself. I couldn't go back. I couldn't connect."

"But religion isn't the only way to connect to a culture," I said. "I mean, I just wish I knew more. I want to *share* this heritage with you.

When you're in hiding, it makes me feel…it makes me feel like I should be too. I don't even know what your maiden name is."

"It's Kumari."

"Kumari," I said, to test the sound with my own tongue.

"Yes, it means 'Princess' in Urdu."

"But mom! That's *cool*."

She laughed softly. "It hasn't been until I've watched you struggle to find your footing that I've realized—maybe I shed some of the most special and unique parts about me. I don't want you to be ashamed of who you are. To know that maybe I played a role in your…confusion or lack of confidence…and maybe that led to…I'm sorry, K."

And because sometimes the parents are the ones who need to be comforted, I said, "Mom, it's okay."

We ate our cake pops and she left.

"*The Isa Project* has an approximate runtime of 90 minutes," my recorded voice said through The Box's sound system. "There will be no intermission. Please silence your cell phones and any other noise-making devices that you have brought with you…including your dates. Thank you for supporting local experimental art and Lincoln DeLuca's senior capstone. Sit back, relax, and enjoy the show!"

This was it. The performance would begin with a video compilation featuring footage from all the loved ones mentioned by the cast and then…we'd take our places onstage. Of all the roles I'd ever played, I was most nervous to play myself.

"Thank you for doing this." The whispered voice tickled my neck.

It was Lincoln, standing so close to me as we peeped through the backstage curtains that the butterflies in my stomach tripled. It was hard to be this close to him and not want to reach out and…

"You're welcome," I said, avoiding the hazel eyes that would tug at my heartstrings.

Lincoln and I had worked peacefully together; I was determined not to repeat history and bail on him again. I sometimes read into his overtly professional demeanor as his way of giving me space; he missed me too, I told myself, but he didn't want to put pressure on me to get back together. After all, I was the one who broke it off. Maybe he expected *me* to make a move if I was experiencing regret. The other conclusion was that he preferred it this way. Maybe he was even relieved to have dodged an extremely high-maintenance bullet like myself. I clearly wasn't ready for a relationship of that magnitude with everything I was working through…

The idealist in me still imagined Switzerland as a feasible possibility. We could go as a platonic couple on a mission, salvaging the years of friendship between us. Although, realistically, I knew that having him and *only him* as my travel companion would stir up emotions that would only leave us more damaged. I hadn't made a firm decision because I was torn between a sense of duty to Isa and the desires of my conflicted heart. Putting it off, however, was not going to be an option for much longer. My thesis was submitted, soon the play would be over, and we'd be walking across the stage to receive our degrees in a week.

"Is it okay if we do the thing?" he asked.

I didn't need clarification.

"Break a leg. Don't make me beg… Drop a line and they'll whine…" we whisper-chanted.

"You're a great director, Abe," I told him when we finished.

And he was—it was abundantly clear that he was born for this type of work and that made me envious. I wished I had the same clarity about my career path. But even with muddled feelings about my own future, I was never distracted from adoring Lincoln as he worked.

"This process has been about *all of us*. Soooo…instead of a director's speech, I've got these post-it notes and markers…" Lincoln said to our cast as we huddled backstage. "Write an anonymous kind word to someone in the cast on these, then stick it on that person's back. Some unfiltered love is better than any pep talk I could give. We've got 20 minutes till places. I want everyone's back covered!"

"You're so brave," one of my notes said.

"I LOVE your hair and you have the best clothes," said another.

"Your aura is enchanting," "Your snort-laugh makes my day!" "Thank you for always asking me how I'm doing," "You have a deep well of compassion," "You're my inspiration."

These little notes would be keepsakes that I would treasure forever.

"And you're a great artist," Lincoln said backstage, seconds before our cue to enter.

I had to shake the flush from my face, squash the fluttering in my chest, and push myself through the curtain. The stage was dark until we took our places, then the spotlights purred to life over each of us.

"My sister. My friend," Lincoln began.

"My flesh. My blood. My legacy. My son," recited Deja.

"My Năinai," "My secret keeper and fuzzy business partner," "My parents," "My first husband. My first love."

"My innocence," I said.

We began to circle each other. Our movements lacking rehearsed choreography, we skid, leaped, spun, and glided as one living organism all the while calling out the names of what we had lost.

"My sister. My friend," "My son," "Năinai," "My secret keeper," "Mom and Dad," "My first love," "My innocence," "Isa Claire," "They named him Marcus but I call him Landon," "Năinai's house, Năinai's youtiao," "Chubbie," "Kourosh," "My bee earring," "Her laughter," "His first steps," "My comfy pants," "Her whiskers," "Family game night," "The smell of his cologne," "My choice."

When the lights went dim, we exited. Only Deja remained onstage to bare her soul. Within her first few lines, the audience was invested. From the look on their faces, I saw them slowly beginning to comprehend the push and pull of Deja's conflict.

"...Christmas cards and photos on his birthday. That's what I get. I don't get to tuck him in. When he says, 'Mommy,' I don't get to say, 'What is it, baby?' I'm his first mom, but I'm just a name. I said I didn't want contact. I thought it would be too hard, but 18 years of waiting is what's hard. They named him Marcus. That's what's on his birth certificate. He's Landon to me. That's what I called him for nine months and that's who he is to me. I only just got a fulltime job and I only just got out of the trap his daddy laid for me. I couldn't give him safety. He's happy, so I'm happy. But 18 years of waiting—that's what's hard."

Jon walked onstage carrying a birthday cake with two fat candles—a number one and a number eight. He lit the candles and disappeared behind the curtain, leaving Deja alone onstage, the flames from the candles the only source of light to illuminate her face.

"Happy birthday, Landon. Mama loves you," Deja said. She blew out the candles and exited the stage.

At the conclusion of Jon's piece, Lenny pushed a cart of hot youtiao—Nǎinai's recipe—out from behind the curtain, offering samples to the audience. Lenny himself spoke of Chubbie as photos of him opening his business were displayed on the projector behind him. A recording of Lenny singing "Here Comes the Sun" while Chubbie mewed in the background as if claiming her spot in the duet, played as he exited.

"I've known I'm gay since I developed a crush on Kenya—my pre-K playdate. I waited until freshman year of college to come out to my parents," Natasha began as she built a Jenga tower onstage. "They wrote it off as a phase—a side effect of letting me get a BFA at a liberal arts college. We haven't spoken since Hanukkah two years ago…when they realized it's not 'just a phase.'

"...The last time I was in Target I had a breakdown when I saw the Jenga display. But forgiving them…showing on Tuesday night for family game night and going back to pretending would be…betraying myself. And who I've always been. It's not a phase. This is me." Natasha knocked down the Jenga tower and walked offstage.

Leonora waxed poetic about Cressida as twinkling lights above the audience elicited gasps of delight.

"She is within me; therefore, I never have cause for fear. I cannot forget the best part of myself; this part that knows the secrets that are only spoken of amongst the stars."

"...people, they assume that arranged marriages can't possibly end in a love story, yes?" Dr. Mirza said underneath the spotlight, "But for me, I have been lucky enough to have two great loves. The second, I found. The first, was arranged by my parents. I had a deep admiration for Kourosh. He was a leader; he took pride in providing for me. He taught me everything I know of commitment. The car crash forced me to step into a new self. I didn't have Kourosh to lead the way. I had to invent my new life on my own."

It was my turn. I entered the bare stage slowly, handing Dr. Mirza the already burning incense. She called it a "esfand" and explained that, in Iranian culture, this ritual was meant to ward off the "evil eye." At her wedding, the esfand was burned right before she walked down the aisle. Holding onto the fragrant embodiment of a long-ago sweet memory, Dr. Mirza walked offstage. With a girlish smile transforming her face, I knew she was imagining Kourosh in his wedding garb.

The stage lights blinded me to the faces of the audience.

Just you read the words. And once you're done, you can let go.

"The girl that looked back at me in the mirror the next morning was not the girl that went to the party. This girl, the new girl in the mirror, had eyes void of color. She'd lost something that was supposed to be given on purpose. I didn't know when or where or with whom, but I imagined candles and flowers and sweet whispers. I wanted sensitivity and caution and gentleness. I was waiting not because I knew what was at stake, but because I wanted to be sure. If I was in love, then how could it be wrong? I would feel liberated, unencumbered, when I gave my womanhood to the person I had been waiting for.

"The girl in the mirror told me *I* was stupid. What *I* did was bad. *I* was wrong. *I* let it happen. She told me that I got what I deserved because fairytales didn't exist. I told her, 'I don't need a fairytale. I would have settled for just having remembered.' She said, 'Too late.' I believed her. Because I guarded myself so carelessly—*so* carelessly that what was stolen could be taken with eyes closed.

"That was over five years ago. After five years, the burden of this story has become too heavy. I've been determined not to be labeled as a victim, but when I faced the truth, my hatred for the ugly R-word didn't come close to the hatred I reserved for myself. I should have, could have said something. I should have, could have stayed home that night. I can come up with an endless list of should haves and could haves for the rest of my days, but then…who stays the victim? Me. The one thing I didn't want to be.

"Victimhood ends as soon as I walk off this stage. As soon as I tear up this paper that holds my story. Victimhood ends today. He stole the color from my eyes and colored how I view the world for too long. I'm painting over that darkness. Victimhood ends now."

On cue, the drop cloth fell from the ceiling and Lincoln walked onstage, carrying my paint kit. I took the box of colors and brushes from him, and we locked eyes. The rings of pink, made prominent under the stage lights, told me that he had been crying. I set the box down, faced the audience, and tore my handwritten story in two. Then into smaller and smaller pieces. The story and all that had happened was just dust. With my attention directed to the drop cloth, I reminded myself of Lincoln's direction, "Don't worry about taking up too much time. Take *all the time*. The audience will be in the palm of your hand."

I began with a jar of deep ocean blue. Leaving the brushes untouched, I stuck my entire palm in. I brought out a dripping clump and threw the paint directly onto the drop cloth. I did the same with the burgundy, the shamrock green, and marigold yellow.

Paint the story with the colors you want to see, I thought as I smeared lilac directly onto the cloth.

You didn't deserve this. You aren't your past. This is not the end of your story were the thoughts that carried scarlet mixed with white creating dark pink to the fabric.

Sweating and covered in paint, I stepped back to observe my work. Without a plan in mind, I had written "I forgive you" across the drop cloth. The audience might've interpreted those words as an olive branch for my abuser, but they weren't for him. By the time I was finished with my painting, I had forgiven myself.

Lenny pulled me into a fatherly hug the moment I entered the dressing room.

"Miss K, I'm so proud of ya. I really am," he said.

"*Beautiful* work, my dear. It felt good, yes?" Dr. Mirza said.

Natasha handed me a towel so I could wipe some of the paint smears from my face, but when I heard the first notes of Jon strumming "High and Dry" onstage, I raced back to the wings to peer through the curtains. I didn't care what I looked like; I couldn't miss Lincoln's piece.

"I lost my sister in stages. First, she cast herself off to a deserted island. I tried to follow, but the waves were too rough for me to reach her. Then, she dove into the ocean and refused to come out. I tried to search for her, but I didn't have goggles. I couldn't see what she was seeing. When she finally resurfaced, I had already steered my ship in a different direction. She went back to that island, and she didn't intend to return. Instead, she went straight up into the sky. She wanted to live on a cloud…in the sun…or wherever it is that angels go.

"But that's what has always bothered me—Isa is no angel. She *was* no angel. She hurt a lot of people with the things that she did. She didn't care about the rules. Sometimes, she scared me. I thought she would leave any of us behind if we weren't onboard for an adventure. I was—I *am*—her little brother. I never wanted to be left behind.

"When we were little, she told me to eat Ella's dog food and it would give me superpowers. She said I'd be able to talk to dogs. I did it. It didn't work. But when we were in middle school, she got up 30 minutes early every day to apply foundation to my forehead. I had terrible acne and she knew I was insecure. Isa said my singing sounded like a dying cow was auditioning for the opera. She called me a nerd when I'd go on about video games or *Star Wars* or *Lord of the Rings*. But Isa would sleep on my bedroom floor when it was storming because, until I was 12, I was scared of thunder.

"Isa's not without fault just because she's dead. She could cut right to the bone if she wanted to get even. But because she was—*is*—my sister, I loved her. I'll always love her. And I hope that wherever she is—the place for non-angels, the place that is more of an in between place for normal-type-people—I hope she knows that my love for her was not based on whether she was good or bad. It just was. It just *is*. Because she's my sister."

Right as the audience began to applaud, our stage manager pulled the rig lines attached to the drop net hidden in the rafters. Five hundred artificial daisies fell from the ceiling, covering the audience, covering the cast as we ran out from behind the wings to take our bows. I wasn't sold on the idea, convinced that real daisies were the only way to pull off this stunt, but real daisies would have maxed out our production's budget by a longshot. I had to hand it to Lincoln—as we all clasped hands and bowed, I couldn't tell a distinction. The daisies raining from the sky provoked enough awe and wonder that I think it would have held up to Isa's standard of whimsy—it didn't matter if it was real.

After the show, the audience was invited to write the names of their lost people, places, and things and stick the notecards all over my painted drop sheet. We'd been given permission to hang the display in the quad until graduation.

"It's sort of like a collage," Jon mused. "And the 'I forgive you'—that was brilliant, K. It's like we're forgiving what's lost for leaving. Does that even make sense? Do you think people will get that?"

"That's the beauty of art," Lincoln said as he approached us. "It doesn't have to make sense. If it made them feel, we did our job. We don't need them to 'get it.'"

By the time most of the audience had trickled out, we went backstage to gather our belongings.

"I wish we could do this more than once!" Deja said. "I haven't had this much fun since I played the Tin Man in elementary school!"

The cast made their rounds, saying not "goodbye" but "see you later."

"I'll lock up," Lincoln said to me. "You catch up with your parents."

"Actually," I said, lingering at the dressing table. "Can we talk? I know Tony and Whitney are waiting but—"

"No, yeah, yeah. Of course."

He dropped his task of sweeping up the dressing room floor and took a seat next to me. The intensity behind his eyes gave the slightest impression of expectancy. I dismissed the thought.

He's just being polite.

Lincoln was always polite. He was always nice. I shouldn't flatter myself by thinking that maybe he was *longing* for an opportunity for us to be alone…

"I…um…I met with Steve," I began.

"What? When? K! *Alone*? You should have—I would have gone with you!"

"No, it's okay. We met in a public place. It was totally fine. It was fine because…Lincoln, he didn't do anything."

His face fell.

"I… Are you sure?" he asked.

"I'm sure."

He sighed and rubbed his neck in the way he does when he's uncomfortable.

"This is…good. Right? But I…I don't know. Now we don't… We'll never know for sure. I just wanted an answer."

"Well…" I pulled the turquoise song book from my purse and placed it in his lap. "We do have answers."

He picked up the book and quizzically opened the cover.

"Is this…? Oh my god. Where did you—"

"Steve had it."

He was already beginning to dive in, but I stopped him.

"Lincoln, there are some things in there that are…not very…well… I want you to read my letter first, okay? Can you promise me you'll do that before you read anything else? Everything you need to know is in that letter."

I pointed to the envelope I tucked inside, and he nodded.

"Thank you," he said softly.

"For what?"

"For finding this. For telling me the truth. You didn't have to give this to me. Especially with us being…um… Thank you."

"Lincoln, you deserve the truth."

I took his hand. Because I didn't know how you were supposed to treat your director/ex-boyfriend/best friend (if we could still call each other friends…) and I was sick of following some made up social protocol. I wanted to hold his hand. He stared at our touching palms for a moment and then met my eyes.

"I've always liked your eyes," he said.

"What?" I was so thrown that I laughed.

"Yeah, they're the richest brown I've ever seen."

"But they're *brown*. You're the one with the cool eyes."

"No," he insisted. "Yours have these flecks of gold. It's like drops of honey in a cup of chai. It's like…a warm bath or something cozy. Something peaceful. They're like…home."

He squeezed my hand and as my heart thudded embarrassingly, I thought that he was leaning in. Was he about to kiss me? Should I also lean in? My palms were sweating like we were teenagers again about to have our first onstage kiss. I was going to make a fool of us both and bang right into his forehead.

"You still have paint in your hair," he whispered.

I reached for my head, and he stood up. Whatever might have happened, didn't. I had to accept that I'd made my decision. I broke things off. I couldn't have it both ways. I couldn't only have him on my terms.

"Well, I should probably get goi—" he started, heading for the door.

"Yeah, same. Mom and Dad are taking me out to—"

"Oh, nice—"

"Yeah," I stuttered, "you didn't want to come or…?"

"Nah, no. I've got plans with Whit and Dad."

"Right." I nodded. "Of course. Well…was it…the play…was it what you'd hoped it'd be?"

The smile that spread across his face nearly brought me to my knees.

"Better. Much better."

16.

What Happens Next

The tiny second story studio watched me as I taped the last box shut. "Misc. mugs and books" I wrote in Sharpie, creating a satisfying scratching noise against the cardboard. The space was almost entirely empty, save for the memory of me that already mixed with the stale air. It needed to prepare for someone else's solitude, so it was time to surrender my keys to the landlord. He'd be there any minute to perform checkout procedures. I wanted to savor the final moments; goodbyes were always difficult for me, and I'd grown to approach every transition, every move, with reverence.

"Thank you," I whispered under my breath to the empty studio. "I needed you."

Next, I'd move back in with my parents for…who knew how long. I'd graduated without a plan. A semester ago the mere idea of this reality would have spurred a panic attack. Now, I just tried to take it all one day at a time. I had survived worse, and I could survive the ambiguity. That's what I did. Through it all, I survived.

When I heard the rustling on my fire escape and the brisk knock on the front door, I assumed it was the landlord, coming at long last to collect the keys and push me into my next chapter in life.

"Just a second!" I called, shooing F. Scott away from the door.

But the landing was deserted. I glanced to my left, then to my right—no one. I peered over the railing just in time to see a forest green Subaru drive away from the curb. Isa's car. *Lincoln's* car, now. I stepped out onto the mat, thinking that I could possibly wave him down, and that's when I heard the crunch of the envelope from beneath my saddle shoes. "Katie," it said. Definitely not in my landlord's burly all capital letter script—this letter was from Lincoln.

"Let's go back to the letter. Read it to me again if you don't mind," Dr. McPherson instructed.

I cleared my throat and shifted my weight in the oversized armchair, manifesting the folded letter from my back pocket. Forty minutes into our hour-long session and there we were again—reading Lincoln's letter for the millionth time since I'd opened it at 11:00 am that morning.

"Dear Katie," I started, but immediately interrupted myself. "Why does he call me that?"

"Does that bother you?" Dr. McPherson asked, pen and clipboard at the ready in case he needed to jot down something telling about my mental state.

"I mean…yeah. I don't like anyone to call me that. And he's, like, the only one that does it. It just feels so…intimate. Like he's family."

"And that disturbs you?"

"It doesn't *disturb* me, but it…I guess it reminds me that he has so much."

"What do you mean by that?" Dr. McPherson pressed.

"He knows everything about me. And…it's scary to be known," I finally articulated.

"I see." Dr. McPherson wrote a brief note and met my eyes once again. "My apologies... Feel free to continue."

I sighed and picked the paper up again.

"Dear Katie... If I loved you any less, I might be able to talk about it more...or in person. But I'm a writer, so I hope you'll forgive me for saying this in a letter."

"He does come in strong. Quoting Jane Austen... Is she one of his favorite authors as well?" Dr. McPherson asked.

I knew I could get him distracted and spend the remainder of our time gabbing about literary references, but today I wanted to cut to the chase. I needed to make a decision about this letter, and I didn't trust myself to make that decision alone.

"No, but he knows I love her, and I told him once that he reminded me of Mr. Knightley... I didn't think he'd actually read any of Austen's books."

Dr. McPherson nodded, jotted down something unreadable on his legal pad, and tried to suppress a smile.

"My husband...I've been trying to get him to pick up an Austen for *years*." He cleared his throat. "Anyway, I apologize. Go on."

"First, I'm so grateful that you shared everything with me in your letter. Having that insight into my sister's life is painful, but a gift that I thought I'd never have. Soooo...thank you. Isa's death is not your fault. I know next to nothing about how life works, but I know we have choices. Isa made a lot of choices that led her to a sad place. She made a lot of choices that hurt all of us. That isn't to say that she wasn't sick, and she wasn't hurting. I guess she didn't have a choice over how her brain made her feel. But you definitely didn't choose to end her life for her."

"He's right about that, as we've discussed," Dr. McPherson said.

"I know," I agreed. "But it's the next part..."

He nodded, encouraging me to continue reading.

"Second, because we do have a choice, I choose to love you— the real you," I continued, the words leaping off the page as my eyes passed over them. "You've hung the moon since we were 14. Over and over and over again I thought about what it would be like if you loved me like I loved you."

I looked up from the letter to see Dr. McPherson's dreamy smile. He straightened as soon as he caught me looking.

"How can that be true, though?" I asked him. "If this is true, then why…why didn't he ever say anything back in high school?"

"Think about it," Dr. McPherson replied, "was there anything…or any*one* that perhaps prevented the two of you from exploring a different sort of relationship?"

I didn't need time to think; he knew that I knew what he was implying. He knew that I knew he was right.

I resumed reading. "You were what got me through some of those dark times in New York. It's obvious, isn't it? I was on that train to Newark because I was trying to get to the airport. I dreamt of getting on a plane all the time back then. In my dreams I was coming back to you. I know that's unfair. You're a person, not a character I dreamt up. You showed a side of yourself that I should have felt privileged to see and I messed up. I wanted my dream girl to make my broken pieces whole and I thought I could do the same for you."

I paused, looking up from the sheet of notebook paper that had the ability to disarm me.

"Why did you stop?"

"Because…do you think that's just some romantic writer bullshit just to lure me in?"

"You have valid concerns," Dr. McPherson said, "but let's be careful that we aren't letting trauma and the manipulation of others speak for Lincoln's intentions. Who's making this judgment? You, with facts you know to be true, or the events of the past? You're smart, K. You can see the distinction."

"I mean, he does have this next part…" I hesitated. "Where he says, 'If you choose not to speak to me again, I'll understand. If you choose not to come with me to Switzerland, I'll understand. But please don't walk away thinking that you are your wounds. They aren't as visible as you think. I choose you for you, not for who I want you to be.

For who you *are*. Please believe that. I choose you without the expectation that you will choose me. I just wanted you to know exactly where I stand in case this is the last interaction we have for another three years. I didn't want to leave you wondering.'"

I didn't bother to refold the paper but placed it gently in my lap.

"And…" Dr. McPherson said, "how does that make you feel?"

Are therapists required to use that line at least one time per session?

"I'm not sure. When I first read it, I was happy about it."

"Tell me about that."

"Well," I began, thinking back to the breathlessness I experienced as I read the line, "You've hung the moon since we were 14," "I thought, 'Oh my god. It's like he'd reading my mind.'"

"How so?"

How could I explain in a way that didn't have me committed for insanity? Every word made me want to dance through the streets like Gene Kelly in *Singing in the Rain.* Those words—it was like I'd heard them before. Not in a cliché way, it wasn't like he used a quote from a movie… Okay, he *did* quote Jane Austen, but he didn't say, "You complete me" or something moronic and questionably codependent like that. Those words, *his* words, were recognizable because I had thought them myself. Not about myself, of course. But about him. Since that goofy grin was first directed at me, I had loved Lincoln DeLuca. All the stuff that happened in the middle—the party junior year, the fallout of our friendship, the panic attack during *Hamlet*, even the weight of responsibility I felt over Isa's death—all of it was filler. What I knew to be true was that I couldn't walk out of Lincoln's life. Not again.

"It made me happy," I fumbled, "because I love him back. And I want him back."

"But?" Dr. McPherson said. "It sounds like there's a but…"

"*But* I don't have solid faith in…anything. I can't trust that…that…what if I accept his apology and run to him like he's my knight in shining armor and he manipulates me? What if I'm too infatuated to see—Jesus Christ—she never even asked me my name! She never asked what 'K' stood for!"

Dr. McPherson didn't ask "Who?" He didn't need to. All of our sessions led back to one person. And even if I knew the longings of her heart, even if I knew her regret and I knew that her child had a name…I couldn't shake the anger that still burned in my chest.

"For so many years, I could have been happier. Lincoln and I—we could have been together. All the wasted time… Isa's always been at the center, preventing me from moving on. I don't—I *won't*—be a puppet again. And now it might be too late. What if I'm, like, irrevocably damaged? How can we have a relationship then?"

"K, I'm going to be rather blunt. And for that, I hope you'll forgive me," Dr. McPherson said, setting his pen and clipboard to the side. "None of us are going to leave this world without a stitch of blame. We've all been hurt and hurt other people. We have a choice when it comes to how we remember those that have left us. Knowing that Isa could be emotionally manipulative, and she most definitely contributed to your being in unsafe environments, does that invalidate the *good* memories?

"You seem to be unable to decide whether to defend Isa or to condemn her. I'm here to tell you that you aren't required to do either. Let the good be good and let the bad be bad. But leave it all in the past. Lincoln is not Isa. Any other romantic pursuit or budding friendship that comes your way—whoever that is and wherever they come from—they are not Isa. And you, K, you are by no means irrevocably damaged. I *know* you know better than to believe that."

Did knowing that Isa wasn't a spotless, wholesome human being make me love the good any less? Did it make it any less real? These were questions that I hadn't directly asked myself. I wanted to say yes. I am a person that burns for authenticity. But the truth is that no, it didn't. And I felt guilty that it didn't. I felt like I *should* hate her, leave her memory in the dust, and harbor resentment towards her for the calamity that she brought upon my life.

And yet, I couldn't. I could feel waves of self-righteous anger, but at the end of the day, what hurt the most—what made me the angriest—was not what Isa did to me, but what she *didn't do*. She didn't stay. I loved those moments still. In my belligerently naive way, I loved the good memories—and they *were* truly good—even more. I loved them despite. I loved them because now I could consciously choose to. I had always chosen to see love where Isa was concerned. Maybe that wasn't such a bad thing. Isa wasn't perfect, but she was a friend unlike any other.

"K, answer me this—why did you stop your suicide attempt?"

"How is that relevant?" I asked, although I knew I wouldn't be able to avoid answering. Dr. McPherson was too slick.

"Indulge me if you would. What made you change your mind?"

Over three years ago. After that fateful performance of *Hamlet*. Walking back to the dorm in the rain. It was all coming back to me. My roommate was gone. The bottle of Tylenol that sat on her bedside table. She was a rugby player. She got muscle aches. I had a different kind of ache and no one there to stop me. I don't know how many I swallowed, but when I started to vomit, I called my dad. When I woke up, he was holding my hand. We were at Vanderbilt, where I would spend my 19th birthday. I swore to him that I would never try to do it again.

"Because I…" I often thought about the answer to this question, although this was the first time I had been asked. "I wanted to know what would happen next. I wanted to see who I would become. That sounds stupid now. I'm just—I'm nothing special—but I was almost nothing at all."

"You have every right to see who you will become. And you have every reason to believe that person is going to be extraordinary."

Extraordinary is going a bit too far, I thought. *Although…*

"All this time I've thought that I let these terrible things happen to me—I even nearly stripped myself of my own life. But *I* was the one that got myself out. *I* picked up the phone to call my dad. *I* stayed in Vanderbilt, *I* came to you, and I *am* getting better."

"You say you don't have faith in anything," Dr. McPherson nudged, "but what I see is a woman who is starting to have faith in herself. People can make big mistakes, but they are always capable of transformation. You have a remarkable ability to adapt."

"I always have," I confirmed because it was true. There was only one thing still nagging at me… "But what if I want him there too? Are you allowed to have both? Belief in yourself. The ability to go it alone and adapt to face the storm. But also, I don't know…the *safe* place that reminds you of these things?"

"If you want to adapt to include a partner into your life, K, I think you can trust yourself to choose that partner. Do you think Lincoln is a safe place?" Dr. McPherson asked.

"He always has been."

Without the mind monsters overcomplicating matters, it was obvious.

"You know I won't tell you what to do. But if I weren't your therapist, if I were, say, just your gay best friend… I'd say, "Go get your Mr. Knightley. And get your ass on that plane to Switzerland."

My eyes widened in delight. I snorted loudly.

"Forgive me. It wasn't professional of me to say ass."

~~Dear Abe,~~

~~Dear Lincoln,~~

~~I loved your letter. It was perfect.~~

Lincoln,

Can we start over? I didn't mean what I said before and I

I had the fuel from chugging a large chai latte and the sugar rush of a gigantic pistachio muffin but still—I was incapacitated at the bird table, completely ill-equipped at expressing myself. Was it possible to stay seated here in my little bubble at Chubbie's and beckon him to me? I didn't have a degree in creative writing; I wrote research papers with APA formatting...how could I even come close to writing something on par with Lincoln's eloquence?

"Men aren't mind readers," Paisley had said on multiple occasions. "You have to be very direct with them to get what you want."

But it would save me a lot of agony if they did have telepathy. Why were words so hard?

"K, I'm about ready to lock up. You want me to show you that video of the kittens I was telling you about before I kick you out?" Elijah asked as he wiped the barista counter.

"Oh yeah, sure," I replied.

He disappeared in the back to retrieve his phone, and I slouched into my rickety old chair. I guess I wasn't going to write this letter tonight. I studied the colorful papier Mache artwork of the tabletop. "The bird table is our favorite," Isa said on my first visit to Chubbie's all those years ago. It never occurred to me to sit anywhere else in the café. No matter what I felt about Isa on any particular day, whenever I'd walk through that door, I flocked to that table as my sought-after retreat from the outside world. White doves, spritely sparrows, daring blue jays...and...what was that?

Etched into the table that I occupied at least four times a week was a distinct scratch right above a pelican's beak. I rubbed it with my thumb, but it didn't go away. Instead, it became bigger. And bigger. Drawing a line then a smaller line on top then...was that the letter "F"? Now "L"? "Y"?

"FLY" the table read.

L...I...T...T...L...E...B...I...R...D

"Fly little bird," I spoke aloud, disregarding the possibility of Elijah witnessing my hysteria.

But it kept going...

I...G...I...V...E...Y...O...U...

"I give you my blessing? Fly, little bird. I give you my blessing!"

Backstage before *Peter Pan*. The last words Isa spoke to me. How she spun me in dizzying circles and played with my hair. She kissed me before I rushed off. The moment I recalled the innocence of that peck, I felt a phantom pressure on my lips. So light, I could almost convince myself that I'd imagined it. Almost.

"Isa?"

There was a stained-glass sconce on the wall opposite—it flickered once. Once for yes. I racked my brain. What was she trying to say? "I give you my blessing." Blessing for what?

"Isa? Is it Lincoln? Should I..."

My phone buzzed.

Lincoln DeLuca [8:57pm]: Hey. Feel free to ignore this. I might have left something for you on your mat. But now I feel dumb because idk if you already moved out... :/

The sconce blinked and I knew what she wanted me to do. Forget the letter—I didn't need a script.

"Whoa, dude! What's going on with that light?" Elijah said, emerging from the breakroom.

"Dunno. But, sorry, Elijah. I have to go! Text me the...thing...you wanted to show me. About Crema and Beans. See you later!"

"K, everything cool?" he asked, but I was already gone—jogging to my car.

Lincoln was, as I predicted, at the swings when I parked at the corner of the playground. Ella, tied to the jungle gym, wagged her tail like crazy when she saw me approaching.

"How did you know I was here?" he asked.

"That…" I said, pointing to Ella who was now sniffing my shoes. "…and I just hoped."

I sat down on the swing next to him and pulled the letter out of my back pocket. The deep creases gave away how many times I'd read and reread it.

"I read your letter."

"You did?"

"Yup. And *you* read *Emma*?"

I raised my eyebrows, highlighting my shock and amusement. He beamed in response.

"I was hoping you'd catch that."

"If I loved you less, I could talk about it more? Abe, that's a classic. Of *course,* I caught that. I'm not just a casual fan, you know. I'm obsessed."

He pivoted his swing so that he was facing me dead-on. His face now serious, he said, "But the other things I said…you read that too, right?"

I nodded.

"I do love you. Do you believe me?"

For all the eloquence I lacked and for all the courage I had denied myself in the past, I was able to manage, "I'm trying. Because I love you too."

And that seemed to be enough.

"There is no try, Katie Statham."

"Oh, shut up," I said, kicking his shin. Even if I wouldn't commit to watching the entire saga with him, I knew a *Star Wars* reference when I heard one.

"Okay, well, I'll just have to prove it to you," he said.

When I smiled, it was glorious to see how his entire face lit up from within—how I had the power to do such a thing. Just Katie, the shy new girl. She was capable of giving someone else the wings to fly.

"Okay then…prove it," I said right before I pressed my lips into his.

On a cliff overlooking Gimmelwald, at an elevation of some 4,000 feet, our shaking hands gripped the little carved box.

"Let's back up a bit," I suggested, "I'm afraid we're going to accidentally throw the whole thing over."

Lincoln nodded and we took a few synchronized steps backwards.

"What are you thinking?" I asked because his silence that morning was odd, but not unexpected…and I always wanted to know everything that was on his mind. I collected his thoughts like they were precious stones.

"I'm thinking…you're so damn beautiful even though I know for a fact that you didn't shower last night."

I gave him a look and he knew what was coming.

"Hey, if you punch me right now, I'll literally careen off this cliff to my doom. Accept the compliment. I beg of you," he laughed and as I fought back a smile. "And also…I'm thinking that I'm gonna miss her. I'm gonna miss having one last thing to do for her. After this…what happens next?"

This act did mark the end of our mission, so to speak, and I felt a surge of melancholia as well. Over the last three weeks, we scoured every inch of Switzerland it seemed and couldn't settle on a location. Of course, it was beautiful—the entire country was a feast for the eyes and a well for the artist's imagination. But we didn't want to let go. Nothing was good enough. Then we checked into the Mountain Hostel. It was like a portal to another world; the pace was slower, the laughter lingered for longer, the meals were prepared with care, and the air was sweeter. Isa had never been to Switzerland, but Gimmelwald was exactly the kind of place that a whimsical soul like herself would have originated. Her smile was in the sunny faces of the daisies lining the hiking trails. Her singing voice whistled in the midday breeze. Her husky laugh would have been unstoppable at the sight of the cows, with their playful bells, parading through town en route to Sefinenalp for the summer.

I sighed because I didn't have an answer. "I guess…what's next is…we keep going. We remember her. That's all we can do."

"But it's not fair," Lincoln said, his eyes watering. "Death isn't fair because memory isn't enough. I want to know what she would have thought of you and me. And I want to know who she would have fallen in love with. Or what crazy thing she would have worn to the Tony's when I got my first nomination. She should be here. Not us. She would have *loved* this."

He extended his arms, gesturing to the enormity of the majestic landscape before us. Rolling lush green hills, meadows sprinkled with wildflowers, and the mountains—God, those mountains. It *was* unfair. The one person who wanted to experience this more than anyone wasn't here. In person, at least. The shivers up and down my spine told me that some unidentifiable remnant of her finally made the pilgrimage.

"It's not fair," I said, for Lincoln's sake but also to the box that I alone held in my hands. "It's never going to be because it wasn't supposed to be this way. Twenty-year-olds aren't supposed to die. We were never supposed to be older than Isa. She was who we looked up to. And kids who grow up in nice neighbors, who go to the best schools…those kids aren't supposed to become drug addicts. That's what we were told…but that's not what happened. That's not how life really works. There's no way to make it right. I wish I knew why these things happen or what to do next, but I don't. All I can say is that, Lincoln…"

I reached for his check, stroking the coarse hairs of the full beard that he'd developed over the last three weeks.

"Lincoln, I am here to stand in the 'I don't know' with you. We'll figure out what happens next. I'm going to miss her too. And I promise you—I will never forget."

We watched the wind tenderly carry the ashes out of our hands. I decided that the very last thing I should do was to keep my heart and my brain where my feet were.

"I love you, Isa!" Lincoln bellowed.

"I love you, Isa!" I echoed.

We dipped our hands back in the box and continued to release our sister, bit by bit, into the place she was always meant to be.

"I love you, Isa!" we shouted.

The ashes exploded in puffy clouds suspended for the blink of an eye in mid-air. I heard her voice— "Come onnnnn!" I saw her porcelain body dashing ahead of me, her wispy white-blonde hair electrifying the darkness. I remember thinking she looked like a sparkler that night. And she was. That's exactly who she was—a firecracker, a lightning bug, a sparkler lit up for the Fourth of July.

The box was empty. We stood for a moment, staring at the dazzling ridges of the ice-capped Swiss Alps, and panting from the exerted yells. The promise was fulfilled. I knew without knowing that Isa wouldn't visit me again. I knew—even if I didn't have a clear understanding of the afterlife or Heaven or Hell or reincarnation—I knew that wherever she was, she was with her daughter. She had to be. That's the only ending I would allow. Lincoln interlaced his fingers with mine.

"You ready?" he asked.

"I'm ready."

This was going forward.

This was what it was to take your heart from the past.

Together, we walked back down the path.

Epilogue

F. Scott almost never forgave me for leaving him with my parents for the two months we spent traveling through Europe. Mom sent me updates with pictures of him looking miserable while being forced to wear cat-sized garments. He seems to have put the past behind him now that he has a cozy window seat all to himself in our Chicago apartment. He presides over the entirety of our 900-square-foot palace like the king of Lincoln Park.

We saw all of Switzerland and went through France and Italy before running out of funds. Then began the parade of part-time survival jobs. I wanted to go back to where I started—back to roaming the galleries at the Art Institute and riding the Ferris wheel on the pier, so we chose Chicago. It felt right, but the first few years weren't easy; we occupied roles as baristas, bookshop cashiers, tutors, cart-pushers, babysitters, set builders, dog walkers, and probably more that I can't remember.

I eventually went back to school and followed the most natural path in the world—art therapy. The School of the Art Institute of Chicago's program gave me the opportunity to focus on addictive disorders. Balancing class, an internship, and work was no small feat. Eventually, last spring to be exact, I went in on an office space with some friends from grad school. I have a window that faces Lake Michigan and together my patients and I use paint to make sense of big emotions. For what I lack in take-home pay, I gain in the pleasure of making a difference.

Lincoln taught writing workshops to everyone from first graders that could barely spell their names to senior citizens in nursing homes before landing a stable gig as the director of education at Chicago Storytellers of Tomorrow, an organization devoted to cultivating young writers. He still freelances on the side—directing and submitting his plays to theaters all over the city. It's a strange week when we aren't occupying two seats in at least one playhouse auditorium. We're still waiting for Broadway to call…I tell him it will be any day now. And I believe that wholeheartedly. I also drag him to museums as often as he'll let me. I started volunteering at the South Asia Institute. I can't wait to take you there one day and tell you all about how your 25% of Pakistani blood is 100% magic.

Your father proposed to me the night we opened *The Isa Project: Stories of Loss in Chicago*. I didn't know at the time that he had a ring in his pocket…or that you were in my belly. Neither of us knew what to expect, but we found that the community was hungry for an opportunity to talk openly about their losses. Chicago is just quirky enough to be receptive to devised works. We perform pop-ups with new groups once a month and plan to keep it going.

We went back to Nashville and had an intimate ceremony at the swings. I wore a $15.00 yellow sundress that I got from a vintage thrift shop near our apartment. Lincoln wore a bowtie and suspenders—I'd never seen him so handsome. It was simple and quiet. It was us. And it was perfect. We announced your arrival over an Italian feast prepared by Whitney and Azrah. You were only the size of an avocado, but everyone flocked to my belly and fell in love with you on the spot. We left our wedding celebration one enormous sapphire richer—your Grandpa Tony found the "Heart of the Ocean" when they finally sold the family's old house. He wanted us to keep it. I will let you wear it someday. As often as you want.

Of course, we had to have a reunion with the original cast of *The Isa Project*. But Leonora made the announcement for us—declaring to the small gathering at Chubbie's that I was "bestowed with an exceptionally gifted child" before we even hugged her hello. She insists that you possess the energy of a friend we both used to know. I don't know if I believe that, but I do believe that you are the driving force behind reuniting a broken family.

    A letter from a long-lost granddaughter with news on the upcoming birth of a future great-granddaughter elicited an invitation for dinner. We will meet them tomorrow. Your Grandma Azrah and Grandpa Tim are not quite ready for contact with their estranged parents and in-laws, but we hope they will be soon.

    You might be wondering why I'm telling you all this and, to be honest, I didn't have an agenda when I began. It just felt good to write it all down. I was afraid I would forget, although that's probably far from possible. These stories, the ones I have written out for you, have shaped me into the type of mommy I will be…and I hope that will be a very good one. I know I'll make mistakes. And I know that, at times, I'll hate myself for those mistakes. But I hope you know that I'll always be trying my best. And, for everything that I'm missing, it'll be made up in the world's most wonderful dad. He is waiting for you too.

    In just two weeks, I'll get to see your face. Gemma Kumari DeLuca, I hope you have your dad's big smile. I hope you have your aunt's sense of freedom. I want you to know that every step I took to get healthy, every hard thing I had the courage to tackle, it has all been for you. I had no idea at the time, but it prepared me for you.

    P.S. I think you'll like the flower box your daddy installed outside your nursery window. Last weekend we filled it with daisies.

Acknowledgements

This book would not exist if it weren't for the encouragement of my husband, Matthew Briggs. Matthew, you are my inspiration. Thank you for reading every new chapter during your breaks at work and thank you for your patience when I would say, "I'll be done with this section in five minutes!" …and wouldn't leave the office for another hour.

My parents, Gerry and Tyna D'Arco, are the kind of parents that encourage imagination, a love of reading, and all artistic inclinations. Thank you.

To my sweet in-laws, Rodney and Kathy—I'm sorry for the curse words. Please still like me.

To my Julia Cameron Crew, Matthew McWilliams and Stephanie Iozzia—lifelong friends are hard to find, and I consider myself very lucky to call you mine.

Ugh, Robert (Snob) Armstrong…I guess I have to thank you too. But in all seriousness, you were my first "theater freak," my first therapist before I could afford to hire a professional, and continue to be my most trusted source for book recs. I can't wait to see *my* name on your stylish NYC apartment bookshelf. "Wonderful tuna, tickle me Elmo, Spam!"

In fond memory of Elise Marie Armstrong.

Resources for Help and Hope

If you or someone you know is thinking about suicide, please call the National Suicide Prevention Hotline at 800-273-8255 right away.

Substance Abuse and Mental Health Services Administration's National Helpline is a free, confidential, 24/7, 365-day-a-year treatment referral and information service for individuals and families facing mental and/or substance use disorders. Call 1-800-662-HELP (4357) or visit https://www.samhsa.gov/find-help/national-helpline for more.

The National Sexual Assault Online Hotline is available 24/7. Get help by calling 800-656-HOPE (4673) or visiting https://www.rainn.org/ today.

Birth mother and adoption resources can be found on Birth Mother Assistance's website: https://www.birthmotherassistance.com/index.htm

For help and healing after an abortion, please visit First Choice Women's Resource Center's website at https://1stchoice.org/women/after-abortion-care/

Bonus Content

To listen to the full-length versions of Isa's songs, please visit: https://on.soundcloud.com/FKkj

Song lyrics by Gina R. Briggs

Music by Matthew Briggs

Made in United States
Orlando, FL
24 October 2022